oswald wynd

The GINGER TREE

PERENNIAL 📖 **CLASSICS**

A hardcover edition of this book was published in 1977 by
Harper & Row, Publishers.

THE GINGER TREE. Copyright © 1977 by Oswald Wynd.
All rights reserved. Printed in the United States of America.
No part of this book may be used or reproduced in any man-
ner whatsoever without written permission except in the case
of brief quotations embodied in critical articles and reviews.
For information, address HarperCollins Publishers, 195 Broadway,
New York, NY 10007.

HarperCollins books may be purchased for educational, business, or sales promotional use. For information, please e-mail the
Special Markets Department at SPsales@harpercollins.com.

First HarperPerennial edition published 1991.

First Perennial Classics edition published 2002.
Perennial Classics are published by Perennial, an imprint of
HarperCollins Publishers.

Library of Congress Cataloging-in-Publication Data

Wynd, Oswald.
    The ginger tree / Oswald Wynd.
      p. cm.—(Perennial classics)
    ISBN 0-06-095967-3
    1. Japan—History—20th century—Fiction. 2. Illegiti-
mate children—Fiction. 3. Scots—Japan—Fiction.
4. Women—Japan—Fiction. 5. Nobility—Fiction.
6. Adultery—Fiction. I. Title

PR6073.Y65 G56 2002
823'.914—dc21

                                              2002016985

HB 08.21.2018

The GINGER TREE

1

&

I was sick yesterday on my birthday, after not having been sick crossing
the Bay of Biscay and even in the storm off Malta. It seems silly to
have been sick in a little sea like the Red Sea, but when I did get to
the deck at sunset, to escape from Mrs Carswell's groaning, the Second Officer came up beside me at the rail and said that I had been
unwell because of the ground swell from Somalia. He said that many
people who can stand up to all sorts of bumping and knocking about
in storms are unable to stand up to a heavy ground swell. He is quite
a nice man, though he must be thirty at least. He has very big hands.
Too big. I did not tell anyone it was my birthday yesterday, not even
Mrs Carswell. She was being sick, too, much worse than me.

The swells are like little hills on the move, completely smooth
and grey. As we go up sideways on one of them you can see the others coming at us from the horizon. The sky is grey, too, and it does
not seem able even to redden up for sunset. I am back in the cabin
writing this, up in my berth above Mrs Carswell, who is still groaning. I would not have believed that anything could creak like this
ship creaks. It is stifling in here. They have put tin things outside the
portholes to catch the breeze, not even from the ship's movement.

I have decided right now that I must not send this notebook to
Mama as I promised. Ever since Port Said I have found myself wanting

to write down things that she must never see. I have heard that people change east of Suez and that could be what is happening to me. The day before yesterday, when I was beginning to feel not too well, I still wanted to eat curry and I have always hated curry. It is almost frightening, that you can travel in a ship and feel yourself changing.

It is not happening to everyone. Most of the passengers are too old to change. Nothing would ever change Mrs Carswell. I wish that, if I must have a chaperone, it did not have to be Mrs Carswell and we did not have to share a cabin.

I left off my new corset two days ago. Now I know I can never send this to Mama. Mrs Carswell has not found out yet since we dress and undress, at least mostly, behind our bunk curtains I just could not get into that corset up here in the heat under the roof, which is why I left it off first time. Then I smuggled it down while she was still sleeping and hid it away in my cabin trunk under the little sofa. Fortunately I have a small waist even without having it held in, and she has not noticed yet, but I will have to be careful. She has the sharpest eyes. They are like jet beads.

Mama would be horrified if she could read me writing like this. Perhaps I do it because there is no one I can talk to on this ship. In the First Class they are all old except the Prices, and Mrs Carswell says the Prices are not suitable. She calls them 'pushing' and thinks they ought to be travelling Second Class because all he is going out to is a position with the Singapore Water Board. Mrs Carswell says that in Singapore they will soon learn their place, because people in the Public Works Department are not acceptable socially. In Hong Kong Mr Carswell is a lawyer, which means that his wife can leave cards at Government House once a year and the Governor's Lady then leaves cards on her. Mrs Carswell is on the tea-party list. She says I will learn about these things in Peking.

In all the things they did for me before I came away no one told me anything about how not to have perspiration. If China is as hot as this, am I going to be damp for the rest of my life? I have used up all my eau de Cologne already and it only makes you feel cool for about five minutes. I cannot ask Mrs Carswell what she has done about perspiration all her years in hot countries. She must have done something? Perhaps not.

SS *Mooldera*,
January 11th, 1903

We were right out in the Indian Ocean before the Captain spoke to me for the first time. I was about to go down from the top deck because of the coal smuts coming from the funnel when he came along from the bridge. He is a big man and very hairy, with the kind of beard that never seems to be trimmed, wisps coming out of it. He does not appear very sociable and I turned away so that he would not have to speak to me but he made a point of coming to the rail and asking if I had my sea legs again after the big swells. I said I had, then told him that I did not like the Indian Ocean very much, was it always this grey colour? He said we were passing through the tail of a monsoon and usually the sea was a wonderful blue. I have not seen any wonderful blues yet, not even in the Mediterranean which was grey, too, only a different kind of grey. This is a hot grey, with vapours off the water. The Captain said that from where we are now all the way to ice in Antarctica there is nothing but sea, four thousand miles of it. He trained in sailing ships on the Australian grain run and they used to go through the Roaring Forties which are just north of the ice and once he was nearly shipwrecked at an island which is all black rock mountains and huge and no one lives there because terrible winds blow all the time. Then he must have thought he was frightening me for he said in a broad accent: 'But dinny fash yersel', lassie, you'll no be shipwrecked.' Though his name is Wilson I had not realized he was Scotch until then, which somehow made me feel safer on this ship.

After the Captain had gone and before I could escape from the smuts, which I was sure were getting in my hair, the Second Officer arrived, at once wanting to know what the Captain had been saying. The Second Officer comes from Cardiff in Wales and his voice is sing-song and he keeps putting one of his hands as near as possible to mine on the rail without actually touching me. He knows I am going to China to get married because Mrs Carswell told him when she found him standing by my deck chair one day just after we left the Suez Canal. While we were still in the Mediterranean he never even looked at me. The heat does make people different.

Last night I went down to dinner by myself because Mrs Carswell could only take some clear soup brought to her by the stewardess, though she was sitting up in her bunk watching me do my hair. I hope she hasn't guessed about the corset. Some other people did not come down to the main saloon either, which left me and the Malacca Judge almost alone at our end of the long main table. The Malacca Judge is very old with a big tummy, and is coming back from his last home leave before retiring. He used to drink whisky with his dinner, but stopped it, I think because he saw Mrs Carswell did not like this. I would not have expected a judge to be worried about what Mrs Carswell might be thinking. Last night he had three whiskies, starting with the soup. The ship was still rolling and those boards they call 'fiddles' were raised all around the tables to keep the plates from landing in our laps. The Judge offered me a glass of wine and of course I refused, but it was strange, I really wanted to say yes. Once or twice I noticed the Captain looking at me from the top of the table. Mr Davies seemed to be doing this quite often from his much smaller table. I don't think he likes the company he has at mealtimes, they are all old, even a woman who dresses young though she must be forty. At night she shows a lot of bosom. Mrs Carswell says she is a slut even though she is the wife of the British Consul in Swatow. Last night her dress had a bodice with a lot of Chinese embroidery on it, very gaudy. I was wearing my brown dress that Mama liked, but I don't. Good enough for this ship, though. I am keeping my new things fresh, most of them still in tissue like the wedding dress. I thought about wearing the voile with spots but decided not to, with Mrs Carswell watching.

SS *Mooldera*,
Next day

There has been quite a fuss in the Second Class. A lady was in her bunk when she saw a huge rat running along the pipes just over her head. In those cabins the partitions do not go right up to the roof and the rats can use the pipes as a road. Apparently the lady just screamed and screamed and they couldn't stop her until the doctor came. Mrs Carswell says it was a wonder *he* was able to do anything. She is quite sure the doctor has something in his past, which is why he is on a ship, but she will not tell me what she thinks this is. Now we have to shut our door at night instead of just pulling the curtain over it to give some draught from the porthole because Mrs Carswell thinks the rats might come to the First Class. I have pipes over my head, too, but they go through small holes in the iron wall and I think I am safe.

Perhaps because I was remembering about that rat I went to the end of our main deck and stood there for quite a long time looking down at the Second Class. They use the deck by the hatches to the holds and only have a small covered piece right at the back over the propeller and Mr Davies says they only have one saloon. They must use this for everything, eating, reading, sewing, etc. They have no piano. We have two, one in the men's smoking-room, which of course I haven't tried, but the one in the drawing-room is very tinny. Just after Gibraltar I tried playing a Chopin mazurka on it but had to stop, for Mrs Carswell does not care for music.

I felt it was rather shameful to stand there staring down at the Second Class passengers. Usually when we take our constitutionals around the deck we just walk quickly past that part, but today something made me stay to watch. There is a young lady with two children, both girls, and always in clean pinafores which cannot be easy to do in cabins like theirs. I would like to talk to her, but there is no way, of course. There are three Catholics, too, priests in black robes. Mr Davies says they are Jesuits. I don't think I have ever seen a Jesuit before. They walk round and round the hatches, their mouths shaping words they are reading from a little book. I can't remember ever having talked to any Catholics, at least not when I knew they were that. There are quite a few of them in Scotland, but I never heard of any in South Edinburgh where we lived. We are all Presbyterians.

SS *Mooldera,*
January 14th, 1903

Tomorrow we reach Colombo in Ceylon which will be my first land in the Far East. There will also be a mail ship leaving for home within a few hours after we arrive, so this is the first chance to get a letter off since Suez and I have been writing to Mama all morning. I can't use many things in this notebook, though I did tell her what the Captain said to me. I did not mention Mr Davies. I also told her about the Lascar sailors washing down the decks quite early in the morning and the sound it makes just over my head which nearly always wakes me. There is not a lot to say. I told some fibs, that I was getting on with my needlework when I haven't touched it, and that I was reading *Daily Thoughts*, which she gave me, each morning after breakfast. I had stopped reading it even before we got near Malta. There is a message for every day and they are all semi-devotional, but I don't care for them somehow. When we were still in the Bay of Biscay Mrs Carswell asked to see what I was reading and I gave her the book, but she gave it back quite quickly, saying the Bible was good enough for her. I haven't seen her reading the Bible. If she carries one somewhere it must be well hidden, for I think I have seen everything else she has. She scatters things. In a small cabin this is a trial. I have never shared sleeping quarters with anyone before, except Margaret Blair when I went to stay with the Blairs near Aviemore, and her room was huge. I didn't mind that, though it still gave me a strange feeling.

Mrs Carswell always has a nap after lunch which she says you must in the tropics. She takes off her dress and puts on a wrapper and lies on the bunk. It is bad enough climbing up to my berth over her at night time, but I won't do it during the day. Also, she likes to eat heavily at what she calls 'tiffin', and this makes her snore. It is horrid in that cabin and I won't ever stay there longer than I have to. Usually I go to my deck chair and sit there. I am reading *St Ronan's Well* by Sir Walter Scott from the ship's library, but I do not find it very interesting. Mama says I am not a natural reader, for I do not like being instructed in a book. Most of the books in Papa's old library were like sermons about something, though they were not sermons about religious matters. I only remember Papa from childhood, but I do know it was a great grief to Mama that he never went to church more than twice a year, if then. And never for Holy Communion. Once, when she was crying about being a lone widow after I had said I would marry Richard and go to China, she said that the Devil had got to Papa through a man called Dr Huxley. I remember the name because I was curious about who Dr Huxley was, but I never found out.

I was reading in my deck chair, the ship scarcely rolling at all, when I realized that the light had changed. For days we have had such a strange light, that greyness, the sun screened. Now it was suddenly much brighter. I went to the rail and straight ahead the greyness from sea to sky ended on a line, and some miles ahead I could see the blue the Captain had talked about. It was glittery enough to hurt my eyes and this seemed to be because where the cloud ended there was a breeze ruffling the water, though where we were it was still quiet and the sea looked oily. I went to the front of the deck and stood there, all alone, the other passengers probably taking their after-lunch naps. As the ship got nearer that light, but was still in shadow, it almost seemed as though suddenly we would be moving from one picture into another. Then there was a great commotion on the water just inside where the sea was still grey, what seemed to be huge fish leaping into the air and falling back again with great splashes.

'Dolphins,' Mr Davies said from behind me, and I jumped. I don't know how long he had been standing there. He must have been watching me while I was watching the sea, which gave me an uneasy feeling. He asked if I would like to go to the ship's bow to watch the dolphins leaping in front of it. The deck below was used by Chinese steerage passengers but we hadn't any as yet so it was all right to use it and we went past hatches and machinery to more steps up over the forecastle where the Lascars live. From an open door came a strange, hot smell that wasn't cooking, I don't know what it was. There was also the sound of a penny whistle, only with better notes, deeper and rather sad. Maybe it was a Lascar playing a tune of home. I wanted to wait on the steps to listen but Mr Davies gripped my arm and pushed me up.

The dolphins seemed to be waiting for us just where the sunlight began, and Mr Davies told me that they like ships and like being watched by the people on them. A few minutes later I had to believe him, the dolphins began to jump back and forth across the *Mooldera's* bow, all of them going much faster than we were, coming curving in with new-moon arc leaps out of the water and then an even bigger leap right across the ship's course which put them only a few feet from us. One of them, and I think it was the same one coming back again and again, turned on his side in the jump and I saw in that shiny black shape a small shining black eye which seemed to be looking straight at me. This sounds silly when put down in writing but suddenly then it was as though things that had been frightening me, and I had not written down in this notebook, or even thought about except far back in my mind, were all right now. That dolphin seemed to be saying that I didn't need to be uneasy about what was going to happen to me in the East. The breeze on the sea was making quite a noise by then and I almost wanted to shout into it, wildly. Of course I didn't. Mr Davies would have thought I had gone mad. When I turned to him with a question he had not been watching the dolphins at all, but staring at me. I wish he wouldn't do that.

The ship moved into sunlight and it was very hot, even with the breeze. Mr Davies said 'Oh my G—!' Of course he is a sailor but I was still very startled he would say that in front of a lady. It made me look to where he was now looking. On the open piece of the bridge I could make out the Captain from his whiskers and he seemed to be watching us through binoculars, while the First Class cross deck beneath him was lined with passengers who must have been wakened from their naps by stewards and stewardesses telling them about the dolphins. I couldn't see Mrs Carswell but I was sure she would hear about me being up at the bow of the ship alone with Mr Davies. However, I am writing this in my bunk by the light of the little lamp here and Mrs Carswell has not said anything so perhaps

her being so aloof from most people on board will keep her from
getting the news.

SS *Mooldera*,
At sea,
January 17th, 1903

Mrs Carswell and I are not speaking. She heard about Mr Davies
and me from the Malacca Judge making one of his jokes at dinner.
Mrs C. never laughs at his jokes and this time she looked like thunder. Later in our cabin she said I had behaved like a *fast* woman and
had I forgotten that I was betrothed to a gentleman of a very distinguished English family? I was cheeky, I suppose, I said yes I knew I
was engaged but I was travelling to be married and not to enter a
nunnery. She said she did not know what was to become of me after
she left this ship at Hong Kong, for there was no one on board she
could put in charge of me to Shanghai. I was very angry. I am
twenty years old, if only just, and can look after myself, so I said why
not get the whiskery Captain to look after me for the last part of the
voyage? For a minute I thought Mrs Carswell was going to strike
me. If she had I would have left the cabin and gone straight to the
Purser to demand some other place to sleep. Maybe she saw in my
eyes what I was thinking, for she seemed to check the words that
had been coming and said instead that her report to my mother on
my behaviour on board the *Mooldera* would bring sorrow into an
Edinburgh home. I said talking of reports made her sound like a
headmistress. After that we both went into our bunks and drew the
curtains. She did not begin to snore soon after the noise she makes
moving about getting out of her clothes, so I expect that anger kept
her awake as it did me.

In the morning I felt uneasy about our quarrel and worried that
she really would write Mama, which I did not want because things
like I am a fast woman would be terribly hurtful. Mama is proper,
too, though not nearly so strict in her thinking as Mrs C., to whom
breathing is almost a sin. I wonder what she would think of her own
snoring if she knew about it? Perhaps Mr Carswell has always been
afraid to tell her?

I got up and washed and so on with the curtains on the lower berth still drawn but with the feeling that I was being watched from behind them. Well if Mrs C. was doing that now she knows about my corsets. However, she can't say anything because if she does I will know she was peeping. It would be a little like someone watching to see if you close your eyes through prayers, if they see you don't they haven't closed their own, so they are unable to mention the matter. I only close mine when I am serious about my prayers, but not for the Minister's prayers. In our church there were some people who kept their eyes shut for the blessing on King Edward and all the members of the Royal Family, but after that, opened them.

I could see the Island of Ceylon from the deck before I went down to breakfast but I wasn't very interested in it. At the table I did not speak one word to the Malacca Judge and I think he knows why. I ate a good breakfast, for I am very hungry these days, the porridge lumpy, but excellent bacon and eggs, and they make lovely crisp hot rolls on board. I had three. Before I was finished Mrs C. came in. We all said good morning very politely. Afterwards I went up on deck and sat in my chair, on the side away from Ceylon. Mrs C. came to me there and said she thought we had both been a little hasty last night and I said yes we had, and for a minute I thought she was going to bend down to kiss me, but she didn't, maybe because she does not care to bend too much with her figure. Anyway, it was a reconciliation and I decided to do what she wanted in Colombo in spite of what Mr Davies had said about going down the coast a little way to a place called Mount Lavinia. He didn't actually make this an invitation, perhaps because he knew he would have to take Mrs C. with us in the train, or carriage, or whatever it is.

SS *Mooldera*,
January 18th, 1903

Well, we have now seen all we are going to of 'India's coral strand'. Perhaps Ceylon is not really India, I have never been very good at geography, though I am becoming more interested in it now. I have taken to carrying this notebook in my work-bag and writing in it when I am pretending to write letters. I did try to write a letter to Margaret Blair in Aviemore, but I wanted more to write in this book so ended up with a postcard to her showing the harbour of Ceylon. That is about all I saw. I went ashore with Mrs C. and we had to wait for her friends' carriage in a very hot shed with a tin roof. When it came the carriage was a rattly old four-wheeler with a black hood up that was smelly, I suppose to keep off the sun, though we had our parasols. The horse was all skin and bones. We drove through streets with white buildings and lots of dark-skinned people in variegated clothes that were quite pretty if too plain for my taste, the women draped like Greek statues in museums, only better covered of course. After that we came to a part with gardens, very thick plantings, but not much colour, or at least not that I saw, mostly some kind of lily. Then the horse pulled us slowly up a sloping drive with palms on each side that reminded me of the pineapples with their tops left on you see in that expensive Princes Street fruit shop sometimes.

Mrs C.'s friends were waiting for us on the steps of a white bungalow with huge verandahs furnished like rooms. Their name was Johnson. Mr Johnson didn't speak much, but his wife did, all the time, mostly to Mrs C. She wasn't interested in me except to ask Mrs C. about whom I was marrying, and she seemed quite surprised when she heard, staring at me rather rudely, I thought. Luncheon took a very long time. Whenever she wanted service Mrs Johnson didn't ring a bell, she clapped her hands and a manservant came in. I think there must have been plenty of servants in that house, I saw three men working in the garden. I wondered if I would soon be clapping my hands when I wanted anything to have people come running. It is rather a strange thought. At home we have only Cook and Jessie, though of course quite a lot of people in South Edinburgh have a good many servants. One of Mama's friends has a page who wears a uniform when he opens the door to ladies on the 'At Home' Thursdays, but the page is really the under gardener. We had tea at the Johnsons', then drove back to the jetty for the last

launch out to the *Mooldera* and that was all I saw of Colombo. Mr
Davies had not gone to Mount Lavinia alone, he was waiting at the
top of the gangway.

SS *Mooldera*,
January 19th, 1903

There has been terrible trouble. Tonight at dinner the dessert was
very good because the ship had taken on a lot of fresh fruit and we
had to taste many strange things, though most of them seemed
insipid to me. The stewards brought us finger bowls for the first
time on this voyage, perhaps because in this calm sea there was no
danger of them spilling. Even Mrs C. tried a fruit, though she had
said when she saw the selection that they might be poison to Western stomachs. In Hong Kong she does not touch anything raw that
comes from China, only vegetables which must be cooked. She was
talking of servant trouble when the Judge, rather suddenly, leaned
over the table to say to me that there was to be a concert that night
in the men's smoking-room and that Mrs Price had agreed to sing,
but she had no one to accompany her on the piano, and would I
oblige? Before I could say anything Mrs C. spoke for me, saying:
'Miss Mackenzie has never been in the smoking-room since we left
Tilbury docks and she has no intention of entering it.' The Judge
was looking at me as though he had not heard Mrs C. at all. I took
a deep breath, then said yes I would certainly accompany Mrs Price
if she had the sheet music for her songs. The Judge thanked me,
never looking at Mrs C., and then added that it would be quite a
large attendance because an invitation had been issued to the Second Class passengers to attend. At this Mrs C. put down her napkin,
stood, and without giving any of us a glance, went out of the
dining-room. The news that the Second Class would be at the concert made me a little uneasy. I had thought they were only allowed
up on our deck for Divine Service, which only three or four of them
attend. This is a Church of England service read from a book by the
First Officer. They say the Captain is without God. The responses
from the congregation are very poor and the singing dreadful, and
usually I don't really take part for the Church of England service is

strange to me, though I suppose I shall have to get used to it when I marry Richard. After the service they serve beef tea on deck if it is calm, and in the hallway if it is rough.

On the stairs up from the dining-room I decided that if I was to accompany Mrs Price before a lot of people I could not do it in the brown dress but would wear the voile with spots which needs a special petticoat. Mrs C. always goes to the ladies drawing-room after dinner for a time before going to bed at half past nine, but this time she was in the cabin, sitting very straight on the little sofa. As soon as I went in she said in a very loud voice: 'Mary Mackenzie, do you consider yourself a true Christian?' I was quite shocked. Even our Minister had not asked me *that* when I was accepted into the South Morningside Church after Infant Baptism. She went on to a lot more, about her duty as my chaperone which was a sacred trust to my dear mother and whose wishes with regard to me Mrs C. knew very well indeed. From what she said and the way she said it the men's smoking-room could have been a place of special wickedness, but I have looked in quite often through the glass doors and all there was to be seen was men reading with cigars in their mouths, or sometimes playing cards or chess. When I spoke I was a little surprised at the way my own voice sounded. I asked Mrs C. if she would kindly go up to the drawing-room as usual because I had to dress for the concert and would like the cabin to myself. I thought for a minute she was going to refuse, but she got up and went through the curtain into the passage. A few seconds later she came back to say: 'It may interest you to know that I have available, should I wish, the means by which to send a message to your intended husband.' When she had gone I was shaking and had to sit down.

At quarter to nine, still feeling upset, I went up the stairs to the main deck and though I had a feeling that Mrs C. would be watching from the drawing-room I did not look in there to see if she was. The doors to the smoking-room had been fastened back, the chairs arranged in rows as for Divine Service in the drawing-room. The piano was in a very bright light. Some of the chairs were already occupied and there were small tables to hold glasses, with two stewards already serving alcoholic drinks. The Judge was in charge and came over to me at once, calling on Mrs Price to join us. She was wearing a dress I had not seen before, green silk, very plain, but a good colour with her hair which is quite bright, not auburn, but with orange-seeming glints through it. Somehow I wasn't so pleased with my voile, there is perhaps too much detail with those ruffles and the colour not quite right, a sort of blue-mauve, the spots white. I couldn't help thinking that with my face flushed pink, as I could feel it was, I was not looking my best. Usually my skin is like ivory, and I have never been threatened by rosy cheeks.

The Judge introduced me to Mrs Price to whom I had not spoken before and she smiled quite sweetly while we exchanged politenesses, after which she gave me her music. On top was 'Pale Hands I Loved Beside the Shalimar', something of a surprise because when I have heard it once or twice it had always been a man's song and I remember that at one Edinburgh musical evening some of the ladies said that it was rather unpleasantly suggestive. Her other song was the 'Londonderry Air' with the Danny Boy words, and her encore 'Where the Mountains of Mourne', etc., which made me wonder if she has Irish connections.

The Judge led us to seats which were not with the others but at an angle to them, so that the audience could look at us even while we were not performing, which I didn't like. It was a surprise to see that one of the other performers was the First Officer who reads the Divine Service, a rather solemn-looking man who does not seem to preside over a very cheerful table in the dining saloon. There was also the ship's doctor who sat down on the other side of me from Mrs Price and we spoke for the first time. He asked me if I was going to sing and I said I was just an accompanist and he told me that for his sins he gave humorous recitations, but did not have a large repertoire because there was no need to increase it, his audiences changing on every voyage. He is a gingery sort of man with almost greenish eyes and doesn't look old when he smiles. Also, he has no moustache, which is a good thing, because I don't like ginger moustaches. I think I would find it very embarrassing to go to him as a doctor, he has a way of looking that is too bold. His name is Dr Waterford. Perhaps Mrs C. is right about something in his past, but if that is the case it seems to sit lightly on him.

While I was talking to the doctor the lady with the two children from the Second Class came in. She was wearing a white dress that was quite pretty and had her hair dressed very well in a simple style. She stood in the doorway looking more frightened than I had felt, and if I had not been a performer I think I would have gone over to welcome her. Fortunately the Judge turned and saw her and he did that, very pleasantly in a nice old-gentlemanly manner. When he wishes to, the Judge can be very agreeable, and I think it is quite wrong of him to goad me in connection with Mrs C., which is what I am beginning to see he is doing. Why? While the lady from the Second Class was being shown to her seat I saw the wife of the Consul in Swatow staring at her. For once I agree with Mrs C. I do not care for that woman. She had on yet another new dress of cream-coloured Shantung silk cut very low in front with a lace collar that was boned to stand up all around her neck almost like the collars you see in pictures of Queen Elizabeth. The collar seemed to me to call attention to her face, which is very hard, and certainly not young. I think she uses paint. Perhaps she smokes in private? Mrs C. says that in these times of lax morals there are ladies who do, though this might just be one of her exaggerations.

Perhaps because I was looking at her the lady from Swatow looked at me, only she was staring. Suddenly I realized that I should have worn my corset under the voile and that she suspected I wasn't, and was just waiting for me to walk over to the piano to make sure, perhaps preparing to say something to the people around her, who were men. I wanted to run from the smoking-room and down to the cabin and I was very hot, and could feel the flush coming again which would make me look dreadful. I wondered for a minute if I might escape by saying that I felt faint and must go out on deck, but put away this idea because it would be running from something I had said I would do. It seemed as though everyone in those other seats was staring at us and from the burning I felt in my face I was sure it was now bright red. Suddenly Dr Waterford leaned towards me and said: 'No one seems to be thinking about refreshment for the entertainers. I feel the need of some Dutch courage myself, and how would you fancy a lemon squash, Miss Mackenzie?'

Though I was sure he only made the suggestion because I looked as if I might burst into flames, I was very grateful for his consideration and thanked him. He went off to the hatch himself instead of calling one of the Goanese stewards, and while he was away the Judge announced the first item which was to be general singing of a song he said we all knew that had been made famous by none other than Miss Marie Lloyd. I did not know the song. I had heard of Miss Lloyd, of course, but Mama does not approve of music halls, so I never saw her on the stage. I have only been to the theatre three times, once to see a Shakespeare play, *The Tempest,* and twice to Gilbert and Sullivan operas. The Judge led the singing in a voice that must have been quite good when he was young, a baritone, and it was mostly the men in the audience who took up the chorus, I did not hear any ladies' voices at all, though the Swatow Consul's wife was waving time with her ivory fan. I knew that Mrs C., if she was listening, would be shocked by the words, which were something about how a little of what you fancy does you good.

The men were still roaring that chorus when Dr Waterford came back with the refreshment, and I thought the lemon squash had rather a queer taste, not as sweet as I had been expecting, but I was grateful for it, and after even a few sips began to feel a little better. The Doctor seemed to be enjoying his Dutch courage, and had been long enough at the hatch to empty a glass before the one in his hand. I noticed that the Swatow lady was drinking what looked very like whisky, too. I knew by then that Mrs C. had been right about one thing, Mama would not have wished me to be at this drinking concert, let alone have me perform. Already some of the men, and they were not from the Second Class, were making loud jokes in one corner and the Judge was forced to call for silence before he announced the next item which was the First Officer reciting 'The

Charge of the Light Brigade' by Lord Tennyson. It is not a piece I care for. During it I sat thinking that I hated the voile dress and would never wear it again.

The next performer was a man who must be more than forty whom I have watched playing shuffleboard, but not spoken to. The Judge said he was a tin mine engineer from somewhere in Malaya, and the man explained before he sang, unaccompanied, that his is quite a lonely life and that he has entertained himself by collecting native songs, the one that he was going to sing being from his Chinese coolies. It was a very strange little tune, if you could call it that, and sung in native language, quite meaningless, but I rather liked it, and I clapped quite hard for an encore which he must have heard, for he looked at me, then smiled and said he would give us a Malay song, this time about a lover lamenting his faithless sweetheart. I had the feeling he looked at me quite often while singing, which made me uncomfortable and some of the men, who perhaps understood the Malaya language, were laughing at the words as though they were suggestive. I didn't like the Malaya song at all. Also, I was beginning to become very nervous again about when it would be the turn of Mrs Price and me, so I didn't pay a great deal of attention to Dr Waterford's performance. It was an extract from *The Pickwick Papers* by Charles Dickens and spoken in low-class English accents with 'welly' for 'very' and such things, which meant I didn't understand a lot of it. During the recitation I finished my glass of lemon squash quite quickly and though I was no cooler from it, I did feel less jumpy.

Though I should have been expecting it, I was still startled to hear the Judge say that now Mrs Price would sing accompanied by Miss Mackenzie at the piano. As I stood up I realized that I had not really looked at the music and also that I hadn't heard the piano played this evening. For all I knew there might be dead keys. When I sat down the stool was so low it was like trying to reach up to a shelf and the audience, seeing this, began to laugh. I had to get up again and spin the stool almost as high as it would go, and then I could not push it back far enough because, like all the furniture on the ship, it was fastened to the floor against rolling. From the way Mrs Price was looking at me it was plain she did not like people to laugh before she started to sing.

I played the introductory bars, the sound like an Italian barrel organ. I was too fast, Mrs Price likes to take her time. She sounded as though a bag of small stones were being jiggled on a string in her throat, and no one could have made out one word that she was singing. One of the hooks at the back of my dress gave way. I could feel the gap, but had to play on wondering how many others would go. The Swatow lady was probably wondering that, too. And maybe the men. I was sure that everyone was watching those hooks and eyes, and not Mrs Price.

The Indian song by Mrs Finden was slow enough but 'Danny Boy' crawled. I thought we would never finish. I felt I should have been grinding the piano slowly with a crank, not trying to get sound from the keys. The worst thing happened then; while there were two stanzas of 'Danny Boy' to go, I became suddenly dizzy. For a moment I thought it might be the ship, then I knew it was not, for the smoking-room was moving around me. I could scarcely read the music and if there had been any new notes I could not have finished the piece. I just managed. Then, during the applause and calls for an encore, I knew I was going to be sick in one minute, or two at the most. I got up and walked past all those faces towards the door. I was swaying. I have never walked like that before in my life, as though my feet were going down on cotton wool, not the carpet. I just kept looking at the doors. I got out into the hallway and just managed to reach the deck, but the railing was too far. I had to stop and bend over.

A lady who could not have been at the concert came out of the drawing-room. I really couldn't see her face but I heard what she said: 'Were you drinking in there? A girl of your age? How disgusting!'

I am writing all this down in my berth above Mrs C., maybe with the idea that if I put everything down and face what happened, that way I may be able to forget. Instead I am waiting for the sound of feet on the deck over my head which will mean that the concert has finished and people are out for a last walk. The Lascars will not wash those boards until the morning. How can I face the other passengers tomorrow?

I don't know when Mrs C. got back to the cabin, her curtains were drawn when I came in. For a long time there was no noise from below at all but now there is a sound that isn't like her usual snoring. I had better put out this light.

2

❧

Letter from Mary Mackenzie to Mrs Isabel Mackenzie

Raffles Hotel,
Singapore,
January 23, 1903

Dearest Mama,

I have very sad news. The lady you found to be my chaperone to the Far East has unfortunately died, which has been a great shock to me as it will be to you. Mrs Carswell did not die on board the SS Mooldera, *but in hospital in Penang, having been taken ill on the night of January 19th while we were still in the Indian Ocean approaching the Strait of Malacca. At dinner she was perhaps a little strained, but it did not seem much to me. She was a lady who always retired early and sometimes I did not accompany her at nine-thirty to our cabin, for, as you know well, I have never been one to sleep early. When I did go down after a last walk about the decks she was already behind the curtains of her berth and later, while I was using a light in my berth to write to you, I heard strange noises from below. For a time I did nothing since I was used to noises in the cabin, but then these became very violent. I found her convulsed and apparently unable to speak. It was very frightening. First I had to*

call a sleepy stewardess, then the doctor, who is a horrid
man. By the time the doctor came it must have been one
a.m. and Mrs Carswell was in great distress and
groaning. He gave her some liquid medicine which had
the effect of making her very sick very often, but no
improvement by morning.

I had to nurse Mrs Carswell assisted by a stewardess
who is old and grumpy and one other passenger, a lady
I had not liked in appearance at all, but who suddenly
came to our cabin as a volunteer when I was at my wit's
end with worry. She is the wife of the British Consul in
Swatow, a Mrs Brinkhill. Before she came I had not had
the slightest desire to make her acquaintance, which
shows that it is not right to make judgements too
quickly. She had seemed to me hard and worldly, but she
became a tower of strength. There are other ladies on
board who might have come to help, but not one of them
did, not so much as a knock on the cabin door with
enquiries though when passing along the passage beyond
they must at times have heard the terrible noise Mrs
Carswell, poor lady, was making. The world is a strange
mix of people of different types and so many look what
they aren't.

When I first agreed to marry Richard and come to
the Far East you said that you feared for me because I
had been brought up in such a sheltered manner and
had never been out in the world. Well, I am having
experience now. I had never thought of myself as a
nurse, but with Mrs Brinkhill to show me how to
manage, I learned a great deal, especially how to meet
up with real unpleasantness without giving way to
disgust and wanting to hide. To be honest I did feel like
that at first, wanting others to take over, but it was Mrs
Brinkhill who helped me to do what had to be done. She
is a wonderful lady. The ship is to be in Singapore for
two days before sailing on to Hong Kong and because

Mrs Brinkhill said we both needed a change from being on board she has taken a room in this very charming hotel. We are now relaxing here, and beyond the open shutters on to a balcony I can hear the crackling of palm fronds in the wind which is a new sound for me, and I like it.

But to tell you about Mrs Carswell. They took her from the ship to hospital in Penang as soon as we had anchored and a tender could be brought alongside. They lowered the gangplank and she was carried down it very early in the morning, just as dawn was coming all bright and red. Penang is a very beautiful harbour and it seemed so strange, the loveliness of nature all around, and a poor woman being carried to her death. I think I knew, though I didn't say it to Mrs Brinkhill as we watched, that she could not live. So you see I am not so sheltered any more. I have seen the face of death. It did not make me want to cry, I was just cold inside.

It is all most tragic. The news has been cabled to Mr Carswell in Hong Kong where he must have been making preparations to welcome home his wife from her trip to England. I do not know much about Mr Carswell, for she rarely spoke of him. However, there were no children in the family. Mrs Brinkhill surprised me by saying that he would marry again soon, that widowers in the Far East always marry again quickly when they lose their wives. Such remarks may make her seem hard, but underneath is a well of kindness. I cannot believe that only a week ago I thought her a lady to be avoided.

Since Mrs Carswell died the ship's doctor has scarcely been seen, perhaps because he knows he did not do much to help her. According to Mrs Brinkhill, the word from the Penang hospital just before we sailed again was that Mrs Carswell had died from dysentery as the result of Colombo fruits eaten on board. For my part I doubt this since she was most careful about eating anything strange and never did in Hong Kong and, though I did see her tasting some kind of melon, it was only from far inside it, at the very centre, which could scarcely carry such germs. Mrs Brinkhill thinks it was probably peritonitis, but we will never know now. Because the trouble just might have been contagious, all my things were moved to another cabin and the one I shared with Mrs Carswell fumigated while we sailed down to Singapore. I was glad of the change, for I would not have cared to go on living in the old cabin with all its associations.

Well, Mama dear, I am sorry this has to be such a sad letter, but you mustn't worry about me. Even though Mrs Carswell has gone I am not deserted and Mrs Brinkhill has really taken over as chaperone. As I told you, she is the wife of a Consul and therefore someone of importance. I am writing this to you in our room in the hotel where I have had breakfast in bed, with the windows open on to all the strange sounds of an Oriental city, the jingling bicycle bells on the rickshas, street cries, and so on. The sun is very bright outside and later we will go for a ride in a carriage about the streets and then visit the famous botanic gardens which are said to be one of the sights of Asia.

The service in this hotel is very good, soft-footed Chinese who seem to know what your every wish is as soon as you think of it. If I am to have servants like this in Peking it will certainly make life very easy in some ways. I had hoped to have a letter from Richard waiting for me here but there wasn't one, so perhaps he missed the mail connections from North China which Mrs Brinkhill says are very uncertain. Even in Swatow where she lives, and which is quite near Hong Kong, there are sometimes whole months in which she has no word from the outside world at all. They take English newspapers which arrive two to three months later in huge bundles, but they read them all in sequence by dates, something her husband insists on. It

*sounds as if her home in Swatow is very pretty but I shan't
have a chance to visit it for the* Mooldera *does not call
there on the way to Shanghai. Mrs Brinkhill has to change
ships in Hong Kong so I will be without her company for
the last days of the voyage. The man I thought was her
husband is not, just an old friend. Her husband is in
Swatow.*

*Well, I must close now. I will write again to catch the
mail from Hong Kong. All my love to you, dear.*

Your ever loving daughter,

Mary

SS *Mooldera,*
January 27th, 1903

Today we passed a huge island in the South China Sea and I am
down in my cabin writing about it before I dress for dinner. Since I
am living on my own there are times when I can wear just a kimono
for coolness if I lock the door. It was Mrs Brinkhill who told me that
it is all right for ladies to do this in the tropic heat, for temporary
relief.

We went to a Singapore shop to buy the kimono and I chose one
that is white cotton with blue flowers on it, very light for easy washing in the basin and hanging to dry by the porthole. Mrs B. also
told me she thinks I have been a martyr to my underclothes, bought
at Maule's Drapery in Edinburgh, which were supposed to be suitable for a tropic climate but Mrs B. says might have been designed
for Eskimos. Mama would be horrified to know that I am abandon-
ing part of my expensive trousseau like this, but then Mama has
never been in a hot country. In the shop I spent the equivalent of
two pounds seven shillings British money.

I have also learned about prickly heat. Mrs B. said that if I hadn't
got it now soon I would, so I admitted that I had it a little, though
I didn't tell her where, but I think she guessed. She said that chafing
is to be avoided at all costs and that I must be very careful about
using the fresh water rinse after my salt baths. I can ask her anything
and she will tell me, without embarrassment between us, or not

much. I have a little, she has none. I am now sitting at her table in the dining saloon which means sitting opposite Mr Davies at meal-times but he does not seem to have much to say for himself in Mrs B.'s company, only staring at me a lot, which I have got used to. A lot of our passengers left the ship at Singapore, including the Malacca Judge whom I was not sorry to lose, and only a few people have joined us, but these include a Mr and Mrs Hansen who are Danish, both very fair and young, which makes a pleasant change. The Danish people must be very carefree socially, for almost imme-diately after we had been introduced Mrs Hansen suggested that I call her Ingrid. I can see that Mrs Brinkhill doesn't care for this quick informality and I don't think she likes the way I am playing shuffleboard with the Hansens at least twice a day. It is my feeling, too, that she somehow arranged that the newcomers were not to sit at our dining table, though there were two places vacant after Sin-gapore. All this is strange, for Mrs Brinkhill is such a generous woman. For instance, I was not allowed to pay one penny towards our bill at Raffles Hotel, though I tried to.

I was writing about the island we saw. It came into view in the late afternoon and we sailed past just before sunset, a big island with quite a high mountain and all a most wonderful bright green that quickly darkened to almost purple. The other day I was trying to describe a tropic sunset to Mama and said that it seemed as if Heaven had spilled down all the colours they had, but of course I had to tear that sheet up for she would have thought it sacrilegious. Travel seems to put more than distance between you and the people at home, an increasing number of things you have seen and thought about which you can't mention for fear they would shock, and this is really sad. I think of Mama doing all the things in one week that she will do in the next week, like those tea-parties.

I am going to a totally different life. For instance, Mrs B. told me about pirates as though they were nothing special. Her boat from Hong Kong to Swatow passes Byas Bay where there is a famous pirate base, and even though these coastal ships have British officers and First Class accommodation protected by iron grilles and so on, they are frequently attacked, usually by accomplices travelling steerage who start things off just before the fast junks appear from behind some island firing cannon. Mrs B. was once in a real battle in which six or seven of the pirates were killed and one of the British officers wounded and she acted as nurse to the wounded man while bullets were flying. I cannot imagine the Edinburgh tea-party ladies being much use during a pirate attack.

The island is called Great Natuna and belongs to the Dutch. The Dutch seem to have a huge empire in these parts that stretches for thousands of miles and includes thousands of islands, some very big like Sumatra. At school we always thought there was only one really big empire and that was ours, on which the sun will never set. I was looking at the island with the silly idea in my mind that it would be nice to be queen of such a place and never leave it when suddenly I remembered Mrs Carswell being carried down the gangplank at Penang looking already dead. I shivered. Mrs B. came up behind me then and asked what was the matter? I told her what I had been thinking about and she said something I will always remember: 'Child, you are travelling towards the lands of sudden death.'

She told me about a huge flood in China near a place called Wuhan in which some say as many as two and a half million people drowned, which is half of all the people in Scotland. Many of the bodies came floating down river to near Shanghai where Mrs B. was at the time.

It *is* whisky she drinks. I believe she must also keep some in her cabin for I have smelt it when I was visiting her there. Some of the things Mrs Carswell thought about Mrs B. are true enough, but I don't mind that at all. Good and bad are not so simple as we are taught. On this ship I have become five years older.

SS *Mooldera*,
Feb. 5th, 1903

When I first heard about the typhoon coming I was rather excited, sure that I must really have my sea legs now so wouldn't be sick, which would make it an adventure. I do not want another adventure like it. The first thing that happened was no ship's officers in the dining saloon for dinner, which seemed odd. Since Mrs Brinkhill left the ship at Hong Kong I have moved back to the main table opposite the Hansens, but Ingrid had a headache, and for some reason Nils was gloomy, though I don't think he was worrying about the coming storm. Afterwards I was going up the main stair when I met Mr Davies coming down it and I asked for news of the typhoon. He didn't at once answer me. His face looked strained. When he finally spoke he was very solemn: 'Miss Mackenzie, I want you to promise me that whatever you may think is happening on this ship you will stay in your berth in your cabin.' I couldn't believe he meant I should stay in my berth in the daytime, but he did, saying that the stewardess would show me how to make bedding rolls that would wedge me into my berth. I said: 'Do you mean the ship's movement could roll me out of my berth?' He said: 'It could throw you out.'

After that I went to the drawing-room, which was empty, as though everyone had gone to cabins to prepare for what was to come. I found the doors to the deck had been locked so there was nothing really I could do but go below myself, to undress and go to bed in the normal way without any padding of blankets. What woke me was my trunk coming out from beneath the berth and sliding over to hit the leg of the sofa. Then, while I lay listening to a roaring noise I had certainly not heard before on this ship, the trunk began to move again, this time rumbling over to crash against the cabin door. As we came back to near level I got up and went to pull aside the curtains over the porthole, only to find that the inner iron shutter which I had never expected to see used was now clamped down against the thick glass beyond it. The ventilation grille over the door which had sometimes let in the sound of men coming down late and noisily from the smoking-room now gave me a variety of other sounds, amongst them a great clattering that sounded like a shelf loaded with pots collapsing in a pantry. There was shouting at a distance, but no words I could make out. I was trying to push the trunk back under the berth when the ship went into a roll much worse than anything I would have believed possible. The ship lifted, then sagged, the sag throwing me first on to the sofa, then against the cabin wall. My trunk followed me, this time breaking the sofa leg. What must have been a monster wave hit the ship just beyond my wall, and this was followed by a shivering twenty times worse than the vibration we had when the *Mooldera* was going at top speed. Then came a roll that had me almost standing on the cabin wall and I was sure the ship was going to capsize.

It seemed to take a long time to get back to my berth and into it. Once there I tried to make that padding of blankets, but this wasn't enough to hold me in and I found a grip for both hands, one of them on the roll board, the other on a small rack fixed to the wall. It was very hot in the cabin, but I think I was perspiring from fear.

Somewhere down the passage a woman began to scream. The sound would die away, then there was another bad roll and she screamed again. Above that roaring noise and the creakings came a sharper tearing sound, as though the very metal plates were being torn from the ship's sides. I was sure that the *Mooldera* could not keep afloat for much longer and that we were all doomed. I prayed to God that He would not let me die on a ship to China. It was a coward's prayer and I am ashamed of it, but I lay with my eyes shut and asked it over and over. Then I thought that perhaps the Jesuits in the Second Class were praying, too, and that might help. I thought of other things, that it was Sunday and in Edinburgh Mama might now be pulling on her gloves and coming out of the house as all the church bells of Morningside said it was time for morning service. On Sunday, with no trams running, all you hear is the feet of people on the pavements going to church, not even the clip-clopping of horses because there is no need to use carriages with so many churches near at hand. When one of the rolls seemed to be becoming too deep for the ship to recover I called out: 'Mama, Mama!' as though she could hear me on her way to church, but I still didn't become as noisy as the screaming woman.

I thought of something else on my berth, but not for hours, as though it needed a long time of me being afraid to bring it out from hiding in my mind. I asked myself why I was coming to China to marry Richard and I couldn't get any answer to that, just a sort of dreadful emptiness. I couldn't see his face, as though my memory refused to bring out a picture of him. And the awful thing is that even now, when I try, I can't seem to *see* him. We didn't exchange photographs. There is just a very small snapshot of him in the Highlands when he was standing beside the horse he had been riding, but it is mostly the horse. What I can remember is that his hair is tight, fair curls over his head, and his side whiskers are not too bushy and he has blue eyes, but I can't see his *whole* face. In the Highlands, at Margaret Blair's, I thought he was the most handsome man I had ever seen and that is only thirteen months ago. Probably he doesn't remember what I look like, either.

There was a letter waiting for me in Hong Kong. My hand shook as I opened the envelope. The words seemed quite formal, but then he is like that. He was most correct in writing to Mama asking for my hand in marriage by the same post as he asked me. In this letter he said he was impatiently waiting to meet me in Tientsin and that it was his great regret that he couldn't come to Shanghai but his military duties prevented this. He has, however, made all the arrangements for me in Shanghai, I am to be met by an assistant Consul he knows there who will see me to my hotel, where I have a two-day wait for the ship that is to take me on to Tientsin. It was a letter full of arrangements. He said he had a hundred things to do to make ready for me. It was quite a long letter but beyond the words I could see that he was writing as I am now doing to Mama, trying to find things to say. I suppose that is the way I would be writing to him, too, and probably I am lucky in that I don't have to, I will be there before any letter.

If I find coming to China was a mistake what is to happen to me? If when we meet we just stare at each other as two strangers what can I do? I could never go back to Edinburgh in humiliation.

SS *Mooldera*,
Feb. 7th, 1903

I have just come down from the deck where it is bitterly cold to my cabin, thawing my fingers on the heating pipes. We have turned into one of the wide mouths of China's greatest river, the Yangtze Kiang, and Shanghai itself is up a side turning from the estuary, past what Mr Davies called the famous Woosung forts, though why they are famous he did not tell me and I was too cold to ask. The river is the colour of weak milky coffee and has flat banks of what looks like marshland. The only interesting thing to be seen are the junks with their ribbed sails like bats' wings.

I am not only down here to get warm but also to get away from Mr Davies who, since the storm, has become something of a nuisance, and thank goodness I'm not still sitting at his table. It isn't what he says so much as the way he looks, which gives me the feeling that at any moment at all he may suddenly say something quite improper to someone in my position and that I won't know what to say in return. So I am rather running away from him, which is horrid of me, because he has been most considerate in a way ever since Mrs Carswell died. He is really a very nice man, and it is such a pity that at his age he isn't long settled with a home life. It makes me nervous when he talks about a sailor's lonely years at sea, always meeting people who will soon go down a gangway and pass away from him forever. He can sometimes be quite poetical, perhaps because he is Welsh, and that's when I become most uneasy. Surely, apart from everything else, he ought to realize that at thirty-two he is remote from me in the generations? I told him that my fiancé is twenty-five, but any mention of Richard makes him frown. Mr Davies would be a very possessive man, I think, if he was given the chance.

Grand Hôtel de Wagon-Lits,
Shanghai,
February 8th, 1903

Well, I am in China for the first time, since Hong Kong is not China proper. Hong Kong is beautiful but this place, from what I have seen of it so far, is quite hideous. My hotel is in the French Concession. I had never heard of Concessions and the assistant Consul who came to meet me had to explain what they are. Apparently the Great Powers have taken pieces of China and established their own laws in these places, the natives only able to come into them as foreigners, which seems rather odd. All the buildings I can see from my window are European and, except for rickshas and those Chinese foreigners walking in the streets, I might not be in the Orient at all. There is a narrow river in front of the city, very dirty and very crowded with shipping. Along its banks are the poor living in boats with all their families and dogs and cats, cooking on braziers in the open exposed to the bitter wind. Mrs Brinkhill told me to expect to see great misery in China and said that I would get used to it. She also said I was to remember that people who don't know any better don't miss the things they haven't got. That is all very well if you live in some remote area, but these poor people here can look across at buildings like my hotel, all lit up with gaiety and high living. I should think this would make them angry. Of course, I must remember that we have our poor, too. Mama would never allow me to go unaccompanied down Leith Walk in Edinburgh or into places like the Canongate and the Grassmarket, these places of great misery. Still, I cannot believe that the poor in Scotland are anything like as poor as these Chinese on boats. The Bible says that the poor are always with us, so perhaps we must just accept that, but I wonder if it is going to be difficult for me to do it in China? I certainly hope that Peking is a prettier city than this.

There was a letter from Richard waiting in this hotel, not so formal as the one to Hong Kong, and he signed it with love, so I am not feeling cold inside even though everything around is strange. The assistant Consul who met me was at Harrow with Richard, very pleasant, though his wife who came with him to the ship stiffish, a plain woman with a thin face, wrapped in furs and wearing a hat of the same skins. I was not asked to their home.

Saying goodbye to Mr Davies was rather sad. He was waiting at the gangway and held my hand for too long, his very hot. He said he hoped God's blessing would go with me into China and quite suddenly that brought tears into my eyes and I had to turn away. When we were getting into the carriage on the jetty I looked back to see him at the rail, and he waved his big hand. I wish him well. He should get a Welsh wife. As he said, it must be sad to go down to the dining saloon on a ship to sit all alone at a table from which the passengers of only yesterday have all gone.

Today is exactly one month since my birthday. I am a changed person from what I was in the Red Sea.

Grand Hôtel de Wagon-Lits,
Shanghai,
Feb. 9th, 1903

This morning I woke up with a headache and in that state which ladies must endure. I had what breakfast I wanted brought to me in bed. It is strange how quickly one comes not to think of these Chinese menservants as men. After the hotels in Singapore and Hong Kong it doesn't bother me at all if one of them comes into the room when I am still in my nightgown, I do not look at him nor he at me. Everything he does is very smooth and quiet and one scarcely knows when they have gone.

I am glad to be alone when this is happening to me. Even at home with Mama it was always a trial, not only because one must never speak of it but also she dislikes having any sign at all brought to her attention. I was so startled when Mrs Brinkhill spoke openly to me of one's problem, as though there was no need for screening with delicacy. I will never forget how frightened I was the first time, which was at school. That was when Margaret Blair helped me and we became such friends. If I ever have a daughter I will not let her have such a shock. The thought of having a daughter is strange.

Grand Hôtel,
Next day

I go aboard the coastal steamer this evening for a sailing at midnight. Last night I was at dinner with the friends Richard wrote about, people called Hamlin who live in a very large house in the British Concession with many servants and grand furnishings in the French Empire style, which makes a very impressive room to enter but not so comfortable to sit in. The only hints of China were in the vases and the servants. At dinner nine courses were offered, but I must have lost my sea appetite suddenly because I couldn't do more than touch most of them. It was a large party into which I had been squeezed out of politeness at the last minute, and the gentleman they had got to keep the numbers right was old, with a red face, his only interest being the contents of the glasses in front of him. Each place setting had five of these and I would have thought Red Face could have found a wine that pleased him, but apparently not, for suddenly he said to our host: 'I say, Willie, none of this stuff has travelled, I've had enough of it. Brandy soda.' This rudeness only made Mr Hamlin laugh, and a servant at once fetched what was wanted.

I asked Mr Hamlin what being a company lawyer in Shanghai meant. He leaned over, patted my hand, and said: 'It means, my dear, that my life is dedicated to protecting innocent British business men from the machinations of the wily Chinee.' I said quite boldly that giving such advice seemed to be profitable, at which he went into shouts of laughter which had his wife looking at him from the other end of the table and clearly not at all pleased. I think Mr Hamlin quite liked me though I am certainly looking far from my best, quite horrified to see the state of my skin in the first large, well-lit mirror I've had the use of for some time. It must have been the salt sea air. Fortunately Mrs Brinkhill warned me about China Skin along with China Tummy and all sorts of other horrors and in Hong Kong I bought a pot of the cream she uses called 'Apple Petal' which you apply nightly and allow to soak into the pores. This is the first time I have used any aids to beauty other than oatmeal soap, and I don't really like the idea much, but perhaps in this part of the world it is essential.

I decided not to wear either the voile or the brown dress to the Hamlins', going down into the trunk for the blue French silk with

Belgian lace in a series of little capes from the shoulders. It is rather low over the bosom and Mama had sewn another piece of lace, on a backing, across the lower part of the square neckline which quite spoiled the dress, so I took it out again. In the Edinburgh shop they said it was a Paris model, and it cost enough to be . . . eleven pounds. Mama, generous in these things, said I must have one dress which was a wild extravagance for the very special occasion and then she began to cry, which was surprising in a shop.

I did not at all like it in the drawing-room when we were waiting for the men to join us after their port. There were nine ladies besides me and all of them seemed to have been too free with the liquid refreshment at dinner, including Mrs Hamlin. She is what Mama would call a handsome woman, certainly very sure of herself and her position in the world. She talks with her head held back, as though her nose was helping her to see you. She is a friend of Richard's mother so is quite old, but does not look as though she had ever been a girl. I had already noticed that in the Far East the ladies are very *rich* in their dressing, with satins and embroidery and so on. There is a great display of jewellery also, to the point of seeming vulgar, though I noticed when visiting Richard's family in Norfolk that this seems socially acceptable even in English country areas in the evening. They wear such plain clothes in the day and then are peacocks at night. I felt like a dull Scottish hen. Of course, I did not have my blue silk then.

When the men joined us the servants set up tables for a Chinese game called Mah Jongg. The ladies seemed surprised that I had never heard of it and one of them said it was becoming all the rage in London. I told her that in Edinburgh we are very slow at taking up *English* fashions, which Mr Hamlin thought an excellent thing, this causing his wife to give him a hard look again. I wonder if they are a happy couple? Certainly they have plenty of this world's goods. They sent a carriage and pair to the hotel for me, with a Chinese coachman in a livery of sorts, this padded for the winter, so that he looked like a very small man inside fat clothing. Most of the people here, though, apparently don't keep carriages, the ladies having their own private rickshas with a private coolie to pull them. This came out because one of the ladies' coolies had just died and she had had him for fifteen years which is apparently quite remarkable, for the pullers are not long-lived. When I asked whether this was because of their work the lady said certainly not, it was because of tuberculosis. She explained that the coolies of Europeans were very well looked after indeed, it was the wealthy Chinese who quite often mistreated theirs.

Mr Hamlin did not play Mah Jongg, sitting by an open coal fire with me. He told me that Peking is lovely, not in the least like Shanghai which is just a business kitchen in which to make money as fast as you can and then leave. In his view anyone who lives here for any other reason must be out of his mind, but Peking, in spite of the Boxer Troubles, is an Imperial city and feels like it. Though the Empress Dowager now pretends to like Europeans Mr Hamlin is quite sure that if she could she would order her people to start killing them again. When I said I seemed to be going to a dangerous city he said that the old lady had too much sense to try anything like the Boxers again, having had her fingers so badly burned only a year or two ago, and that I would find her capital one of the most interesting places in the world in which to live.

By the time I got back to the hotel it was after midnight and I sat for a long time in front of the dressing-table mirror which has movable side pieces and a bright electrolier over it. I am not beautiful. My hair is just ordinary brown. I think my eyes are best, brown, too, but really quite large and with lashes. And I haven't a big nose, for which I am thankful because from his pictures Papa had. It would have been an awful thing to inherit. Three men have wanted to marry me and I said yes to the third. Mama wanted me to say yes to the second. If I had married George I would have had a very safe life in Edinburgh.

I have decided I don't like the way I am doing my hair, the bun on top makes it look like one of those loaves of bread they call Sally Lunns. Still, this is the way Richard saw me, so I had better leave it just now.

Letter from Mary Mackenzie to her mother,
Mrs Isabel Mackenzie

SS Ching Wha,
At sea,
Feb. 11th, 1903

Dearest Mama,

*I am so ashamed of that short letter written on the
Mooldera just before we reached Shanghai, but my excuse
is that I was still rather upset by the typhoon. I won't
describe that again and you must not worry about my
travelling in ships because having seen what they can
endure and survive I will not easily be so frightened
again. In Shanghai I spent most of the time resting in my
hotel before embarking on this coastal ship which is very
small compared with the Mooldera, only eight cabins in
the First Class accommodation and eleven passengers
occupying them, though the steerage is packed with what I
suppose must be hundreds. In spite of its name this is a
British ship with British officers, the Captain and two
others, plus a Scotch Engineer from Troon. The other
passengers are an American Methodist missionary and his
wife who are returning to a city called Sian-Fu which they
had to flee from during the Boxer Troubles. The husband
is rather anti-British in his attitudes, calling us ruthless
imperialists, which does not make him the most agreeable
of table companions. I think he resents having to travel on
a British ship because there are no American ones on this
route. Three Catholic priests who were in the Second Class
on the Mooldera are now in the First Class here (there is
no Second), but all except the youngest seem to live in
another world with their little books of prayers which they
must say. They are not at my table in the small dining-
room but the youngest priest talks to me sometimes when
we meet on deck, about the weather and so on. The other
passengers in the First are all Chinese who take their*

meals in their cabins and no exercise, so we scarcely ever see them.

This Captain, unlike the one on the Mooldera, is a very merry man, only half English, his mother Norwegian. He is from Newcastle and a little like a Scotchman in his attitudes, and with a peculiar sense of humour which I enjoy. I think that usually not many people laugh at his jokes which makes him like me rather, because I do. Also, having lived in the Far East for twenty years without once having returned to Britain—his wife is in Shanghai—he can tell me many things about China which are most useful.

I am writing this because the ship touches at a place called Wei-Hai-Wei before Tientsin where I can post a letter. I think of you so often, wondering what you are doing, and whether you are still giving your every other Thursday 'At Homes'? Did you go to hear Handel's Messiah once again this year as usual? It is so strange to think that I am now on the opposite side of this spinning world and that this means at least a six weeks' journey and months for the post. They say that the new Trans-Siberian railway service will mean that it will soon be possible to be in Europe from the Far East within twelve days, which seems almost unbelievable, but I don't know that I could endure sitting in a hot, smoky carriage for all that time. The sea journey offers a good deal of variety and interest.

As you can imagine I am so excited about meeting Richard in no time at all now. He will be waiting for this ship in Tientsin and we will go from there by train together to Peking. You must not worry about your daughter coming so far to marry, I am sure we will be happy and make a good life. Cook and Jessie are, I know, looking after you as always and you must give them my warmest greetings. Do you still have the same gardener? Oh well, if he has gone you will soon get

another. I am writing this in my narrow bunk and my
arm has got cramp so, dearest Mother, I will say goodbye
for now.

    Your ever loving daughter,
    Mary

                                  SS *Ching Wha*,
                                  Feb. 11th, 1903

Tonight before getting into bed to write this I said my prayers, which I have not done since the typhoon. It is a habit you can get out of. On the *Mooldera* I had to do it privately up in my berth after undressing, which was such a struggle in itself that quite often I forgot. Somehow the words you say at home in your prayers are not right for China, and I wonder if this is going to be a continuing trouble to me? Perhaps it is the missionaries and the priests on this ship which have made me think of these things but I cannot escape the feeling that my faith is now being tested. In Edinburgh it is easy to believe in Heaven as a reward for the good life carefully lived, but from what I have seen of the Far East I am having doubts of what had once seemed certain. For instance, those people on boats in the Shanghai river. No doubt many of the people living in that way lead sinful lives as we would see it, but surely it is in ignorance? And if that is the case are these sins that would put them in Hell as punishment? Perhaps there is an excuse in ignorance and they would not suffer as we who *know* would suffer justly.

    I feel so far from home and Mama right now. I am sitting here staring at the rust stains which come through on bolt heads from the iron plates, wondering if I believe in Heaven and Hell? Perhaps it is not necessary to believe in either to believe in God? If that were so I would feel better, yet every Minister I have ever listened to would say that the Christian must believe in life after death and rewards for goodness and punishment for evil, and that if one did not one could not be a Christian. How can millions and millions of people be so proud as to believe they are *worth* being kept by God forever and ever?

    Mama would die if she knew I had put down words like this.

Sometimes at night in this creaking ship I feel so far inside myself, with no help from anything outside, that I wonder if this is the way things must be even when I am married? Perhaps these are just a traveller's thoughts because one is so unsettled and all you have of your own is in a trunk and two cases. Maybe I will feel better when I am once again with faces I will see every day for a long time. I think of Cook in Mama's house, who has been with us ever since we came to Edinburgh and who always sings hymns when she is baking. She only goes to church rarely but believes firmly that when she dies she will go to Heaven which is, for her, a little two-roomed cottage in Perthshire, or what looks like it, with a brook running through the garden. She told me once she could see every detail. I wonder what Mama sees when she thinks of Heaven? I have no vision of it at all.

Perhaps there is a lot of Papa in me and Mama has always been afraid of this. I know very little about him except that I think Mama was half angry with him because he was not a good business man like Grandfather had been and that before Papa died suddenly he had allowed the factory to run down so there wasn't nearly as much money as Mama had expected. However, she has always been very generous with me; after paying for my trousseau and steamer tickets she gave me two hundred pounds, which I said was far too much, fifty would have been enough to get me to China and my husband's protection. She insisted, saying a young lady must have a little nest egg to give her a feeling of security. I was quite nervous about carrying so much money and have spent very little of it, only about ten pounds so far, which has included purchases on the way and tips to stewards and stewardesses on board the *Mooldera*. I think I should reach Peking with a least a hundred and eighty pounds, which is more than some quite respectable people have to live on for one year.

SS *Ching Wha*,
Feb. 13th, 1903

We are now anchored in the harbour of Wei-Hai-Wei which is a piece of British China I had never heard of. I asked the Captain at luncheon how we came to own it and he said we only took it five years ago. When will we stop taking places in the world? The way we do it is the reason why the American missionary doesn't like the British, and in a way I cannot blame him here. The Captain said that this is a good harbour and after the Japanese moved out in 1898 after their war with China was over it seemed a good idea for us to move in before the Chinese had a chance to come creeping back. They say that Queen Victoria didn't want us to take any more of China and when informed about her new possession said: 'We do not wish to hear about it.' But that may only have been the Captain's story. I know I should not listen to jokes about the Royal Family but I had to laugh when the Captain said that the Queen gave a large piece of Borneo to Rajah Brooke because she thought his need was greater than hers. The Captain is very irreverent and I don't think the other officers like it, particularly the Second Officer, who is very patriotic and serious. Mama wouldn't care for the Captain's jokes, either, and Mrs C. would have left the dining saloon.

It is strange how soon we forget the dead. Though I lived so close to her for weeks on end, and could scarcely move without her watching, I now only remember Mrs C. from something like this and in honesty do not greatly respect her memory. This is perhaps very wrong of me.

From the deck one can see the walled city of Wei-Hai-Wei itself and I must say our new colony is very pretty, the harbour closed in by the island of Liu Kung Tao on which is our naval base. There are quite high hills all around, some with terraced rice fields, and a good deal of pine forest. The air is extremely cold, but dry, and though snow has fallen recently the sun is strong and bright. There are six warships of our China Squadron anchored near and I watched a liberty boat going ashore from one of them. There was not time for us to land though some passengers left us by tender, including one First Class Chinese with a pigtail. The steerage people took no notice at all of the unloading going on all around them, continuing with their deck cooking over braziers. I asked the Captain if he wasn't nervous about having his ship set on fire by an overturned brazier and he said he lived in terror of it, but had hoses ready which he had used more than once to spray both cooks and their stoves. However, the Chinese become seasick quicker than most races so that if the sea is at all rough they do not eat.

I find watching them cook down there quite fascinating and it seems to go on all day. This morning the youngest priest came up beside me at the rail and said in his quiet voice: 'Is this how you like to watch the world, Miss Mackenzie? From an upper deck?' I thought that was rather cheeky of him even if he does wear a robe and is addressed as Father Anthony, which I find so strange and never could do to one so young, so I call him nothing. But when, half angry, I looked at him, he was smiling. It is a gentle smile but gives me the feeling that it is a little put on from his theological training. He is very fair with thin hair that will not last long, though this will not matter to him. I realized that he had not meant to be superior but had a real interest in what I might be thinking. Suddenly I was bold in a way I could never have been a month ago. I said: 'In Moukden you expect to be right in the middle of the world?' His answer to that was a nod, which wasn't very satisfactory, which somehow prodded me to go on and I said: 'For every convert you make in China ten thousand will be born who will not be converted.' As soon as that was out I thought how dreadful of me, but he wasn't angry, just nodded and after a moment said in a quiet voice again: 'All we can hope for is to be a leaven.'

I felt terrible because I could see that he was sincerely humble and his being willing to spend his whole life on something that seems hopeless was a kind of rebuke to me. I was a little frightened, too, because I knew then that I would never be able to follow a straight line in life as he was doing. I will probably always be of weak faith. When I pray it is for God to stop a storm.

SS Ching Wha,
Feb. 14th, 1903

It is early morning and I am writing this because I can't get to sleep again. Tomorrow we reach Taku Bar and then go up river to Tientsin where Richard and I meet. All the way from Wei-Hai-Wei it has been bitterly cold, the wind now reaching us from Siberia, like a stab to the lungs when you step out on deck. Even with the heating pipes clanking from the hot water being pushed through them it is still so cold in this cabin I have had to massage my fingers.

These days I find I can look back at the past with new eyes, suddenly seeming to understand things that I missed at the time. I have been thinking about my visit to Richard's mother. Mama had refused to come with me, saying that if I was going all the way to China to get married it would be a good experience for me to travel to Norfolk unaccompanied. It was quite a difficult journey, with two changes, one at Peterborough and again at King's Lynn, and when I reached the station of Swaffham where I expected to be met all I found was the family carriage and coachman. I did not know then that Lady Collingsworth was a semi-invalid with rheumatism, so was quite unhappy on the long drive sitting alone in the back of a vehicle that was not in very good condition, more like a hackney in Edinburgh than a private conveyance. Also, the countryside was strange after Scotland, so flat and to my eyes uninteresting. The house of Mannington itself seemed almost suffocated by old trees, a brick building, not stone, and so dark inside that if there had not been a fire on in the hall I would have seen nothing until my eyes became accustomed to the gloom. The house is undoubtedly very damp on that low-lying ground and needs fires in all the rooms even in summer, though there was never one in my bedroom and the sheets were clammy. Lady Collingsworth and Sir John, Richard's eldest brother, were very kind in a way but I can see now clearly enough that I was being inspected that first evening and for the next three days as well. I can also see myself as they must have seen me. In spite of my school which did its best to cure me of a Scotch accent I still have one because Mama has stayed quite broad in the way she speaks even since moving to Edinburgh, and the moment I came home for holidays it was to lapse into the old way of speaking. Lady Collingsworth pretended not to notice my accent, but Sir John kept asking me to repeat things, which was embarrassing. He is still a bachelor but as Lady C. said to one day when we were alone at tea, he expects to do his duty soon. I thought the lady in

question was a neighbour called Elizabeth who came to Mannington three times while I was there, but with my new eyes I think she
was curious about me because she had been after Richard herself.
She is quite pretty but with too colourful a skin from hunting and
with very broad hips that I expect come from horse riding. I do not
think I passed Elizabeth's examination either.

3

Letter from Mary Mackenzie to her mother,
Mrs Isabel Mackenzie

c/o P.O. Box 103,
Legation Quarter,
Peking, China,
Feb. 17th, 1903

Dearest Mama,
    This will probably be my address for some time
because the house in which Richard and I are to live
when we are married isn't yet available. It is in the
native city and still occupied by a German couple so I
haven't even seen the outside as yet. There is no place for
us in the Legation Quarter itself which was terribly
devastated during the Boxer Troubles, many of the
houses completely destroyed by Chinese guns or fires after
the bombardments. The most important residence, Sir
Robert Hart's, was burned to the ground with all the
records in it of the Chinese Customs which he has been
in charge of for many years. However, the new Legation
Quarter is to be fortified with a strong wall and in
front of this a very wide space that is never to be built
on, this to give a clear field of fire if there should ever be

any more troubles. Perhaps I shouldn't be telling you all this, but there is no need to be nervous about me, the city is now totally pacified. The Allied troops who stayed a long time to make quite certain of this have left only recently.

As we came alongside the wharf at Tientsin it didn't seem as though I was arriving in a Chinese city at all, all the buildings seemed European, one with a sign saying Astor House Hotel and another Gaiety Theatre. Except for rickshas waiting on the dock, and some palanquins, there was nothing really strange at all except perhaps that everyone waiting for us seemed to be wearing furs, men and women alike. I was expecting Richard to stand out from the crowd because he would be wearing a uniform, but he wasn't, also in a fur coat, a long one, which made him look like a Cossack especially since he was wearing a fur hat to match! He was up the gangway as soon as it was lowered and then came striding down the deck to meet me, pulling off that hat and just dropping it in order to take both my hands and welcome me to China with a kiss. I was a little surprised that he did this in front of all those people because he is always correct, as you know, but I was glad, too.

That night I spent at the Astor House Hotel and Richard had a room at another hotel, but we dined together at the Astor, a small table by a window that was hung with rich red curtains. There was an orchestra playing, three instruments. Except for the Chinese waiters, called 'boys', that room could have been in Edinburgh. At first we were a little shy together, but soon I was telling him about my journey and the sad death of my chaperone, and Mrs Brinkhill, the typhoon and so on. I suppose I was chattering but Richard didn't seem to mind and he kept me going with questions. Then, when we had finished the meal, I think he must have tipped the orchestra, for suddenly they began playing 'Tales from the Vienna Woods', a bit squeaky for they are Russians, and Richard took out a little box with my ring that he didn't think it was safe to send to Scotland. So I put on my engagement ring to Austrian music and I hope that was a good omen, though I know you don't believe in such things. The stone is a Korean amethyst which Richard says is not to be confused with the ordinary amethysts we see at home, but a much richer colour and more valuable, of course. It is set in seed pearls. He had it specially made in Shanghai to the measurement I sent and the fit is perfect.

The next day we did not meet for breakfast, but at about eleven Richard arrived in a carriage and though it was cold it was sunny, and we drove with the hood down and well wrapped up in a huge bearskin rug that was smelly, but warm. Richard was interested in all the sites where battles had been fought for the control of Tientsin during the Boxer Troubles and we stopped on an iron bridge across a narrow river where the fighting had been very intense. What interested me was the river itself. I could scarcely see water between the sampans and small junks packed into it on which families were living out their lives. It was really a floating slum cutting across the main shopping street of Tientsin in which there are many fine shops and buildings, these all restored for business again. I wonder where the people in the boats went to during the Boxer fighting, perhaps they just stayed where they were, hoping for no stray bullets. Mrs Brinkhill told me that I would soon get used to the poverty in China, but I haven't yet. It is not confined to special places as it is with us, you see it everywhere, and have quite horrid reminders sometimes. Right outside the Astor Hotel there was a beggar on the pavement with a greatly disfigured face and stumps for hands. Richard said he was a leper but that I wasn't to worry about such things because a lot of the beggars become quite rich and return at night to comfortable houses. He also said that in China nothing is what it seems, and I was to remember that. I am not sure I know what he meant.

That afternoon we took the train to Peking, sitting opposite each other on rattan seats that were cold and slippery. There was nothing much to see, just flat fields with clusters of mounds in odd places in nearly all of them. These are graves. The Chinese country people bury their dead in the family fields and then plough all around them. I saw one or two fields that seemed more graves than ploughed land, and couldn't help thinking that it was wasteful agriculture.

What we talked about on the train was Mannington. I have found already that a way to make Richard happy is to talk about his home, which he loves above all things. In a way it is a pity he is a third son so cannot hope to inherit. I think he would have made a better 'laird' of the Collingsworth estates than his brother. Sir John seemed to me, though quite nice, a slow man who was really only doing his duty about his inheritance, and I don't think he really cares much for hunting which in Norfolk makes you odd, I believe. The English families are run in such set ways, the eldest son inheriting all the property while the others must go into the Church or the Army. It is all laid down before you are born and no one ever thinks of varying the pattern by leaving everything to a second son, or a third, as a father might well do in Scotland if he was displeased with his eldest. I didn't say this to you at home but at Mannington I felt that there are so many differences between the Scotch and the English that we might be French and Spaniards in our separate ways. A Scotch wife to an Englishman must expect that her husband is going to seem a foreigner.

Our wedding is the first in Peking since the Boxer Troubles so there is going to be quite a fuss. An English Bishop will be up from Shanghai on tour at the time and

*will perform the ceremony. I do not much care for the
Anglican Church way of doing things, but I suppose I will
just have to put up with it, though after we are married I
shall attend a* Protestant *service as often as possible.*

*I must give you my first impression of Peking. It was
dusk when we went in rickshas from the station towards
the walls and a huge gate in them. My ricksha and the
ones behind carrying Richard and my luggage, had to
slow down to make way for a* camel. *The camel had a big
load on side packs and bells on its neck and it almost
pushed past me in the ricksha as though to show that in
China camels have priority over Europeans. I said to the
camel: 'By all means go first,' and Richard called out
that he hadn't heard what I said. I couldn't very well tell
him that his fiancée had started talking to camels.*

*I asked whether the gate was the Hatamen, but it
wasn't. The Captain of the* Ching Wha *told me that the
Empress Dowager, returning to Peking after her exile as a
result of the Boxer Troubles, had entered the city by the
Hatamen Gate with all the foreigners she had tried to put
to death up on a parapet watching her return. From her
palanquin she noticed them up there and the Old Lady
bowed very deeply to the people she had meant to kill.*

*I must not tell you these stories or you will be worried
again, but such tales do not make me nervous. I am
staying until the wedding, the final date depending on the
Bishop, with the British Second Secretary and his wife, a
Mr and Mrs Harding. This house, like most, had some
serious damage during the siege, a shell through the roof
for one thing, but this has now been repaired. Damage to
a once-beautiful garden will take much longer to heal,
burning timbers scorched the trees and shrubs and only a
few survived, as is the case with most Quarter gardens. It
is such a pity because they must have been very beautiful. I
climbed yesterday with Richard up on to the wall behind*

us here, and the view showed Peking as a city of gardens. I
have yet to visit the outer precincts of the Winter Palace
where the public are permitted.

I am thinking of being extravagant and buying a fur
coat since everyone has at least one, some eight or ten,
particularly rich Chinese ladies. Mrs Harding took me to
the one shop where it is safe to try on these furs, elsewhere is a
real risk of catching smallpox. I liked very much an almost
black Manchurian wildcat, very long and sleek. It cost
fifteen pounds but Mrs Harding says she thinks she can get it
for twelve if we bargain cleverly. I shall leave that to her.
Your loving daughter,
Mary

Legation Quarter,
Peking,
February 22nd, 1903

I am back to the notebooks I never thought I would write in again
after I was with Richard. For the last four days it has been nothing
but parties, first an evening here for me to meet some of the diplomats of all nations, though mostly of the lesser ranks in the legations. Then we went to a reception at the home of the British
Minister, Sir Claude Macdonald, who organized the defence against
the Boxers and is expected to be moved shortly to another post.
Lady Macdonald is in England but Sir Claude was most charming
to me, saying he is looking forward to a splendid wedding which
will do them all good. He asked me if I was related to the Mackenzies of Achtarn who are distant connections of his but I had to say
that my family had lived on the East Coast for some time and so had
lost contact with Highland relations. At that his eyebrows shot up as
though I had surprised him. He is a big man who dresses in fancy
waistcoats as if formal occasions bother him a little, though I expect
that in diplomatic uniform he will be most splendid. Against him all
Chinese must appear very small physically. He is really like a Highland Chieftain and though very friendly is also grand. I think

Richard feels it a little that he was not here during the Boxer Troubles which makes a division between him and all those who were. I have noticed that he does not like too much Boxer talk, though interested enough in the *way* battles were fought.

Mr and Mrs Harding are being very kind to me, though I do not see much of him. When we meet at meals they both talk to me but don't seem to talk much to each other, as though they are no longer finding things to talk about. I suppose this must happen, but it is rather sad. It is not easy for a husband and wife to have interests together in Peking. Tennis is played here in the Quarter during the summer, but there are no winter activities such as there used to be, like skating outside the city walls and sometimes race meetings, because that area is still unsafe for Europeans. One can't go riding out there, either. What everyone complains about most is not being able to go to temples in the Western Hills because of bandits and some Boxers still wandering about. Those temples used to be hired for weekends or longer stays and the priests just moved out temporarily. I am not sure I would care for a holiday in a Buddhist church but when I said this to the wife of the First Secretary she told me that their temples are not nearly so sacred as our churches and that they adapt quite easily for picnics or as holiday houses. When I asked about the consecration of these buildings I learned that the Chinese do not bother about such things, though I am beginning to wonder a little whether the foreigners in this country pay enough attention to native customs and practices? Christians seem very sure of themselves when surrounded by other religions. This is right, of course, but somehow it makes me a little uncomfortable.

Legation Quarter,
Feb. 24th, 1903

Last night Richard and I went, with the Hardings, to dinner with the First Secretary of the French Legation, a Monsieur and Madame de Chamonpierre. According to Mrs Harding he is really Le Vicomte de Chamonpierre but does not use the title since his country is now a republic, and he is not in favour of inherited rank. Mrs

Harding suggested that this was an affectation, but now that I have met Monsieur and Madame I do not think so. Though we were introduced at Sir Claude's reception I did not really get a chance to talk to them, but I noticed Madame's dress, which was of stiff silk, very plain, only striking in cut and colour, a deep cerise which made her stand out in the room. She is very dark, not beautiful, rather a big nose, but it is her eyes you notice which on first meeting seem to be searching at once to see what you are made of. I cannot guess what she discovered I was made of, but it is flattering to find her giving me the kind of attention which she does not give Mrs Harding. Perhaps there is something still in the Auld Alliance between France and Scotland? It may, of course, be only kindness because she sees me as young and helpless in a new place, but I think not. Towards Richard she is slightly teasing in a way I'm surprised he accepts so easily. He didn't seem at all embarrassed when Madame said she hoped I realized what a responsibility I was taking on, marrying the most beautiful man in Peking. I cannot imagine Richard allowing an Englishwoman to call him *beautiful*, but perhaps he excuses such expressions from her because that is the way she speaks English, as though every word was directly translated from the French.

The important guest at dinner was Sir Robert Hart, who Richard says is the most respected Englishman in China and who could have received Sir Claude's position as British Minister if he had wanted it, but did not, for he regards being Controller of Chinese Customs as much more important. It would seem he does not often go to dinner-parties at the level of Legation Secretaries, but makes an exception in the case of the de Chamonpierres, something that I can see irritates Mrs Harding very much. I did not exchange a word with Sir Robert all evening, partly because I was at the other end of the table at dinner, but later in the drawing-room he never came near my chair, as though military attachés' fiancées did not exist for him. I had been warned by Mrs Harding that for this evening I would probably be seated next to our host, but that I must not regard this as anything more than an exception to the usual rules of entertaining in which a Second Secretary's wife takes precedence over the wife of the military attaché. I do not think that Mrs Harding much cares for the de Chamonpierres' informality and she said afterwards that she did not enjoy the spectacle of the hostess totally controlling the conversation at dinner and after.

Madame did *not* control the conversation in that way, but what she did do was join in what Mrs Harding would regard as men's talk and make that the talk of the table. After the tea-parties I liked this very much, though I did not say so to Mrs H. Madame does not care for the Russians and was quite vehement about them. She says that if they are not stopped they will not only take over Manchuria, where their influence is very strong already, but the whole of North China and probably Korea as well. She says the Czar is a useless puppet under the control of scoundrelly Ministers, and that it will be quite shocking if the European powers with interests in China allow Japan to go to war by itself to stop the advance of Russian Imperialism. At this point Richard said that if Japan took on the Russian giant she would be committing suicide but Madame wouldn't have that, claiming that one Japanese soldier was worth three Russians. She added that a Captain Kurihama had told her it would be an honour to die in so worthy a cause as fighting the Russians. Everyone except me seemed to know who Captain Kurihama was, and I noticed Richard frowning, as though the name disturbed him in some way. I was quite silent. I have never heard anyone, least of all a woman, talking about Royalty the way Madame was talking about the Czar who is, after all, closely related to our Royal Family.

It was an interesting evening. I will never be able to, but I would still like to guide the talk at my own dinner table as Madame does. Richard, though, would hate that. We walked home from the dinner, only a short distance and the night fine, this all right for Mrs Harding who had her sables, but in my cloth coat I was quite chilled. I was beside Mr Harding who had been sparing of personal opinions during my stay in his house and, perhaps to provoke him, I asked what he thought of Madame? He said at once that she intended to make her husband French Ambassador to London or Berlin and though he wasn't a betting man he would back her all the way to do it. This made me laugh. Richard looked around, I think because he had heard, and though the street was ill lit I had a feeling he was staring at me. Could he perhaps be wondering whether a Scotch wife will try to make him a General or a Field Marshal?

Another thing that Madame de Chamonpierre has done for me is to make me dissatisfied with the way I dress. I would like her for a friend. As we were leaving she said: 'You will call me Marie.' So I shall.

Letter from Mary Mackenzie to her mother

Legation Quarter,
Peking,
Feb. 28th, 1903

Dearest Mama,

I can now give you the address of my home-to-be in Peking even though I still haven't seen it. If this seems strange it is because as soon as the house became available, the day before yesterday, Richard moved in from his bachelor quarters and so far Mrs Harding has not been free to accompany me as chaperone. It is very necessary to observe all the proprieties here for the gossip is like a village and I do not wish to give any excuse for talk about what I am doing. I'm sure you will approve of this.

My address after the wedding will be 157 Hutung Feng-huang. It may surprise you that our house has a number just as at home, though the Chinese system of numbering is rather erratic and Richard tells me that our neighbour on one side is eighty-four and on the other one hundred and twenty-three. The hutung means lane and Feng-huang is translated rather vaguely as fabulous bird, which I gather means a bird that is both male and female. So your daughter will be living in the lane of the fabulous bird. I expect that, like so many narrow streets in this city, it will be rather smelly, for there is a system of open drains along the edges of all of them. Even in the

*winter freeze-up these are noticeable and what they will be
like under summer heat I cannot imagine, for they only
get washed out by rain. However, we seem to be behind
quite a high wall, a little compound of our own, so that
may help.*

*Our house has quite an interesting history. The
Germans have now returned home and Richard bought
over their furniture, paying a hundred and twenty
pounds for everything, which is quite a bargain even if a
lot of the things are not to my taste. I can make changes
slowly. We are really very lucky for houses are hard to find
in Peking since the destruction. Before the Boxer Troubles
ours belonged to quite a high court official (it has
fourteen rooms not including kitchen and servants'
quarters) who was one of the men backing the Empress
Dowager in her wicked policies against Europeans. After
order had been restored the Allies demanded the execution
of certain ringleaders of the Boxers and the owner of our
house was one of the ones who had his head cut off at a
public execution. I don't know what happened to the dead
man's family for the house was empty when the Germans
found it. If all this seems rather gruesome to you then you
must remember that the Boxers were ruthless and cruel
and certain reparations were called for.*

*Richard has so far engaged a houseboy, a kind of
butler, and a cook and a handyman, which does not seem
many servants for the kind of life we must live here, but
no doubt I will be able to arrange for more when I have
taken charge. We will go straight to the house after the
wedding for there is to be no honeymoon. With the state of
the country there is no place we could go to except
Tientsin, which would be rather foolish for I didn't think
it was an attractive city in spite of the European shops.*

*As you can imagine I am most anxious to see my new
home and find it a little trying that Mrs Harding hasn't
been able to make the time to come with me. Still, I must*

not complain for they have been most kind to me during this waiting period. I have tried not to get in the way but I remember what you said when I came back after being with the Blairs in Aviemore for ten days, that any guest for more than a week becomes a nuisance. Alas, I fear I am being that, but though I suggested going to the hotel in the Quarter they would not hear of it.

I have met a French lady in their Legation who will, I think, be a good friend to me. When I called to leave cards for Richard and me after dining there she had me in and we had tea and talked for two hours. She is most entertaining about diplomatic life, a sharp tongue but a kind heart, like many Scotchwomen.

There is one thing that is troubling me a little and on which I suppose it might be said I have made a stand, perhaps foolish. The delay in our wedding is because the Bishop of Shanghai is due to come to Peking and Richard arranged that he should conduct the ceremony. Apparently this Bishop is very High Church Episcopal, what they call Anglo-Catholic, and even uses incense. When he heard that I was a Presbyterian he let it be known that he does not perform mixed marriages himself, but his Curate would do it, since I am a Christian. It may have been wrong of me but when I first heard this from Richard I was angry, though I couldn't really believe it. Then it was confirmed by Mrs Harding. What is expected of me is that I make a statement rejecting the Church of Scotland and accepting the Church of England as my faith. It is almost as if I was being asked to go over to Rome. If our union is to be consecrated by this Bishop I cannot remain a Presbyterian. What I said was: 'Very well, I will take the Curate.' Now Richard is angry with me, and of course I can see why, this being the first wedding in the Quarter since the Troubles, and Sir Claude has offered his home for the reception, an honour we never expected. Richard clearly thinks I am mad not to be willing to make a statement that I will adhere to my husband's religion, but it is not just that, I do not want to become an English Episcopalian. Why should I? I have been baptized. I told Richard that when King Edward comes to Scotland to shoot grouse he automatically becomes a Presbyterian and Richard couldn't believe this until he found out from someone in the Legation that it is true, but even then he will scarcely accept it.

I am not asking for your advice because long before I could receive it I will be a wife, one way or the other, so the decision will be mine alone. Last night I was awake for hours trying to make it, but could not. You must not trouble yourself about this, in a way it is a storm in a teacup. Though it is also a question of principle. Or will you think your daughter is just being silly, or worse, refusing to obey her future husband?

I have bought the black Manchurian wildcat coat. Mrs Harding has five fur coats but I think she likes mine better than any of hers except her sables, which are beautiful. From little hints that come from time to time I think she is quite a rich woman in her own right. Also, she has that air of not having to listen to her husband unless she wishes to. The dinner gong has just gone, so must close.

Your loving daughter,

Mary

PS (after dinner) Mrs Harding, who is a skilled bargainer, got the fur coat reduced to just over nine pounds in British money which means I have not been so extravagant after all, since a coat which will last me the rest of my life has cost less than the blue dress you got for me.

Legation Quarter,
Peking, China,
March 2nd, 1903

This morning Marie de Chamonpierre sent a messenger with a 'chitty' asking me to come to tea this afternoon, and naturally I was very happy to. She received me most pleasantly, saying that to really enjoy afternoon tea in the English manner she feels she must have someone from England to share it with her. Like everyone, she talks about England when she means Great Britain, but I have stopped telling people that Scotland is not part of England, it does no good. Her boudoir was very hot from steam heating in pipes in the American style and I found the atmosphere stuffy, made more so by many plants on stands and a huge pot of heavily scented lilies. Marie was wearing a negligée which was quite revealing and was certainly more comfortable than I was in outdoor clothes. When we had been served tea she asked if I would be shocked if she now indulged in her secret vice. I had no idea at all what she meant until she opened a box and took out a long, black cigarette.

Only two months ago if I had seen a lady do that in her Edinburgh drawing-room I would have been shocked but today all I felt was a kind of surprise and then I thought that there is no reason for women to be ashamed for doing something in private that men do openly everywhere. I cannot, however, imagine a world in which ladies would use smoking-rooms as men do, but having a cigarette behind closed doors doesn't seem a matter to cause scandal, though Marie says it would in Legation circles. Her husband knows, of course, but has only asked that his wife's smoking be a rumour about which no one is ever allowed to have actual evidence. It was a great compliment to me that I should be taken into her confidence like this, and it can only mean she is certain I would never give her away, which I never will. I don't think Marie has many close friends amongst the other Legation ladies even though she was here during the Boxer Troubles and worked very hard for the wounded. Little things Mrs Harding has said suggest she is not too popular and, of course, there is that prejudice that French means Fast. Perhaps French women are not generally liked by their own sex because they are too successful with men.

She teased me about Richard, saying that since he came to Peking she has always tried to get him for her dinner-parties since he is better decoration than the most elaborate floral arrangement. She also said that when his engagement to me was announced here the youngest daughter of the Belgian Minister collapsed at a tea-party on hearing the news and soon afterwards left for Europe to take the waters at Baden-Baden. I told Marie that I was sure most of the ladies here had no idea at all what Richard had seen in me, at which she seemed a little surprised, as though she thought that I, of all people, ought to know what had made my fiancé propose marriage, but now I am not sure that I do. Marie began to talk of what she called the 'science' of marriage, at which I felt she was not candid in the way Mrs Brinkhill used to be, veiling what she really meant, though this could be that she is at times a little uncertain in her English and does not wish to be misunderstood.

I was just going to ask her advice about changing my hairstyle when suddenly she switched to religion, which I would not have expected of her. She said she came from Bordeaux, though educated in Paris, and that she had cousins in that city who were French Protestants, so she could understand my feelings. I was too surprised to say anything at all and she went on about how religion affected one's life in the diplomatic service. This seemed to be that it is essential for those who officially represent their countries abroad to be adherents of that country's main religion. She said that, though Catholic by birth, had she been a Protestant like her cousins when her marriage was being arranged, she would have seen the essential need to convert to the Roman Faith for the sake of her husband's career. I then asked if her husband had been a Protestant would she have deserted the Catholic Church to worship with him? She said she couldn't answer me since this wasn't a thing that could ever happen in France. I said I had heard there were many atheists in France and she agreed that was true, but there were none in the diplomatic corps.

I wasn't angry with Marie for raising something that is really no concern of hers, because it was quite plain that Richard had asked her to do this. I am angry with *him*. However, I think I kept very calm and listened while she went on about how Richard was in no way concerned about what my religion was in private so long as I was English Episcopalian in public. She also said that I must see how important it was to him and to his career to be married by a

Bishop, to which I replied it was becoming important to me *not* to be married by a Bishop, at least on the conditions laid down. We did not quarrel, but I think she was quite startled that I could be so sharp. I tried to explain it was a matter of feeling rather than reason, but Marie said she had heard that Scotch people were stubborn, and now she had proof of that. We parted pleasantly enough, though she did not come to the door with me. That could be because she does not like to appear in a negligée in the front part of her house. I am wondering now if our friendship will develop quite so fast in future? Marie would always see things from Richard's point of view because he is a man.

4

⚭

157 Hutung Feng-huang,
Peking, China,
March 11th, 1903

Dearest Mama,

My news will make you have a little cry, I know, for I am now Mrs Richard Collingsworth. I thought about sending you a cable when the Bishop's sudden arrival here fixed the date, but felt that it might give you a lonely feeling to know the day and hour of my marriage which you could not attend. I hope I did the right thing? No, I was not married by the Bishop and have not renounced my faith. There was a sort of compromise in which the Bishop agreed to bless the union, with his Curate performing the actual ceremony. So that is the way it was even though the arrangement made Richard cross for a while.

Everything was very simple. There was no one suitable for me to have as a bridesmaid so I asked Mrs Harding to be matron of honour, and for her husband to give me away, which may not have been very conventional, but in China you can't always do things the correct way. I did not much care for the Anglican service, but 'tholed it' as

Jessie would say, only stipulating that they must sing the twenty-third psalm in the Scottish metrical version which no one knew except me, so it made rather a poor sound with the small organ having to work very hard to make it any kind of sound at all. Being winter, the flowers were mostly plants and so on, loaned from houses in the Legation Quarter, but the church looked attractive. It was chilly at first, because the stove had smoked from a blocked chimney when lit and had to be let out for cleaning before it could be lit again, so the heat had not reached the altar when I did and I had to promise to love and obey Richard for the rest of my life through teeth that were almost chattering. However, since the English marriage service takes much longer than the Scotch, by the time we turned for Richard and me to come down the aisle together the packed church had warmed things up and I don't think I looked blue with cold.

If it is lucky to have the sun shine on your wedding day then Richard and I should be happy for we came out into the most beautiful winter sunshine, hard cold, and much snow lying from a heavy fall two days earlier which made everything very clean and glittering. Richard and I got into the open carriage loaned by Sir Claude, the Minister, for the short journey to his residence, and there was a procession behind us of ladies in rickshas, though most of the gentlemen walked. Two years ago never in my wildest dreams would I have seen fifty rickshas, each holding a European lady wrapped in furs, at my wedding. Though I had worn my new coat to the church I refused to wear it during the drive to the reception, with Richard saying that exposing myself like that was the way to get pneumonia. I wasn't really cold, for as you will remember my wedding dress has a high boned collar and, being of silk, quite a little warmth. Anyway, I sat under the Minister's fur rug but looked the bride, I hope, from the waist up.

These days there are not many Chinese to be seen on the streets of the Quarter, and those who do come in are either servants or on business, so there were very few to watch this 'foreign' ceremony. The natives who were about didn't look at us. I am told this is something quite new since the Boxer Troubles, that before them Europeans, especially ladies, were the object of endless curiosity wherever they went. Not now. It is almost as though there was a conspiracy not to notice us. A short time ago I went to the street of the silversmiths with Mrs Harding, who was having two condiment sets and an epergne made for her dining table, and though I was conscious of being watched, whenever I turned suddenly to see who was doing that, all I saw was downcast eyes. It is disturbing in a way to have people all around you pretending you aren't there, and this makes what happened to me as I was driving as a new bride somehow seem important.

The carriage went around a corner into a street quite empty except for one old woman walking along the very edge of the roadway by the drainage ditch. I think she was possibly a sewing woman from one of the legations, for she was carrying a small, cloth-wrapped bundle. She must have been quite good class, too, fallen on evil days, for she had the bound feet which is said to promote the swaying flower walk Chinese men find attractive. In older women this becomes a painful hobble on twisted bones full of rheumatism. The sound of the carriage made the old lady look up, but instead of at once dropping her eyes again she stopped by a gate and stepped back on to the boards over the drainage ditch, keeping her head high and watching. It was me she was looking at. We passed quite close to her. It is hard to tell Chinese ages but I would say from the lines on her face that she must have been at least seventy, though her hair was still jet black, dyed probably, and pulled straight back to a tight bun on her neck. Her padded long jacket and trousers were of grey material and looked cheap, but in her ears were two pieces of what I am sure was very good quality green jade, perhaps an only treasure left she would never part with.

I smiled at her. In a moment she smiled back. I don't think she had any upper teeth left, but it was still a sweet smile and I know, as if we had been able to communicate without words, that she was suddenly remembering a day long ago when she had been carried in a palanquin to the house of her Lord, a man she had almost certainly never seen before, bringing with her all the fears, hidden behind a smooth face, of a young girl who is being plunged into strangeness. I had been quite composed during all the preparations for marriage and the ceremony itself, but in that moment I felt tears come into my eyes. Maybe there were tears in that old lady's eyes, too, I don't know, for we passed and were gone. I have only spoken of this to you, Mama, and never will to anyone else.

Sir Claude must have travelled by another route in a ricksha for he was at his residence to greet us, so the first to kiss your daughter on her wedding day, after the groom, was His Britannic Majesty's Minister to the Imperial Court of the Dowager Empress of China. Though he himself is a Scotch Episcopalian, I am quite sure that I heard his voice in church trying to give some body to the metrical twenty-third psalm.

In a way the reception was a little lonely because there was no one at it who had known me for more than a few weeks, but Mrs Harding, rather a formal lady, quite surprised me by the support she gave, as though she realized how I was feeling. Also, there was Marie de Chamonpierre of whom I have written before, from the French Legation. She has been a useful guide to me in many ways and is very gay and bright, her dinner-parties never a little dull like most of them here, or at least the ones I have been to. There is not much else to do in winter time when we are confined to a small district under the

shadow of the city wall, with only daytime excursions to
the native parts. As a newcomer I have to watch my step a
little as I do not wish to become part of any cliques. It is
interesting, though, the levels of contacts between the
various legations, some in states of alliance with others,
like the nations they represent, others only exchanging stiff
formalities. My friend Marie hates the Russians, who she
says are up to no good in Manchuria, with designs on
Korea and China as well, and she backs the Japanese to
defeat them if it ever comes to open conflict, though
Richard says this is ridiculous and just woman's talk,
much as he admires Marie. The French here are on very
good terms with the Japanese, whom they are encouraging
to flex their muscles, and so are the British up to a point,
though with more restraint, perhaps. Richard is quite
friendly with the German Military Attaché, but on the
whole we British are cautious with this contact, too, for
they are so often our rivals in matters concerning China.
All these are things I have to know about if I am to
become a hostess in Peking. You can never give a simple
dinner-party here, even at small parties there is always the
matter of diplomatic precedence to be considered, the
ladies even more strict about these than the men. A
military attaché's position, too, is a little curious, in that
he is not really permanently part of the diplomatic service,
and may be returned to ordinary duties with his regiment
at any time, which with Richard would be England. I
don't think he wishes this, however, so we may be in the
Far East for a good many years.

I will leave a description of our house of the dragon
screen to another letter, in which I will give you all the
details of how we live in it. Our houseboy, Yao Tsu, has a
squint eye which made me uneasy at first, but I am
growing used to it. All this later.

Your loving daughter,
Mary (Collingsworth)

The House of the Dragon Screen,
Peking,
March 24th, 1903

I suppose other people have had honeymoons like ours, going straight to a house in a Far Eastern city, the house situated so far from the rest of the foreign community that friends can't just drop in. Also, people have probably felt it was best to leave us alone for a time, though I wish they had not. The only contact with the Quarter since we came here is a huge bunch of purple iris (where did they come from in Peking at this time of year?) with a chitty from Marie de Chamonpierre sending her love. Unfortunately the flowers look a bit odd in the drawing-room, which is upholstered mostly in red plush, though they do match the lapis lazuli plate which seems to be Richard's only treasure. Richard, of course, is at the Legation every day, but in spite of his having been a gay bachelor here, he does not seem to have had many close friends, and I don't get much news of what is happening from him. The Legation squash courts have been repaired now and Richard plays on them three days a week, which means that he does not get back here until well after eight. By the time we have had dinner he is so sleepy that he just goes straight to bed.

It seems to me sometimes that I might as well have been a Chinese bride. Since coming here I have only been out of the gate once and that was last Sunday when, as a surprise, Richard had rickshas at the door after lunch and we went in them to a place called Coal Hill, which is more a mound than a hill, and from which you can see the tile roofs of the Winter Palace stretching like the waves of the sea over what seems to be a third of the city. In summer I am sure it is a very fine view with the leaves out on the trees of Peking's famous gardens, but there is still no hint of spring here, some snow and an icy wind blowing straight from the Gobi Desert. In spite of muff and heavy gloves my hands were like ice and my feet lead. I said to Richard that to get warm it might be a good idea if I pulled the ricksha for a while, which he did not find amusing. It was not a successful expedition. All I wanted to do was get back to the huge stove in our drawing-room which, though the ugliest thing in an ugly room, is still the real heart of our draughty Chinese house and sits glowing on cheap Manchurian coal like a private sun. If I could I would eat all my meals by it, but we have them in the dining-room where there is a much smaller stove, allowed to die down when we aren't using the place, which means that when we do I sit in my carved German chair with a wind whistling around my ankles. When I think of the fires kept well built up by Jessie in Edinburgh I could almost weep.

Never in my life have I been so conscious of myself sitting around doing nothing. I won't pretend that I attended to the house in any real way at home, though Mama did see that I had some lessons from Cook on how to prepare simple dishes, but there I never seemed to have enough time to spend on the things I wanted to do. Here there is nothing to do. I expected at once to take over the running of my household only to find that this is quite impossible. According to Richard, everything must be done through the houseboy. Since Yao only knows six words of English and I know as yet only three of Chinese, one of these to tell the ricksha coolie to go more slowly, it is not easy for me to give any orders. It is not that Yao has no wish to be helpful, he tries to be, and sometimes gives me his smile, which is a sad one, as though it came straight from a life that has been hard all the way, as I expect it has. I think that though he is a gloomy man to look at, and appears to have a slight palsy in that his hands always shake a little, we have been lucky with him, for I am sure his heart is kind, which is not always the case with servants, especially new ones.

The cook I never see. It is apparently the custom of the country that you never go into your kitchen, or at least the lady of the house never does. Our arrangement here is that Richard inspects the kitchen for cleanliness once a week and from what he sees then gives orders. He is studying Mandarin and has a teacher coming to his office at the Legation most mornings, though how well he speaks I would not know. I have seen ricksha coolies and others staring at him with blank looks while he seemed to think he was making everything plain. Marie has told me that she will never attempt to learn any Chinese, that it is risky for a woman to try to because a word like 'eat', pronounced in a slightly different tone from the correct one, immediately takes on a completely new and sometimes shocking meaning. I think Mrs Harding quite fancies herself as a linguist, but once or twice I saw her servants, particularly the houseboy, looking as though trying not to laugh. So perhaps Marie is right here, though I intend to have Yao teach me some simple things for I don't think he would deliberately expose me to ridicule.

Mama gave me no advice on marriage as from a mother to her daughter and all I can remember is that she once said the honeymoon can be a trying time. What I think she must have meant by that was a picture of staying in some hotel with all the other guests knowing you were newly married and watching with curiosity when you came into the dining-room for breakfast, and so on. She could have had no idea what was waiting for her daughter on her honeymoon and I had no idea of it either. For instance, I thought that once I was married there would be no time again for writing in notebooks and that the account of my travel out to China would be kept as a curiosity for later years. Actually I have nothing to do but write in this book, or letters home, but already letters home, even to someone of my own age like Margaret Blair, are difficult simply because half the things I might mention would have no meaning to them at all.

Soon I must raise the question of the furnishings of this house with Richard because we cannot continue living in it as it is with the things left by his Germans. I am not surprised they were glad to get a hundred and twenty pounds, I wouldn't have given them fifty. I can't seem to open the question of money with Richard, though this must come soon and an understanding be reached. So far he has paid all the bills and given me nothing. Not that I expected an allowance from him and so on at this stage, but he must surely know that I cannot go on indefinitely on what Mama gave me for travel? I think he is a man who will always be careful with money. I have certainly never seen him being free and easy with it, he carries his silver and copper coins in a purse. One of my cousins now living in Dundee always does this, too, and is quite mean, his wife an object of pity within the family.

It is really strange to be in my first home as a wife and not have much idea how things are run. It would seem that Richard gets a rough idea of what our meals are to be from the cook, and he says I am to put any suggestions I have through him, but I have no idea what the cook's capabilities are. Since we came here we seem to have been eating nothing but chicken, no doubt the cheapest meat in the market. I can't go to the market myself, not because this is forbidden to European ladies, but because there is a system of cheating on household accounts that has long been accepted by all, which Richard says is not really cheating in the usual sense, in that it is a sort of ten per cent tip on everything to the cook or houseboy who does the buying. I am told that there is no point in expecting European ideas of honesty because you won't get it, so that you might as well keep wages as low as possible and just accept the unseen commission. This principle applies in the Legation Quarter too, of course, where Sir Claude's cook takes twenty per cent because it is the house of a Minister.

Richard says that Yao even gets his commission from the ricksha coolies who charge us more than the fare for natives and then pay the houseboy, who summons them, the difference. Apparently if I were to take him shopping with me as a translator he would get a commission from every place I went into, whether I bought anything or not. In all this talk Richard and I came very near to discussing the money situation between ourselves, but still did not. I feel he is constantly shying away from the subject. This means, of course, that I cannot do anything about the house until I know where we stand and what I might spend. I have no idea what his salary is and whether or not this is supplemented by an income from his family in Norfolk.

I must *do* something soon. I cannot go on sitting here writing letters or talking to paper as I do in these notebooks.

Letter from Mary Mackenzie to her mother

> The House of the Dragon Screen,
> 157 Hutung Feng-Huang,
> Peking, China,
> March 29th, 1903

Dearest Mama,

I cannot believe that it is more than two weeks since I last wrote to you and promised a description of this house. First, you must not put 'The House of the Dragon Screen' on your envelopes; that is not official. To be quite honest it is just a name I started using because I thought it sounded good on a letter to Margaret Blair. The house really has no name, even though it did belong to the high official who lost his head. It is approached down the narrow lane and has a high wall above a drainage ditch. Poor Richard, when we came here from the wedding reception and he wanted everything to seem just right, there was a huge heap of dumped rubbish in the drain, including a dead kitten. I pretended I had not seen it, but he knew I had.

The gate itself is pretty, with a tiled roof that has a charming curved line. The gates are wide enough (double) to let a carriage through, but are never opened, you go through a smaller door in one that is like a hatch. The woodwork was once bright red, now much faded. The first thing you see inside is our dragon screen, about eight feet high, of stone, on which the dragon's tail starts up in one corner with body and clawed feet seeming to crawl down it to the bottom through an intricate pattern of carved flowers and leaves. It really was put there to keep out devils because in China devils cannot go around corners so if they come in from the outside world with you that screen stops them. You will think I am living in a really heathen country when I tell you that I am sure our houseboy holds the little hatch door open for half a minute after we have come through it in order to make sure that the thwarted devils have a chance to get out again. I haven't said anything about this to Richard who seems to have little sympathy for Chinese superstitions, only believing in English ones, like the ghost at Mannington. You must not think me flippant if I say I think I would prefer Chinese devils to a Mannington headless lady.

Inside I am afraid the house is not what I would like, though it has possibilities. You cross a paved courtyard beyond the screen in which are large ornamental rocks and nothing else, at least in winter. There is a narrow porch, then the front hall, this large and square, with the dining-room on one side and the huge drawing-room on the other. The less said the better about the furnishings: a man's choice I have no intention of putting up with for long. There are eleven bedrooms, though only two furnished at the moment. Heating is by coal stoves. There is no real garden to this house as such, just a series of courtyards with earth in them and nothing else except two porcelain seats in one, the kind you sometimes see in Edinburgh front halls that have been brought from China. The servants have houses built against the outer wall on the kitchen side, and though I haven't seen into them I believe they have two rooms each. The cook and his wife have three children (I have never seen Mrs Cook) and the handyman and his wife also have three, so you will see that I am not alone inside these walls when Richard is away, though the whole place sprawls so much I rarely hear a sound from children's voices or anything like that. There is no back gate, everyone must come by the devil screen, including tradesmen, though there are not many of them, things mostly bought at market and carried home by our servants. There is a ricksha stance not far away from our gate so that we can always have this

conveyance available, indeed there is no other in Peking
except palanquins, and I don't really see myself being
carried in one of those. The ricksha coolies sit waiting day
and night in a little hut which has a charcoal brazier in
front of it. I don't think it is a healthy life, for the man I
always get has terrible bouts of coughing sometimes.
However, rickshas and their pullers are just accepted as a
necessity of life.

I wonder if I will ever get used to the beggars? There is
nothing to fear, really, for they do not approach you, just
sit by the ditches, bundles of dirty rags, sometimes silent
and motionless, but more often swaying and muttering
what sounds like an incantation, though perhaps it is a
prayer for alms. I have been told not to notice them, and
have never really been in a position to give them anything,
passing in a ricksha and so on, but when the opportunity
arises I will give some money. What their living must be
like I cannot imagine. In China life is cheap. This is
something you feel very sharply very soon. For many just to
be able to exist seems a privilege.

If this makes you want to give to foreign missions at
church, do so, but as yet I have seen nothing of the work of
missionaries. There seems to be little contact between them
and the diplomatic services. I would think that only a
very brave person could be a missionary in China, for so
many of them were killed by the Boxers in remote places. It
must be hard to try to love people you know would murder
you if there was a change in the wind.

Dearest Mama, I hope this has not been a depressing
letter. I am still getting used to many strange things and
seeing them yet with raw eyes. In time I am sure I will not
notice. Remember me to Jessie and Cook. Tell them that
no Chinese servants could ever make such a comfortable,
warm home as they do.

All my love to you,
Mary

The House of the Dragon Screen,
Peking,
April 2nd, 1903

I have just had Marie here almost all afternoon, our first visitor, who came without sending a chitty first to say to expect her. She did not think much of this house, though pretending to for my sake, saying that our dragon screen was the best she had seen, but on the threshold of the drawing-room exclaimed, as though she could not stop herself: *'Dieu! Un wagon de chemin-de-fer!'* I know what she means, the room *is* like an open-style railway carriage, long and quite narrow, and with windows down both sides facing each other, one set looking on to the front court rocks, the other on to an inner court that is quite empty. When Richard opened the door to this room for me for the first time I could scarcely conceal dismay. The furniture left by the German couple is quite dreadful and the huge stove on its zinc base hideous, even if it is a good heater.

Marie was very gay about the stove. She said that it defeats the mind to imagine anyone importing such a thing from Europe, and that it must have been set dead centre in the hold of the ship that brought it, otherwise it would have caused a list that could have been quite fatal in a typhoon. She believes that since the stove reached China it must not be neglected, but featured in our room, though on a new base of pale green tiles she knows where to get. According to her, that stove could do wonderful work as a social ice-breaker, and redecoration and refurnishing should seem to be completely deferential to the monster, everything else in exquisite good taste to point up the joke. She was quite sure that soft green is the colour I want, starting with specially woven Tientsin carpet, the curtains to be hand-woven brocade. Richard would be horrified by the estimates for what Marie thinks is necessary.

She insisted on seeing the whole house before tea was brought in, though with so many empty rooms the tour did not take long. Marie tested the mattress in my room and said that the hardness might not matter now but it soon would. I think I prefer the way Mrs Brinkhill dealt with delicate matters, head on, not flirting with them. Richard's room seemed a total surprise to her, perhaps because it is almost entirely furnished with his regimental officer's equipment, folding camp bed, canvas washing basin and chair, plus a card table pushed against one wall, a small hanging mirror above it. There are no curtains at the window, which is of a Chinese lattice type opening in, and no stove either, the hole for the pipe blocked up. Though the weather has been bitter since we came here he sleeps with his window open always, the draught swirling down the passage to me. Marie said who would have believed the beautiful Richard was at heart an ascetic? I said nothing.

Yao's shaking hands set the teacups rattling as he carried in the tray and Marie thinks he has some disease of the nerves which would make it foolish of us to keep him because there is no greater nuisance in China than unwell servants who feel they have a family claim on you. If we got rid of him quickly he would not have any right to feel this. Her advice may be sound enough but already I have a kind of affection for Yao.

The cakes were not very good and Marie asked about our cook. I had to tell her that I have had practically no dealings with the man and had only been in the kitchen twice, and that really only to look in from the door. Somewhat to my surprise she did not approve of this. Having seen her in her boudoir, I would have thought that kitchens would be the last thing to interest her, but it must be her French instincts, for she insists on going down to prepare certain sauces and even some dishes from family recipes which she says she is not giving to any cook, so while she is there he is not even permitted to watch. Also, she taught the man how to make proper bread. She could not stand what she calls Peking bread, of the kind I had at the Hardings' and have here, too, which tastes as though the dough had been artificially soured during the kneading. Before the Boxer Troubles there was a good French bakery in Peking, but that has not opened again. Another thing that Marie says I must insist on is seeing that all salad ingredients are immersed in a solution of potassium permanganate before serving and this will *not* be done in a Chinese-managed kitchen unless it is made quite clear that instant dismissal will result from any failure to observe this rule. From untreated raw vegetables you can get cholera and intestinal worms, to mention just two of the possibilities.

After tea, at which she drank many cups, she excused herself and I had to show her down the corridor to the little room and also our bathroom next to it, both missed on our earlier tour. She came back to me with an expression which said she had not liked what she had just experienced, no surprise really, but I did not expect any comment. However, she said at once that our sanitary arrangements were a horror, to which I agreed, but pointed out that they were quite as bad at the Hardings' so that this was what I had come to expect in China. Marie announced that this was *not* to be expected in China, and that Edith Harding, like all the truly rich, was totally mean about spending money, even on essentials. If Richard and I were to entertain, as we must soon do, it was quite impossible that we show our guests to such facilities. In the first place what was essential was a chemical closet of the kind with which her house was equipped and which could be ordered from a shop in Tientsin. She also said that to have water heated by a stove built on to the *outside* of the house was something from the eighteenth century and that even in Peking one could have taps to a basin and a paraffin heater.

By this time I had heard rather too much of Marie's suggested improvements and said that we did not wish to do too much to the house since we didn't know how long we would be in Peking. To this her reply was that one must live in a decently civilized manner wherever one was and why should I not do what she had done when she was first married, which was to demand from her husband that he take the equipping and furnishing of their first home from the money she had brought him as a dowry? It was quite wrong to let a new husband think this money was simply his to do with what he wanted, it had been paid by the bride's parents to secure the complete comfort of their daughter. I must have been staring at her, for she asked what was the matter?

What I said then was rather awkward, something about the practice of dowries having more or less died out in Britain. It was she who stared then, before bursting out laughing. According to what she calls her certain knowledge, there is not one man in the British

Legation in Peking, with the possible exception of Sir Claude himself, who had not most carefully married for money. Marie said that there might not be with us, as in France, precise rules any more for these marriage settlements, but they were settlements none the less, and absolutely vital to young men making a career in diplomacy because nearly all of them were the younger sons of good families who had only their names to offer the world, no financial backing. Mr Harding was an example of this, a distinguished Essex family, his brother a baronet, but penniless, so he had been obliged to fend for himself, searching for and finding Edith. Who would have had Edith if she had been without a fortune? Madame Harding might attempt the grand manner now she was on the road to becoming a Lady when her husband, in old age, was knighted, but she was actually nothing but the daughter of a Midlands manufacturer of iron bolts, and quite without any social standing in English society.

I felt myself becoming very warm and knew that my face was colouring up in the way it had done at that concert on the *Mooldera*. Marie noticed, of course, her tone changed, becoming quiet, as though she was suddenly worried: 'Surely, *ma chère*, your mother must have discussed such things at the time when your marriage to Richard was arranged?' I said the marriage had not been arranged and no dowry talked about because there couldn't be one from my family, which is poor.

Marie looked really astounded, clearly finding it difficult to say anything, though what she did manage was a considerable shock: 'Mary, what of your family factory?' I had to draw in a deep breath then. I knew very well indeed that I had certainly not spoken of that factory to her or anyone else in Peking, and the only one who could have done so was Richard. After having been so very hot I felt suddenly as though there was a frozen lump in my stomach.

I wanted her to go and she sensed this, rising, talking about other things as we waited for Yao to bring in her coat, saying that from the first time we met she had wanted us to be as sisters because at once she had felt real sympathy between us, even our names being almost the same. Her coat was brought and I helped her into it, beautiful matched leopardskins to almost floor-length trimmed with silver fox at hem, neck and cuffs. Her hat, which she had not taken off, was a small round pillbox, also leopard, worn tilted down on to her forehead. Even with the sick feeling I had then I could appreciate how elegant she always is, of course at great cost. Perhaps her wardrobe is also paid for from her dowry?

Near the door Marie paused to pick up the purple dish Richard says he had found in a bazaar. The dish is translucent like a cake of Pear's Soap, with a dragon curving around it. I said something about the plate having to go if we decided on Marie's green colour scheme. She said it was priceless. I didn't see how that could be since it had been bought in a bazaar. Marie looked at me, rather hard I thought, then said that it was of a type only done on Imperial Court order or, by special permission, for the very highest princely families. I then asked how she thought Richard could possibly have come by such a piece and she said: 'Loot from the Winter Palace.' She laughed and added: 'He probably won it at cards from another officer. One who had helped at the sacking of Peking. Richard is very good at cards. Didn't you know?'

Marie has been very kind to me, but I came back from seeing her off at the gate with the feeling of having been pulled about like some article in the January bargain sales.

The House of the Dragon Screen,
April 5, 1903

I had been expecting signs of spring in April, but it has been snowing all night, and is still doing it, the frost hard. It is so quiet one might be in the country, not a sound coming in from our lane. Until a short time ago there was the noise of our handyman sweeping snow from the path to the gate. He was heaping it up against those rocks that are supposed to be ornamental, a broom and a shovel his tools, but not working very hard with either, stopping often to blow on his hands, which were bare, though the rest of his body was covered by a long padded robe and a cap with earflaps lowered which didn't leave much of his face exposed. He was using the shovel when he looked up suddenly and saw me at the drawing-room window. I raised my hand in a sort of wave, but he must have taken this as a signal to go away, for at once he picked up his tools and disappeared behind the dragon screen, beyond which is a door to the servants' courtyard.

All I know about him is that his name is Ching Hen. I haven't even seen Mrs Ching Hen because the dragon screen hides all the comings and goings from the servants' side of the compound to the lane. I am beginning to see that the huge piece of stone has more uses than just keeping the devils at bay.

I am writing this by the crackling stove. Though I can't hear any sounds of it, there must be a wind for there is a huge draught in the iron chimney and this is red hot where it leaves the stove. Quite often I look at that pipe and think how easily it could glow right up to the wooden ceiling and set it alight. This house, behind its high walls and built almost up to them, would burn like paper and sticks in a grate the moment you set a match to them.

Richard does not like seeing me at breakfast, so Yao brings a tray to my room. Already we have contrived a system of not meeting before Richard leaves for the Legation, though this is sometimes quite trying for me if he leaves later than usual and spends too long in the bathroom. Richard has the kind of nature which brightens as the day goes on but is very dark in the morning. The trouble is I am quite cheerful then and in Edinburgh was often an early riser, even as early as the servants, sometimes helping with the housework, dusting and so on. Here I am not supposed to do anything, at least while Richard is about, so I tidy my room. It is not a room I would ever become fond of, even if a great deal of money was spent on it. The two windows face a brick wall just ten feet away and the only sun that comes in, at least in winter, is if I open the door to the passage which runs alongside the courtyard and has windows to the floor. Later, when there are flowers out there, it may be quite attractive, but I wonder if I will ever get away from the feeling that the house is like a prison? Or perhaps a fort in enemy territory.

If I have become fond of anything in these rooms it is this huge, ugly stove. It has isinglass windows on the fuelling door which put a patch of colour on the carpet the Germans left, and when that door is opened for coals the whole stove roars: 'Yes, feed me and I'll do my job!' It does that, too. Within an hour of its ventilators being opened in the morning this big room is warm.

I have been thinking about friendship, how it is usually an accident. Marie is becoming my friend because we are both here in Peking and most of the Legation ladies are slightly suspicious of her. I think this is partly because she is too clever for them, but more because she is popular with their husbands. She is taking me up because she cannot be entertaining to men all the time. If she and her husband had been living in London, and we had met there, she would not have looked at me twice in a place so full of interesting distractions.

I wonder if Richard does not care to see me in the morning because he has no wish to be reminded of the night before when he visited my room? I have no wish to be reminded of it either.

Letter from Mary Mackenzie to her mother

House of the Dragon Screen,
157 Hutung Feng-huang,
Peking, China,
April 17th, 1903

Dearest Mama,

  I know it is a terrible time since I last wrote and my
excuses are poor, but I think of you so often, and wonder
what you are doing just at that hour, trying to imagine
this, that you are settling by the fire for tea, for instance, or
that on an Edinburgh April day you are visiting friends.
Suddenly, as I was beginning to feel shut away behind these
walls like a Chinese wife, things have started to happen.
First, it is the spring. We had snow in the early part of this
month, but now there is fruit blossom out in gardens—
though not in ours—and we can ride in our rickshas
without those smelly fur rugs tucked in around us. All the
snow has melted and the city feels clean and washed, though
I don't think it will stay like this for long. I find that I am
seeing a hundred things that I never noticed with winter

clamped down, like how the ends of many of the curved tile roofs have little animal figures marching in a procession towards a bigger figure on the last tile, which is usually a hen with a devil on its back. These are called bongs. Even going down our lane, which can be quite squalid at ground level, if you look up you see the most beautiful roof patterns and sections of wood carving though I do get a little tired of dragons everywhere. It is as though all the Chinese had experienced the same bad dream.

One day my friend Madame de Chamonpierre got the loan of the French Minister's carriage and called for me in the afternoon and we drove through an eastern gate out to the Temple of Heaven where, on ceremonial occasions, the Emperor worships. What he worships, or why, I am not very sure, and Marie didn't know either. There was no way to find out because we had no guide and the coachman only understands 'go slower' or 'go faster' in French. However, we got out and walked for quite a long way over paving, through which grew tall weeds, to what Marie thought was the Altar of Heaven, this reached through a gate that had what seemed to be stone wings sprouting from the top portion. After that were steps up three different levels to a circular platform offering a view down to what was the temple itself, this set against a circle of trees coming into bud. In that whole huge area we saw not another human being, only pigeons, which was a little eerie. You would have thought that in a place where the Emperor sometimes comes to worship there would have been priests about, or at least someone to pull up the weeds. Marie would not go down to the actual temple because she was reminded of the Boxer Troubles by what she says is the most frightening thing in China, a sudden deep silence where there should be continuous noise. It was certainly silent at the Temple of Heaven and we were quite glad to get back into the carriage again and hear the clip-clop of horses' hooves.

I have been to the Russian Legation, though not to meet their Minister who is away in Vladivostok. Our host was the First Secretary, who is a Count, and wore enough medals to have fought in ten wars, though he does not look like a man who has ever fought in any. As Marie had told me to expect, we talked about nothing interesting and the men drank too much vodka, which is their whisky, only apparently quite tasteless. I wondered what was the point of drinking it until Richard took me away quite suddenly because, as Marie said afterwards, our Russian colleagues were becoming too relaxed suddenly.

Then there was a dinner-party at the de Chamonpierres', very elegantly done, with twelve guests, at which one of my table partners was another Count, this time a Japanese one. He is military attaché at their Legation here, and during the Boxer Troubles became one of the heroes of the defence, in that he led a party of Japanese marines through the streets of the Chinese city, this seething with Boxers, to the relief of a Catholic mission which he helped to defend when he got there. Of the twenty men he took with him seven were killed, and Captain Count Kurihama was wounded in the leg and has a scar on one temple where a bullet grazed his scalp. He should have been a very interesting man to talk to but I could scarcely get him to say a word. Marie explained afterwards that they are brought up never to have their meals with the women of the household and that it is impossible for them to get used to sitting at table with females. Marie says that quite often, at formal dinners in her house, she has had the feeling that Count Kurihama was about to order her back to the kitchen where she belongs while the men are at the serious business of eating and drinking. Clearly she had placed me next to him to see if a Scotch girl could get any reaction from a Japanese Count, but I failed. The peak of our conversation was reached when I asked if Kurihama was a place name, as

*with our aristocracy, or a family one, and after thinking
for about five minutes he said one word: 'Family.' Not the
most sparkling of dinner partners. I have a feeling he
knows English quite well, but is keeping this a diplomatic
secret.*

*I must soon be considering giving our first dinner-
party at Dragon Screen House, and I can promise you,
Mama dear, that the idea quite terrifies me. Have you
any Scotch recipes that could make chicken taste different?
I am quite sure that the beef we get here is not that at all,
not even old oxen, but camel. Our cook serves it in a
sloppy stew which has clearly simmered for hours but it is
still like chewing parcel string. Peking is supposed to be a
paradise for food, and may be in some of the Chinese
restaurants, but only very few of the Legation people are
going to these again, and Richard has never taken me. Is
there any way, do you think, that I could make a Chinese
cook produce a good Scotch meal from simple recipes?
There is now open again quite a reasonable European
grocery store where you can get most things, at a price, so
if you have any ideas please send them. Your last letter,
via the Trans-Siberian railway, reached me in less than a
month, which means there is still time, since I will not be
entertaining until Richard comes back from a mission.*

*He leaves for Chinwangtao at the end of this month to
make a report to the Admiral of the British China Fleet.
I do not know what this is about. Richard says it is part of
the routine contact between the services, but Marie looks
mysterious. I would so like to impress her with that Scotch
meal, for she thinks we live on porridge three times a day
during the week and steamed mince on Sunday. She says
she had a Scotch nanny who told her this was our life in
the 'frozen north'. Marie would amuse you, I think, she is
very gay and bright.*

Loads of love, Mama dear,
Mary

House of the Dragon Screen,
April 23rd, 1903

Yesterday I had Edith Harding to tea. I was absolutely ashamed that, after having shown me such hospitality for so long, as well as being matron of honour at our marriage, I had not had her to see the house. I suppose my idea was that I would try to do something to the place before she visited, but beyond pushing furniture about I have done nothing at all. Also, I am quite sure that Marie will have let Edith know that she has been here *twice*. It is not that there is any competition over me, or any real interest in me, either, between the ladies, it is just that I am a novelty in this place. I suppose until I die I will be that first bride after the Boxer Troubles, remembered for this distinction when my name has been forgotten.

Edith arrived wearing one of those unfortunate brown dresses of which she is so fond. Somebody really should tell her that when you are wispy in appearance brown does nothing to flatter. Wicked Marie, after seeing Edith—who is very thin—arrive at a dinner-party in a browny-grey evening dress made like a tube said it was like watching a very big earthworm come in from the garden. I must find out what Marie says about me behind my back, and I am sure Edith will be most willing to tell me.

She seemed slightly surprised that I was looking quite well and the reason for this came out over her second cup of tea when she said that she had found her own honeymoon very upsetting, but that perhaps going straight to one's own home was the best idea. She and Mr Harding went to a hotel at Torquay in June when it rained for a week. I said that it had snowed for the better part of the first two weeks of my married life, at which she said that adverse climatic conditions meant that you got to know your husband quite well sooner than you would have done if the weather had been favourable for outdoor activities. I thought for one moment she had made rather a doubtful joke, but she was quite serious. Edith does not make jokes of any kind.

I have wronged her in the sense that I have thought her cold. She has always been rather formal with me, as though only a certain degree of intimacy was permissible with an engaged girl living under her roof. But I can see quite clearly that now I am under my husband's roof she feels free to make a bid for closer friendship, even perhaps for the sort of intimacy which I do not wish. There were suggestions, very delicately put certainly, that we might discuss areas of married life that I could never discuss with anyone, except perhaps Mrs Brinkhill, who seemed to travel through life with a trunkful of worldly wisdom she was ready to open for those she liked. I didn't have to rebuff Edith in any way, her curiosity about Richard and me was under several veils and she only lifted a corner of one of them, dropping it at once when she saw my reaction.

The odd thing is that, though I wouldn't have believed it possible only a few weeks ago that I should feel this, there are certain things that perhaps I would like to talk about to someone I *really* trusted. Surely all that is written in prose and poetry of love and romance cannot lead only to the experience that has been mine? And I am beginning to have a curiosity that seems to me unhealthy, a way now of looking at other women and their husbands, wondering if there is some kind of secret happiness between them? If there is, they do not show any signs of it that I can see.

I must make arrangements to keep my notebooks secure, it would be dreadful if Richard found one. I do not know enough of him yet to be sure whether or not he would be the gentleman and decline to read what was not intended for his eyes, but I have a feeling he might not be so gallant. I will have to get a box with a lock. It is like a schoolgirl silliness. I should stop this vice of putting down what has happened to me, yet I believe it would be like trying to give up opium. When I am thirty, will I want to read about the follies of being twenty? If I have children, would I one day want them to open that box and see the records of what their mother was, perhaps to their shame?

Edith either senses that we are not too well off or thinks the financial arrangements in our married state have yet to be clearly settled, for she began to suggest very economical ways in which I could set about doing things to our drawing-room and when I told her about Madame's extravagant ideas for the same project she said that Madame had been a spoiled child turned into a spoiled woman and that sometimes the way she tried to queen it at her own dinners made Edith feel quite ill. When I thought about Marie queening it, what I remembered was a look that Monsieur de Chamonpierre sent down to his wife past all his guests, a look which seemed to say that the other women around the table tired his eyes which could only be refreshed by Marie. The message seemed to me so plain that I turned my head to catch Marie's response. There was none. She was being charming to the First Secretary of the German Legation, tapping his wrist lightly. She has told me she detests the man. Perhaps it is better to have no inclination to despatch such eye messages than to despatch them for no response.

Before she left Edith promised to lend me her sewing woman who is quite skilled at upholstery work, an unusual thing in China where the natives all sit on hard wooden chairs. Edith really is being very good, I must try to like her more. I wonder if I could persuade her not to consider brown when buying dress materials? She had come in furs, in spite of the sun shining, not the sables, Mongolian fox that could easily be some kind of long-haired rabbit, probably one of the bargains of which she is so proud. I am pretty sure that if you are the kind of person who would spend money cheerfully if you had any means that you will never have much. It is the rich who gloat over bargains, Edith's coat is a great mistake, almost piebald in colouring and quite wrong for her, which meant that from a short distance away it was difficult to see where the coat ended and she began.

> House of the Dragon Screen,
> Peking,
> May 3rd, 1903

Last night, when he visited me, I asked him to stay, and instead of going back to his room at once, he did, for perhaps half an hour. There was kindness between us. Then, when he had gone, I began to cry very quietly. I don't know what is the matter with me.

He has gone now to Chinwangtao. He went in ordinary clothes to see an admiral, which seemed strange to me, but he says the visit is informal. The suit was very like the one in which I had first seen him coming in from the Scottish moors, it may have been the same one. Suddenly I wanted to go to the station with him, saying that Yao could fetch another ricksha in a minute and I could pick up a coat in the hall. He told me not to be foolish.

I stood in front of our red gate watching the back of his ricksha bouncing towards the place where our lane bends, not expecting that he would turn to look back, but he did, and waved his hand. My heart gave a bump. Then I became conscious of the Chinese passing in the lane looking at me curiously, which was strange because I have become so accustomed to not being stared at in this city. Perhaps, because we live in this lane, we are now accepted by the people round about and when I went through the hatch in the gate and saw the dragon screen the carving no longer looked foreign and weird, almost as though it was now at work keeping those devils out for me, too. Then I remembered that it had not kept the devils out for the court official who had lost his head.

House of the Dragon Screen,
Peking,
May 5th, 1903

This morning I did something Richard would not have approved of. I called Yao in about ten-thirty and put on a little performance as an actress, pretending that I was in a market buying things, picking up vegetables and so on, the object of all this being to tell him that when he went shopping I was going with him. For some time he watched me with a look of almost panic on his face, as though he thought I had gone mad after only two nights of being deprived of my husband and then, when the idea began to dawn, a strange thing happened, he laughed. Whatever Yao's life history has been his face says that there has been very little in it to laugh over, and though I have no belief in my talents as an actress it is something to have produced that laughter. Soon we were laughing together, a demented servant and his demented mistress, not the kind of carry-on that would have been approved of in Edinburgh or the Legation Quarter. I don't care. It pleased me to be able to laugh with Yao though if Mr Ching Hen happened to be sweeping up in the outer courtyard at the time there is now a scandal in the kitchen quarters. I must see that I do *not* make Yao laugh when Richard is here. Am I going to become one of those women who is too familiar with servants and so earns their contempt?

Anyway, we went to market, Yao and I, down the Lane of the Fabulous Bird, a Scotchwoman and her servant both carrying baskets. There was the question of how we should walk in the lane and we started out like children playing Indians, with me the leader, which seemed very silly indeed, so I waited for him and we went along side by side with him looking very nervous probably for fear the familiarity might be reported back to Mrs Yao. Perhaps I shouldn't have insisted we walk like that but I have always hated seeing dogs trained to heel, and the idea of servants doing this is much worse.

One thing I haven't quite got used to yet is the Peking smell. It is everywhere you go, almost as though contained by the city walls, not one of the spicy smells that are supposed to be a feature of the Orient, but more like rancid butter that has been slightly heated in a pan. The smell seems to come from everywhere, but is particularly pungent rising from the fur rug that is put over your knees in rickshas. It is as though the whole city had been dipped in some substance which gives off this reek, faint in some places, strong in others. I noticed it when Richard and I were up on Coal Hill on that bitterly freezing day, though there was no hint of it at the Temple of Heaven outside the walls.

Yao and I must have walked half a mile to the market, which was a simple enough arrangement on what looked like a piece of waste ground though there was a sort of gate, this made of upright wooden poles with a sign stuck across the top and banners hanging from it with Chinese writing in huge characters. Beyond were the stalls, all of a portable kind, with the carts that had brought them in the background. Here the butcher worked in the open, chopping and cutting on a fat slab of wood with clouds of flies rising at every movement he made. Flies were a solid skin over pieces of meat hanging behind him. It was the same at the fishmonger's, flies thick on a huge cod even as it was being cleaned and filleted. The insides were not being put in a bucket for disposal, but in a container on the counter, and while I watched an old woman shoved over a coin and received some fish entrails in a jar she was carrying. I longed to know what tasty dish was going to be made from her purchase. I would have thought that the vegetable stalls would have interested the flies less, but they were there too in thousands. I certainly saw the need for that washing in potassium permanganate and am rather put off the idea of salads of any kind, particularly since I learned how these crops are fertilized, with what cannot be talked about put straight at the roots of the growing plants. Perhaps we are too fussy about many things in the West, and there are certainly no signs that the Chinese, as a result of poisoning themselves, are dying out. Marie thinks that by the end of this century they will have swamped the world, even the Russians, for she says that two Chinese are born for every one of the rest of us. I don't know where she gets her statistics from and I am a little suspicious of them.

All my attention was on the stalls and their vendors, so that for some time I just didn't notice the interest in me, and this was partially, I suppose, that I had grown so used to not being looked at in Peking, at least not openly, which rather gave the feeling that you could go anywhere and be invisible. But not in the market. There wasn't a big crowd, I expect most housewives and servants had shopped earlier, and those there were not all women, some very well-robed men, which surprised me as much as it would have done to see a gentleman shopping in an Edinburgh grocer's. One of the men was quite openly asking Yao questions about the foreigner while he frankly stared at me, Yao not a little embarrassed by this. There was no feeling of hostility at all, but for all that, from having been relaxed, I felt myself stiffening up, self-conscious suddenly, particularly of the clothes I was wearing.

I had put on a simple dress with a light coat over it, my hair tucked up into a felt hat, no parasol, and I had left home feeling that I was drab enough not to be an object of interest to anyone, but standing in that market I felt that what I was wearing was ridiculous. These people, in far from their best clothes, had a kind of elegance, the men in long robes split only at the ankles, the women with three-quarter length tunics over trousers, their heads bare, the hair simply dressed, the only jewellery in ears, no brooches or other fussy ornaments. I seemed to be all bumps in my clothing, my skirts far too long even though in Peking we have these made an inch or two off the ground so as not to sweep the dirty lanes and streets. It was as if I understood then just how weird we must look to them from their own simplicity of style, all fuss and furbelows. In China we ought to wear Chinese clothes, like some of the missionaries do in the interior, but I can imagine how the Legation dinner tables would react to that idea. Suddenly I wanted to say to these people, please look your fill, I am indeed a curiosity.

I am probably showing the first symptoms of China Head, a disease amongst Europeans in this country which results in them being sent away from the Far East and never allowed to return. If this is my complaint Richard is going to be sadly embarrassed, and I thought just how angry he would be if he could see me in this place with a shopping basket hanging over my arm while Yao, keeping his good eye on me, tried to inspect a piece of fly-covered ox with the squinting one.

> At the de Chamonpierres',
> Legation Quarter,
> Peking,
> May 6th, 1903

I am writing this in bed. Living here is very luxurious, my breakfast tray set with the most beautiful Limoges china, so fine I was afraid hot coffee might crack the cup. I would have preferred tea but in a French house tea is just a British joke in the middle of the afternoon. Marie swept me away from home, first with a chitty warning me that she was coming to do it, then arriving, breathless, because I was her only hope to make up the numbers at a dinner-party they were giving last night which was a difficult mix of guests and only the little Scotch, as Armand calls me, could solve things. All nonsense, of course, pure French flattery of the kind they do automatically when they have a mind to, but still very pleasant to receive. I think Marie is so lucky with Armand, and wonder if she really appreciates him? They say French men are all loose living, but I would be very surprised if Armand has any interest in any other Legation ladies. There is talk that all the Legation bachelors go to Chinese women, but this is not a matter I want to hear too much about because it makes me uneasy when I am in the company of someone I know is behaving wickedly. I find it so difficult to look at them while we are engaged in ordinary conversation, which I know is very silly of me and is something I will almost certainly grow out of soon in this life. Anyway, I cannot imagine Armand going out to Chinese women and will not consider the idea.

I didn't feel that my contribution to the success of the de Chamonpierre dinner-party was quite so important when I found that my task was once again to attempt to make Count Kurihama say a few words while we were at table. It was quite clear that he didn't want to, and I didn't score a very startling success. I said I had seen pictures of beautiful Mount Fuji and longed to see it for myself. To this he said: 'Ah.' I asked if he had ever climbed the famous mountain and he said: 'No.' I then wondered why he had not and he said: 'Too busy become soldier.' I am sure he speaks English like that because he thinks it is the way people expect a Japanese to speak English and suddenly, to my own complete surprise, I said this to him. For the first time, I think, he looked straight at me. Then he laughed. It was rather like getting a laugh from Yao, it changed the Count's face completely for half a minute, no, about three seconds, making him seem almost a boy. Though he did not tell me this, Marie did afterwards, he is leaving Peking next week to return to Japan for active military duty. Marie is quite sure that in the coming war between Russia and Japan Count Kurihama is sure to distinguish himself. I don't know why she is so obsessed with the idea of this war, which she thinks France and Britain should be preparing to join on Japan's side against what she calls the savage bear. She has been in Japan on holiday and says it is like paradise. I have been given a novel to read set there called *Madame Chrysanthème* by Pierre Loti. I looked at it last night before I slept. It seems to be very French in that the heroine is a woman of doubtful virtue.

After having been forced to endure me throughout dinner I was expecting Count Kurihama to steer well clear in the drawing-room, which made it quite a surprise when, as the gentlemen joined us, he took a firm course to a place by my side, as though he had deliberately planned to do this. He drank his coffee and sipped his brandy, sitting with a ramrod military back, and in a true Japanese silence, staring towards one of the few open fireplaces in Peking. This gave me a view of one side of his head if I wanted it, on which there was a decided cheekbone flush from the drink he had consumed. I matched his silence, aware as I did this of Marie looking at me from across the room, perhaps considering coming to my rescue and sweeping me away to another grouping. However, this was not necessary. The Count, having finished both coffee and brandy, turned his head and said in slow but still perfect English, except that he could not make an 'l' sound, using 'r's for these so that the sentence came out as: 'Prease teru me about Scotrand.' It was quite a tall order, but I began by saying that we also had a sacred mountain called Ben Nevis which is also often snow-capped. He seemed mildly interested and asked if it was a volcano? I told him that all our volcanoes had gone to sleep some millions of years ago, for which we were very thankful, though we still had earthquakes at a place called Comrie and I had experienced one while staying in a hotel near there with my mother. The Count then said that at his home in Tokyo there is usually an earthquake every ten days or so, small ones, but that if as long as a month or two goes by with no shake people become nervous, expecting a big one. I asked what happens in a big one and was told that people get knocked off their feet and tiles come down from the roof. It all sounds rather terrifying and I asked him if the earthquakes were the result of volcanic activity but he said no, Japan was mounted on the back of a huge dragon which was subject to uneasy dreams. I think he meant this as a joke, but he didn't laugh, so I didn't either. Really, he is an odd man. I found myself wanting to make him smile again but was not successful.

Marie has just left after coming in suddenly to see me just as I was thinking about getting up and making use of her civilized bathroom. She was wearing a peignoir, of apricot colour, with much lace, and sat on my bed to suggest that I should not go home today, but stay on with them until Richard gets back. I said that I expected him tomorrow, at which she looked wise and said I'd be lucky if I saw him in ten days because, as everyone in the Quarter knew well, he had not gone to Chinwangtao, only passed through it on the way to Moukden, where his mission was to report on Russian activities in Manchuria, which report would then be sent to London in the diplomatic bag. I wasn't to be distressed that he had not told me himself for he had been under orders to tell no one. I said it was not much of a secret if the whole of the Quarter knew what he was doing, and if this was true, what about the Russians? Marie laughed and said that of course the Russians knew what he was up to, and would be waiting for him in Moukden, but since the territory is still officially Chinese there was nothing they could do to stop Richard's activities, only watch him from the moment he got off the train. He would expect to be spied on, but that wouldn't keep him from collecting what he needed for this report.

Naturally all this didn't make me too happy and I told Marie I wouldn't stay on with them because I wanted to use the time while Richard is away to get on with doing a number of things to the house. This was a mistake because Marie immediately volunteered to come and give me her good advice, but then fortunately remembered that her social calendar for the next few days was practically bursting. I wish she did not give me the feeling that I have been 'taken up' by her. I am certain it is something that rather sets the other Legation ladies against me, and that I don't like, either for my own sake, or for Richard's. I am not good yet at handling people and situations.

5

Letter from Mary Mackenzie to her mother

157 Hutung Feng-huang,
Peking, China,
May 19th, 1903

Dearest Mama,

*I have some rather exciting news for you, or at least it
is exciting for me! Richard was away from Peking on
military business and was only just back when he came
home one evening to say that the Empress Dowager Tsz'e
Hsi (you pronounce that with the tip of your tongue
almost against the back of your upper teeth) had sent a
command to the Legations that she wished to meet a few
of our younger wives. For some time now, and to help
wipe out memories of the Boxer Troubles, Her Majesty has
been giving tea-parties to the wives of European
diplomats, but only at the higher levels, Ministers' and
First Secretaries' wives and so on. The numbers were
fixed, as though only a few foreign women could be risked
in the Winter Palace at one time, and usually only half a
dozen would go, this leading to some unpleasant feeling
amongst the ladies who felt that the upper levels of our
society were keeping the privilege to themselves. Perhaps it
is that the Empress of all China, and real ruler of this*

*country since the Emperor is a nothing, has got tired of
seeing the same faces at her parties, for her new
invitation, though not actually naming me, said that she
understood there had been a wedding in the Quarter
recently, and that she wished to see the bride, also any
other ladies of about that age.*

*There is a great shortage of ladies about my age!
At the German Legation there is one wife of twenty-six
and at the Italian another of twenty-seven, but that is
all, so the friend with whom I stayed when I first came,
Edith Harding, was included though she must be at
least thirty-three or -four, with two sons at school in
England. My French friend Marie, though really still
quite young, had already contrived to get herself to one
of the tea-parties, so was not eligible this time, and
finally it was decided to send just the four of us instead
of the usual six.*

*The great day is tomorrow. Our audience is not to be
held at the Winter Palace within the city walls, but at the
Summer Palace some distance outside, this built by the
Empress only about fifteen years ago, at immense cost,
and some say using the money raised throughout the
Empire to help improve the Chinese Navy. The story goes
that when Sir Robert Hart, the British controller of
Chinese Customs, asked Her Majesty what new ships had
been built with the money raised the Empress pointed to a
marble boat at the edge of an artificial lake and asked if
he did not think that was a pretty warship? The Lady
Tsz'e Hsi is certainly no ordinary ruler, amongst other
things suspected of using poison from time to time to
advance her position. Her Co-Regent, the former
Emperor's chief wife, died very suddenly, leaving all the
power in the hands of Tsz'e Hsi and she is said to keep her
own son as a virtual prisoner. There is no doubt that she
was totally behind the Boxers' plan to wipe out all the
foreigners in China. I remember that when we had*

*Catherine the Great at school in history I thought her the
most ruthless woman who has ever been, but perhaps this
title ought to be given to the Lady with whom I am to sip
tea tomorrow (green, I should think). Not the wildest
imaginings of either of us could have foreseen, when you
bought that blue dress for me in Edinburgh, that it
would be worn for* this *special occasion. If it seems too
formal for teatime, apparently the custom with these
audiences is to dress as for the evening because Her
Imperial Majesty likes to see her European guests as
jewelled as possible. In this she is going to be sadly
disappointed with me!*

*The four of us leave the Legation Quarter in the
British Minister's carriage at two p.m., accompanied to
the Hatamen Gate by Legation guards, where our escort
will become a troop of mounted Imperial Cavalry. You
can imagine that I am feeling excited, this is likely to be
the nearest I shall ever get to royalty in any country unless,
of course, Richard is one day knighted at Buckingham
Palace, though I do not feel in my bones that this is going
to happen.*

May 20th.

*I was so exhausted last night when I got home I could not
eat a thing, much less write anything down for you,
Mama, but today my memories are still very fresh and I
will try my best to give you a clear picture of what
happened. First, there was a slight let-down. The Legation
guard to the Hatamen Gate consisted of only two soldiers
mounted behind us like postillions and apparently under
the impression that what they said, and the language they
used, was quite inaudible to the ladies in front. This,
unfortunately, was not the case. Then, when we reached
the Hatamen and had driven through the tunnel under
that massive pile of stone, we found that the Imperial*

Cavalry, whom I had pictured as elaborately garbed with coloured banners flowing from their spears, were in fact two rather elderly-seeming men mounted on sad-looking ponies. China is often like this, you look for great pomp and show, but there is none, and when you are least expecting it there is suddenly a glittering display that seems out of keeping with the occasion, like a funeral. There is no dignity about these ceremonies at all, just a wild display of vulgarity, as though the idea was to show how rich the deceased had been, this with tinsel glitter and dozens of hired mourners who scream with grief for a fixed fee.

The drive was over dreadfully rutted roads and the four of us nearly had our heads knocked together, which was not good for our hats. Rather strangely, court etiquette had obliged us to wear these with evening dress, and mine was that small one you called too pert in the shop and did not want me to have, but if you must wear a hat with evening dress it would seem sensible to put on as small a one as possible. The other ladies, however, had not felt this, Mrs Harding wearing almost a whole flower border, while the two opposite were in very wide, floppy brims that in a stiff breeze became like sails out of control. After the first few miles we were obliged to stop the Minister's carriage to have the back hood raised, which saw us completing the journey in considerable warmth and not able to see much out of the two smallish windows which had to be almost completely shut on their straps. I wasn't much troubled, though, about no view, for from what I have seen of the country around Peking it is dull, with almost everything in the way of trees cut down or stunted by the poor for use as fuel in winter.

We were given no instructions in Chinese Imperial Court etiquette, simply told that we were to follow the *instructions of Prince Tai, a court chamberlain. The Prince has been in Europe twice, sent there by the Empress on missions before the Boxer uprising, to which he was strongly opposed, almost losing his head because of this. Luckily for the Empress, she did not issue the order to have this done and the Prince became chief go-between in negotiations with the Allies after the capture of Peking. Apparently these ladies' tea-parties are one of his ideas for improved relations with foreigners.*

We were the first tea-party at the Summer Palace, the others having been given at the Empress's winter home within the city, and during the drive I began to get the feeling that those responsible for making the arrangements for us had been rather carefree about this. Our route led through an area in which bandits and still roaming bands of Boxers are reported from time to time and I could not really feel that our elderly escorts, with their slung rifles, would be much use if we ran into one of these. I did not, of course, say anything to the others about this, but I think Edith Harding was having similar thoughts, and from time to time she kept pressing against her lips a handkerchief heavily scented with eau de Cologne.

However, we arrived safely, driving through what looked rather like a triumphal arch, not part of any wall, just standing by itself, this set beyond a vast lake quite choked with lotus plants, though no blooms. As we got down from the carriage what I noticed at once was the perfect symmetry of the scene ahead, first a white marble bridge, gently arching, then marble steps to another gate, its tiles of Imperial yellow, then the roof of a second gate beyond this appearing over the first. Towering above all, on a hill, was a five-story pagoda on a broad stone base, this flanked by two little pavilions on their own mounds, perfectly matched and looking rather like fantastical summerhouses. Everything was

matched in this way, the trees flanking the approach to
the marble bridge pines of exactly the same size and
shape. The sun was shining and everywhere was colour,
not from flower beds, but from roofs and columns, a
wild gaiety that still remained dignified because of the
balance of everything.

It is as though a thousand artists had been brought
together and were able, under strict discipline, to work
a miracle of harmony. When you speak of a palace you
think of a building, but this is a whole city by a lake
and climbing up a hill, with all its parts, pagodas,
temples, woods, seeming to fit perfectly each with the
other, so that nothing jars on the eye. Nervous as I was,
I still felt, as we set foot on that shining, alabaster-like
bridge, a sort of wild delight in this loveliness. Maybe
the Empress should have spent the money on ships for her
Navy built in Glasgow but, however much Richard
would disapprove of this, I can't help wondering if
perhaps she was not right to squander vast sums on this
beauty. Ships become out of date and are discarded, but
a Summer Palace floating on its hill will endure
forever.

Really, Mama, I wish I were a poet and could sing
of this place, that is how I still feel about it, looking
back, and know I will forty years from now if I am still
alive. Perhaps it can best be described by music. You
know how Handel, of whom you are so fond, goes on
with repeated phrases that are so well based on what has
gone before that you expect or expect almost what is to
come, and when it does, feel a kind of satisfaction
because the theme is half recognized, though not
completely, there is a surprise element, too. Well, the
Summer Palace is like that, you are never totally
surprised once you have got the idea of the design in
your mind, turning your head to receive one half a
surprise, the other half the completion of a pattern

recognized. Oh, I am putting it so badly, but on that bridge I suddenly understood how some people are affected by a kind of madness about China, so that afterwards nothing can ever make up to them for being away from it. The poverty is terrible, and the suffering I have seen, even from my sheltered life, does not bear thinking about. Richard says I am not to think about it, but I do, stabbed by the sight of a beggar with rotting limbs inside a heap of rags mumbling away to indifferent passers-by, or my ricksha coolie coughing as he waits for me somewhere, so that I wonder if he ever gets enough to eat, or is ever, in winter, warm enough. These are only two of a thousand miseries on every hand. And yet, despite these things, there seem to come moments, and not just at something outstanding like the Summer Palace, when everything that is around you is suddenly perfect, like a painting in which the picture is filled with exquisite detail, only this picture is alive, moving and there is a kind of strange music with it. You will think I am being wildly fanciful and wondering what has happened to your daughter, and I am not quite sure what has, but perhaps after so short a time I am already coming to have a love for this country. I long to be able to speak to the people properly, learning the language with a teacher, but Richard says this is quite unnecessary for me, and won't hear of it.

I am sure you are impatient with me for taking such a long time to get to the Empress, but it took us a long time to reach her from the alabaster bridge. Four ladies walked flanked by four Chinese men, who were dressed in long grey silk robes and may have been minor court officials or superior servants. They did not speak amongst themselves or to us, and I had the feeling they did not really approve of what they had to do, all of them wearing little round black caps, and two only with pigtails, the symbol of the Old China that has now become unfashionable, perhaps because most of the heads that were cut off after the Boxer Troubles, and exhibited, had pigtails. Our escort did not so much guide as herd us and I could see that the other ladies were a little unnerved by this. For my part I seemed to have got over nerves, my attention taken up by what I saw at each turning, another vista of garden with a pavilion in one corner, or a moon gate, or a long, long gallery of painted columns with delicate carving at the top of the pillars but a total plainness beneath. In the courtyards, and sometimes out in the gardens, were huge bronze animals, and lamps and what I suppose were enormous incense burners.

Prince Tai was waiting for us in an open area in front of a heavily roofed building that looked as if all those tiles might soon crush it into the ground, the only thing in the whole palace precincts which didn't seem light and gay. I had been expecting the Prince to be wearing a gorgeous Mandarin coat, but he was in European morning dress, probably in our honour, a short little man, with very short legs, and Richard would not have thought much of his tailor. He spoke excellent English but at a very slow pace, strange from a Chinese who always seem in their own language to be jabbering away at electric tramcar speed. He told us that Her Imperial Majesty was waiting and we were to follow him, but gave no instructions at all on protocol, perhaps there being none he could give us in a circumstance so outlandish as foreign ladies about to approach the Sacred Throne of the Manchus. He opened one half of huge lacquered doors himself, beyond which I expected to find an ante-chamber opening into another ante-chamber and so on, but no, we were in the salon of the audience itself.

It was a very long room. I am not good at measurements, but perhaps it was as long as our church in Morningside, and like it had side aisles, these beyond wooden columns lacquered bright red. The main part of the hall was completely unfurnished, a huge expanse of polished wooden floor with a raised dais at the far end on which was the dragon throne, or one of them, in this case a carved black ebony chair. The one seated figure was surrounded by at least fifteen court ladies in brilliant embroidered tunics, all of them standing absolutely motionless. The figure in the chair, wearing more sombre colours, didn't move either.

As we walked forward bare boards creaked under our feet. They are said to be laid like this to give warning of approaching assassins, and certainly the sound was loud enough, the only sound, until suddenly there was a louder noise from an orchestra of flutes, fiddles and wooden clappers half hidden back in one of the aisles. About six feet from the platform four Hong Kong wicker chairs had been set in a half circle, each with its own table on which were cakes and sweetmeats. The chairs reminded me of the palm court at Peebles Hydro where we holidayed three years ago, tables laid there for tea, too, and the same chairs waiting, with music from behind a screen of greenery. And there was that Prussian aristocratic lady staying at the same time, the Baroness Von something or other, who behaved with such queenly arrogance, special seats reserved for her and her entourage, and everyone kowtowing as she moved down to her throne. This, rather oddly, was what I was thinking of as I approached an Empress, and I did not, as expected, find myself shivering with nerves.

Just before we reached those chairs Edith Harding must have picked up a signal from Prince Tai which I didn't see, for she went down into a very low curtsey,

*followed immediately by the other two, my performance
coming rather late. Up on the platform no one moved, as
though those glittering figures were taking part in a
tableau picture, everyone waiting for the curtain to drop
so they could breathe again, only here there was no
curtain. Against that rigid stillness a movement from the
Empress was startling, one hand lifted from her lap.*

*It was not an ordinary hand, but a glittering of gold
talons. I had heard about those nail shields but a first
sight of them was startling. They were about a foot and a
half long, perhaps more on the main fingers, and even if
the gold was beaten quite thin, those protectors of nails
that are never cut must have weighed a great deal.
Because of them the Imperial Lady can do nothing for
herself, she must be fed, dressed, everything, by court
ladies in constant attendance, even put to bed with those
nail guards still on. For a minute or two I just stood
there thinking what this meant, and staring at those
hands which were back in her lap, like ribbed fans folded.
Every morsel of food that went into her mouth had to be
put there by others; the Empress who, next to King
Edward, rules over more people on earth than anyone
else, is almost as helpless as a cripple without arms. It is
perhaps no wonder that she behaves sometimes like a mad
woman.*

*The orchestra which had burst out so suddenly went
silent again and Prince Tai bade us be seated. Four
European ladies sat down in chairs that creaked almost as
loudly as the boards had done. We had not been instructed
that we were not to look directly at Tsz'e Hsi, so I did this,
getting an impression of a very small body under stiff
robes covered with dark embroidery. Her face was very
white, almost certainly with paint, and there was
something quite eerie about that pallor, even her lips
almost grey. What seemed to be rather thin black hair was*

drawn tight to a bun on the neck, exposing ears that were noticeably large against such a small head, and in which she wore what I think were opals. I have never seen Chinese ladies wearing diamonds, perhaps because these are not available in the country.

It was soon plain that one of the things the Imperial Court simply did not know how to do was be informal. In their lives there is a rule for everything, but this party was completely outside any of those regulations drummed into them and it was my guess that they stood rigid because they were terrified of doing anything at all. Also, a slight mistake in etiquette or procedure, which with our Royal Family would be ignored or dismissed with only a mild rebuke, in China could mean banishment from Court and total disgrace to all the lady-in-waiting's family. With Tsz'e Hsi's reputation, a cup of poisoned tea might come into it.

I had expected the proceedings, whatever they were to be, to be opened by some kind of a speech from Prince Tai, so you can imagine my surprise when, into silence, came a series of squeaks that might have been made by a large mouse. The Empress was talking from the dragon throne, but though I could see those grey lips moving, the sound almost seemed to come from the side aisles somewhere. It was a long message to which we all listened not comprehending one word and then, as abruptly as they had started, the squeaks stopped. Prince Tai, all this time standing to one side looking a little like a funeral director, now moved forward and began a translation. He told us that the Empress welcomed us with her whole heart, and that she was filled with only goodwill towards our countries and the people who came from them to live in the Celestial Capital. It was the Imperial wish that we and her subjects would live in total harmony and deep affection forever, with the mistaken past totally forgotten. Her Imperial Majesty had issued edicts that this was to be

*the feeling of all her people in all parts of the Chinese
Empire.*

*There was a lot more in this manner and then the
Prince announced that tea would be served, after which
would come informal conversation. The tea turned out to
be us sipping from too big, handleless cups, while the court
watched. With those nail guards the Empress could never
take any kind of refreshment in public, so presumably
none of her attendants were allowed to either. I felt
terribly sorry for those ladies who were still playing living
statues in that carefully arranged grouping around an
old lady in a chair. Prince Tai didn't get any tea either,
or a seat.*

*Informal conversation did not get off to a very good
start, one reason for this being that the German wife
speaks very little English and the Italian wife none at
all, and when Prince Tai tried them with French, they
both bowed from the sitting position as though they
understood all right, but neither uttered one word.
Edith Harding, usually so much in control of things,
wasn't very fluent either and could not seem to get
beyond some not particularly interesting talk about the
weather. This left me with my mind as blank as Edith's
seemed to be but suddenly my good fairy, if I have one,
came to my rescue with a topic that ought to interest
someone who had spent so much money on it, the
Summer Palace. Since I had been so impressed I must
have sounded quite convincing, and as Prince Tai's
translation travelled up to the dragon throne I was very
conscious of Tsz'e Hsi's eyes on me, though her head
never moved.*

*When I had finished about the beauties of her
residence, and the Prince had completed his translation,
the mouse voice sounded out again, but this time the
words had a crackle in them, of command. I was to come
up on the platform and approach Her Imperial Majesty,*

*which I did, suddenly very uneasy, by a flight of three
steps at the side, the Prince my escort. Without being told
to, I went into that low curtsey which really needs a
special training I haven't had, but for some reason I did
not want to bow, especially the kind of bow that would
have been called for here, amounting to almost total
abasement. When I had straightened up again I stayed
where I was, about five feet or so from the throne, and in
a position which forced the Empress to turn her head to
look at me, which she did. What I looked at were her
hands. One of the finger guards moved, as though the
owner of that fan had been about to open it, then
decided not to.*

*Prince Tai said Her Majesty had a present for me,
and a servant brought it, a box about six inches long
covered in padded black silk. The Prince told me to open
the box, presumably because Tsz'e Hsi wanted to see my
reaction to her gift, so I lifted the lid. On more padded
silk, this time white, was a pair of earrings, jade and gold.
The jade is obviously of the finest quality, long pendant
pears of it, in shape very like those awful dangles Aunt
Elsie always wears to go with her boned high-necked
collars, and which on me would look even worse. I tried
my best to look pleased and said that the earrings would be
treasures in my family forever, and, while I got all that
out, the Empress stared at me.*

*I think it must be enamel on her face that stretches
away wrinkles and leaves no expression, and in that mask
her eyes seemed terribly alive, not old eyes at all, but full of
a kind of dreadful energy and purpose. This may sound
ridiculous, but I felt that she was looking at me greedily
because I am young, thinking what she could still do if she
had my youth, and angry because there was no way even
an Empress could steal from me, for her own use, the years
I have ahead. I think I understand now why she keeps the
Emperor a prisoner and a puppet. He is young, too. She*

cannot bear to think of a world in which she is dead and
gone.

     Richard has just come, I can hear him talking to the
houseboy in the front court. This letter has been far too
long as it is, so I will just close it quickly as:
     Your ever loving daughter,
     Mary

157 Hutung Feng-huang,
Peking,
July 12th, 1903

After I had written to Mama about my visit to the Imperial Court,
and posted it, I knew that I had said things in the letter that I
should not have done. Today this was confirmed by Mama's reply,
reaching us by the swift Trans-Siberian service in which she says she
is both angered and distressed by what seems to have happened to
me. I appear to her to have suddenly grown hard and worldly, given
to making would-be clever remarks about people which do nothing
but show up the deficiencies in my own character. At my age I
should be showing respect to those who are older, and therefore
wiser, than me.

I am a fool to have written to Mama as though she was a friend,
not Mama. It is as if I had forgotten, in half a year, what she is really
like and how she has always lived. Fortunately, as usual the post
came after Richard had gone to the Legation. He reads all letters
that come to me, as a husband's right. But he will not read this one.
I set a match to it and watched it burn in the empty drawing-room
stove. In future I will always be the dutiful daughter and write to
Mama about the weather and what a lovely evening we had at the
Italian Legation. Perhaps it is as well that I have been checked in
this way, because if I had not Mama might soon have been reading
between the lines that I do not find being married to Richard what
I hoped for in coming to China. I was a fool there, too. Why do we
have to make such terrible decisions for our whole lives when we are
too young to know what we are doing? The big mistakes are hung
around your neck and you have to wear them forever.

157 Hutung Feng-huang,
Peking,
July 17th, 1903

I changed my mind and went after all to see Dr Zimmerman the American who is doing duty while Dr Hotchkiss is on holiday in Japan. He was quite kind, and confirmed what I suspected. I am with child. I shall tell Richard tonight. Perhaps this will end what I do not want. I could not ask the doctor whether this is necessary. Marie, who has no children, can be of no help to me now. Edith would be of too much help. Oh, this house with its high walls holding in the summer heat!

6

The Temple of Ultimate Peace,
Western Hills, China,
August 9th, 1904

In spite of its high-flown name this building has rats, huge ones from
the noise they make in the ceiling. Beneath the rats we live in near
luxury, as one always expects with Marie and Armand, four servants
from their Peking house plus Jane's amah from ours. The camping
furniture, or at least what Armand *calls* camping furniture, is
extremely comfortable, all manner of canvas chairs and some smaller
wicker ones, folding tables, mattresses inflated by bicycle pumps,
even rugs over the worm-eaten floors. Food supplies reach us by
pack mule from Peking every second or third day and we drink what
Armand says is the only thing for really hot weather, champagne.
He has devised a cooling arrangement in a little stream that comes
down through the rocks behind us.

I am beginning now to feel the charm of the Western Hills,
though not at all attracted by them at first, wondering what all the
fuss was about beyond the fact that they offer an escape from that
cooped-up feeling we all get in Peking. I am used enough to bare
hills in Scotland, but those are green and these, on approach, a
burned-up browny yellow, seeming completely part of a landscape
dedicated to dust storms from the Gobi Desert. It is only when you
get in amongst them that you discover almost secret-seeming glens
in which the natural growth has escaped the terrible woodcutters of

China. Great clumps of bamboo flourish up to a height of twenty feet, with tree-sized rhododendrons and magnolias which must be wonderful in bloom. The temple garden here was once cultivated, though long since left to ruin, and Armand has found in it what he says may be a Ginkgo tree. He is something of a botanist and has pressed the leaves to have them identified. Apparently the Ginkgo is something from another geological age, long since extinct everywhere except in China, a kind of link between conifers and ferns. Armand says fossils of its leaves have been found on the Island of Mull in Scotland. He is a man of strange areas of knowledge suddenly revealed but none of these revelations ever really noticed by Marie. Perhaps he is so kind to me because I *do* notice, but then again in fairness to Marie she clearly sees things in Richard which I do not, for he is certainly much more light-hearted in her company than he ever seems to be with me. This might be because their backgrounds are similar, both from *old* families, if in different countries, whereas the Mackenzies of South Edinburgh could not even name a great-grandfather or, indeed, have ever heard much about grandfathers. This is something that Richard will never understand about me, that I live without ancestors, whereas his life at Mannington was surrounded by innumerable generations of them, all in dark paintings watching as he went up the stairs to bed as a boy. It is probably a particularly terrible thing to live in the Far East without ancestors, where they are so highly prized, but in honesty I cannot feel that I miss them.

In a way this is a rather sad holiday, the first and probably the last I will ever have with the de Chamonpierres, who leave for Washington at the end of September. Since that is an Embassy, not just a Legation, this is a real promotion for Armand, and Marie already sees herself as a hostess in America, astonishing the capital with her splendid entertainments and gourmet food, at which I can see Armand wincing a little for, though they must be very well off indeed, he is a man who worries about expenditure, I think. Anyone married to Marie would!

However, Armand spends money in his own way, and has just announced that his first purchase in America is to be a motor-car, at which Marie declares she has never ridden in one of the horrible, smelly things and has no intention of ever doing so, which means that she will have to have her carriage and pair as well. Though Marie and I each have our reservations about the other, I am very fond of these two and for me Peking will be desolate without them. Marie says that in due course Richard will probably be transferred to Washington also, and then we will be together again. She says that she *wishes* this to be and that when, in her life, she has seriously wished hard for something it has always happened.

This must be a nice gift to possess. I don't have it, and am without much hope that a British Military Attaché will be sent to America to watch what their Army is doing, this simply because it has done very little since the Spanish-American War when they acquired the Philippines as their first colony. It seems to me that as a people they are most unlikely these days to become involved in wars abroad, having plenty in their own huge country to keep them occupied. Still, one never knows, and after all Marie was right about the Japanese and Russians going to war, for we are now right in the middle of one of the bloodiest struggles in human history between them.

Richard's last letter was from a Russian headquarters at a place called Anping. Though he seems to believe that the Russians will win in the end, I think he would prefer to be watching the fighting from the Japanese side, for most of the war has been attacks by them with the Russians just defending positions. He seems to think very little of the Czar's Viceroy in the Far East, Admiral Alexeiev, though he does have a better opinion of Kuropatkin whom he thinks is just playing for time bringing in more Russian reinforcements via the Trans-Siberian railway. The sheer might of Russia is bound to triumph in the end for, as Armand told me the other day, the Czar has a standing peacetime army of well over a million men without calling up the reserves, while it is said that the Japanese are already desperate for manpower. I don't see how gallantry alone can give them victory.

Marie found out through the Japanese Legation that Count Kurihama has been wounded yet again in the Battle of the Yalu. I'm sorry to hear this, remembering how he said, with a serious face, that Japan was mounted on a dragon subject to uneasy dreams. Apparently the Count has now been made a full Colonel and received a high decoration from his Emperor, which I'm sure he deserved. Marie is certain he will become a general very soon.

It is strange being in China during this war which is being fought over who is to have control of Manchuria, and the Chinese, with battles raging on their territory, have no say in the matter at all. It is humiliating for them to have to stay passive while their own land is being ravaged, the more so because of their defeat of not so many years ago at the hands of Japan. The Empress Dowager and her advisers remain completely silent about the whole matter, as though it were not happening not so very far north of us. She has again moved her whole court, which is like moving a city, out to the Summer Palace which we can see from some of the higher bridle paths amongst our temples. The only thing that really affects us here is the slowness of mails from home now the Trans-Siberian railway has been requisitioned for military use only. Everything for us has to come by sea via Suez, and there seem to be delays here, too, for Mama's last letter was dated nearly two months earlier. All this makes home seem very far away and I'm not sure I really think of it as home any more. After not quite a year and a half in China I feel sometimes that it is at least ten years since I left Scotland. From Mama's letters nothing has changed there. The changes are all in me.

> The Temple of Ultimate Peace,
> Western Hills, China,
> August 10th, 1904

I seem to have caught the writing disease again, which may be because I wake up early and Marie is such a late riser. Armand gets up early, too, but immediately goes off on a long walk on which I have wanted to accompany him sometimes, but never suggested this, pretty sure that Marie wouldn't like the idea. Also, I have always made a point of supervising Meng's preparation of Jane's first morning feed, though I know I don't really need to do this since Amah is so devoted to the infant. Actually Jane is putting on weight fast at last, the cooler air up here undoubtedly suits her, and she no longer looks what I have always thought her, a 'peakit' baby, as we say in Scotland. I tell Meng not to be continually screening the child from the sun, a little of which won't harm her, but Meng goes on keeping her in the shade. Perhaps I am wrong to trust Meng as much as I do, but Marie says it always happens with amahs in China and does the baby no harm, not that Marie knows much about raising children. I don't think she minds one bit about not being a mother, though I have no idea how Armand feels about having no heir for the de Chamonpierre name. This is probably something that worries a man of family. I know how disappointed Richard was that Jane was a girl, and it is almost as though the infant does not recognize him as her father, she never laughs when he comes towards her as she sometimes does with me, though more often with Meng. On the rare occasions when he picks her up she quite often screams, and I'm sure he has noticed this. I had always thought that girl babies had a special feeling for their fathers even from a very early age. I can certainly remember this from my own childhood even though Papa died when I was quite young. With him I felt safe from many things, including punishments, for he never lifted a hand to me, leaving this to Mama.

I still have guilt feelings about not being able to breastfeed Jane. I think it angered Richard that a daughter of the Collingsworths had to be suckled by a *Chinese* wet-nurse, as though this might be the source of some strange contagion. I know that Edith did not approve at all, she wanted me to use some special artificial infant feeds that can be obtained these days from Tientsin, but the wet-nurse was a cheerful, kind woman and I'm sure that Jane took no harm from her milk. It was when we started on the artificial feeds too soon, this by Richard's orders, that she failed to put on weight.

The Temple of Ultimate Peace,
Western Hills, China,
August 18th, 1904

There is absolutely nothing to do here, and though one or two of the temples nearby are occupied by others from the Legations we have no contact with our neighbours, perhaps because we are rather isolated, for there are rumours of partying elsewhere. It is a terrible thing to say, but the news of the war, with thousands dying, reaches us as something unreal, in which it is hard to believe. Armand comes back from his botanical excursions as though from some secret excitement and will talk, if made to by me, about China as an astonishing reservoir of sometimes unique plants, which is somehow hard to believe when one looks at hills which appear to be covered with nothing but sun-scorched grass.

The other day there was a slight sandstorm from the Gobi Desert, but only touching us lightly here and apparently not nearly so bad in Peking as the ones we had last summer. However, though lucky in our escape, these temples cannot be closed up in any effective way and, though we lowered shutters and so on, we were still eating grit with our salads and everything had a layer of something much more solid than dust. I covered Jane's cot and mosquito net with wet cloths that would hold the sand and keep it from getting through to the bedding, and the whole time we were under assault from the sand cloud, about two hours, Meng insisted on carrying Jane about with her and never staying still, as though movement was somehow a kind of protection against the attack of these devils from the desert.

I am reading a great deal, more steadily than I ever have, and as though she knew I would be driven to this here Marie brought along almost all her library of what Armand calls her dream literature about Japan, though fortunately not more Pierre Loti which I would have had to struggle through in French. Greater than Loti, Marie says, is Lafcadio Hearn, who writes in English about the land he adopted, and he certainly does make it seem almost Marie's paradise, though there were things in one of the books, *Kokoro*, which disturbed me and continue to. One evening after dinner we discussed these matters in a general way, though Armand has only read one-half of one of Mr Hearn's books, stopping because he prefers plants to fairy stories. What we discussed was reincarnation.

It may be the result of my Scots education, but I had never ˙d of this before, the theory that we all have many lives and are returned to a new life in a condition that somehow reflects what we were and what we have done in a previous existence. It is a strictly un-Christian doctrine, of course, or I thought it must be until Armand said that once it was not, part of Christian teaching by some sects, and then rejected as improper doctrine at a church council.

I must admit the idea attracts me a little, that the mistakes we make in one life, or perhaps the seeming complete waste of it, are not all, but that we can profit by these errors when we come back again and, by some instinct carried over from another living, not make the same mistakes again.

Marie also quite likes the idea but Armand says it in no way accounts for natural increase, and that with the world population becoming larger all the time there must be a factory busy manufacturing new souls to send out as well as despatching the old ones for a new turn, at which Marie said nonsense, the new souls might not be new at all, but old ones coming to earth for the first time from another planet. At this point Armand said that if we would excuse him he would go to bed, which he did after warning us to put out all the lamps, and Marie and I went on talking about reincarnation until I suddenly had the thought of Mama coming from another life into her present one, and I wondered what she was being rewarded for, or perhaps punished by being given me. Marie prodded at my thoughts until she got this one out and after I had told her a little of what Mama is like we both began to giggle, and then went on to play a game in which we tried to think of what various people in the Legation Quarter had been last time, and what they were likely to be next. We were soon laughing so loudly that Armand came back again in his dressing-gown and Jane woke and started to howl.

Marie says that what we were last time and what we will be next is the most brilliant drawing-room game ever invented and she is determined to play it next time they give a formal dinner to the German Minister, who is a Prussian with a steel spine. She also wants to try it on the Russians, saying that the game ought to be as effective as that ice-breaking ship they used on Lake Baikal in Siberia to get the trains over in winter.

In one of Marie's Japan books there was a story that was quite horrible, but somehow fascinating. It was about a couple who were so poor that there was almost nothing for them to eat and when their baby was born, rather than let it starve slowly, the father took the infant to a stream and drowned it. They continued so poor that starvation stayed a threat and the man drowned two more babies. Then things improved for the couple and the wife had her fourth child which they kept and it thrived, growing fat. Both parents doted on the son they had been able to keep, and one day the father was bouncing a ball for the baby when he was so overcome with love that he stopped and said out loud that the Gods had favoured them at last with this great gift of the infant. The child looked up and said clearly: 'I'm glad you feel like that now, Father, for I tried to come to you and Mother three times before and you always drowned me.' The father ran away, becoming quite mad.

Mama would think I am becoming quite mad, too, even to think about such things.

Western Hills,
September 7th, 1904

Armand is just back from Peking where he has been for the last ten days. He brought the news that there has been a great Japanese victory over the Russians at a place called Liao-Yang and that as a result the Czar's armies are in retreat on Moukden. There was no word of Richard at the British Legation and I have not had a letter for three weeks, but I am not worried because it seems that the Russian withdrawal north is quite orderly and, of course, Richard will be with headquarters and not near the actual fighting. There is apparently considerable excitement and some unrest in Peking as the result of the Japanese triumph, for the Empress Dowager would much rather have the Russians the dominant influence in Manchuria. She hates the Japanese and there are hotheads at court who would like to see China entering the war on the side of the Russians to drive the Japanese out and Armand believes that the old lady has been listening to them and is tempted. He also thinks that it would be unwise for us to return to Peking at the moment because it is known that the British and French favour the Japanese and there are signs of feeling against us because of this in the Imperial City. When we do go back, Jane and I, with Amah, are to stay in the Legation Quarter with the de Chamonpierres until Richard returns, though this won't be very convenient for Marie, who has all her packing to do before the end of the month. It was decided that we will stay on in the temple for another week or ten days, and Armand is going to stay with us. Marie told me afterwards that he has brought a rifle to have here, as well as others to supply some of the Legation people in other temples. I do not really mind all this for myself, because I can't believe that anything will happen to us up in these hills, but I worry a little about Jane. With Richard away she is my complete responsibility.

Western Hills,
September 11th, 1904

Nothing has happened, the sun shines, it is hot at midday but cooling down sharply by sunset. No more rumours or any news of the war have reached us, yet over everything there hangs this curious feeling of something about to happen that can only be bad. I don't know whether Armand or Marie feel it, too, they give no sign if they do, and everything seems perfectly normal. I forget about my feeling for hours and then suddenly there is that lead lump sitting in my stomach. It may be nerves. With her usual good cheer Edith told me to expect to be depressed for a long time after my baby was born, that it took her a year to really recover from the births of both her sons. I'm sure the doctor would say that this is nonsense and it is certainly nonsense for me. Admittedly I did have a bad time with Jane. As the British nurse at the Legation hospital was putting my baby in my arms for the first time she said: 'Well, Mrs Collingsworth, I'm relieved, too, that she is here at last. It was beginning to look as though she didn't want to come.'

I have thought of that often. Supposing it were just possible that Jane had decided too late she didn't want to come to Richard and me? This is just a crazy idea from one of Marie's books, yet I couldn't have blamed the poor little thing if she had wanted to change her mind.

Western Hills,
September 12th, 1904

I got up this morning before sunrise after a night of broken sleep, something that doesn't happen to me often. I am rather ashamed that I don't always wake when Jane cries, but this could be because I know Meng is there to look after everything. I suppose we are lucky to have these faithful amahs on duty practically all the time, but I sometimes wonder if it is good for the mother or the child?

I did my hair in what was almost the dark, putting on a skirt I have been wearing a lot up here, of flowered Japanese cotton in a pattern Mama would think far too gaudy for a lady. Because it was chill in the bedroom and likely to be chillier outside I added a grey Shetland cardigan which Mama sent me from Jenner's on Princes Street last Christmas, this over a white blouse, the whole an outfit Marie would not have cared for very much since she believes that even casual clothes should remember elegance. I don't think she really likes the country, though she pretends to; she is only at ease in a city. One of the things I like about this half-camping in a temple is that there are no mirrors about in which you can see how dreadful you are looking. I'm sure Marie misses mirrors, her house is hung with them, in the drawing-room one reflects another, and you turn to see at least fifty reproductions of yourself stretching away into the distance. This is all right if you are in looks and wearing the right dress, but not good for the spirits on off-days.

A temple is easy to get out of without making a noise, and just as easy for an intruder to enter, which was my thought as I went down three steps into the garden. We are really very isolated up in these hills, a long way even from the nearest village and certainly from any kind of help should it turn out that the area is not free yet of brigands or roving bands of ex-Boxers. In so far as I know, only two or three of the other temples are now occupied by Europeans, most back to the city again. I think another year I will suggest to Richard

that we holiday in Wei-Hai-Wei under the British flag, the place certainly looked attractive from the ship. Perhaps responsibility for
Jane is making me more nervous than I ought to be, but I am getting a little jumpy about this place, marvellous as it has been to stay
here with Armand and Marie.

It had rained during the night, not much, but enough to lay the
dust, the paths firm. I haven't walked very much since we came and
don't really know where all the tracks lead to, but I chose the one
that climbed straight through the middle of a dense clump of enormous bamboos, and in that light it felt almost like going into a tunnel. When I came out on the other side, the path now much steeper,
the sun was just rising over the saw-edged ridge of hills to the east,
a sudden brightness quite dazzling. Birds, particularly one kind
which Armand says is a Chinese species of finch, set up a terrific
chattering, as though they had all slept in and were scolding each
other. My way now climbed through masses of huge rhododendrons and above these a kind of oak tree which grows in the shelter
of these glens. I had stopped, standing quite still, when there was a
rustling and a long green snake came weaving out on to the path
moving slowly, seeming unaware of me. It stopped, too, as if for a
warm up in the sunshine, but it wasn't sudden heat that was making
it sluggish: well down from the pointed head was a very large bump
that could only be from a toad or perhaps one of the temple rats.
The snake was digesting its breakfast, and would probably be doing
that for a long time. One never really knows whether these creatures
are poisonous, or I don't, though I could see that this was far too
big to be any type of adder. I'm not really frightened of snakes just
because they are snakes, at the same time I was not going to challenge that one even though it had eaten, and I was about to turn
back into the bamboo when I heard a sound underneath the bird
noise, only audible because it was continuous, certainly a human
voice in a kind of drone that didn't even seem to take breaks for
breathing. It reminded me of that endless whining from the Peking
beggars, except that this was pitched much lower, a voice that in a
singer would be classed baritone. The sound was coming from
somewhere above, though I couldn't really place direction through

that thick growth all around. The reptile barring my path seemed disturbed by this sound, too, and with forked tongue probing out in front, a pointed green head parted grasses and then slowly towed a long body, distorted by that swelling, out of sight, leaving me free to go on climbing if I wanted to.

I was beginning to be really curious about this incantation to the dawn. It might be one of the priests displaced from his temple now camping out in the woods until the foreign devils had gone back to the city and he could once again say his prayers under a roof. I moved carefully, kicking no stones, the drone becoming more prominent as that first rush of bird sound died down. The path levelled out, with an offshoot from it leading to another painted temple like ours, except much smaller and with what had once been its garden even more of a ruin. On a rocky outthrust, hidden from the path below and only just visible when I was a little way above him, sat the worshipper.

He was facing the sunrise, sideways to me, and completely unaware of anyone on the path, a man with the cropped head of a priest and in a white robe which is a colour you only expect to see for mourning in China. I recognized the Buddhist posture for prayer, the seated on lotus leaf position, legs tucked in tailor fashion, hands held palms together in front of his chest at about waist level, the drone of the chanting not broken by regular, low bows. There was something lying beside him on a straw mat which I couldn't make out until I had gone a little higher. It was a crutch.

Suddenly I thought I knew what that crutch meant: a leper. He wore the white of death while putting up another hopeless petition that a new day might bring him some relief. Leprosy still produces a kind of panic in me in spite of all you hear about it being a very slow contagion. The most dreadful thing about the disease is that long-drawn-out destruction of the body while the mind remains intact. I had the panic thought that summer visitors to these temples might be coming to a secret leper colony and that it wasn't priests who cleared out temporarily to provide holiday homes.

The man moved, the prayer pose suddenly abandoned. I watched quite frozen while he groped for the crutch with one hand, remembering then how some of these cripples from the disease can still move with astonishing speed. There is a horrible story about a leper beggar suddenly getting up and chasing a European woman, catching hold of her with his good hand and laughing as he rubbed the crumbling stump of what had been his other hand against the bare flesh of her arm.

I had the sensation then you get in wild dreams, of wanting to run from a horror, but being unable to move, and while I stood there the man in white somehow managed to stand on one leg, propping himself up on the crutch while he bent over to roll up the straw mat. It seemed almost to be a drill, as though he had practised all the necessary movements, none wasted, and it was only when he had straightened, with the mat under one arm that I saw what he was wearing was a Japanese kimono. The sun caught a scar on one side of his head. It was Count Kurihama. I am sure he didn't see me as he swung himself up towards the little temple. He never looked in my direction.

I have not told Marie or Armand that one of the heroes of the Russo-Japanese war is living just up the hill from us. I don't really know why I am being secretive about this. It may be from a feeling that the man in the white robe would not wish to come to a picnic dinner-party given in his honour. Armand, coming back from one of his botanical expeditions, may well meet the Count, in which case his privacy will be ended, but I am not going to bring that about. I was back here lying on my camp bed by the time I heard Armand setting out for one of his early morning walks. The rats usually go silent as it becomes light, but this morning they went into a great flurry of activity, plus loud squeaking. Though they don't seem to come down into the rooms I am always nervous about one of them getting at Jane under the tight mosquito netting stretched over her cot, and I got up again to have a look at her, quietly pushing open the sliding door.

Meng was asleep in a corner between two quilts but even through the mesh of the net I could see that Jane had her eyes open. She sometimes comes awake like this and instead of at once crying for her feed, just lies perfectly still looking up at the ceiling.

It could have been the rats that wakened her, but if she had been frightened she would have cried. There was plenty of light, and Jane must have seen me bending over the cot, but I had the feeling she did not want to be picked up, was neither hungry nor in need of comfort. Sometimes, like this, Jane does not suggest the helpless infant at all. Only a few days ago Marie said something that quite disturbed me: 'You know, I have seen your baby lying laughing at her own jokes.' Perhaps they are Collingsworth jokes. Jane is going to be as fair as Richard.

Western Hills,
September 13th, 1904

All the time we have been here Marie and Armand have insisted on using English, at least in my presence, which means most of the day. They say this is practice for Washington. His accent is much less noticeable than hers, he seems to have trained himself to be able to think in English, too. With Marie you have to wait sometimes while she chooses the right word for the French one in her mind. Armand says that, next to the British, the French are the most arrogant people in the world about learning other languages. According to him, the real reason why Napoleon wanted to conquer us was that he was certain God speaks French and it was therefore maddening for him to know that across only twenty miles of channel were the British who had no doubts at all that the Almighty had always used English to communicate with man, even when He was dictating the tablets of the Law to Moses.

I find Armand most entertaining, more so really than Marie. He never fights to rule the conversation like his wife, but waits for the right moment to say something, and when he does it often stings with wit. Mama would be outraged by almost everything Armand says and at first I, too, was a little shocked at times. But no longer. He has a warm heart. I think he finds me restful, perhaps because I do not advertise myself. I really have nothing to advertise.

Now they are quarrelling, in French. It is noisy, but I am sure that anger for both of them does not go deep. When Richard and I disagree we don't say much, but there is a column of coldness in me and in him, too, because I can feel it. It is better to shout at each other. Marie wants back at once to Peking and people again, she is utterly bored stuck in a temple in the Chinese hills where the only excitement is some kind of new leaf from a prehistoric tree. Armand has just told her that she will return to the city when he thinks it is right that she should, and not a minute before. It sounds as though she has upset the table on which her patience cards were set out. I think I had better go for a walk.

In the evening.
There is something wrong with the wick of this lamp, it keeps smoking and blackening the chimney. I went on my walk. Count Kurihama's temple looked deserted as I passed. It is the highest of all, the last building on this hill. Up there the winter winds have stunted the trees and I saw a pine with its branches touching the ground, like arms put down for support. It was very hot this afternoon but I went on climbing to get the view back over the plains to Peking, for I have been told you can sometimes see the sinking sun reflected in such a way that it looks as though the city was burning. Flies kept me company and a horrible, much bigger insect repeatedly swept down like a kestrel on its prey, some relation of what we call a cleg in Scotland, but even more vicious. I was wearing a white canvas hat with a floppy brim but could have done with more shelter from the glare, which seemed to radiate off the leaves and the very earth of the path. I have given up carrying a parasol in China. There are times when these are useful, but I think we look so silly holding the frilled-edged things over our heads, especially when riding in rickshas from which they stick up in Chinese street traffic like flags of identification. I took with me one of Armand's sticks because I have no intention of meeting another snake on these paths without some weapon.

The end of the trees and the point from which I could get my view was probably less than half a mile beyond the last temple, but it felt more in that heat and because of the steep climb. I came around a clump of wind-flattened rhoddys to find Count Kurihama half leaning, half standing against a rock outcrop, as though he was taking from it as little support as possible. His crutch was propped beside him but he wasn't touching it. He must have been hearing my coming for some minutes.

I didn't need to imagine how I was looking, my face moist, and not just my face, either. He had obviously been standing for some time where the breeze reached him, hatless, his face, very brown except for the white scar. His dress was almost formal, a white pongee suit, light enough, but with a button up to the neck collar which gave it the look of a uniform. The only casual things about him were his shoes, white canvas with rubber soles. I could see that most of his weight was on one leg, though the other was still put quite firmly on the ground.

I might have pretended complete astonishment that he was here in the Western Hills, but have no confidence in myself as an actress, so all that happened was a polite exchange of good afternoons as though we had been neighbours meeting when one of us was out to post a letter. I then said that it was very hot and moved into the shade of the rock, though some distance from him. My heart was thumping from the exertion of the climb and I used one of the large men's handkerchiefs that I now always carry in the hot weather, patting my forehead and cheeks. The view I had come to see was hidden by a haze.

It was a shock when the Count suddenly apologized for having said his prayers at a point so near the path, thus disturbing my early walk. He had not thought European ladies came out alone to see the sunrise. I don't know whether he was mocking me or not. I said that we had heard about his wound and hoped it wasn't troubling him too much now. He said no, it was nothing. Without looking at him, I asked where he had been hit. The wound was in his upper leg, made by a piece of shrapnel, but all that was necessary now for a complete cure was exercise. He added that it was shameful for a soldier to live in idleness while others were fighting for their Emperor. I wondered why he had come to China instead of convalescing in Japan and his answer was that he hated hospitals and rest homes. Also, he wanted to be quite alone for some time in order to offer prayers of apology to the men under his command who had died. It might not have been necessary for so many of them to die if he had given better orders.

During all this we didn't look at each other, or at least I didn't look at him, and I am sure that he, too, was staring down at the plain. I had never heard of a soldier sending messages to the spirits of those killed under his command asking to be forgiven for his errors as their leader. It seemed wild and strange to me, but it also suggested a kind of brotherhood that was utterly different from the way in which I have heard Richard speak of the men under him when he was with the regiment. Perhaps this is the secret of Japanese success against the Russians, that military rank does not prevent a man from being one in spirit with all those serving the same cause.

We began then to talk about the war, or rather I asked questions and he answered them. He has no doubt at all that, in spite of the huge numbers of men the Russians are sending east via the Trans-Siberian railway, the withdrawal on Moukden indicates their complete defeat soon. He said the defensive war is always the lost war, and that any lines drawn up just to hold the enemy's attack mean inevitably that the enemy will break through. He has complete contempt for the way the Russian fleet has refused to do battle, mostly staying hidden in Port Arthur. The rumours of a huge new Russian fleet coming from Europe do not trouble him, either; he says that if it ever arrives in these waters Admiral Togo will sink all their ships. The arrogance of that was a strange contrast to his humbleness over the men under him who had died.

I was sure his leg was giving him pain, but that he would never show the slightest sign of this in front of me. I thought of the rough path he had to use to get back to his temple, but knew what he would say if I offered to give him help down it. I said that I would have to be getting back and that I was staying with Armand and Marie. He showed no interest in them. I did not think he had any interest in me until I had said goodbye and was already on the path down, with my back to him. He called out: 'Mrs Collingsworth, please come to tea tomorrow afternoon.'

He would never have issued such an invitation to a Japanese wife. Perhaps they think we are all loose women at heart.

Western Hills,
Sept. 14

God forgive me, I went to him. I have no excuse for myself. He kept saying 'Good, good?' making this a question. I did not really answer him, but I wanted to. All I can think of in this madness that has taken me is his body. Armand and Marie still do not know he is here. I won't tell them. I will never tell anyone. We have five more days. His name is Kentaro.

Western Hills,
Sept. 17

I stayed too long today. I'm sure Armand is beginning to wonder about my walks, always taken in the heat of the afternoon. Supposing he should decide to have a look at the empty temple above ours, in case there were some interesting plants in its old garden? He may have done this. We would not have known if he had.

Western Hills,
Sept. 18

I think Armand knows. There are a number of ways he could have found out. Kentaro has supplies delivered to his temple only once a week, but a pack mule came up yesterday, past our temple. Armand was out walking at the time and could easily have seen where it went. I cannot look at him. I don't think he has told Marie. I am certainly not going to stay with them in Peking, I could not. I am glad they go to America soon. Kentaro and I have only one more day. It is impossible for us to meet in Peking, and he is only to be there for a short time before he goes back to Korea for headquarters duty until he is fit for the front again. I can only pray that the war is over by then. His leg still hurts him badly. He has never let me see the wound, always with a fresh bandage on when I come. I do not know whether this is love. I do not know.

Our last day. I did not care if I stayed too long. I did not care how Armand looked at me when I got back, or Marie. Kentaro sat out on the verandah wearing only a loin-cloth, his bandaged leg thrust out in front of him. After a while I put on the cotton kimono he gave me to use and went to him. He had a sheet of white paper flat on the boards and was using a long brush dipped in black ink for the sweeping strokes of Chinese characters. When I asked what he was writing he said a poem. After he seemed to have finished I asked for a translation. He said the poem was not one he should have been writing in this place. I wanted to know what he meant by that and he told me he had come here to prepare himself for duty. He had broken solitude. I asked if he was ashamed of this and he said not as much as he should be. It was like having riddles given back instead of answers. I asked again for a translation of the poem and in careful printing, as though he needed this to help him, he wrote down the Japanese words in English letters. Afterwards, taking a long time, he used the brush again to write the English words:

Kono yama no ura ni	At the back of this mountain
Uguwisu no uta	The song of the nightingale,
Myonichi hidoi kaze	Tomorrow will there only be
Narimasho?	The violent wind?

I began to cry. He caught hold of me and said: 'Do not cry, Mary.' I cannot believe that we will never meet again. I cannot believe that today is today and tomorrow is nothing. It must not happen like that. What can we do?

I came back down the hill carrying his poem rolled like a scroll. He did not watch me go, turning back into the temple. It was nearly sunset. When I got here the trees were shadowing the verandah but I could see the glow of Marie's cigarette from one of the chairs. No one called out to me.

I went by a side way to my room and sat on the camp bed looking at a wall. Next door Meng was singing to Jane, a harsh voice that sounds as if the vocal cords had been strained at some time, but the baby seems to like it. The singing became softer as Jane showed signs of going to sleep. I waited for Marie to come in to say how disgusted they were with me, but she did not. It was Armand who called me to supper. We had it on the card table with the usual two candles stuck in bottles which Marie says are better than the glaring lamp. Armand mixed the salad and made the dressing as carefully as usual. I did not try to explain why I had been away from two until nearly six, saying very little. The talk between them was in French, mostly Marie going on about what they would and would not take to Washington. I ought to beg them not to talk about me in the Legation Quarter before they go. I don't think they will, but I have spoiled a friendship. If there was any explanation I would give it, but I have none for myself.

I am afraid to put out this light and lie back. If only there was something you could do to make yourself numb.

We did not have any wine at supper, the champagne is finished. I want away from these hills. I will never come back to them again. I must blot out the picture of a path climbing through bamboo. I must never say a name. I must never say it. I will not look at the scroll.

7

157 Hutung Feng-huang,
Peking, China,
November 27th, 1904

Dr Hotchkiss is looking as though he needs another long leave in Eng-
land, too old for active duty in the Far East, but not too old to be
practically certain about my condition. I am to have another child.
The doctor told me how delighted my husband would be, and we
might hope for a boy this time. He asked when Richard would be
back from his duties with the Russian forces and I told him that my
husband was now sealed up in Port Arthur by the Japanese siege of
the place. He said this was unfortunate but that I should try to get
the news to Richard some way, for it ought to make him very happy.

Recently a few devils have been getting around our stone screen
and one of them seemed to have travelled to the surgery with me. I
said that I didn't think my news would make Richard very happy
since I hadn't seen him since July. Dr Hotchkiss was turning away as
I spoke. He stopped dead but did not turn back to look at me.
There was no need for him to do any arithmetic in his head; the
woman now sitting up on his leather-covered sofa was nothing like
five months pregnant.

When I saw him walking slowly over to the washbasin I felt sick
with shame. He washed his hands, then went to the desk and was a
long time writing a prescription which he said, determinedly keeping his voice normal, that I could have made up at the new phar-

macy which had just opened. For all that he has been in medicine for nearly forty years, he has stayed a simple man who believes that the rules for living are all laid down and properly indexed, so that in any situation you have only to look up the regulations which apply to your case and abide by them. As I have not done.

While I dressed I thought about Mama receiving the news, as she must one day, that her second grandchild was half-Japanese and born out of wedlock. I could not begin to picture how she would take it in that house where the windows have a layer of lace against the glass to foil prying eyes, and all the talk, at least Mama's, is carefully watched to provide nothing at all that wagging tongues might use. She will probably hate me. I cannot see her having any other feelings but deep anger. I hope I am wrong.

Dr Hotchkiss tried very hard to be kind. Without exactly reminding me that his surgery is as sacred as the Confessional which Marie uses so blithely, he said he would help in any way he could and was there anything I wished to tell him? I shook my head. I am sure he was relieved that I had not burdened him further with a confidence.

> 157 Hutung Feng-huang,
> Peking,
> December 13, 1904

I have had a letter from Mama, in answer to one I wrote from the Western Hills, in which she is quite shocked that I took Jane to such a dangerous place, and what would Richard think if he knew? Also, she wondered if it was quite wise to make such close friends of a *French* couple in a place where there were many British available? She says she loses sleep over the thought that we are so near to that horrible war in Manchuria and that in spite of what many people in Britain are saying about them, she cannot feel any sympathy for the Japanese. After all, the Czar's family are cousins of our own Royal House, and in recent years the Japanese have seemed rather pushing and too sure of themselves, which could bode ill for the future.

Every word that Mama writes now seems to come to me from a place that is a thousand light years from where I live. I suppose if you look at a map the war in Manchuria does seem to be taking place quite near to us, but in Peking everything has quietened down again, the Empress Dowager having decided against listening to the wild voices urging her to action. She is now back in the city after having prolonged her stay at the Summer Palace, which may have been because she was making up her mind as to whether or not she should take China into the war.

I get the news from Edith Harding who has been faithful in attending me here, which I'm sure she would not have been if Marie had said anything to her or to anyone about what happened in the Western Hills. I did not go to any of the farewell parties for the de Chamonpierres, even the one which Edith gave, rather grudgingly I thought, my excuses quite acceptable; one that while there was any remnant of unrest in the city I did not like leaving Jane at night here; and two, that if I went to the Quarter in the evening it meant some reluctant husband being detailed off to see me safely home again. No one was so desperately anxious to have me as a guest that they tried to beat down these defences.

I know that I should not stay sealed up in this house the way I am doing, and a few times I have gone for a ricksha ride just to get out, but I have been uneasy until I was in through this gate again. It is not that I care for the house very much, and I haven't tried to do to it the things I could have while Richard was away, but it is the only shelter I have. For how long?

When I try to look at the future I can't see a thing. This has never happened to me before; even when I had no idea what was coming I could imagine something. I could always make up a picture to fill up the empty space on the wall in front of me. Now I can't. That wall stays blank. I had a dream in which I went up to it and touched it, and it dissolved away like steam blowing from a kettle, but beyond me again was another blank white wall waiting and I knew if I went up and touched that one it would dissolve, too.

It must be that for all of us there has to be an apology available that we can make to ourselves for anything we do. It doesn't matter so much about an apology to others, pride may block this, but we must have that one for ourselves, to be able to say: 'Yes, I did that, *but* . . . ' If you can't put the 'but' after what you did then you are in a sort of way lost. There is no 'but' that I did not know what I was doing when I went up that path to take tea with Kentaro. I went knowing what he was going to think of any woman who accepted an invitation issued as he had done. In his eyes she was there to be used. Also, I don't think I really wanted what was to come, for I had no idea of what this was going to mean to me. I wanted an end to what I had, to Richard, to my life here in Peking, to the Legation Quarter, to growing old in a narrow groove that might lead me one day to sitting in a house like Mannington, like his mother does, with a few people she knows and accepts because of how and where they were born, and a whole world beyond of which she knows nothing. You kiss your cousins and never complain about the arthritis which is crippling you.

This is what Richard would want for me. His worry is that I will not fit in as his wife should, so I have to be trained to make certain I do. It would have been so much wiser for him to have married someone who had already received the necessary training and was fixed in it. He has never really been at ease with me, even for short periods, or I with him. Perhaps this is why he always waited to come down the passage to my bed in the dark. The lamp was out and he would never let me light even a candle. He came when he had to, perhaps half hating me, because he felt his need a weakness.

Oh God, I do not hate him! I did not want to hurt him by what I did, it was not anger at Richard, it was the trap we both are in. I wanted to tear it open. Well, I have. I sit now in the wreckage made by me, waiting. I can do nothing but wait. What else is there? Should I take Jane and run, to have my half-Japanese baby in Scotland, from my mother's house?

157 Hutung Feng-huang,
Peking,
Dec. 15, 1904

Yao knows. I do not think it is because I show much yet, and I have been careful about what I wear. There is an almost unmanlike gentleness in him that you would never expect from a gaunt figure and that strange, off-putting face. Marie could never stand him. She said it gave her the shivers to have him open the hatch to her, and certainly those unbalanced eyes are a bit alarming to have peering at you through the observation slit. His shaking is considerably better these days. My few words of Chinese and his few of English mean that we can never really say anything to each other, not even the communication of a mistress to her servant, but somehow words are not really necessary. I have known he was my friend ever since that day when I made him laugh. I still do not see much of the others, Yao manages everything, ruling the house in Richard's absence and, in the long evenings when he should be in his own quarters, makes little visits to the drawing-room to see if I need anything. He is now watching what I eat, and if I clearly like something I get it again and again, too often. My appetite is very good. I have none of those bouts of feeling dreadfully ill that I had from early days with Jane. Perhaps these will come.

Jane continues to put on weight. There is a stove in her nursery which keeps it very warm, but I have her playpen brought to the drawing-room each afternoon, insisting that Meng take time off and leave the child with me. Jane seems quite content with the arrangement, she cries very little these days, and I find myself conducting one-sided conversations with her. It is probably very silly but she does not seem to mind.

We ought to get out more, but it is very hard to establish a baby's routine of the European kind. For one thing we have no baby carriage, there would be no point in it, the lane's rough-surfaced and there are no parks to go to. She was put outside in the summer, but now, though the winter sunshine is bright enough, it is below zero all the time, the air wonderfully dry, but still icy. So we hibernate, Jane and I. Only Edith comes to visit from the Quarter. The others have probably forgotten I exist and I have no wish to do anything to remind them. With Armand and Marie gone, I'm sure that every Legation party is exactly like every other party. Edith tells me that the successors to the de Chamonpierres have arrived but she does not think they will be so popular. I look at Edith sometimes when she is here and wonder what she will be saying about me in a few months' time. Could I find sanctuary with them if I need it? I think not.

> 157 Hutung Feng-huang,
> Peking,
> Dec. 17, 1904

A letter from Marie written on board the SS *Empress of Japan* bound for Vancouver has taken its time in reaching me. It is four pages of Marie's chatter which is not as effective in the written word as it is spoken, but then the purpose of her letter is plain enough; she wrote to reassure me, without even one reference to our time in the Western Hills, that there will never be from Armand or from her the slightest hint forthcoming about what happened up there. It is very good of her, but I can see now that she probably had her own reasons for great discretion on the matter while still in Peking. Probably I am being ungenerous towards a good friend. These days I don't feel very generous towards anyone.

It is almost two years exactly since I went up the gangway of the SS *Mooldera* at Tilbury. That girl would have been horrified at the idea of being forced to share a cabin with the woman I have become.

> 157 Hutung Feng-huang,
> Peking,
> Dec. 19, 1904

Still no letter from Richard and the Quarter has had no word from him either. I sent a chitty in requesting that the Legation let me know anything they heard and had a reply from Sir Claude himself, very kind, saying that if they had been in possession of any reliable information they would certainly have passed it on to me, but they really know nothing. The explosions of mines laid in the waters outside the harbour of Port Arthur have damaged the submarine cables, which are no longer operating, and of course the overland telegraph lines have been cut, the only news coming out being by the occasional courier who manages to get through, plus the stories of Chinese refugees from the fighting areas, of whom there are a great many. The official reports are all from the Japanese side, and speak of great slaughter, both in their ranks and the Russian. Apparently, after being repulsed in various areas around the outer defences of Port Arthur, the Japanese have now taken to mining and have blown up some forts by this method. As Sir Claude said, it is turning into one of the most savage and brutal wars in human history. He assures me that the Legation is very much aware of me living alone in the Chinese city, and that if I am at all unhappy about this arrangement I am to let him know and some place will be found for me in the Quarter. I will thank him for his very real kindness, but what he suggests is the last thing I want at the moment.

Sir Claude did not sound as though he was very worried about Richard's safety. I'm not either. I don't really allow myself to think about him, because when I do a kind of dread comes, too. I haven't been successful in putting Kentaro out of my mind. With his wound healed, he will have demanded to get back to active service with his regiment, and if he is not killed we still will never meet again. There can be no help for me from there. I do not dream about him, but quite often, awake in the night, I give way to the temptation of going back to that temple high above the others, and we are lying side by side resting from the heat of the afternoon, and our own, not touching, except that he has my hand lightly cupped in his. Behind us, beyond a shutter half closed, a cicada is making its loud, harsh sound.

157 Hutung Feng-huang,
Peking,
Dec. 21, 1904

A chitty from Edith Harding saying that I must certainly come to them for Christmas since there would now seem to be no hope of Richard getting home, and that they will somehow make room for Meng in the servants' quarters so that Jane can be properly looked after while I am there. Edith has a real talent for making her words ring with Christian charity while at the same time clearly showing that duty is prodding her along a course she would avoid if it were at all possible. I sent her servant back with the message that her great kindness was more of what I had come to expect from her, but that I was suffering from a digestive complaint which, though not serious, made it sensible for me to be very quiet over the festive season. There could have been no more polite rejection of the Harding plum pudding, and, half an hour after the servant left here with my note, I received by telepathic communication Edith's sigh of relief. I think her next visit here will now be postponed until into the new year, but I am not happy about that prospect for I am beginning to show, and even with let-out waistbands and loose skirts she is likely to spot my condition, with the kind of reaction I can only too easily imagine.

If I have any plans at all just now, and I cannot really pretend that I do, these are that Richard should be the first to know. Somehow I don't want him to come back to a Legation Quarter yattering with the news. And how the bored Mah Jongg women will seize on it.

157 Hutung Feng-huang,
Peking,
Dec. 22, 1904

The Legation, reminded of my existence by my note to them, have sent me a huge batch of the newspapers that Richard used to bring home, the newest of these dated three months ago. In an old London *Times* was a detailed account by their correspondent with the Japanese forces of the early stages of the battle for Liao-Yang in which Kentaro was wounded. The casualty lists that during the summer and autumn had been breakfast reading for the people at home suddenly came alive to me. I remembered twice seeing the blood seeping through those bandages from a wound that wasn't healing, perhaps because of the way he was forcing himself to walk on that leg. I read the names of those villages through which he had probably marched with his men, An-ping, Hsiao-tun-tzu, as though they were stations along a railway line I travelled often, though in the names I saw blood and ruins. This is Kentaro's second war in only a few years. He said he is a soldier not a poet, yet he wrote that poem I dare not look at.

157 Hutung Feng-huang,
Peking,
Dec. 27th, 1904

Jane has not been well. I remembered something Edith once said about how doctors out here have to see so many of their small European patients buried in our lonely Far Eastern cemeteries, and suddenly I was terrified by the thought that I might be going to be punished through Jane. Dr Hotchkiss has been here twice, once on Christmas day. He did not seem too worried about Jane and may have been wanting to check up on me. I had nothing to report, just a little morning sickness that wore off quite quickly. He started to tell me that I was being lucky this time, then stopped. Jane is better, but we don't bring her out of the nursery to the stove in here, so I sit by it alone, thinking about what I have done to Jane and Richard, and to myself, as well as others. I wonder what the baby I am carrying will look like? I am sure it is a boy.

This afternoon I forced myself to write to Mama. I filled my letter with lies, descriptions of the life I am not leading. Afterwards I did something that I remembered from school, a thing that a girl whom we all thought a little crazy about religion used to do. She said that if you needed guidance all you had to do was close your eyes, open the Bible at random, put down your finger on a page, and there would be a message. I put down my finger and opened my eyes to read: *My beloved is unto me as a bundle of myrrh, that lieth betwixt my breasts. My beloved is unto me as a cluster of henna-flowers in the vineyards of En-gedi.* I was mocked.

157 Hutung Feng-huang,
Peking,
January 3rd, 1905

Edith came this afternoon, quite late, at about half past five, a time when I thought she would never be out in the city alone in her ricksha. I was bathing Jane in the nursery. I have been doing that, wanting to do things for the child that I don't have to. Meng does not like it. She does not like me. She has seen my condition. It will be the talk of the servants' quarters except when Yao is with them. He would not allow it. The news may have got back to the Quarter via servants, who are a network amongst themselves, and when I saw Edith I was sure this had happened, that she had come to see for herself whether the gossip was true. But it was something else.

General Stessel, the Russian in command of Port Arthur, has surrendered the city. It happened after one of the major forts had been blown up by Japanese mining, almost everyone in it killed. Edith said she had come to me at once because she had feared that if I heard about this when I was alone I might start imagining that Richard had been in the fort as an observer. At the Legation they say this is very unlikely, his was a headquarters role, and that we can expect him home in a matter of days, or at the latest by the middle of the month.

I thought then of what it might mean to me if Richard had been killed, how I might escape that way and have my baby quietly in some place like Hong Kong where I was not known and there could be no scandal. Then I felt sick that I wished him dead as a convenience to me.

Edith seemed alarmed. She made me sit down and drink some sherry, which is all we have in the house. I had been wearing a wrapper over my dress for bathing Jane, and kept this loose, watching to see from her face whether Edith was inspecting me. I don't think she was. In my own cowardice I am starting to suspect everyone. I will not be able to go on hiding here much longer.

8

Grand Hôtel de Pekin,
Peking,
Feb. 2, 1905

I have been put out. Richard is paying for my room here until passage
can be arranged for me from Tientsin to Shanghai and then back to
Britain on some P & O ship. He said I did not deserve steerage but
he would send me Second Class. He called me a whore. It was his
right to do that. I am not to see Jane again. He said there isn't a
court in the world which would not uphold his right to protect his
daughter from a depraved mother. He would not let me into Jane's
nursery for the last time to see her. I begged just to be allowed to
see her from the door but he would not allow it, standing to bar
the way.

This past month has been horrible. I was expecting him every
day, but he went from Port Arthur to Wei-Hai-Wei and settled into
a hotel there to write his report for the War Office. Because this was
highly confidential he did not even let the Legation know where he
was, let alone me. He arrived about six this evening, with no warning that he was coming. Meng had just taken Jane back to the nursery from the pen by the drawing-room stove and when he came in I
got up. We didn't say a word, just stood staring at each other. I was
too frightened to speak.

He had heard nothing, so at least that was the way I wanted it.
He has time to think how he will face the world. No one will blame

him. An unfortunate marriage, the husband away on active duty and the wife, beneath him in social station, behaving as one really might expect such a woman would do. I wonder if they will soon be talking about how I refused to say the words needed to be married by a Bishop?

I thought he was going to start hitting me when I would not tell him who the man was. He began to hurl names at me of men in the Legation Quarter, probably the ones who were known to go to Chinese women but he thought might have found me more convenient during his absence. I hadn't even spoken to most of them. I saw what trouble he was going to make for himself and others, so I told him. For what seemed a very long time he just stood there staring at me, then he went to the door that leads into the passage by our bedrooms. A moment later I heard him vomiting.

What will he do with Jane? Send her back to Mannington? Will she be raised in that house amongst the dark portraits? I'm sure he is right about the law, especially in England, and that the Collingsworths will be able to keep me from ever seeing Jane again, at least until she is of age and can choose to if she wants. But she won't want to by then. While I begged for that look at her from the nursery door he said I would soon be able to look as much as I wanted at my half-Jap bastard.

I went into my room then and began to pack. I brought everything I will take from that house, including my cabin trunk. What I have in the world, here in this hotel room, doesn't look very much, that little trunk, one big suitcase and one small. He didn't give me any money. I still have twenty-six pounds from what Mama gave me more than two years ago. I never had any money from him regularly. He would give me some every now and then, but he paid all the household bills, and the servants.

Why am I putting all this down? I may be looking for small excuses for myself. But there aren't any. Now, sitting here, feeling sick, I love Kentaro Kurihama whom I will never see again. And by all the judgements I am wicked because of this. So I must be.

Three rickshas in a row took me away from the Lane of the Fabulous Bird. I was in the first, my luggage in the second, Yao in the third. While Richard is still responsible for me, which I suppose is while I remain in this city, I was not allowed to travel through the streets of Peking at night unaccompanied. At the hotel Yao helped the page with my luggage, carrying the trunk between them inside, then up to my room.

I went into the lobby where the clock said twenty minutes past eight. There was considerable noise from the dining-room, people at dinner, and the undermanager told me I could have a meal with the others, or in my room. My voice sounded quite normal when I said I did not want anything, though it seemed to me that I was having to pull it out of a lump of ice. Yao was waiting at the door of my room. He bowed, and when his head came up the one eye focused on me had tears in it. I have never expected to see any Chinese man weeping for me. Both his hands were folded together in front of his chest. I put my hands on his and held them there for a moment, but I could not say anything. He knows how few my words in Chinese are.

It is now nearly midnight. I will not go downstairs tomorrow. I hope I won't have to see anyone before my train leaves for Tientsin, though that may be a few days until a ship sails for Shanghai. Jane almost never cries at night now, but if she should Meng would be too far away to hear her. Perhaps Richard will arrange for the amah to sleep in the nursery? I hope he doesn't think he must change amahs because Meng has seen and heard too much. Jane needs someone she knows. I wish I could pray, but He would never listen.

9

Letter from Mary Mackenzie to Madam de
Chamonpierre in Washington, DC, USA

13 Tsukiji San Chome,
Tokyo, Japan,
April 8th, 1905

Dear Marie,

*Never in my life have I been so grateful for a letter as
I am for yours. It came nearly a week ago and I have re-
read it every day, several times. I suppose I had guessed
that you would have had the news from Peking of what
happened to me, but the last thing I was expecting was
that you should write as you have done, saying you worry
about me continuously. I do not deserve such friends as
Armand and you after what I have done, and I am so
thankful to you both. No one else has written since I came
here, and I haven't been expecting anyone to, which made
your letter seem like a kind of miracle, meaning that I
have not been totally wiped out of mind by everyone I used
to know. If parts of this letter do not seem very balanced
and sensible then please forgive me and remember that
ever since I came here, and except for my two little maids,
I have seen no one to talk to. I can't really talk to my
maids either, who don't know any English, though*

Japanese seems to be a much simpler language to speak than Chinese and I am trying to learn it. Since it would seem probably that I will live the rest of my life in this country I had better, hadn't I?

Though you don't say where you got your news of me I think it must have been Edith, and it was clever of you to write me care of the Japanese Legation in Peking. If I have done nothing else I have at least given the Quarter something new to talk about, and they ought to be a little bit grateful to me for that. You will have heard, I suppose, that I just disappeared from my hotel room before Richard even had time to start making the arrangements to have me sent home to Scotland. The morning after I was put out of the house in the lane a young man from the Japanese Legation called to see me at the hotel. I refused to go down to the lobby, and just had him brought up to my bedroom, since I was now beyond the pale, which made it quite pointless for me to worry about what was or was not respectable. What the young man had to tell me was that Count Kurihama had not simply gone back to Korea forgetting all about me. I know you always admired him so it will not surprise you that in the circumstances he did what seems very much the honourable thing, that is, left word that I was to be watched—indeed, almost spied on— and that if anything went wrong with me I was to be helped.

I have had plenty of time to think about this since, and it does not do me much credit that he seems to have believed that if nothing happened as a result of our affair to expose it, I would just go on living with my husband, putting away the Western Hills as something to be forgotten. His opinion of me doesn't appear to be any higher than my own, for when I am really honest I know that this is exactly what I would have done, hiding my secret and continuing to live as Richard's wife, using as an excuse the fact that Jane needed me.

Marie, I don't think you ever felt that I was truly devoted to Jane as a mother ought to be, and you made excuses for me by saying that the child seemed remarkably independent even as an infant, and so on. I know this sounds now as though I am inventing things to suit myself, but when the end came with Richard the thing I minded most was the thought of my daughter left with him, of being cut off from her forever. It was almost a surprise that this was the thing that had stunned me and brought me close to complete despair, not the fact of being disgraced as a wife before the world. Now Richard already seems far away, that house in the lane a place where I lived long ago, but Jane I think of as now, wondering what has happened to her, and whether Richard has taken her away from Peking, back to Britain to leave my child with his mother? If you can find out anything about this for me, please do, and you are clever at finding things out.

You will be wondering how I left Peking. The Japanese Legation arranged everything. I was only the one night in that hotel and left it without hearing from Richard again, travelling to Tientsin with an escort who disliked the job he had to do, the young man regarding wives who are faithless to their husbands as creatures only deserving to die. Richard could not have wished me in better company for that journey! My escort put me on board a Japanese freighter at Tientsin and then left, thankfully, to return to more normal duties. On the ship it was much the same. I stayed mostly in my cabin, but when I did go out and met any of the crew they were curtly polite, no more. I felt almost as though I was a prisoner even though keys weren't turned in locks behind me. However, some of this may have been imagination. I was in a state of disgust with myself.

As for my first impressions of your beloved Japan, well, I had very few. In the first place we arrived at

Shimonoseki quite late at night and my first walk on the soil of Nippon was along a concrete station platform that seemed endless, past the longest train I have ever seen, with red bands marking the third class carriages, blue for the second and white for first. I was put in a first class compartment by another young man who had met the ship and didn't seem to have any kinder feelings towards erring wives than had the one from the Legation. At dawn we passed endless tea plantations, at least I think it was tea, the bushes looked like the ones I had seen in my school geography of estates in Ceylon. Then there was a city called Nagoya, where my escort appeared suddenly at my compartment door with a boxed meal he must have bought on the platform. One of the boxes held cold congealed rice and the other quite a pretty array of raw fish and highly coloured pickles which tasted horrible even though I was hungry. As you might expect, I am always hungry these days, though here I get bread and butter and milk even though the rest of my diet is basically Japanese, for my two maids don't know how to prepare anything else and at the moment I don't seem able to teach them, I just let things slide. In fact that is what I have been doing ever since I came to this pretty little house, making no decisions, just allowing things to happen from outside, though not much does. You must not think I am in low spirits all the time, I am not; it is just as though my life was becalmed, sails flapping, and I can only wait to see if there will be a wind tomorrow.

I go out sometimes in the evening about dusk, accompanied by one of my maids whose name is Misao San, very sweet, not yet twenty, given to endless chirping like a sparrow. She seems to think that if she talks at me continuously in the end I will begin to understand, and there may be something in this for I am already recognizing words, hoping soon to be able to fit them into sentences, something I should have done long ago but for *this laziness in mind and body. Just one street over from this house is the Sumida river and there is a sort of bund within two or three minutes' walk where quite large ships tie up, some steamers, though mostly three-masted schooners which I suppose are in the coastal trade. Tsukiji used to be the Foreign Concession, but the Japanese did not for long allow concessions on their soil and now there are only a few European-type houses left in it.*

I have not seen Count Kurihama since I came here. He is still in Korea, I believe, and probably at the front though I have had no actual news of him at all. At the moment I am very big with this child, much bigger than I was with Jane, and quite hideous. There are no mirrors of the kind you like in this house, but I have a small one which tells me too much. Even my face seems swollen.

I can hear you asking why I did this, why I came to Japan to be the courtesan of a man who is married with four children? In fact I don't even know whether this is what he intends for me, it could well be that I am only in this house he has provided until I have my baby. St Luke's hospital is just around the corner and I am to go there. Maybe you will laugh when you hear that it is run by Presbyterians, though they are American Presbyterians who are perhaps kinder to fallen women than Scotch ones. A Japanese doctor from the hospital has been to see me three times, very gentle, and speaking some English, though I am not sure whether he will deliver my baby himself. I could easily find out, but I haven't asked, no questions to anyone is part of this drifting from which I must recover as soon as I have had the baby.

The only one I have written to besides you is my mother. I had to tell her that I was here under the protection of a Japanese gentleman. She will call me what Richard did, only in her mind, the word itself has never passed her lips. You told me that Bordeaux is very proper bourgeois, but I am sure Edinburgh is ten times more so. My Mama will

never make contact with me again, I feel that. I pray that
what has happened will not make her really ill so that I
would have that on my conscience, too.

I did not mean to wail at you, and I have not yet told
you why I did what I have done. The alternatives were
impossible. Richard was to send me to Edinburgh,
returning me to Mama. I had twenty-six pounds of my
own money and that was all. I thought about getting on a
ship for home, then leaving it at Hong Kong or Singapore
and trying to get work. But what work? I have no
training in anything. I can't even cook properly, so
couldn't go as a servant. And who wants European
servants in the Far East? Even if there had been
something I might do in one of these places, who would
take on a woman in my condition? Marie, there is
nothing more helpless in a world made for men than a
woman heavy with the child she should not be carrying.
The Count provided me with an escape and I took it,
that's all. I know that I must make a future for myself
but at the moment I can't even see a hint of what this is
to be.

You must not think that what happened at the temple
had anything to do with you. You could not possibly
protect me from something you did not even know about
until it was too late, so do not have such thoughts. But
write to me. I promise that when I answer next time I
will be back in something like my old character, not this
dreadful drifter. Last night, thinking about Armand
and you in that temple in the hills, I remembered our
jokes and laughter and, remembering, wept.

I am so glad that you are enjoying Washington and
that Armand has his Pierce-Arrow motor-car, which
sounds very grand. I was surprised, though, that you ride
in it, and not behind a pair of horses. Do you really think
carriages are doomed, to be replaced by these machines? It
is hard to believe, and twenty-five miles an hour indeed

sounds a dreadful speed when you are not on rails. I had never heard of the electric brougham you say Armand wishes to buy for you, but if they are slower they are probably safer. Do ladies steer these themselves, or must there always be a driver? I believe there are some motorcars in Tokyo, though I have never seen one in Tsukiji, it is all rickshas and handcarts here, with oxen to pull the heavy loads. In Japan everything seems to move faster than in China, the people in a hurry to get somewhere. You will be happy to know that I am reading more than I used to. There is an English library at the hospital which the doctor told me about and I send a chitty with Misao San saying what would interest me, and the maid returns laden down with a good selection. I am in the middle of a novel by Mrs Humphrey Ward who, according to her publishers, is the most famous woman writer in the world though, ignorant me, I had never heard of her.

Forgive me, Marie, and please write. I promise I will never use your name with other people to bring you any embarrassment from having known me once. My very sincere regards to dear, kind Armand. Thank you so much.

Your grateful friend,
Mary

13 Tsukiji San Chome,
Tokyo,
April 17, 1905

My baby will be born in less than two months and though my body is aware of this, my mind does not seem to be. It is difficult for anyone from the West to be serious about life while living in a Japanese house. My first impression of 13 Tsukiji is the one I still have, that it really is not a house at all, but a flimsy box around a game played to quite simple rules. The game is entertaining most of the time, but can become very boring. Sometimes it is much

more than just boring. I have lived in a completely Japanese manner since coming here, sleeping between quilts at night, sitting on
cushions on the matting by day, eating off a table only raised six
inches from the floor and, in the colder weather, freezing, my feet
icy as I huddled over a charcoal brazier from which rose suffocating fumes.

Every evening at dusk my two maids, Misao and Fukuda, make
another move in their charming little pretence that they are running a house, closing it all up for the night with wooden shutters
along the verandahs, these our security against the greatly feared
dorubos. At first I thought, from the serious way this word was
thrust through laughter, that it meant some form of dreaded devil,
but my phrase-book says 'robbers'. I can't really see what a burglar
breaking into one of the countless thousands of shut boxes in this
city could hope to steal, beyond money that is, for there is practically nothing in them. I arrived here with little enough and yet the
contents of one small cabin trunk and two suitcases presented
almost unsurmountable storage difficulties, this in a house with six
rooms including the kitchen, but not a single drawer in any of
them. There are cupboards behind sliding doors but these are
almost filled during the day by the quilts that will be your bed at
night.

One thing the Japanese house does not consider is any kind of
comfort for a woman carrying a child, and I don't think this is only
because I am a Western woman carrying a child. What you cannot
do in this condition is loll about on floor cushions, and if you
attempt to sit up straight on one of them your back soon protests. I
tried explaining to my maids that I must have one chair of some
sort, but the best they could do as a result of my pantomime was
produce a stout box that had once contained Australian apples, with
a cushion on top. Once again there was no support for my back.
Finally I appealed to Dr Ikeda and a chair duly arrived, quite light,
made of wicker with a back, though low, which is adequate.

During the days, in this pleasant warm weather, I have my chair
out on the boards of the narrow verandahs, but it was in the
evening when the problem arose, my chair having to be moved

inside and, with my great weight added to it, the four legs prodding holes in the beautiful straw matting, something that brought my happy little maids near to tears, as though holes in the matting were the only thing that caused real distress in their lives. From my point of view this wasn't a very satisfactory arrangement either, for the legs set on softness didn't make my perch too secure. In the end we solved the problem by breaking up the apple box and laying its boards on the matting as support for the chair's feet. This arrangement is all right, except that I can't ever move my chair from its fixed position, and Misao San in particular continues to behave as though both chair and the boards under it outraged everything she had been brought up to believe in. Also, it has added to her not very arduous work. When the shutters have all been slid away along their runners and stowed into the boxes where they are kept by day, poor Misao has then to come in and carry my very light chair eight feet out on to the verandah, after which she takes the four boards away to the kitchen, returning with a hand broom and pan to sweep carefully around where the chair has been. The rest of the room is only swept once a week, though the wooden verandahs are polished daily with greasy cloths that I sometimes suspect have been recently used to dry my dishes.

I don't go into my Tokyo kitchen either, it seems wisest not to since there is nothing I could possibly do in there anyway. It has an earth floor with two steps down to it from the level of the rest of the downstairs, and in place of a cookstove three fat charcoal-burning braziers on which heat temperatures are controlled by using a stiff paper fan vigorously for fast cooking, or not using it at all for simmering. Any kind of baking is unknown, not a hint of an oven anywhere, but Fukuda San can fry things very well and is especially good with fish done in batter, which I learned early is called 'sakana tempura' so I could order it often. The water supply is piped to a tap over a cement sink with an open drain under it that I suspect has a serious leak somewhere, allowing seepage into our ornamental pond. The goldfish that Misao San keeps bringing home from the evening fairs have regularly to be fished out quite dead. The one modern feature of that kitchen and this house is electric light, this a total surprise to me coming from Peking's lamps and my mother's gas fixtures in Edinburgh. Large sections of Tokyo are now lit by this method, thanks to German enterprise, not British, and there is also a system of electric tramcars which, on still nights, can be heard clanking away in the distance along the Ginza, though the lines do not come down into Tsukiji as yet. The sanitary arrangements might be said to be slightly better than those in Peking, but not much.

There are times when I feel almost content here, which I suppose ought to shame me. It is as though I am then able to close all the doors in my mind except the one opening into this living, so that I have no past and no future, and with a great excuse for unthinking laziness in my pregnancy. At night the winds of the world sometimes probe for cracks in the tightly closed shutters, but Misao and Fukuda have left no gaps and I am safe between my two quilts. I do not even think of Kentaro who has provided me with this.

13 Tsukiji San Chome,
Tokyo,
April 27th, 1905

Dr Ikeda has been three times this week. I'm sure he is well paid to give me every attention, but this seems too often. I think he is worried about the position of the baby. He asks me questions about where I feel movement when it happens and I don't think my answers satisfy him. He must be the quietest doctor in the world. His English is good enough but he never uses a word that is not necessary. I have no idea what he thinks of me as a person or as a patient, though I try to do what he tells me. Until recently he had me taking exercise every day, like walks to the Bund, but now he doesn't seem to want me to move about very much.

I get quite frightened sometimes, more so than I think I did with Jane, though one forgets. I am not sure whether, if he was willing to, I would want Dr Ikeda to tell me exactly what he thinks is wrong. I am such an awful coward.

I do a lot of reading, but not always with my complete attention, and sometimes I seem to see my old lives beyond the words, first with Mama in Edinburgh, then with Richard, and Jane lying in her cot looking at me, but all these as pictures seen through dusty glass. I have strange dreams: the other night I was walking along Princes Street wearing the blue evening dress Mama bought me, though it was sunshine and clearly morning. Someone was with me but I couldn't see who it was, as though unable to turn my head to look. What I did see was the fashionable Saturday crowd, the ladies pretending to shop, but really showing off their new outfits and then planning to meet friends for coffee in one of the restaurants. Princes Street has that slight dip in the middle so that at certain points you can actually see all the people promenading for at least half a mile ahead of you, and I was at one of those places when suddenly, directly in front of me, a yawning black hole opened up. Then beyond it coming towards me were people laughing and talking, and who couldn't have seen that hole at all, but I was right on its crumbling edge, and knew that I was going to fall in and be swallowed up. That was when I woke soaking with perspiration. Unlike most dreams, I just couldn't forget this one quickly.

Sometimes I think of the little, unimportant-seeming accidents that have changed my life, like going to stay with Margaret Blair and meeting Richard, one chance in ten thousand really. Then there was a morning walk up a path through a clump of Chinese bamboo to Kentaro. Because such slight things can swing me completely off into another way of living, am I some special kind of fool? Do other people, too, make their lives from little accidents like these? I suspect that those who really succeed in living are the ones who don't let accidents happen to them, who plot their days like a ship's course on a chart, and never take their eyes off the compass.

13 Tsukiji San Chome,
Tokyo,
May 29, 1905

I have not been well, quite a lot of vomiting. Dr Ikeda has kept me in bed for the last week, lying flat most of the time. Today I have been propped up against another rolled quilt at my back, reading the papers.

Unlike Peking there is a daily newspaper in English here, the *Japan Advertiser* and it is rather strange to again have world news quite soon after the events have happened. Yesterday there was a great battle between the Russian fleet which has sailed here all the way from Europe and the Japanese Navy. Just as Kentaro said he would, Admiral Togo has utterly defeated the Russians, sinking most of their ships. What had seemed the invincible power of the Czar has been broken and, in the Far East at least, apparently destroyed forever. The editorial in the paper says that the war on land cannot go on for much longer either, which means that Japan's total victory is now a certainty. In the future she will have to be classed as one of the great powers of the world.

Lying here in my wood and paper house, served by two kind but really very silly girls, I wonder how this can be. Though I have not seen much of the country, I have the feeling that it is a very poor land, if not so poor as China. On my walks to the Bund there is a bridge I never use now, going some distance to another to avoid it, because at one end sits a leper beggar, the same bundle of rags I saw so often in Peking, and the same droned petition as you pass. The leper is a man and he sometimes has a small child with him, also in rags, the child trained to scream, or perhaps pinched to make him do it, when anyone approaches the bridge. The disease has almost completely destroyed one side of the man's face, it looks as though the inside of his mouth had been turned outside. Whenever we have gone that way I have always given him something, though I haven't much money, just my twenty-six pounds turned into nearly two hundred and fifty yen. However, all you give a beggar is a few sen. Misao thinks it quite unnecessary to give him anything. She and that shapeless wreck on the bridge are also part of these people who will soon have defeated one of the greatest nations in the West. Then I think of Kentaro praying his apologies to the souls of the men under his command who had been killed. To consider that God may be on the side of such a man, and thousands like him, is disturbing.

13 Tsukiji San Chome,
Tokyo,
June 4, 1905

I had an uneasy night and fell asleep only after Fukuda San was up and banging about the kitchen. The noise she makes doing anything, which is a great deal, did not wake me, but a sharp, loud voice in our little vestibule did. It was a woman and she almost seemed to be shouting. A moment later, though the words were Japanese, I was sure the user was not, it was Japanese spoken with a marked English accent. I heard Misao trying to interrupt that voice, but with no success, and I was suddenly very uneasy, conscious of only two layers of papered doors between me and the entrance area. If it had been a European house I'm pretty sure there would have been no stopping our visitor, that she would have come surging along the verandah to the room in which I lay, but the matting meant that the attack could not really be a surprise one, the lady would have to unlace or unbutton her shoes. I heard Misao say the phrase which I already recognize from its constant use: '*Choto maté kudasai*'—please wait a little—and a moment later the maid slid back the screen, which meant that I lay exposed to the garden. The visitor, foiled at the entrance, might at any moment make her appearance through a gate in the bamboo fence. There was something about that woman's loud, positive Japanese which made me certain she would be very difficult to stave off.

Misao had brought a calling card. On it was: 'Miss Alicia Basset-Hill' and, also printed, up in one corner: 'Society for the Propagation of the Christian Gospel'. 'PTO' was in pencil. The message on the back was as positive as the voice: 'Have been meaning to call, but have had pneumonia.'

The lady was almost certainly a neighbour. I knew there were a few foreigners living in the Tsukiji area but in my brief walks had seen no sign of any of them, and of course the language barrier means I get no real gossip from my maids. What I felt then, and am still feeling, was almost sheer panic. It looks as though arrangements have been made to spy on me here in Tokyo. My first thought was that Mama had done this, then I was sure it was Richard. In Peking

I had heard talk about so-called undesirable Britons, who cause embarrassment in foreign countries by what they do or the way they live, simply being sent home by the Consular people on orders from the Embassy. I hadn't registered at the Embassy in Tokyo, behaving like someone in hiding, which is really what I am doing in a way.

I didn't say a word to the waiting Misao, knowing too well that a whisper would travel through those thin walls, but shook my head violently, giving the card back with signs that it was to be returned to the visitor. Misao seemed to take fright at my agitation and went down the verandah. A moment later I heard more of the loud, confident English-Japanese, then a clicking on the flagstones of the front walk, after which the outer gate slid open and shut on its noisy metal runners. Misao San brought me a present from Miss Basset-Hill, a tin of Huntley and Palmer's assorted biscuits. I'm afraid that a meeting with this woman cannot be avoided.

10

§

I fell into that black hole which in my dream I saw opening in front of
me. I remember Dr Ikeda peering down. He seemed a long way up,
a face at the mouth of a vertical cave. One of the nurses told me that
after the operation he was always coming in to see how I was doing.
She half admitted that she thought I was dying. They had to cut the
baby from me, there was no other way. Nearly four weeks later I am
still in pain from that, but insisted on breastfeeding my child as soon
as I was conscious enough from the drugs they gave me. My baby is
a boy, of course. He has some dark hair and a powerful voice,
already with two slaves, Misao and Fukuda, three, if I am to be
counted. It is easy to see that the maids are delighted the child looks
like a Japanese. I keep thinking about names for him, but have got
nowhere on that important matter.

Perhaps I should have him christened, though I do not think
Presbyterians are supposed to believe that infants who die unbap-
tized go to hell. I certainly don't, and probably it is quite wrong to
even consider baptism when his father is of such a different faith.

I have only written to Mama twice since coming to Japan, with
no reply. Ought I to let her know she has a grandson or would the
news shock everyone in that house? Miss Bassett-Hill sent in a huge
net bag of oranges the day after I got back from hospital. She must
have known that I came home with a baby I am not entitled to by

my marriage, and as a missionary ought to be shocked, especially as a single lady missionary. So why the oranges unless she has some commission to see me whatever I do? The thought of her makes me uneasy.

Tsukiji, Tokyo,
July 23

The terrible heat of the last ten days was broken by a violent thunderstorm last night, this seemed determined to stay circling over the Sumida River area and directly above us. The crashing sounded like the world breaking up. I had the maids for company, Misao letting out almost continuous squeaks of terror, but the baby slept solidly through it all in a way that amazed the three of us. Twice the electric light flickered and went out, but it came on again moments later. Rain was suddenly a cloudburst. Though the canal on the opposite side of our street should have acted as a drain it didn't, and soon we had flooding over the lip of our outer gate, geysers spouting through the slats like the overflow of a reservoir. In minutes our entrance area was under water and the fishpond in the garden overflowed, but what looked like the beginnings of disaster was all gone by morning, the air fresh, the sun bringing heat without the muggy humidity we have been enduring. I was sitting out on the verandah in my chair and Misao had the baby on a mat in the garden when I heard her asking him if he was her friend: '*Anata boku no o-tomodachi desu ka?*' My baby showed his gums, and there was his name—Tomo. The maids are delighted with it.

This afternoon I decided I have been playing the invalid for long enough and I went for an enormous long walk, which was down the stepping-stones to the gate, through this and across the road to the canal bank where I stood looking down at mud left by a retreating tide, feeling that I had come far enough. A commotion at our gate didn't make me turn at once but when I did it was to see a ricksha there with its shafts lowered and for a moment I thought I had been caught and Miss Bassett-Hill was lurking under the raised hood. However, what came out was not a person, but a huge parcel which Misao and Fukuda collected between them, apparently excited. By the time I had joined my maids the parcel was sitting in the middle of the living-room matting, the baby still out in the sun, for the time being neglected. It was obvious that the parcel as such was a suitable object for deep respect, almost veneration, Misao and Fukuda both sitting on their legs staring at it. I settled into my chair and then had practically to prod them into getting on with untying the string around brown paper, which was done with a solemn adherence to ritual. First I was handed a folded white and red paper symbol which indicated a gift and then a label on which was one word printed in English—'Mary'—together with an address written with a black brush in Japanese. There was a second layer of wrapping under the brown paper, but what was eventually revealed was a red cloth fish.

It was a very big fish, at least three feet long, about one and a half wide, and standing a couple of feet off its carved wooden base on which were decorations, in bright green, of artificial seaweed and water ferns. Fins and tails were of cloth, sewn on, but the scales and head were stylized hand painting. I had guessed the fish was stuffed with something before it was pushed over matting to me and Misao had demonstrated how you got inside, via a slit under the tail portion. I put in my hand and pulled. Out came yard upon yard of a heavy silk crêpe in a soft grey tone as a background to huge flaring blooms of paeony flowers and a design of leaves, the material obviously intended for the most exotic of kimonos. With the last folds came something else, a wallet of gold brocade. Inside were twenty new one-hundred-yen notes.

From my reading in Marie's books on Japan I knew that the fish is the symbol of the male child. I sat in my wicker chair out on the boards of the verandah, watched by my bright-eyed maids, wondering if this was Kentaro's way of acknowledging the birth of a son? It could also be my whore's price, two thousand yen leaving him free to wash his hands of me and Tomo. I looked at the silk again. No respectable woman in this country would ever be seen wearing that heavy crêpe splashed with gaudy flowers. It could only be made up into the kimono for a courtesan.

Last night I did not sleep. One says this often enough meaning that one did not sleep well, but I never closed my eyes. Every hour I heard the night watchman coming down our street, striking his wooden clappers together and shouting that he was busy watching for burglars but had seen none and we were not to worry.

I kept thinking about what I could do with two thousand yen. It is exactly the money Mama insisted I carry out into the world from Edinburgh. Now I have it again. A thousand dollars is a lot more than most of the emigrants from Europe have to take with them to a new world but I've heard that the Americans are strict about refusing to admit the morally depraved. I'm sure that if I went to their Consul that is how he would classify me. Also, Tomo is a Japanese by birth, I couldn't just take him anywhere I wanted to go. And wouldn't it be wrong to bring up a half-Eastern child in the West? My thoughts kept going round and round, getting me nowhere.

I am continuing to breastfeed Tomo but don't mean to go on doing this for as long as Japanese women, which apparently can be for years. Usually, holding him, I am content not to think, wanting only these minutes. He rarely cries except when he needs something, and with three women in attendance he gets it quickly. I look at him lying back on the matting doing those upside down bicycle exercises and remember Jane, who was not a whiner, not really much of a crier, either, but never joyous-seeming like my son. It is as if Tomo knew he had been born to a golden future. Nothing could be less probable in his case, but he seems quite certain of it. Again I have that weird feeling my baby knows things which are hidden from me. It is, of course, imagination.

The war in Manchuria drags on, though there is talk of the Americans arranging a peace between Russia and Japan. I woke up the other night suddenly wondering what would happen to me if Kentaro was killed. How selfish I am getting. I keep telling myself that it is for Tomo that I am frightened, but this isn't true, women with children may be doubly fearful on their account, but half the fear is still for themselves.

Yesterday I went with Misao San by ricksha to a branch of the Yokohama Specie Bank not far from the Ginza where I opened an account with one thousand eight hundred yen, keeping two hundred which I intend to spend getting to know Tokyo and my place in it, if any. Already I can see one possible future for me, quite the most pleasant of a variety of things that could happen, this to be Kentaro's second wife. It is quite unnecessary here for a man to wait until his first wife is dead before he takes another, the concubine and her children occupying a separate house and having quite an established place in society. The present Crown Prince is not the son of the Empress, but a child by the Emperor Meiji and a court lady, a young man who could not possibly be heir to the throne in any other country but this. Most concubines are successful geisha who have retired from their profession to live with a protector. The legal wives don't seem to protest against these arrangements.

No one who was a decent Christian could possibly consider the life that I am willing to let become mine. I seem to have lost all sense of shame. Does this mean that I am slowly being destroyed?

Tsukiji, Tokyo,
August 9th

Something I have been dreading has happened, a note from Miss Bassett-Hill asking me to lunch day after tomorrow. She says that since I have been seen abroad she hopes that I am now fully recovered from my recent confinement and illness after it. The note, delivered by hand, starts 'Dear Mrs Collingsworth' so she must know all about me and this almost certainly means that they also do at the British Embassy. Why should a single lady missionary want to associate with someone who has lost her character, unless it is to spy on her? It can't just be kindness. She has probably been instructed by the Embassy to find out all she can about me so they can build up a case to put to the Japanese to have me deported. Richard could well be behind this. I want to say I can't go, but that would show I am afraid, so I must, and try to brazen things out, something I am not trained to do. If I refuse this time she will only come at me again.

Tsukiji, Tokyo,
August 11, 1905

I don't really know what to think about what happened to me today. Miss Bassett-Hill's house is Japanese style, only a little bigger than this but in a much larger garden, and stuffed with furniture from England. Thick carpets are laid over the matting though you still take off your shoes in the entrance, and I couldn't believe her drawing-room when I saw it, desks, bookcases, a plush-covered sofa and chairs all crowded in, and all seeming very insecure on the soft flooring underneath. A high bookcase trembled every time I moved in my chair and I had the feeling flimsy walls were going to topple in on us under the weight of framed portraits, Miss Bassett-Hill apparently needing to bring all these reminders of her ancestors with her to the wilds of the Orient. There wasn't one thing in that room beyond basic design and woodwork which hinted at Japan, even the sliding paper doors glazed to suggest french windows. In what had once been the alcove for formal ornament was a huge roll-top desk over which hung an electric light shaded by green beads knitted together.

For a moment or two I didn't realize there was a third person in the room, a woman sitting in a rocking-chair with a fixed base, only the upper portion movable on springs. These creaked as she stood. The lady was wearing a plain white blouse and a brown skirt showing her ankles, as though it had shrunk from many washings. Her black hair was dressed in the Sally Lunn loaf style I wore out to China but abandoned soon after in favour of combing straight back to a bun low on my neck. The other guest, if she was that, seemed to have lost a few vital hairpins, a not very elaborate coiffure still in acute danger of suddenly collapsing, many stray tendrils already loose. It was only when my eyes adjusted from the brightness out on the verandah that I realized the lady was Japanese. Our hostess, dressed in a total black which looked like mourning for the sins of this world, introduced us.

'Baroness Sannotera, Mrs Collingsworth. I was sure you two would like to meet. And now I must go and see what my terrible cook is doing to the lunch.' She added in her high, thin, almost piercing voice: 'The Baroness has recently been released from prison.'

The one thing I was sure of in that moment was the lunch-party was going to be very different from anything I had imagined. Miss Bassett-Hill left and the Baroness, not showing any embarrassment over that introduction, moved to a side table, saying over a shoulder, 'I'm sure Alicia would want you to have a sherry.'

I needed something. As the Baroness turned with two glasses in her hand she added, once again in perfect English: 'When one is associating with former jailbirds, it is always useful to know how long they were in for. I was sentenced for six months but only served three because of family influence and despite the fact that it was my third conviction.'

I felt I was being challenged to ask why she had been in prison, so I did. The reply was immediate: 'For staring at the Emperor Meiji.'

Even when she explained this was a little hard to believe, but apparently it is absolutely forbidden by law to look directly at the Emperor, who is, of course, regarded as a god. When his carriage passes in the streets the crowds are expected to bow very low and keep that position until it is well out of range. All windows in upper stories are out of bounds and during state processions the police stand facing the crowds, on the outlook for anyone disobeying the edict. The Baroness had chosen a very prominent spot near the bridge over the moat around the palace and when Emperor Meiji had been driving to a state opening of parliament had very conspicuously stood erect while everyone else was bent double. She had also shouted at His Imperial Majesty that Japanese women must be freed from slavery. There had been a great scandal leading to a prosecution and the Baroness had not only received many death threats, but also gifts of ceremonial short swords from patriotic societies with suggestions that she take her own life to atone for the shame brought on her family and her country. Her two previous convictions were for creating an obstruction outside the office of one of Tokyo's daily papers during a campaign for votes for women, and a jail sentence of three months, later reduced to two, for having stated in a lecture that the Emperor is not divine and should not be worshipped.

I didn't have to account for myself to Baroness Sannotera, Miss Bassett-Hill had told her all she knows about me, which is obviously a great deal. The Baroness described how she had joined the Suffragettes during her stay in England, almost as the direct result of witnessing the junketing in London on the relief of Mafeking, that celebration of a victory in yet another stupid war that need never have been fought if women had their proper say in the conduct of world affairs. I was thinking this lady was bound for more jail sentences if she went on expressing these thoughts in Japan when our hostess called us into the next room, saying as we joined her:

'The French may have taken to Japan, but their wines have not. I was hoping for a good deal from this bottle, but once again my hopes have been dashed.'

Miss Bassett-Hill is not some kind of spy for the Embassy or my relations; she learned about me from Dr Ikeda at St Luke's where she does volunteer work twice a week. It was an extraordinary party. I will always be able to see that erect figure in black sitting at the head of a table which also wobbled on soft matting, telling us about the habit of some missionaries of returning statistics on the number of converts made each year and her comment on her own work.

'I doubt very much whether, as the result of my thirty years here, I could confirm *one* convert. The Japanese don't seem to care for Anglicanism. Perhaps they can't begin to understand it. I'm not sure that I do myself. And of course, there is the fact that I am *very* High Church.'

At the gate, as she was getting into her ricksha, the Baroness turned to me.

'Two disreputable women like us ought to be friends. What do you think?'

I think yes. We are going to the Kabuki theatre together next week.

Tsukiji, Tokyo,
August 16th

If Aiko Sannotera is a foretaste of what is going to happen to Japanese women in the twentieth century, then Japanese men are going to have to live through a revolutionary experience. To me she is like a door opened into the world again after a long time when I was shut into the cell of myself. My maids are terrified of her, they could perhaps accept such an un-female approach to living in a foreign woman, but that a Japanese, and a Baroness at that, should be so emancipated shocks them utterly. The grand-daughter of a Finance Minister, who ought to be behaving like a great lady, talks to them like an equal instead of using the language for servants, and this, too, is totally unnerving.

Aiko was divorced six years ago by her husband, who she says was remarkably patient but finally could not stand her any longer, at least as his wife, for they are still friends and it is he who contrives to have her jail sentences shortened. Also, the gods had punished a female rebel by making her barren, and though her husband had been quite willing to adopt an heir to carry on the Sannotera name, Aiko had suggested that he really ought to have a try with another woman and she is glad this has been successful, the Baron now has two sons and a daughter.

We went to the Kabuki last night, sitting in one of the little boxes on matting in an area that would be the centre stalls in Europe, surrounded by families packed into other little railed boxes, most people eating solidly, which is necessary to sustain you through an eight-hour performance, though you can vary your attention to the stage with family gossip and in the case of one party of business men attended by geisha, with something rather different from that. I thoroughly enjoyed a theatre in which, while an actor is about to disembowel himself against a background of paper cherry blossoms, people in the box next to us could become totally concerned with curing grandpapa of hiccups resulting from too much rice wine.

The action of the play must have reminded Aiko of her own family history. In rather a loud voice which even pushed through the shrieks of the dying actor, she told me how her grandfather, the Finance Minister, had been murdered. Four swordsmen had chopped their way into the family home, killing first the gate attendant, then two serving maids, then Aiko's grandmother who tried to protect her bedridden husband, finally reaching the old man himself whom they literally carved to pieces. The crime for which he was slaughtered was having resisted attempts by the Army and Navy to corner more finance for their expansion.

It is easy to see from where Aiko gets her stubborn refusal to be intimidated by the powers that be. And I can see, too, why she thinks Japan is ripe for a thousand reforms to take the country out of what she calls feudalism in new clothes. She isn't a restful woman to be with, your mind isn't allowed to go slack in her company, and this is what I need. I have rested too much and too long.

Tsukiji, Tokyo,
August 20

Aiko was here this afternoon. She is marvellous with Tomo when I wouldn't have expected her to have any instinctive feeling for children at all. She must know Kentaro since the Japanese upper classes seem quite close knit, but she has never mentioned him. This is not to spare my feelings, she spares nobody's feelings, but I suspect because she finds quite unbearable the idea of my subservience to the whims of a Japanese man. What she would probably like me to do is wrap my son in a quilt and carry him out into a Tokyo night, putting behind me forever my dependence on the male.

As a 'new' woman there is one thing Aiko forgets, that she was born into a wealthy family and married a rich man, her idealism never threatened by not knowing how she was going to eat tomorrow. I'm not trying to diminish her or make excuses for myself, she would die for a cause that was important in her eyes, but at the same time would see nothing odd in having her last meal before execution sent in from an expensive restaurant on a gilded lacquer tray, all this paid for by her ex-husband. I think that already we like each other as much for the areas of what seems to each the absurd in the other as for anything else. It is not a close sympathy in all things, or ever likely to be, but already a kind of warfare. In time I will make her a stronger and more worthy adversary. In only ten days she has brought me back into real living again, and for this I will be forever grateful.

Tsukiji, Tokyo,
August 24, 1905

The Russo-Japan war is over, a peace treaty signed yesterday in America at Portsmouth, New Hampshire. Kentaro may soon be back in Tokyo. I try not to think about what this could mean for me and for Tomo.

Today I went alone to the Ginza for the first time, buying some home-style cakes at Fugetsudo's, delicious little macaroons made with real ground almonds, and after that walking through a four-storey department store called Matsuzakara. This had many sections full of imports from Europe where richly dressed matrons seemed to be spending money wildly, perhaps the wives of war profiteers who have been receiving bad publicity in the papers recently.

At Maruzen's, the bookshop, I got a copy of Basil Hall Chamberlain's *Things Japanese* which Aiko recommended, saying it is full of plain home truths for the people in this country. I also found a second-hand Shakespeare, complete works in one volume and far too small print, but last night I read *Macbeth* straight through because I couldn't stop, with Tomo making little puppy-like noises in his sleep as though the light disturbed him.

I don't suppose we are meant to have much sympathy for Macbeth, but I did, as though I could feel everything that happened to him from those first thoughts of murder in his mind, these the beginnings of his destruction. The most terrible thing in the play is the idea of the Fates hounding, the witches their instrument, so that you know there is no escape for Macbeth, his doom inevitable. This is a little like the idea of God strict Presbyterians in Scotland still have, that He has chosen you for hell or heaven before you are born. It is a really wicked thing to pin on God. I cannot believe in Fate as we see it in *Macbeth*. I was not inevitably destined to climb a Chinese hill path and allow a Japanese soldier to make me with child. What I did then was from my own choice, I cannot blame God or the Fates, just myself. And often, looking at Tomo, I am glad.

11

*Letter from Mary Mackenzie to Madame de
Chamonpierre in Washington, DC, USA*

13 Tsukiji San Chome,
Tokyo, Japan,
September 16, 1905

Dear Marie,

*Once again it was marvellous to hear from you and I
can't thank you enough for having acted as my 'detective',
which I know has put you to a lot of trouble, whatever you
may say about that.*

*I had guessed, of course, that Jane was almost
certainly at Mannington with Richard's mother, and all
I can really hope for now is that she is enough like her
father, or grows up enough like him, for that world to be
completely right for her. It is certainly stable enough. I
hope, for her sake, that Jane in no way takes after me,
and I am sure that Lady Collingsworth will do her
utmost to make sure that this does not happen. I am glad,
too, that Richard will not be posted back to China after
his leave in England. It troubles me to think of the
damage I have probably done to his career prospects, but
surely it will be understood that he is in no way to blame?
No word of a divorce has reached me, but I suppose that*

*under English law this could be done without any
notification to me at all.*

*My son Tomo is very well. He has been healthy from the
first though it was not an easy delivery, his position in the
womb wrong, I am still not very clear in what way, but
the doctors at the very good hospital here had to operate
just before term, which means I will never be able to have
another child. As someone who is now part of what you
would call the* demimonde *this is probably a good thing. I
am not troubled about it. With Tomo I run the risk of
becoming a doting mother, which is something I must
watch. My two maids appear to take few things in this life
very seriously except babies, particularly boy babies, so not
only can I safely leave Tomo with them, the problem will
soon be to keep them from totally spoiling the child.
Already he is like a little prince who has only to express a
whim to have it immediately satisfied. It is quite
extraordinary how early infants begin to sense their power
and to use it.*

*I am no longer isolated in this house as I was when I
first wrote, having now two friends, one English lady and
one Japanese, the latter a Baroness of somewhat unique
character for this country. She has taken me out into the
world of Tokyo and even beyond, for next month we go to
some hill in the country for a ceremonial viewing of the
autumn colours of maple trees. The Baroness wears
European dress all the time . . . if you can call it that . . .
and we ought to make a curious pair of sightseers,
arousing considerable interest as we have already done on
various expeditions, including the theatre. So you see, I
am not growing in on myself as I think you would have
expected me to since you thought I shut myself up in that
Peking house. Tokyo I like, it is not beautiful with its
endless miles of little grey wood two-storey houses, but it is
full of life and much richer than China in simple
entertainments for all the people, which cost little and*

sometimes nothing at all. I go regularly to the night markets which open up every evening with portable stalls along the main street, the Ginza. These are lit by acetylene flares and practically everything available on this earth can be bought at them. There also seem to be festivals of some kind or another every other week, most of these based on temples, but very light-hearted. It is my impression that the Japanese take religion very casually, believing in little beyond ghosts. It is a great country for ghosts, everything is haunted, including trees.

Of Count Kurihama I have heard nothing. He is probably concerned with what now looks as though it would become a permanent Japanese occupation of Korea, something that should please you since you believe that they ought to rule Asia. I am not sure about that, even though my baby is half-Japanese.

You say nothing of Armand's Pierce-Arrow? I hope he hasn't been having trouble with it. From what I read in the papers these vehicles are expensive luxuries. A number of new rich Japanese, war profiteers mostly, called narikin, have imported motor-cars, but they are continually breaking down or rolling off narrow tracks into rice fields and having to be pulled out again by patient oxen. I am thinking of getting a bicycle. Aiko, the Baroness, has just bought one, a lady's model with three-speed gears, on which she is now whizzing about the streets of Tokyo, I fear to the great danger of lives and property, liable to have some very dramatic accident shortly!

As you can see, I am in much better spirits than when I last wrote. The autumn is lovely here, sunny days and cool nights. A neighbour plays the samisen in the evening, a stringed instrument on which geishas are skilled, so perhaps I should learn to play one. It makes cool, twanging notes that have a kind of deep sadness, not like anything I heard in China, and there is also a bamboo flute which sounds like a rich contralto voice.

You ask about earthquakes. There have been some, but mostly small, setting up a rattling more than a violent movement of the earth and in this light wooden house I really wasn't frightened at all. It is the huge fires, called the flowers of Yedo, which are terrifying; they sweep whole wards of the city, producing dreadful fire storms. Since I have been here six thousand houses were burned down in one night in the Ueno district. Though Ueno is a considerable distance from us here the sky overhead was blood red through all the hours of darkness. They say that the canals which crisscross this area are a protection, but burning wood embers, wind borne, can travel for miles. Aiko tells me that in the last fifty years, and except for the central portion around the Imperial Palace, almost the whole of this city has, at various times, been burned down and rebuilt. Naturally enough, the people here seem to have no great feeling for the permanence of material things, and if you are a city dweller the chances of losing everything you possess at least once in a lifetime are very high indeed. Many know this two and three times.

The Baroness must be the only Japanese woman who thinks it a bad thing that her country won the war against Russia. She says it only inflates their swelling conceit after the defeat of China years earlier. She tells me that there are even some military hotheads who say that it will be Britain they take on next, in spite of that treaty of friendship and alliance. I'm sure that, though you are French, you will agree that if ever the Japanese try that they will be in for a nasty shock.

Thanks so much for writing to me, and please do it again soon. Better still, on your next leave from Washington why not another visit to your beloved Japan? These days the travel involved is becoming nothing, only five days or so on the train from where you are to Vancouver and from there just another twelve to Yokohama. The world is getting much too fast for me, I

*have decided I am a slow person, but it does mean that
all kinds of things that were impossible a few years ago are
easy today. Perhaps in fifty years we will be travelling in
flying machines. I recently read in our English-language
paper that two Americans are rumoured to have flown
twenty-four miles in only half an hour at some secret
testing ground, but I must say I find this hard to believe.
One wonders whatever next. My love to Armand and
to you.*

   Sincerely,

   Mary

*PS Armand is not to risk your life speeding in the Pierce-
Arrow. The papers also tell me that the automobile is
becoming quite a menace in American streets and even
on country roads.*

13 Tsukiji San Chome,
Tokyo, Japan,
September 19th, 1905

After lunch today Aiko came on her bicycle to give me a riding les-
son. The only place for this was the street in front of our house
which at that time was completely empty. Misao and Fukuda came
out to see the circus. They still cannot make Aiko out. That a foreigner behaves as though mad is to be expected, but this is their first
experience of a Japanese who had caught the infection of that
lunacy. Also, Aiko's voice isn't really very ladylike by local standards,
she can be heard across a crowded room when she thinks she is talking to you alone. As an instructress she bellowed, there is no other
word for it. Finally, by paying no attention at all to what she told me
to do, I managed to stay on for all of thirty yards and was really
going quite well when I hit a stone which swerved the front wheel,
giving me the choice of falling off or going straight into the canal. I
fell off, with the maids coming clattering to my rescue crying: '*Ara!
Ara!*' while wicked Aiko just stood by the gate laughing.

After this we sent for two rickshas and, leaving the bicycle with
its back wheel padlocked, rode up to the Ginza pulled by two *kuru-*

maya men who must have thought we were both foreigners and who enlivened the journey, at least for Aiko, by a shouted exchange as they padded along on the subject of the likely morals of their two passengers, conclusions not very complimentary. Aiko was furious, but contained herself until we got to Matsuzakara's store, when she then let out a stream of what I don't think was very high-class Japanese, at which their jaw muscles went slack. I know she did not tip them.

We went up in the newly installed American electric elevator which clanked and gave me the feeling that it might go on strike at any moment and simply drop us four or five floors to the cellar. Our destination was the ladies' foreign gown department which Aiko says dresses a number of the court ladies, as it used to do her when she was one of them. All I can say to that is that it can't be a very well-dressed Court. A number of the 'models', mounted on what appeared to be headless sewing dummies, were the last word in 1890 styles and looked as though they had been sitting there ever since, collecting dust. Aiko noticed my reaction and told me about a garden party she had once attended where the ladies were mostly dressed by this department in 'foreign style', and where one of them was wearing an enormous cartwheel hat decorated with ostrich plumes. The moths had got at the hat and every time the lady bowed a plume fell out. Palace protocol is strict at these parties, demanding that you stay in the place to which you have been assigned by rank, and by the time the occasion was drawing to its close the court lady, still bowing, was surrounded by a kind of witches' circle of ostrich feathers.

Aiko was on the hunt for what she called a useful two-piece she could wear for cycling and though we had a good look there was nothing remotely approximating to this. I was even more serious about looking than she, for Aiko is now threatening to scandalize Tokyo by sending to London or New York for a pair of the bicycle bloomers that are currently the fashion for more daring ladies. I'm quite certain that if she wore those here the police would arrest her on suspicion of being an anarchist. There are times when I wonder if she is not one of these at heart.

In the end the saleslady, herself wearing a charming dark kimono, poor advertising for what she had to sell, took us into a curtained booth and presented 'fashion' books in which we were to search for a suitable made to measure outfit. The books weren't dated and the patterns could well have been the sort of thing Mama might have ordered about the time I was born. Finally we were bowed from the department with Aiko no nearer than she had been to a replacement for worn and shrunken tweeds brought from England many years ago, but still nearer to being up to the minute than Matsuzakara's offerings.

Tsukiji, Tokyo,
Sept. 23

I gave my first luncheon-party, with the same guest list as the only other Tokyo luncheon-party I have been to, Aiko and Miss Bassett-Hill. Since I have no dining-room we had it Japanese style on a low table about which we sat on cushions, the meal a compromise between my ambitions for it and what I knew Fukuda San had hopes of achieving, the main dish one of her flattish omelettes, this time considerably flatter than usual, with pieces of chicken poking out of it as though trying to escape from being held down under an eggy blanket. We started safely enough with a tin of Crosse and Blackwell's imported consommé which I picked up, at a price, in Matsuzakara's new luxury food department, finishing with the delicious soft persimmons which are in season just now, and very cheap, I got six for ten sen which Fukuda says was far too much to pay. A wine I did not attempt, certain that whatever I got would disappoint Miss Bassett-Hill, and was glad afterwards when I saw her wince over her first sip of imported Best British Sherry.

Miss Bassett-Hill wishes me to call her Alicia, I suspect not so much as an indication of our increasing intimacy as the fact that it embarrasses her to have to call someone in my position *Mrs* Collingsworth or Mackenzie, so prefers to use Mary. I think she had a slight struggle with her conscience about a relationship with someone who apparently holds lightly vows taken in an Anglican service and blessed by a Bishop, also High Church. However, she is by nature incapable of being truly censorious or casting even so much as a small pebble at hardened sinners, which is probably why the list of her converts will never be very long. In spite of that gaunt, black look she is a dear, and very merry as well, the setting for her laughter making it the more catching because it seems so highly improbable. In many ways I would like to copy her, though without wearing the clear markings of spinsterhood which I never could now anyway. Alicia is what Aiko never can be, highly civilized.

My guests did not leave until nearly four, refusing tea, Aiko riding off on two wheels.

12

§

13 Tsukiji San Chome,
Tokyo,
Sept. 26, 1905

Kentaro came yesterday. I was out in the garden by the fishpond with
Tomo on a quilt beside me. Misao was sewing up the pieces of a
winter kimono she had stripped down for washing and dried on a
board to save ironing. We heard the gate, but thought it was the
bean curd seller. Fukuda received him in the vestibule, telling him
where I was. He came suddenly around the end of the bamboo
fencing and stood looking at me. I had never seen him in Japanese
dress, except light kimonos, the full *hakama* and over-garment
making him seem taller and at the same time almost square. What
he was wearing was in muted tones of browns and greys which
made him look like one of the *samurais* I had seen portrayed at the
Kabuki, all he lacked was the topknot headdress and two swords
pushing out one side of the haori coat.

Misao, in a kind of panic, gathered up her sewing and went scut-
tling between Kentaro and me along the stepping-stones, bowing
all the way. She mounted the verandah and disappeared. Kentaro
came forward slowly, his eyes on me. It was almost as though he had
not yet seen Tomo, the baby drowsy under the last rays of afternoon
sun, not moving. I got up, pushing against an ornamental rock to
do it. What I said was in Japanese, a phrase of welcome I have heard

my maids use many times: '*Dozo o-hairi nasai.*' Without smiling he said in English: 'What are you inviting me into, Mary? The pond?'

I think I held out my hands, I don't really know. At any rate he took both of mine in his, which now seems a strange thing for a Japanese man to have done, for you never see them touch their women unless it is to shove them on, or when loading up a wife with whatever has to be carried. Kentaro and I stood holding hands, looking at each other. What I felt was a kind of hunger. I remembered feeling it as I walked up a path in the Western Hills. Afterwards it was the thing I tried to put from my mind first, before all the other things that had to go, too, if I was truly to own myself again. I don't want to own myself. I don't have to try to now.

I was the one who first looked at Tomo. Kentaro seemed almost reluctant to do this himself, letting go my hand and turning slowly. He must have stared for nearly a minute, then said: '*Yappari nihon-jin desu ne?*' The half question was not really for me, but I answered it: 'Yes, he is a Japanese.'

Kentaro looked startled. It might almost have been that by beginning to learn his language I was in some way invading a part of his life he wanted to keep away from me. He asked if I had a teacher and I told him I had picked up what I knew from the maids, carefully not mentioning Aiko. It isn't just instinct which tells me he isn't going to like the news about my friendship with the unconventional Baroness.

When Kentaro said he would have supper here I knew he meant to stay the night. I carried Tomo inside, putting him down on a quilt inside a square of slats I had ordered made by a local carpenter. Kentaro followed me up on to the matting and suddenly said in a loud voice: 'What's that thing?' I explained that it was to keep the boy safe, that soon he would be crawling about and could fall off the verandah on to one of the paving stones, a height of more than two feet. Kentaro said abruptly, almost with violence: 'Take it away! My son is not to be put in a cage.' Then he added that he would watch over our baby while I was out helping the maids prepare the meal.

It was a dismissal. He wanted to be alone with the child. He had not asked Tomo's name and I hadn't used it in front of him. Perhaps what I chose to call our son didn't matter?

I went out of the room and stood in the narrow passage behind the vestibule, suddenly wanting to be able to hate Kentaro. I had been ordered out into the woman's role, leaving the master of the house sitting by the fire box to smoke a cigarette. I could hear the maids twittering with excitement in the kitchen, but the last thing I could have done was join them there where there was absolutely nothing for me to do. Misao, usually a sweet child, can also have the black sulks, and what those two wanted now was to be alone, working together in a great clatter of gossip about Kentaro. Any suggestion from me about a supper dish would be deeply resented. They were Japanese, didn't I think they knew what a Japanese man would like to eat?

I could have gone out for a walk, but instead climbed the stairs to the little bedroom I am using. Here the pushed back *shoji* gave me what I am coming to think of as a Japanese view, nothing open at all, a hemmed-in pattern of curving tiled roofs plus the tops of trees coming up from our little garden and the tightly fenced gardens of neighbours. With the canal beyond the road it would have been possible to have quite an open vista, but the house had been built to face almost west and all I could see, unless I craned my neck, was the samisen player's unpruned kiri tree, whose sprawling branches and elephant ear leaves shelter the nests of a hundred sparrows.

I sat down in the Japanese manner, something I have been practising, and which is no longer as painful as it was, my behind supported by my heels. You don't often see men sitting like this, in fact I never have, it was probably devised by them as a means of keeping their women docile through continuing discomfort. The odd thing is that when a woman sits any other way in these houses she looks quite dreadful, a sprawling hoyden, as completely out of keeping with her background as my wooden pregnancy chair which these days is kept well out of sight at the end of one of the verandahs. I sometimes use it still in the evening but in the morning it is always tidied away again out of sight, without any queries as to whether I might want to sit on it during the day. What was tolerated while I was carrying Tomo is now an object of a contest between the maids, particularly Misao, and me. In this little war of wills the two Japanese girls are quite as stubborn as I am, and I feel that I am only being loaned the use of this house, allowed to play strange games in it like having two ladies to lunch, but that it really belongs, by the right of their race, to Misao and Fukuda. One thing I have not done is respond to Misao's suggestions, made in the half mime language we have evolved, that she be allowed to turn that brightly flowered silk into a kimono for me. I have no intention of being seen, or allowing Kentaro to see me, decked out in the kind of costume by which one can always identify the whore at the Kabuki theatre.

No sound came from below as I settled by the low, open window with its miniature balcony on which Misao had set a dwarf pine in a blue glazed pot where it would benefit from the autumn rains. Tomo certainly wasn't protesting at being alone with his father and I half wondered if there was some mysterious form of communication possible between males, and the baby was quietly expressing relief at this reprieve from an endless association with doting females. Just recently I have realized that there can be something a little frightening about having a child that half belongs to another race, as though from the very start, almost while its eyes are still unseeing, you can sense the areas of total strangeness that will always remain. With Jane I had imagined that she looked at me with eyes holding knowledge that could never have been gained just from her tiny experience of living, but with Tomo it isn't that, something hurtful, the inevitability of being pushed out and a door shut behind you, just as Kentaro had pushed me out and sent me about a woman's business. But a woman's business isn't available here, I cannot cook and scrub and forget.

The sunset was beautiful. Though we are quite near the Ginza and the business centre, the noises of the city are never very loud. Rather more it is the sense of the river near, the hootings of small steamers and tugboats, these sometimes sternly answered by the great bronze bell at the Hongwanji temple. In the house next door the samisen began, as it often does at the sad hour. Though I have never seen her I imagine the player to be an elderly widow, that slow twanging seems like an endless song of life past, and perhaps only half regretted, so full of pain. I sat listening and my resentment stilled, as though I had been reminded that it was quite pointless, and after a time my body began to ache all over as it does when held in that position, but I didn't move, I didn't relax, the disciplines of this country have already begun to seep into my blood.

I heard when Misao dared to disturb the Lord and Master below with the suggestion that he might like his supper. I waited until I was sure there had been time for her to set up the table, and then descended the almost ladder stair without being summoned, to find Kentaro seated cross-legged in the baby's corner of the room making origami paper toys, a little processional of completed ones marching towards the small quilt. The sight seemed to stop my heart.

The samurai who had suddenly called on us had taken off his haori coat which Misao must have tidied away, and appeared utterly intent on what he was doing, entertaining an infant. Tomo was lying on his stomach, a position he only rarely rolls himself into, and I was sure his father's hands must have turned him over, settling him like that. Tomo lay absolutely still, black eyes fixed on fingers working paper. I thought I had come in silently but Kentaro turned his head and then smiled. It was the smile I remembered from the temple, which ripped away a soldier's years.

Later we made so much noise in that little upstairs room that it might almost have been one of the small earthquakes. Tomo, left below, woke and started to yell. I tried to get up to go to him but Kentaro held me. After a while we heard Misao coming from the maids' room and then her voice singing the little song she uses often, this always seeming to me like a cross between a lullaby and a marching tune.

Tsukiji, Tokyo,
October 9th, 1905

I spend my days waiting for him to come. He never tells me when he is going to, sets no times, makes no promises. On Tuesday he brought me what a Japanese woman might use as a sash ornament, a gold brooch with three small rubies. I have a feeling that the maids are watching me in a way they never have before, something intense now about their curiosity which makes me uncomfortable. There can be no doubt at all that Tomo recognizes his father, the baby's interest when Kentaro arrives quite marked.

This morning I tried to put some kind of normal control over feeling by writing to Marie, attempting the light view of things in the way I have done quite easily before, but the words wouldn't come. I have heard nothing from Aiko and am sure she is keeping away because she knows Kentaro is back and visiting me. I still haven't said anything about her to him, there has been no occasion to, and he never asks me questions about anything. Though he is almost always kind, I have the feeling there is no room in his life for him to consider me too deeply. This may be unfair. But there is no understanding between us of what the other is thinking. He may be completely incurious about what is in my mind. The second wife is for relaxation, you have a duty towards her, but it is a much lighter duty than you bear towards a first wife. Perhaps this is something I'm imagining from my own uncertain situation. It is uncertain because, though I am now sure Kentaro will always look after me, I want more than what we are giving each other. I don't really know what that more could be, but I want it anyway.

Tsukiji, Tokyo,
Oct. 11, 1905

I'm sure Kentaro knows I cannot have any more children and is glad of this. He must have seen Dr Ikeda. Is it possible that this was something arranged, that after Tomo there could be no others? No, that could not be, not in a hospital like St Luke's. And I have heard that Dr Ikeda is a Christian. I must not let myself think these things.

Yesterday Kentaro told me that Fukuda San will be leaving at the end of the month. Her mother is ill at home in Sagami Prefecture, and needs to be looked after. Somehow this seems an excuse that has been used often before and it leaves me wondering whether, for some reason, he does not approve of the girl? I thought I noticed the other day that Fukuda had been crying, but this was possibly from worry about her mother. I shall miss her. She is in many ways more mature than Misao, and though Misao is really Tomo's nurse I feel much happier about leaving the baby when I know that Fukuda will be there to look after him. In fact I just don't go out unless I'm sure both of them will be home and, even then, on outings with Aiko I'm suddenly hit by spasms of worry about all the things that might happen, including fire, that great bogey of Tokyo life which has come to haunt me, too. The earthquakes are just Kentaro's dragon twitching. In a brick house I might be nervous but only light wood and paper round about gives the feeling that you wouldn't be trapped. Alicia says that the heavy tile roofs are the real danger, that they sometimes come down all in one piece over the collapsed framework of the houses, like a lid.

Since Kentaro's return I haven't once been in the city, only going for walks down to the river, sometimes with Misao carrying Tomo tied on her back in the Japanese fashion. I don't really approve of this method of taking the baby out for it seems likely that Aiko is right when she says that tiny legs straddled across a woman's spine have made countless generations here bow-legged. There is no doubt that Kentaro is slightly so, in spite of all the hard exercise to which he has subjected his body.

I am a sort of half prisoner in this house again, after having broken free for a time, Kentaro never suggesting that we go anywhere together. It is not the thing for men of his class in society to be seen in public with their wives of either category, first or second. It is as though, having expensively established a woman in a house, they expect to find her in it at any time of day or night.

One of the things I am determined to do, whether this is approved of or not, is learn the language properly. I cannot go on living in a country in which I am unable to really communicate with the people. I want a teacher, and may even learn to read and write in spite of all those thousands of characters that have to be memorized if you are going to do this.

The nights are beginning to have a real chill now, winter with its huddling over charcoal braziers not far off. I can't see why one couldn't have a coal or wood stove in these houses. It could be mounted on a cement base and though not very pretty, what a comfort when Tokyo's wet snow is coming down outside. I will mention this to Kentaro when he is in a better mood. He is odd just now, not coming sometimes for two days, once not for three, saying very little while with me, as though he was here to forget what was troubling him, probably a family matter. I have to keep reminding myself that he has another complete world in his other Tokyo house, and, with four children, no doubt many problems about which he would never speak to me. He has never mentioned his other family and I'm quite certain has never told his wife about Tomo. Of course she knows about me and the boy just as I know about her.

I wrote a longish letter to Mama, to which there will be no reply, of course. I have never been able to write to her at any length before since coming to Japan but suddenly she has become utterly remote. I remember that world in Edinburgh only through a kind of haze of what has happened since, so am released to talk to her on paper as though we were only quite friendly acquaintances instead of me being the daughter she has lost to total sin. I was reading over what I had written when suddenly the thought came . . . supposing Tomo should some day write to me like this, from the great and safe distance of strangeness? Tears came to my eyes, half for Mama, half for me. I hope I am not getting too emotional. Kentaro won't like it if I show signs of this.

In spite of the shrinking sun this garden is still warm in the early afternoon and I was out there today in my wicker chair reading translations of Japanese poems, these having been put into English by a professor of Literature at Tokyo University who comes from Oxford. It is his idea that all poetry must be made to rhyme and it seems to me he has made jingles out of the sentiments. Kentaro arrived suddenly as he often does and just took the book out of my hand, standing for minutes to turn over the pages. Then he handed the poems back and said one word: '*Kusai.*' Fukuda uses that word every time I bring home cheese from a Ginza shop. The meaning is, it stinks.

I suggested he write me another poem, like the Western Hills one. He stared down: 'You kept that, Mary?' I said that of course I had and that if he didn't like the idea of writing poetry in cold blood, then we could have a little competition between us, which is after all a favourite Japanese game. He finds it very difficult to refuse a direct challenge of any kind, so at once sat down cross-legged on the paving, accepting paper and pencil. However, inspiration came to me first. In the pool, half hidden by floating leaves, was one of Misao's goldfish, poisoned as usual. I wrote, refusing to follow the Oxford professor into rhyme:

> *Dirty pond,*
> *Dead fish.*

I handed the sheet to Kentaro and then watched the change come almost slowly into his face, the boyish look there again just before a great bellow of laughter. He threw himself back flat, his body shaking. We both laughed until we were practically weeping. Laughter between two is sometimes a closer act of love than any other.

Tsukiji, Tokyo,
Nov. 8th, 1905

Fukuda San stayed an extra week, which makes me think that her mother's illness can't have been so very serious. But she has now gone, dry-eyed when she bowed her farewells before going off in a ricksha with her bundles around her, but not looking at me either. We have parted forever without my knowing whether she even liked me a little. The only thing I am sure of is that she was devoted to Tomo. The replacement arrived two hours after Fukuda had disappeared, a much older woman, solemn and correct in a dark brown kimono and black haori. I could see that Misao disliked her at sight, and I at once had the feeling that with Okuma San in the kitchen the atmosphere in this little house is certain to change, and not for the better. However, it is only fair to give her a reasonable trial before I complain. Kentaro says the lady 'understands' foreign cooking, whatever that may mean, and no doubt if I am served delicate soufflés somehow contrived on a charcoal brazier I will soon be regarding Okuma San as a treasure beyond price.

Some days before she went I asked Kentaro if I should tip Fukuda and he said it wasn't necessary, she was well looked after. I then added that I would be tipping her out of money I had brought from Scotland and not from the cash inside his fish which was now safely in a bank earning interest, at which he suddenly grinned and said I could do what I liked. Kentaro is in no way mean about money. After Richard, I suppose I was expecting all men to be this, at least a little, but Kentaro seems to have a samurai's disdain for pelf. It could, of course, be a rich man's indifference to something he has never had to bother about.

I gave Fukuda twenty yen, which I'm sure is much more than she earned in a month. She was most reluctant to accept the money, almost as though she did not want to take anything from me, so finally I just left the envelope in the kitchen and went away. It was not returned to me.

I can never quite get accustomed to the way we can share a house and living patterns with someone for a long time so that, at least in physical terms, we think we know them well, and suddenly a door is shut or a gate closed and we never see them again, and soon never think of them either. Poor Yao of the unbalanced eyes who wept on our parting is rarely remembered by me and I'm sure he doesn't now think of me either, yet he was a real support in time of trouble, offering kindness when I had no right to expect it anywhere. It seems such a waste that we lose people this way. Even Jane, my daughter, is now just a shape beyond a screen, like a performer in that drawing-room game we used to play of hanging up a sheet to make shadow pictures on it. I sometimes wonder if under the disguises I wear to make myself bearable to me I am really hard and selfish, pursuing what I want and brushing aside anything that is likely to hinder me in achieving this. I have pretended that what happened at the temple was almost an accident, something beyond my control. But could it be that I wanted Kentaro from that moment at Marie's when he said there was a dragon under Japan? A few nights ago before we became sleepy I nearly asked him when he had first been interested in me. But I didn't, I think because I was afraid of his answer—that he noticed me when I became available. He would not have put it quite like that, but near enough.

13

⅌

*Letter from Mary Mackenzie to Sir Claude
Macdonald, British Ambassador in Tokyo.*

> *St Luke's Hospital,*
> *Tsukiji, Tokyo,*
> *Jan. 11th, 1906*

Dear Sir Claude,
The last thing I ever thought I would do was make a
personal appeal to you. I will never forget your great
kindness to me in Peking at the time I married Richard,
but as a result of what I did later you may well regret
that kindness. I have no right to ask for your help now, but
I do it because I am quite desperate, with no one else to
turn to.

I do not know what you will have heard about me and
what I am supposed to have done, but whatever stories
may be circulating I am not, as I am sure most people
believe, out of my mind. It has been politely called a
nervous collapse. I am in a private room here and
everyone is most kind, but I am watched. If this letter
reaches you it will be because I have been able to bribe a
cleaner to post it. The nurses or doctors would probably
take any letters I wrote, promising to post them, but not
doing this. Perhaps I am wrong here, but I do not think so.

*They say I tried to murder my maid. That is not true.
I must beg you to bear with me while I explain the
circumstances in which I did what I did. It may have
been a temporary madness of a kind, but it was the result
of having endured a week of misery so dreadful that it
cannot really be understood by anyone who has not been
through something like it. My son was taken from me. I
have no doubts now that this was deliberate, and had been
planned for some time, many little things point to that,
though in the days leading up to what happened I did not
notice one of the warning signs. Now, almost three weeks
later, I still do not know where my baby is, but what is so
horrible is that I am quite sure that everyone with whom I
have been in contact, the doctors, nurses, the police, all
know a great deal more than I do about what has
happened to my son but are under orders not to tell me. Is
it any wonder, Sir Claude, that I have been behaving as
though I was out of my mind?*

*I will tell you exactly what happened, and this is the
truth whatever you may have heard from the police or
read in the papers. On the day they took Tomo it was
raining, cold, threatening snow. I had been expecting a
visit from the man under whose protection I came to
Tokyo. He had not been for three days, and I was sure he
would come that afternoon. Misao, my maid, who was
also the baby's nurse, suggested that Tomo had not been
out in the fresh air at all that day and she would take him
on her back to the river before it became dark. I helped her
tie my baby on her back and then cover him with the loose
outer haori coat she wore, so that only his head was
sticking out. I went with them to the gate and watched
them go down the road towards the bridge over the canal.
That was the last I saw of Tomo.*

*When they were not back in about an hour I went out
to hunt for them, spending some time walking along the
embankment of the Sumida river. Then, because Misao*

*might have come home another way, I returned. My new
cook was there but no Misao or the baby. I was sure there
had been an accident. I sent Cook for the police. They
came. It was the first of what seemed like a hundred visits.
One man not in uniform spoke quite good English but
seemed to be trying to trip me up in what I had to tell
him, not really wanting to help. I asked them to get in
touch with my protector but was told that he had left the
day before to take up military duties in Korea. My only
real friends in Tokyo are an elderly English lady whom I
could not burden with my troubles, and a Japanese lady
who has been in trouble with the police because of her views
on some matters. She would have helped me and the next
day I went to the hotel where she lives, but she had gone to
Osaka and they had no address for her there. Or they said
they did not. After that I went to the doctor who has
attended me since I came to Japan and is still looking
after me here. He was kind and promised to help. All that
help amounted to was pills to make me sleep. They did not
make me sleep. The police said there was no trace of Misao,
and there had been no accident involving a maid with a
child on her back, no such patients at any of the hospitals.*

*Sir Claude, I lost my daughter through what I did.
Now I have lost my son, too. You can imagine what my
feelings were like during that first week which now seems
like a hundred years ago, and at the same time just
yesterday. I went out in the city on my searches, always
with the hope that when I came home there would be Tomo
brought back to me by some miracle. Instead there was
only the empty house and the cook, a woman who has no
kindness for me at all. I know now that she was carefully
chosen to replace the girl who would have helped me, but
who had been sent away. God knows, I have felt alone
quite often since I came from Edinburgh to the Far East,
but never like this, a woman walking the streets of a city
in which she could not speak much of the language,*

*looking for her son, going to the police time and time
again to beg them to help. There was no help for me
anywhere except from the English lady who wanted me to
come and stay with her. I think now that probably she
guessed what had happened to Tomo, though she has not
admitted this on her visits to me here in this room where I
am a prisoner. It was kind of her to offer to take me in,
but I had to go back to the little house in case there was the
miracle of Tomo's return.*

*They have taken my son to give him to someone else to
bring up. This was beginning to dawn on me by the end of
that week and as I lay on my quilts in the dark. I may
have slept sometimes during those earlier nights, but I do
not think so. Quite often I was sick. I had not eaten much,
though the cook kept bringing me food, as though this was
her duty and she would do it. I will admit that I hated
her. For the rest of my life I will see her cold face as she
brought in a tray laden with 'foreign' cooking that was
supposed to be what I wanted.*

*Sir Claude, I am very sorry to be making this such a
long letter, but if you are to help me you must understand
what really happened. The stories about what I did are
not true. The facts are that I heard our outer gate being
opened about one in the morning, far too late for the cook
to be coming back from the bathhouse. My quilts were
downstairs and I got up, going to the kitchen door,
opening it very quietly. The sliding door to the maid's
room was directly opposite and I was sure I heard
whispering behind those screens. I crossed the kitchen very
quietly and listened again. There was whispering, and I
was quite sure I recognized both the voices. I banged back
the door, Misao was kneeling on the matting in front of a
wicker basket, packing her clothes. She had come back
secretly to collect her things. She had never disappeared.*

*That was when I behaved like the mad woman they say
I am. Is it any wonder? Misao tried to run for the door*

*from the maid's room to the front court, but I caught her
and threw her down on the matting. I admit I was
shouting. I called the name of my son and then said;
'Doko? Doko? Doko?' which as you know means
'Where?' I am quite certain that was all I said. I know I
never said I would kill her. It is true I did bang her head
up and down, but it was against the soft matting, not
against a wooden pillar as the police say. She was not hurt
in any way. How could she have been, for she broke from
me and ran across the kitchen to the main part of the
house. I did follow her, but I was not carrying a knife as
they say I was. I did not pick up a knife as I ran through
the kitchen. The one they found must have been snatched
up by Misao. She had been meaning to use it to defend
herself against me. I thought she had gone into the
downstairs room where I had been lying but instead she
went up, probably remembering that the shutters up there
were much easier to open. I was still below when I heard
these sliding back. Stupidly I went up the stairs, instead of
going out into the garden. She jumped down. By the time
I got to the gate the street was empty, but I ran along it.
From a corner I saw a ricksha turning another corner.
She had come in that in order to carry away her things. I
couldn't run after it. I had to rest against a fence. By the
time I got back to the house the cook had been to the police
station which is quite near us, and there was a policeman
waiting for me. Very soon the man who spoke English
arrived and began questions again. Some of my answers
may have sounded wild. I was under guard all night
and then in the morning I was brought here. All this is
the truth.*

*Sir Claude, I am not sure whether or not, after
coming to Japan the way I did, I am still a British
subject, though I think I must be. I have, or did have in
the house—the police may have taken it—a British
passport in my maiden name of Mackenzie which I did*

*not return when I married Richard and was entered on
his passport as his wife. If that entitles me to ask for your
assistance then all I want from you is to find out what
has happened to Tomo. I do not ask for the Embassy to
try to get him back for me, which I realize would be
difficult, seeing Tomo's father is a Japanese and my baby
was born here. But it will be some easing of my mind just
to know where he is and how he is being looked after. Not
knowing is a nightmare from which I feel I will never
wake. Surely, as Ambassador, there is something the
Japanese authorities would tell you if you asked them?
I beg that you will do this.*

> *Yours very sincerely,*
> *Mary Mackenzie*

St Luke's Hospital,
Tsukiji, Tokyo,
January 17, 1906

They have brought me the notebook and the fountain pen I asked
for, perhaps because they are curious to see what a mad woman will
write in it. I hope they enjoy reading me talking to myself on paper
because there is no one else I can talk to.

Alicia came yesterday. In a way I have been keeping her outside
what has happened, in control enough to do that, and for her own
sake as well as mine. She may be a High Anglican but a large part of
her has become completely Japanese, and it is with that part of herself that she is looking at me now, thinking that to see someone in
my position is very sad indeed, but also that what has happened may
be for the best in the end. If I accused her of thinking that Tomo
will be happiest in the care of those to whom he has been given she
would be shocked, the English part of her coming into play again.
But the Japanese part would not be shocked. There is nothing
strange in this. In a very short time I have found myself picking up
some Japanese ways of thinking and doing things, and Alicia has
been here for thirty years, with only three visits to England in that
time, none of which she really enjoyed. So she is mostly High Angli-

can Japanese, which can't be so very far from being High Shinto Japanese, the same worship of ancestors.

I must be better to be able to write like this. In a way I am if I don't think of Tomo as anything more than my lost baby, and stop there. But if I go further and remember him lying on a quilt exercising his legs, then all the little bricks of carefully built up pretended strength crumble into nothing and I am back in the pain again, hopeless and helpless.

There has been no answer to my letter to Sir Claude. Perhaps it didn't get there. Alicia says that Aiko is still in Osaka, or somewhere away from Tokyo. Though we didn't either of us say it, what we both think is that she could well be occupying a cell in a southern jail, more of a prisoner than I am. Dr Ikeda spent longer with me this morning than usual, as though there was something on his mind he wanted to talk about but couldn't because he has never found talk easy either in English or his own language. Whatever part he has played recently, either willingly or because he had no choice, I believe that now he wishes me well, and more than that perhaps. There is a kind of bond between a woman and the doctor who has delivered her child, in my case Tomo's life so literally in his hands because I could do nothing.

It may be that he wants to explain why I am being kept in this hospital when it is obvious there is no physical reason for it. In that case he needn't bother, because I can find the answer for myself. I am here on orders from on high, not just the Chief of Police in Tokyo either, well above that. I know now that Kentaro is a member of one of the old aristocratic families who still have the power to do almost what they like without being challenged. He would not want his mistress to be taken into custody on a charge of attempted murder. Anyway, it is a charge that would be difficult to prove in any honest court, Misao's word against mine. The cook had run out of the house to get the police and was not a witness of anything except my banging Misao's head on the matting. I am sure that woman would lie against me quite happily, but I am quite convinced now that the Kurihamas want to avoid all publicity on this matter, just in case the real reason for what happened came

out, as it would, because I would see that it did. Kentaro knows me
well enough to guess how I would react in court. So I am being
'protected' in hospital, free to sit in a chair by the window looking
at what passes for a garden in the courtyard. In a country of beautiful gardens this is a very dreary one. When the weather permits
patients sometimes walk in it for a little, tottering around like ailing
prisoners in an exercise yard.

                                        St Luke's Hospital,
                                        Tokyo,
                                        January 23, 1906

Aiko was not in an Osaka jail, though certainly risking arrest again
in speaking to such women's organizations as exist in cities like
Himeji and Hiroshima of their rights under the Emperor Meiji's
Constitution. It appears that they have some, though the men have
been at great pains to make sure that the women don't hear about
this. As an angel of enlightenment Aiko is both dangerous and in
danger, as well she knows.

I admire her. She was born to the kind of life I would just have
accepted and enjoyed, but acceptance is not in her nature. Only a
hundred women in Japan like Aiko could threaten a man's world,
and the men know it. There were detectives wherever she went in
the south, in plain clothes, but not bothering to hide themselves
from her, the same faces at the back of halls, watching and listening.
She is sure they have orders to arrest her if she ever so much as men-
tions the name of Emperor Meiji again, so has to contrive her lectures on the constitution—which he is supposed to have given his
people—with no reference to him at all. Having now had some
experience of the Japanese police, I really am frightened for her.

We didn't for a long time talk about anything personal to either
of us, the conversation stilted. It was plain that she had to force herself to come here today, which is entirely my fault for, from the
moment when Kentaro came back, I made no attempt to get in
touch with her. I have earned her contempt as the woman who was
prepared to sit behind a wooden fence waiting her Lord's pleasure.

She knows as well as I do that if Tomo had been left to me I would still be sitting behind that fence.

We were talking about nothing really, I think it was the food in the hospital, when suddenly what has happened hit me again as it does often still when I think I am on guard against feeling. I just want Tomo. I cried out, as though it was torn from me: 'What have they done with him, Aiko?'

She had not been looking at me, but did then. It seemed as though there was something like fear in her eyes. It was quite a long time before she said: 'Didn't Kurihama ever give you a hint what he meant for the boy?' I shook my head. I told her that it had been a joy to me that he seemed so fond of Tomo, accepting him.

Aiko began to talk, quite fast. It was my misfortune that the Count had accepted my son by him, because this meant accepting Tomo as a Kurihama. Legitimacy does not matter in the least in Japan. What might have mattered would have been a son who looked like a Westerner. If I had been ginger-haired and green-eyed and Tomo had been born with both these things the Baron would never have acknowledged him as Kurihama blood. I had lost my baby because he looked completely like a Japanese. An accepted son of the Count was a candidate for adoption into a good family, probably somewhere away from the capital, Kyoto perhaps, or Osaka. He would become a *yoshi*, an adopted son, and as such take the family name of his adoptive parents and in due course marry their daughter. Aiko, being almost brutal about it, outlined what I had known vaguely from reading, that all the better families were prepared to keep their names going in this way. And there were few in the country, on the outlook for an adopted heir to their line, who would turn away from a baby of the Kurihama blood even though the mother was a foreigner.

The sickness I felt then made my protest feeble: 'Women have no rights at all in this country?' Aiko's answer was harsh. 'No. And not too many in yours, either. You lost your daughter, didn't you?'

I have not wept often since Tomo was taken. Once or twice I seemed to wake up crying, my cheeks wet, but mostly it was as though the terrible bleakness of my thoughts dried up tears, denying me that relief. But with Aiko sitting opposite I began to cry, not noisily, not with any retching sobs, but still something I couldn't control. Quite suddenly she got up and came over to kneel by my chair. I was leaning forward and she put an arm around my shoulder. She said: 'Mary, Mary,' and then, awkwardly, almost as though it was something she had never done before, or had done to her, pulled my head down on to her shoulder. And that was how I wept, for what seemed a long time. My misery was eased a little.

St Luke's Hospital,
Tokyo,
February 3rd, 1906

The British Embassy got my letter all right and after considering it for two weeks have returned it to me inside a large, important-looking envelope. Before I opened it I stared at King Edward's embossed crest, wondering if any of his subjects had ever got further from their monarch in mind and body than I have. The pages I had written under stress fell out to rebuke me for having appealed to officialdom in highly personal language. Their letter continued the rebuke. It was not from Sir Claude, but signed by the First Secretary, who hoped that I would find my communication to His Excellency enclosed and then went on in polite, formal language to state that His Britannic Majesty's Plenipotentiary in Japan was washing his hands of any responsibility of any kind for Mary Mackenzie, or Mary Collingsworth, or whatever she might now call herself. I am recommended to approach the British Consul who, under certain circumstances, is in the position to arrange the repatriation of British subjects to the homeland. It is pointed out that my son is a Japanese by birth, as well as by an admitted paternity, which could not be contested, and in these circumstances according to both British and Japanese legal practice the nationality of the mother is irrelevant. In the view of the First Secretary my son has not disappeared, but has been removed from the custody of his mother by a person, or persons, with the authority to do this. I will appreciate that the situation is complicated by the fact that the child is illegitimate and can only be legitimized at some future date if he remains in this country. For the British Embassy in any way to interfere in such a situation is totally out of the question as the Secretary is sure I will, on reflection, appreciate. He repeats his earlier suggestion that my present distresses might be alleviated, at least to some extent, by making immediate contact with the British Consul.

I am putting all this down as I remember it because I was foolish enough to tear up the First Secretary's letter the moment I had read it. There was also the suggestion that if, by any chance, I succeeded in finding my son and then attempted to take him out of the country, I could be committing a criminal offence under Japanese law. What he meant was that the Embassy wouldn't be sending me any food parcels to the jail.

A fortnight ago, or even a week ago, that letter would have plunged me into the pit. Today I was almost ready for it. Everyone wants me out of Japan fast, even at the cost of the British taxpayer having to find the money for my Second Class passage on a P & O liner to London. I am *not* going. The Japanese can try to deport me if they like, but somehow I don't think they will try that, because as a deportee I might manage to talk to a reporter of the *Japan Advertiser* whose editor is also the Tokyo correspondent of the London *Times*. Given publicity, my case just might make quite a nasty little footnote to the Treaty of Alliance and Friendship so recently signed between Great Britain and Japan. If that would seem to be making myself far too important, there is also the fact that the last thing Kentaro wants is a strong, harsh light beamed on himself and the Kurihama family. This appears very cold and calculating. It is how I must be now if I am to survive.

So far I am the only one who knows this, but I am leaving St Luke's hospital today. The clothes I had on when they brought me here are hanging in the wardrobe and during the quiet hour after lunch I shall put them on, then walk down to the entrance where there are always rickshas available.

Okatsu Hotel,
Ekoro Machi,
Azabu-Ku, Tokyo,
February 4th, 1906

Aiko's hotel is a very bad one, with a smell of frying greeting you in the entrance area. The bedroom in which I am writing this is not actually dirty, but it has an air of neglect, as though the maids really have no idea how to maintain 'foreign' furnishings. I will sleep tonight in the first bed I have used in Japan. This has a hair mattress and sagging springs. The only quite pretty things are the ewer and basin on the washstand, these of blue Dutch pottery, nicely shaped. I wonder how they got here? The walls are paper thin and someone with a cigarette cough is next door.

Aiko is in Sendai, as I knew, the reception clerk made a little uneasy by my query as to whether she would be back tomorrow. He will be even more uneasy when the police arrive with questions about me. Perhaps the same detective who watches over Aiko will do for us both now, though there is no need for the Japanese to economize with manpower.

Sitting here with my notebook open on a yellowed, machine-lace tablecover, I ought to be feeling depressed, but I am not. The excitement which seemed to sweep me out of the hospital, and then on to the house Kentaro had rented for his foreign woman, still holds. It is almost like a picture I have seen of Hawaiian swimmers riding those boards on the crests of monster waves, the whole thing a matter of balance, the least loss of this toppling you off. I mean to keep my balance. I shall also keep the money Kentaro gave me and use it. I have earned it, after all.

As I had expected, Okuma San was in the little house acting as caretaker, her surprise and shock producing the first real expression I had seen on her face. She had no explanations from me, I simply went in and ordered her to bring to the downstairs room my little cabin trunk which had been stored in an outhouse. I packed the suitcase upstairs and carried it down myself. There was a bad moment when I was taking off its nail a scroll painting of storks I had bought at the night stalls; one of Tomo's balls fell off a shelf and rolled over the matting. Then, on a ledge, I saw a row of those origami toys Kentaro had made for his son.

Okuma brought the trunk, panting and blowing, after which she scuttled off without a word. A moment later I heard the clatter of her clogs crossing the courtyard and I went after her fast, in stockinged feet over the flagstones. She was trying to get the ricksha man to go away. I shouted the worst words I know in Japanese: '*Dame! Bakayaro! Ike!*' She fled, probably for the police station. If she returned with a policeman it was to find the little house empty.

It will not, of course, take the police any time to find me, the reception clerk has probably already reported my arrival here, but I have no doubts at all that official red tape will work in my favour. Before any step is taken to keep me in semi-custody again the matter will have to be referred to Kentaro in Korea. An attempt to get me out of this hotel, even at night, could be a cause for scandal. Also, it will be known that I was in touch with the British Embassy, if to no avail. I think the police will receive instructions to do nothing meantime, except surveillance. The weapons available to me are flimsy, but I believe I am learning how to use them.

I think I understand Kentaro a lot better than he understands me. I tried to hate him for a time, to escape from pain that way, but I wasn't able to. He knew perfectly well that he could never have reasoned me into accepting the idea of Tomo being adopted into a Japanese family, so he did his duty again, and it may be that the way he timed it, just before he was posted, means that he could not bear to be here to see the suffering he had to inflict on me. I may be flattering myself that he cares as much as that. It could be that he is hoping that in time I will come to understand why he had to do what he did. I understand it now, but what I cannot do, and never will be able to do, is believe that it was for the best, which is why I cannot live under his protection any longer, and never will again.

I have gone back to praying, not for myself, as on that ship in a typhoon, but for Tomo. I have no sense that these prayers are being answered. When I think about it, I don't believe that I ever prayed for Jane, even when most miserable about her. Perhaps it was from a feeling that anyone who is being looked after by the Collingsworths of Norfolk has no need for God's succour as well.

Okatsu Hotel,
Tokyo,
Feb. 6th

Aiko completely disapproves of my plans, her objections might well be Mama's. Aiko would be willing to die for any principle to which she was totally committed but her dedication is still set very firmly against a background of family origins and her place in society. In spite of her divorce she remains *the* Baroness Sannotera, obviously regarding the new Baroness as a woman of little account beyond her function of childbearing. Behind all Aiko's zeal I sense a kind of charity, good works done by a superior for her inferiors. Privately, too, I am sure she regards most Japanese women as stupidly cow-like in their docility to the male; she would like to lead them in great processions with banners flying, and they stay home sewing up their kimonos and sweeping the matting, refusing to march behind anyone. Her mild respect for my brave gesture of leaving Kentaro's protection would be completely destroyed if she realized I am still paying for board and lodging with his money, and will continue to do so until my little hoard of this is used up, only declaring my independence by refusing to accept any *more* money from him if he offers it. Though she approves of my getting some kind of work—and even being paid for that work—it must still be something suitable for a woman of my class. What she declines to see is that, if I ever had a class in her sense, I stepped right outside it by becoming Kentaro's lover.

I must have her help in my plans, for I need an interpreter. I also need the Baroness's grand manner to help me batter down the opposition, which I am sure will be formidable. A grand manner is something I am no good at as yet, and doubt if I ever will be, which would have been a real disadvantage as a Collingsworth wife. The ladies in those Mannington portraits look as though, with advancing years, they had all grown into dragons established behind the family solid silver tea service. The people who appear to take to me do so because I seem such a nice little thing, totally unlikely ever to challenge them in any way, or to fight for my status according to protocols. I can see now that there was this in my friendship with Marie, no threat at all from me to the queen of Peking society who was acknowledged as such by all the men, if none of the women.

It is so easy to love those who can never menace us. I think now of that dreadful supper up at the temple when both Marie and Armand knew I had just come from my lover, and Marie's stony ignoring of me through the meal. She was outraged not by a moral lapse so much as the idea that someone on whom she had bestowed her affection had dared to step right outside the role assigned them. I think she also found Kentaro attractive and couldn't understand what he saw in me. Perhaps I was later forgiven when she guessed at what may be the truth, that the Count Kurihama simply took what was on offer. Still, he must have found me acceptable, I have his poem though I have lost his son.

Okatsu Hotel,
Tokyo,
Feb. 10th

I was quite exhausted when we got back here after what was clearly Aiko's triumph against great odds. It is when I am weakened by tiredness like this that all I want is my baby back, at any price to me personally. I took off the things I had put on so carefully for our appointment at Matsuzakara's Department Store and lay along the bed. I have no photograph of my son and I took nothing that had been his from the house, I will never see Tomo grow, I will never see the changing face moving out of childhood towards the man. Already he is recognizing someone else as his mother. I hate Kentaro. I *hate* him!

It is sometimes best to give way to feeling, not to try to control it. Just since writing that I am calmer. I don't know whether it is true that I hate him. His duty, once he has seen this clearly, or thinks he has, is the most sacred thing in his life. Everything else must be sacrificed to it. Working every day is what I need, to come back each night so worn out I'll be unable to think about anything.

Aiko won't tell me what preparations she had made for today's interview at Matsuzakara's but I think that finally having agreed to help me she set about this rather differently from the way she tackles most things, making use of contacts that normally she would scorn, these probably including her ex-husband. At two P.M. we went up in the elevator to the private offices of Mr Hiro Matsuzakara, received by his male secretary in a room that except for a desk, a few chairs and a carpeted floor was otherwise entirely Japanese, with inner paper screens hiding the windows of a modern building, the place for formal ornament holding a small plum tree in blossom and a scroll painting of a waterfall.

Aiko may have been forced to wait in police stations but she is not accustomed to doing it in the ante-rooms of Tokyo business executives of the new rich class, and I had the feeling, as clearly did the nervous young man, that suddenly she would push up from her chair and go sailing over to bang open that inner sliding door before we were summoned. She is very frightening to Japanese men, they seem to sense at once that she is likely to do the opposite of what they have a right to expect from our sex.

It is hard for me to tell the age of Japanese men but I would put Mr Hiro Matsuzakara in his early sixties, a round face, clipped hair, spectacles magnifying small eyes that are not benign. He knew a great deal about Aiko, though she would have disdained to know much about him, and they did not like each other. Instead of sitting awkwardly on the edge of her chair like a Japanese lady should, she was pushed back in it, her legs braced on the floor, as though this posture helped her to throw words across a huge, blackwood desk on which there was very little beyond a small vase containing a single, forced iris. They both talked very fast by turns, ignoring me, and I felt like a girl being introduced to a new school she knows she isn't going to like. The head of the school didn't want me to join them, either, and the fact that he has taken me on shows the pressures that must have been on him, Aiko's former friends obviously still willing to help her on a non-controversial matter like finding someone a job. Quite suddenly Mr Matsuzakara's head jerked around towards me and he used speech in marked contrast to the rapid fire Japanese, each word groped for and drawn forth with great travail.

'How—you—seru—crowses?'

It was a good half minute before I realized he was asking how I meant to sell his gowns. He had sent me that signal in near English to let me know that I didn't have to use my interpreter. I had absolutely no idea how I would sell anything, but had the good sense to stick to the housekeeping side at first, the way his merchandise was being offered to the public in the gown department, to my mind very badly indeed in comparison with other departments in the store. From this I warmed up to say that the gowns themselves were anything from ten to twenty years out of date, the dresses on his dummies would now be available in London only from a theatrical costumier. Aiko had to translate theatrical costumier, but there were no other interruptions, Mr Matsuzakara staring straight at me as he listened, only an occasional glint from spectacles indicating that his head had moved even fractionally. He was not unlike the frog on lotus leaf which is a common subject in their painting, that complete motionlessness likely to be ended by a sudden, huge leap. The thought of Mr Matsuzakara leaping in my direction over the top of his desk ought to have put me off what I had to say, but for some reason it didn't. I was heard out, then there was a long pause, then the secretary was called and someone called Hinobe was summoned to audience. Mr Matsuzakara explained who would be joining us.

'Hinobe he in charge Engurish crowses for raidy.'

We didn't have long to wait before the manager of the foreign gown department joined us. He was a man in his late forties or perhaps early fifties, grey in spite of black hair, grey European business suit, grey skin, slightly stooped as he stood, after three bows to his employer, only a short distance inside the room. Some say that the Japanese face is expressionless, but I no longer find it that. Mr Hinobe was looking at me with a deep hatred I feel pretty certain will never diminish.

14

༄

Letter from Mary Mackenzie to Madame de
Chamonpierre in Washington, DC, USA

97 Nishi Kogura Machi,
Otsuka, Tokyo,
Dec. 3, 1906

My Dearest Marie,
    You really are a faithful friend. I hadn't written to
you for a year but the moment you get a letter, and in
spite of your busy life in Washington, you sit down and
write to me. I can't tell you what this means, living as I
do. Thank you very much, too, for what you said about
Tomo, and also for what you didn't say. I know that a
good many people here think that it was all for the best,
though of course they don't put this into words to me. I
won't pretend that I am over the pain of it, but I have
adjusted, and that's something, I suppose.
    You say I didn't tell you much about my life here.
There really isn't all that much to tell. This is a tiny house
in a suburb where no one else wants to live, the place
practically falling down so I pay a very small rent. I get
up in the morning at seven to leave here at eight for an
hour's tram ride into the centre of the city. My
employment at Matsuzakara's means that at nine, or

soon after, I have started a long day of fitting European clothes on to Japanese women whose bodies were never meant to model our fashions. At one I go to lunch in a small restaurant behind the Ginza where the 'foreign' food is eatable, if not much more. At about five-thirty, or six, I get on a tram again for the ride back to Otsuka where my maid of all work has a supper of sorts ready for me.

The house has one room upstairs and two down and since the maid has to have one of the downstairs ones I am rarely separated from her by more than one thickness of paper. We are so close physically that I am sure, sometimes, that I can hear Hanako thinking!

What do I do for amusement? Well, I told you about my friend the Baroness and once in a blue moon we go to the theatre together, this really part of my Japanese lessons. Then there was a glorious three days in early autumn when I claimed a holiday from my reluctant employers and we went together to the Baroness's ex-husband's villa at Kamakura. I swam every day and sampled how the Japanese rich live, which believe me is very well in a discreet sort of way, their sprawling mansions hidden behind drab fences and modest gates so as not to irritate the proletariat, who are people like me. What the new Baroness thinks of these amiable relations between her husband and his first spouse, leading to the lending of houses, I have no idea, though I can guess.

I am very poor. What they pay me at Matsuzakara's is considered remarkable as a salary for a woman, but is still a pittance. However, I manage, and food is cheap here. I shop myself on Sundays, the store having adopted the European practice of closing on that day, though nothing in my suburb seems to close on any day and if you decide to do your marketing at ten p.m. you still find plenty of places open in which to do it. I no longer ride in rickshas, just take tramcars, the network now extended all *over the city and very efficient if very crowded. Almost always I have to stand on the ride in to work and the same all the way home again, which is a little trying after a day on your feet.*

I read a great deal, anything I can get. I picked up six volumes of the Encyclopaedia Britannica, tenth edition, at a night stall, these from KYS to PAY, and am reading them straight through so one day I shall be one of the world's best-informed women on all matters between KYS and PAY. Six volumes out of twenty-eight will be, after all, quite a slice of human knowledge. Then there are my Japanese lessons, given to me in return for English lessons, by a student at Waseda University who was what I believe is now called a 'pick-up' in America, this on a tramcar, shameless of me, but a woman in my position can be shameless and not lose any sleep.

I shall certainly not lose any sleep over Akira Suzuki, who is nineteen, very sweet, but has not learned to laugh much, deadly serious about German moral philosophy, especially someone called Kant. Since my volume KYS misses Kant by quite some distance I am not able to engage in discussions with Akira on this subject, a disappointment to him. At the end of our fifth or sixth session here in this little house he said suddenly that he thought a foreign wife would greatly help him in his career as a Professor of European Philosophy and would I consider marrying him? I was able to deal with that little problem by saying that in so far as I knew I was still married. He then waited for three more lessons before presenting me with what I thought was a book of colour prints, but turned out to be a series of very specific pictures of intimate physical relations between men and women. My reaction to a not very subtle suggestion of another form of close association was to wrap Akira's present in a ceremonial cloth, known as a furoshiki, *returning this to him next week along with a small bag of oranges. He is*

*very fond of the fruit. I am now waiting, but without
much nervousness, for his next move. It seems ridiculous
that I am not quite five years older than this boy, I seem to
feel a lifetime between us.*

*The situation at my work is rather curious. There is no
doubt at all that in the ten months I have been in the
department business has greatly improved. This has a
great deal to do with me, not necessarily as a result of my
skill as a saleswoman, though I am not bad, but there is
great interest in a foreign woman employed by a Japanese
store. There have been one or two newspaper stories about
this which brought a lot of women to stare, some of whom I
trapped, with a ruthlessness that might surprise you, into
buying a dress. The clothes were dreadful when I came
here, but are much better now. I found that the idea of
sending a buyer to Europe had never been thought of and
when I suggested that it might be worth the money to the
proprietor he was horrified, saying that it was up to me to
produce the designs that would be made up by a whole
team of Japanese women and girls kept up under the roof,
working both by machine and hand for long hours. So
that is what I am doing, though most of my 'designs' are
paper patterns straight from English home sewing
magazines. Occasionally I try something of my own, and
one or two of these 'models' have been quite successful in a
small way. The main thing is to design for short legs.*

*I have now persuaded Mr Matsuzakara to open a
corset department next door to 'gowns', something that
had never been thought of, and a great lack, believe me.
The Japanese figure has to be quite brutally bullied into
anything even approximating a European shape and we
are starting to make our own corsets up under the roof,
too. There is plenty of whalebone available from the new
Japanese whaling fleet.*

*So here I am, already senior saleslady and part time
designer, with a staff of two under me, a young girl who*

*suggests that she may one day have a mind of her own,
and one frightened matron, widowed, who wouldn't say
boo to a goose for fear of losing her employment. I am no
longer in fear of losing mine, though the manager of the
department would like nothing better than to discharge
me. However he knows, and more importantly Mr
Matsuzakara knows, that if they did get rid of me I
would simply walk down the Ginza to the rival store, the
much bigger Mitsukoshi's, who have already approached
me in a very oblique and Oriental way. It was as a result
of this approach that I got a rise in my salary from Mr
Matsuzakara.*

*I now receive considerable attention from this
gentleman, who keeps visiting our department as though
it interested him more than any of the others and chatting
to me in his quite terrible English, usually completely
ignoring the section manager, a Mr Hinobe. From what I
know of the Japanese male it is just possible that the old
man is contemplating enlivening his declining years by
taking a new concubine, and is considering me as a
possible candidate.*

*It is really quite extraordinary that someone as lazy as
I am, who didn't even learn to cook at home in
Edinburgh, and for years was used to doing literally
nothing, now finds that she really enjoys business. What I
do is hard on my feet, but I think I have a flair for it.
And as a sort of by-product of my work I am dressing
rather well these days, the sewing slaves up under the roof
seem to quite like me and, of course, I must be an
advertisement for the department. When you have your
holiday in Japan, Marie, you shall have a most elegant
gown made here of raw Nagano silk, which is my
favourite material.*

*You will think I have ambitions to be a couturière?
The Maison Mackenzie just behind the Ginza, perhaps?
There is certainly the money here to support an enterprise*

*like that, with more and more Japanese women going into
European dress.*

*I hope this long letter will let you see that my life in
Tokyo is not without its interests, sometimes even small
excitements. I have no news at all of my son. The idea is
that I never shall. The main reason now for my staying on
in this country is no longer that I am afraid to go
anywhere else, but a continuing hope that one day, here,
Tomo will be restored to me. I am still sometimes woken in
the night by the clappers of the watchman going his
rounds, coming straight from a dream in which I was
playing with my baby on straw matting. In those
moments, with my maid Hanako snoring below, I am the
loneliest woman on earth. But I have tested friends for
whom I sometimes thank the God who may be there. My
love to you and Armand.*

  Yours,
  Mary

       97 Nisha Kogura Machi
       Otsuka, Tokyo,
       November 9th, 1907

I am still feeling a kind of shock. If I write down what happened I
may see that it doesn't matter very much. Perhaps it is something I
should have been expecting but I never even thought about the
possibility.

The important visitor in Hinobe's little office beyond the
department was dressed in a matron's sombre kimono and dark
sash, her overgarment almost black except for a white flecking
through the silk. Her hair was not in one of the traditional coiffures,
but unoiled, and brought to a bun on the back of her neck rather in
the way I wear mine, this not flattering to a roundish face. She was
sitting on the edge of her chair, straight-backed, but not because
foreign furniture made her uneasy as is so often the case, the lady
was contemptuous of this form of support. On the desk was a lacquer tray holding two cups of green tea and a plate of biscuits. I was

quite certain that the lady had politely declined these offerings but if Hinobe had been snubbed he was showing no signs of being cast down, his eyes glowing with an excitement he couldn't suppress. He saw me come in but decided not to acknowledge me for at least a minute, his usual performance, so I gave mine, which was to announce myself after only twenty seconds.

He pretended to be startled by my arrival even though I had been sent for and was elaborately polite, but in the language reserved for use to inferiors. All this was just an intensification of the almost continuous warfare between us. I was invited to sit down, but since this would have meant fetching a chair from the other side of his desk, I did not. Quite slowly the visitor rose, turned, looked at me, then bowed.

I have now learned a great deal about Japanese bows. A book could be written on the art, which is subject to stricter rules than flower arranging. There are bows for one's social equals, these variable according to the circumstances of the meeting, and for one's superiors, bows for servants, tradesmen, even tram conductors, men's bows to women, always shallow, women's to men, always very deep, plus a huge assortment of women's bows for other women, these a complete language in themselves. Without saying one word a lady can place you exactly where she thinks you ought to be and more fool you if you don't know that you are being assigned your status, as newcomers to what seems the world's politest country never do. The visitor's bow was really very generous, classifying me as almost a lady, if not quite. Hinobe suddenly threw the bomb on which I had heard a fuse sizzling.

'The honourable lady who is now with us is none other than the Countess Kurihama.'

Hinobe, along with everyone else employed in this store, plus a high percentage of the people who come up to the department just to stare, knows the circumstances under which I came to Japan. These have been discreetly publicized, I expect on Mr Hiro Matsuzakara's orders. There was nothing I could do about that, so I accepted it. What I find it impossible to accept is the Countess's open curiosity, this strong enough to make her visit the store just to have a look at me. No wonder I had rated almost a lady on the bowing scale; by her vulgar action she had demoted herself, and she knew it. Hinobe's voice went almost falsetto with joy:

'The Countess has done us a great honour. Her husband, Colonel the Count Kurihama, has just been appointed military attaché to the Japanese Embassy in London and the lady has come to us, most graciously, to have a wardrobe made for her English life. You understand?'

I understood all right. For weeks I will have to be in attendance on this woman, countless fittings from corsets upwards, for day dresses, ball dresses, court gowns, hats, shoes even. Every time Kentaro goes out with his wife in London he will be looking at his mistress's handiwork. I don't think he sent her to me, I think she came herself rather than go to the Russian woman from Harbin who is now doing my job, rather badly I hear, at Mitsukoshi's.

From London we have imported adjustable dressmaker's 'shapes', wire frames designed to be altered by recorded measurements to an exact duplicate of a client's figure. I use them for any original, or semi-original designing I do, and our workroom girls now rely on them absolutely. The measurements are very detailed and I have trained a fitter to take them, but Hinobe, almost as though he had been so instructed by the Countess, insisted that I attended to her personally. That tiny changing room, with Kentaro's wife standing there in only a thin under kimono, created in me the kind of tension I found almost unbearable. I just couldn't get into my professional self at all. At one stage I was actually trembling, and I am sure she noticed.

She could tell me where Tomo is now, and how my baby is, but if I asked would deny any knowledge of my son by her husband. I didn't feel malice from her exactly, but at the same time I knew it gave her pleasure to have me on my knees beside her with a tape in my hands. She treated me as I learned to treat Chinese servants, you accept what they do for you without really noticing them as people. When I asked the Countess to turn around or raise an arm she did so, smiling slightly, but saying nothing, her eyes fixed on herself in a mirror. I am sure she looked at me sometimes, but I never caught her doing it.

97 Nishi Kogura Machi,
Otsuka, Tokyo,
Nov. 17th

Hinobe miscalculated badly today, just how badly has yet to be seen. I used the excuse of a slight cold to stay out of the way when the Countess Kurihama was here for the first fitting of a ball gown, sending in one of the girls from the workroom. I have no way of knowing whether the Countess complained about this, but I was called into Hinobe's office to find him in a towering rage. Who did I think I was, ordering in a chit of a girl for an important client like the Lady Kurihama? He used language that would have been an affront to a street woman, shouting. I was just about to walk out without saying anything when Hiro Matsuzakara walked in, the old man arriving on a typhoon of fury, so he must have been listening. I didn't wait to see Hinobe wither under the blast, leaving, but not to go to the Countess in her booth.

97 Nishi Kogura Machi,
Otsuka, Tokyo,
Nov. 18th

There was no Hinobe in the gown department this morning. At eleven the speaking tube called me to Mr Matsuzakara's office. Tea was waiting, with rice biscuits. I am to be the new head of the department at a salary of one hundred and eighty yen a month. It is an almost unbelievable appointment for a woman in Japan, the old man as good as telling me this, saying there would be great opposition to the arrangement, but that he was prepared to move with the times and give me a chance to prove myself. He knows perfectly well that I have already proved myself, otherwise he wouldn't have dreamed of moving with the times. He also knows that if I had been forced to go on working under Hinobe for much longer I would have walked out of his store, no longer in the least nervous about whether or not I could get other work in Tokyo. In the afternoon I found that Hinobe has been put in charge of the toy department at the back of the first floor. We shouldn't have to see each other often, if at all. I think the sewing girls are happy about the change. I owe them a great deal. If they had wanted to they could have made what I do here quite impossible.

Nov. 19th

The Countess Kurihama came in for another fitting. I did not attend her. As she was leaving we bowed and in my best Japanese I hoped she was satisfied with the progress so far on her projected wardrobe? With great sweetness she said that she was. Kipling wrote those lines about Judy O'Grady and the Colonel's lady being sisters under the skin. The Countess and I are *not*.

15

97 Nishi Kogura Machi,
Otsuka, Tokyo,
Dec. 8th, 1907

I must stop letting this horrible business haunt me. That poor woman was unbalanced, not surprising when you consider she had been Hinobe's wife for twenty years. I wish I could sleep. My nightmares are the kind you see when lying wide-eyed in the darkness. Last night I was driven almost to distraction by the gnawing of a mouse on the wood frame of the matting. When I thumped on the straw it would stop for a moment, then begin again. I'm not usually worried by mice, but I was sure that this one, so determined, was going to tear a hole in the straw and then start to work on the wadding of my quilt.

I knew there was something wrong with that woman for a good many seconds before I saw the knife. She just wasn't the kind to have any interest in our department, shabby, her brown kimono out of date in styling, with much longer sleeve pouches than you see these days, the perfect place in which to keep a knife. She must have identified me from a description Hinobe had given her, and had to see me full face, Western dress not enough, since all the salesgirls wear it too now. It was that stare which gave me the warning, plus the look in her eyes before she turned away and pretended to be interested in a long winter coat on one of our new wax models. A lot of women come to the department just to poke around, and with no intention of buying, so many in fact that I have had to evolve a drill for dealing with them. On a signal from me, or on her own initiative, one of the salesgirls attaches herself to the unwelcome visitor and gradually edges her out, just as a Scottish sheep dog might do. My brightest assistant, Emburi San, was coming forward when the woman dived straight at me. The blade in her hand was a good five inches long, raised well above her head for a slash down. The glove counter saved me. I jerked back behind it and the woman had to swing out in a bid to reach me. Emburi San, moving like a cat after a bird, struck the knife out of the woman's hand.

I felt terror for a moment or two, of course, but it isn't these moments themselves that haunt me now, it is the horrible circumstances surrounding them. Hinobe cut his own throat at night and bled to death seated under the pines in the outer precincts of the Imperial Palace which are open to the public. He was found by a park keeper in the morning, and wrapped in oilskin cloth beside him, in case it should rain and spoil the calligraphy, was his last message. He was joining his ancestors because he had no wish to continue living in a Japan where a faithful employee of many years' standing could be replaced by a foreign woman who had led an immoral life.

I can't read Japanese yet well enough for the newspapers and I have made Aiko promise to pass on everything that is being said about me in the Tokyo press, but I am sure she is not doing this. My maid Hanako pretends to be illiterate, or nearly, but I have seen her with newspapers and I know she is getting stories that are not reaching me through Aiko. The *Japan Advertiser* was discreet enough, calling me Mrs Mary Mackenzie, and avoiding the sensational, but its circulation is small and from the little Aiko has told me I would be a fool not to guess that the big dailies here started with headlines and are probably still running the story in the back pages. The Japanese press does not use photographs, or not that I have seen, and I don't think I have had my picture taken when I didn't know it, but I still feel I am being stared at in a way I never was before. I don't think I am imagining the hostility behind those stares, either.

If I believed in the Fates, which I don't, I would see them really enjoying a game with me. First I am allowed to find some quiet niche and settle into it, then, with no warning, they kick me out. I can almost hear the sound of laughter.

Hiro Matsuzakara has appeared to stand nobly behind me through this time, risking press criticism of himself and his store by continuing to employ a woman who has been the cause of a man's death. The fact is that I am still in the department for one simple reason, the scandal has brought in more than the curious to stare, it has at least doubled our actual customers, considerable numbers of the new rich ladies in Tokyo suddenly deciding that it is quite chic to get your clothes from a semi-murderess.

Dec. 14th

Aiko has just gone. She meant to frighten me and has. She wants me to come to live in her hotel again because she doesn't think I am safe here. She admitted not reporting most of the things that have been published in the Japanese press about me. My involvement in Hinobe's suicide has provoked more than just a small wave of anti-foreign feeling. One of the papers, in particular, has been doing its best to keep these feelings on the boil, with letters, articles and even editorials about subtle Western influences seeping in to undermine the foundations of Japanese national life. Though I am not exactly the text for these sermons, my name keeps cropping up in them. Aiko claims to have heard yesterday from a very reliable source that the British Embassy is anxious to get rid of me as a source of embarrassment here, and they have offered to make all the arrangements for getting me out of the country if I am officially deported by the Japanese Foreign Office. I don't know whether or not to believe this.

Yesterday the Countess Kurihama cancelled the order for her foreign wardrobe, taking two of the dresses we had finished for her but presumably going to that Russian at Mitsukoshi's for the rest. Mr Matsuzakara didn't seem as worried about the loss of this client as I had expected but then why should he, with all the other orders pouring in?

I am not leaving this house and going to a hotel. I have a feeling that my best chance of pulling out of this situation quickly is by continuing as normal, going to work and coming home. In a way getting off the tram and coming down the lane to my house is like returning to a village. The shops along the way, the fishmonger and the greengrocer and so on, know me and on Sunday I went into them as usual, sensing no hostility of any kind. It could be that this village of my lane is not in sympathy with the rest of Tokyo on the matter of me, and is prepared to show this by kindness. Certainly the local dogs no longer bark at me as I pass and a neighbour's fat cat comes, on sunny days, to pay informal calls.

Dec. 19th

My maid Hanako has gone. She must have started packing soon after I left for the store this morning, an honest girl who took nothing but her own things. Akira Suzuki has not appeared for one of our exchange language lessons for well over two weeks now.

Aiko met me for lunch today in the little restaurant I always use, not by arrangement, she just showed up. She now has another worry on my account, having decided for reasons she wouldn't give me that it is the secret societies, particularly the Black Dragon, which are not allowing the echoes of the Hinobe story to die away. According to her, the police force is riddled with members of these societies, all of them extremely nationalist and anti-foreign, some even believing that Japan should never have been opened up to the outside world at all. There doesn't seem to be much logic in their thinking for these societies now support the militarists who have been so successful outside Japan in recent years. Aiko, of course, is remembering the brutal murder of her grandfather which makes her take a pretty extreme view of things, but when I asked her point blank if she thought the Black Dragon might try to finish the job Hinobe's wife had started, she shied away from a direct answer to this, hinting that there might be some moves to frighten me out of Japan.

After all this at lunch finding Hanako gone hasn't been good for my nerves, particularly after that other experience I had of a servant disappearing. But I am not going to spend any part of my life hiding in a hotel bedroom. It would probably be useless to try to find another servant, so I will just have to bring home simple things for supper and learn how to light and keep going a charcoal brazier.

How brave I am! Later tonight I will probably be lying curled with terror, especially if one of Tokyo's sudden winds gets up to rattle the wooden shutters.

Dec. 21st

I think I am being followed. I try to put it down to imagination because I haven't really seen the man, if it is a man. It is more a sense of someone pacing me at a distance, even downtown, at midday. I have tried tricks to catch the follower but, except on the Ginza, there are no plate glass windows to act as mirrors. Side-street shops all have their wares spilling out on to the roadway under awnings and it isn't easy to slip into one of them for a quick look back. Probably I should suspect a case of nerves and go to Dr Ikeda for something to quieten them. Or buy a bottle of whisky.

The decorations for the New Year will be going up next week, bamboo and pine branches by every gate and every shop. I would like to do as others do, but don't know how to arrange for this without a maid to tell me. Matsuzakara's are staging an 'English' Christmas this year, trying to force on the Japanese yet another occasion when they must exchange gifts. There is even to be a tree and Santa Claus, and I am continually being asked for advice on matters about which I know little, for Christmas is not greatly celebrated in Scotland. All that Mama ever did was go to church in the morning. We gave little presents, certainly, but there was no tree and no plum pudding, making that kind of a fuss still regarded as part of Popish practices. The thought of being alone at Christmas doesn't worry me at all, but I do dread the idea of an empty house on New Year's day.

Dec. 23rd

There was an earthquake last night. The weather should have made me expect it, for after snow earlier in the month it was suddenly mild again, almost muggy, what my Tsukiji maids used to call an earthquake-coming day. It came about one-thirty a.m. while I was lying awake, first a hush as though the night sounds of the city had been switched off, then a rumble that could have been a heavily laden train crossing an iron bridge. As soon as the jolting began I knew this one was going to be different from the other quakes I have been through. I got into the wadded kimono I use as a dressing-gown and was on the steep stairs down when the bumping became like being in a railway carriage shunted by a drunken engine driver. I was thrown about, then lost my footing and slid down on to a square of matting where I felt as though I was being bounced in a blanket. Above the creakings and groanings of my house I could hear shouts from neighbours already outside in their gardens. My tiny one offered a real risk of being hit by a falling tile but I still had to get out into it. There was a great clattering of things falling off shelves in the kitchen as I made for the sliding outer door, switching on a light on the way. This showed the one feature of my garden, a large camellia bush, doing a weird dance, as though suddenly possessed by some passing devil and wildly animated to the tips of its shiny, winter-enduring leaves.

It wasn't easy to stand, I had to straddle my legs to do it, this half way to the garden gate where, with luck, falling roofs would miss me. Beyond the wooden fencing that encloses me like a package people were still shouting, and lights blazed all around, which was rather comforting for it meant still no break in the electric wires. The shake eased before this could happen and I was staring at the gate when a shadow near it moved. The gate opened to let the shadow out into the lane, then closed again.

I tell myself that it could have been one of Tokyo's many burglars on the prowl. I should go to the police, but I don't trust them any more than Aiko does, and anyway, what could they do? There are hundreds of robbers active on any one Tokyo night.

Dec. 25th

Matsuzakara's 'English' Christmas has been a great success, Santa Claus's beard rather wispy, like a Chinese sage's, and I found the music inadequate, an Edison Phonograph installed in the entrance hall with a girl in continuous attendance to wind the handle. Apparently there was only one seasonal wax cylinder available, this of 'Jingle Bells'. I have heard these machines in Scotland, one of Mama's friends was foolish enough to buy one. They may be interesting as a novelty but it is quite impossible to imagine any real music-lover listening to that tinny scraping for long. I was glad the sound hadn't the strength to reach up to our department via the store's open central well, though throughout the day, whenever I looked down from above, it was to see an apparently amazed crowd clustered around the horn. I suppose, if we must have new inventions all the time, it is better to produce playthings of this kind than new war instruments, but if the phonograph ever becomes really popular and widely used, it could be a horrible nuisance. The world does not need more noise, we have too much now.

I didn't have to cook supper tonight, this was provided by the store for employees who stayed on for the late opening, which was all of us, for we were 'invited' to by Mr Matsuzakara himself and you don't refuse his invitations. Our meal was sent in, boxed, from what must have been a fairly good restaurant because for once the sliced octopus tentacle was edible, if not exactly delicious. It appeared to have been steamed soft. Usually my teeth just are not sharp enough to gnaw through what feels like the leather tongue of a Scottish farm worker's boot. If the Japanese hope to encourage foreign visitors to this country the cuisine will have to be greatly improved. Western travellers are simply not going to wax enthusiastic over seaweed wrapped around a lump of cold rice, no matter how exquisitely this is served up in lacquer bowls and garnished with other supposedly edible forms of marine flora. A visual entertainment offered as a meal can be the cause of grave disappointment.

I suppose being alone in a little Japanese house on Christmas night ought to make me feel melancholy, but it doesn't, I am in bed with a hot drink made from powdered milk, conscious mainly of very sore feet.

Dec. 27th

I *have* been followed and there has been someone watching my house, but not a plain clothes policeman or a thug sent by the Black Dragon Society. When you have been reprieved from fear it is usually quite easy to laugh, but I am not laughing yet.

I came home weary and wasn't really thinking of anything at all as I opened the gate but without seeing or hearing anything unusual I knew there was someone in the shadows of the little garden. I nearly turned back into the safety of lights and shops but then had the almost fatalistic feeling that whatever had been haunting me must be faced some time.

My gate is fitted into a low frame which means you have to bend down to get through. It is very dilapidated, sliding on rusted iron runners, prone to coming off these and jamming. I stepped through, pulled the slatted wood shut again, but at the same time contrived to jerk it off those runners. Then I went up over the flag-stones to the front door which is also sliding and can only be locked from the outside by a padlock. I couldn't find the key to this and had to grope for it in my handbag, expecting at every moment to hear a step behind me. I got the door open and almost fell into the cement-floored vestibule, remembering then how the light in there had shown up the dancing camellia during the earthquake. If I left the door wide, light would shine right down to the gate. I found the switch, then turned.

There was a shape at the gate again, trying to get out. I snatched up a bamboo and oil-paper umbrella, running out with it. The man had his back to me, trying to pull the gate off its runners, when I hit him on the side of the head with my weapon. It was a mad thing to do, if he had been carrying a knife he could easily have used it on me then. But Akira Suzuki wasn't carrying anything. He turned, staring at me as though I was some kind of devil. I could see three red marks on one cheek from the ribs of the umbrella.

He didn't want to come back to the house with me, but I made him, taking him to the kitchen, setting him to fanning alight one of the charcoal braziers. I was hungry. Without trying to talk to him at all I prepared the fish I had brought home for frying. There was enough for two and when it was ready I asked if he wanted any, but he shook his head. I put on a kettle and he continued fanning to boil it while I ate. The kitchen is the coldest part of a house that in winter, with no heating on all day, never seems to lose its icy chill. The cooking braziers don't do much to warm things up unless they have been going for hours, which they never are now. Akira was shivering. I gave him tea and he took a biscuit.

I didn't really have many questions to ask; what I needed was just a few more pieces to fit into a jigsaw and he supplied them. Akira was one of those outer fringe relations who, in Japanese family life, are dependent on the centre core, in this case Kentaro. They were second cousins. Kurihama money was paying the fees at Waseda University. A meeting on a tramcar had been no accident, this boy Kentaro's continuing contact with me. It didn't matter that I had no contact with him. The little tests to which I had been subjected outside of English and Japanese lessons had been devised by the Count, my ex-lover keeping tabs on me, trying to find out what I had in mind beyond studying a language and selling dresses and coming home to a cold house, whether I would perhaps contemplate marrying again, and if that was impossible, be willing to consider taking an available young lover. I wonder if Kentaro chose that book of lewd drawings himself?

January 27th, 1908

Today a registered letter was delivered to my office in Matsuzakara's. Inside was a small blue book which gave me a credit of five thousand yen on the Nihonbashi Branch of the Yokohama Specie Bank. I re-sealed the packet and sent it back to the bank by a store courier, along with a letter to the manager stating that I wished the money to be transferred to an account opened in the name of my son by Count Kentaro Kurihama. I regretted being unable to supply them with my son's adoptive name, but had no doubt that if they would apply to the Count he would be able to let them have this information, as well as my child's present address.

Feb. 8th, 1908

I am twenty-five. Yesterday the *Japan Advertiser* carried a short item stating that Colonel the Count Kurihama and the Countess, together with two of their four children, had sailed on the *Haruna Maru* for London where the Count is to take up his new appointment as First Military Attaché at the Japanese Embassy.

16

97 Nishi Kogura Machi,
Otsuka, Tokyo,
January 17th, 1909

97 Nishi Kogura Machi,
Otsuka, Tokyo,
January 17th, 1909

I never imagined that I would return to this really rather horrid little house with a sense of joy, but last night in the ricksha coming from Tokyo Central Station, with my luggage following in another ricksha, I felt like singing, the tune in my head, absurdly: 'Scots wha hae wi' Wallace bled', which Alicia once told me Japanese Methodists have turned into a hymn. With me it was a hymn of praise to be back in the capital after a sentence of seven months hard labour in the Osaka branch of Matsuzakara's. I really wasn't far off tears as we turned into this lane with its very mixed smells, its still-open shops spilling wares out across the boarded-over drains, and men naked except for G-strings coming back almost parboiled from the bath-house. It was home. Even the dogs appeared to remember me and didn't bark. After what felt like an age of being an object of suspicion, derision sometimes, this was near bliss.

Before I left for the store this morning the postman arrived with a circular, to tell me that I had honourably returned and wanting to know how I had found Osaka? I said I had found it dreadful, at which he went back towards the gate roaring with laughter. As he slid it open he called out: 'You have become a true daughter of Yedo, lady.' I think he may be right.

It is absurd to label a mass of people anywhere as all of a kind, but that is none the less how I found them in Osaka, hardshelled, interested in making money and nothing else that I could see, the city a huge area of packed ugliness with apparently no lighter side to the living in it, unless you call a brothel quarter reputed to be twice the size of Tokyo's Yoshiwara the lighter side.

As I as good as told him this morning, old Hiro was mad to imagine that a foreign dress department in the branch down there would be profitable. Osaka business men don't want their wives decked out in Western clothes, they keep them at home scrubbing and cooking and having the yearly baby, certainly never wasting a penny of their husbands' money on fripperies. A little research would have shown clearly enough that, in the unlikely event of an Osaka woman being allowed to deck herself out in alien finery, there is absolutely no place in the city where she can go to show it off.

A cloud hangs over my pleasure at being back in Tokyo, in fact more than one. The biggest is that my seven months' work in Osaka has resulted in a complete failure, and Hiro is going to close down what was my department there, turning it over to men's dark serge European business suits for which there is a brisk demand. Though he has been polite enough, for him, all this has certainly put a big red debit against Mary Mackenzie as a success within the Matsuzakara business.

A second cloud which came up this morning is the fact that takings here have not fallen off under the management of the department by Emburi San. She is a dear girl, but behind her welcome I caught the glint in her eye of someone who knows now that she is perfectly capable of running things without me. It will also have occurred to Hiro that a Japanese girl, who earns about half of what he pays me, has been successful in my role for seven months. Also, as a 'foreign' attraction I am not nearly so interesting as I was a few years ago, if in the least interesting. The department could coast for a very long time on the ideas I have put into it, and it could be that Emburi San is capable of producing new ideas that would work as well as mine have done. I don't believe, either, that these days Mitsukoshi's down the Ginza are just waiting to snap me up if I am no longer wanted here. Even in the relatively short time I have been in the country I notice a marked change in attitudes to things foreign; these were once almost an object of veneration but now the feeling about is that anything done in the West can be done here, too, perhaps better.

So far they haven't quite proved themselves on this. We have a sewing machine manufactured locally, selling for half the price of an imported model, but it keeps breaking down and none of the girls will now use it. However, I am sure these initial snags will be ironed out before long. Already the world is beginning to take Japanese goods, cheap cottons from Osaka flooding India, greatly undercutting British manufactures. It is in an industrial city like Osaka that you really feel their intense, concentrated drive to conquer as a people, which is perhaps one reason why I don't like the place, quite aside from its hideousness. In the new Japan which is coming foreigners will have no role at all. There will be no need for a 'Boxer' uprising to drive the aliens out by force, here it will simply become unprofitable for outsiders to stay.

97 Nishi Kogura Machi,
Otsuka, Tokyo,
January 23, 1909

I called on Alicia today, whom I hadn't seen for nine months, finding her looking quite a bit older suddenly, but still crackling with her usual wicked wit. She is certainly no dried-up old spinster, and her problem at the moment is what to do about new American neighbours who, though not missionaries themselves, are renting a mission house just a short distance from Alicia's. Her new neighbours apparently regard her as a pathetic, lonely old exile, and a considerable part of her life is now spent resisting their hospitality, which reminded me of how I had once resisted hers! In the autumn last year they had her to what they call 'Thanksgiving Day' which, according to Alicia, is an annual ceremony to praise God for having delivered them from the British. The ritual is observed with a meal larger even than the traditional English Christmas dinner, and poor Alicia came home to be violently sick, and then off colour for a week after this. She says they are enormously kind but that one of the things for which she has never felt a deep need is sympathy for her deprivation in not having ever experienced a husband, plus domestic bliss. She claims to be at her wits' end in stratagems to fend them off, the wife continually showing up with parcels of 'cookies', which again reminded me of Alicia's early attentions to a very unresponsive me.

I am to help her with the problem of these Dales by coming to lunch along with them next week. We discussed a suitable menu, Alicia wondering what on earth to give them to eat since they seem to favour all kinds of things never seen on her table like boiled maize, which you have to gnaw off a cob as it drips butter, and mashed sweet potatoes. I couldn't very well suggest roast beef and Yorkshire pudding, for I've had experience of Alicia's cook's raw meat and burnt leather, this almost certain to send the Americans home for their week of indigestion. I suggested cold meats from the new delicatessen which has opened up on the Ginza, but Alicia thought it would be rather odd to serve Jewish food in a High Anglican household to people she suspected of being Baptists.

97 Nishi Kogura Machi,
Otsuka, Tokyo,
January 30, 1909

I have met the Dales. Every time Emma Lou or Bob Dale used Alicia's first name, which was often, Alicia's eyebrows shot up towards her hairline, an unnoticed protest at the intimacy. She persisted in calling them Mr and Mrs Dale, but this was no leash at all on their informality. Emma Lou comes from a place called Pasadena in California which she had no intention of ever leaving, still rather shocked to find herself suddenly in Tokyo. He is from Nebraska, a state apparently held in some contempt by Californians, Emma Lou making more than a few references to her husband's farm boy background. I did not at once realize that Hicksville was not actually the name of the village in which Bob was born, but a generic term for places of that size in the Middle West of America. Alicia *never* realized this, and kept asking polite questions about the population of

Hicksville and what the weather was like. Emma Lou said the weather was continual tornadoes and the people went underground into reinforced cellars while their houses were torn away above them. Bob's retort was that at least they didn't have earthquakes which, in view of what happened only two years ago in San Francisco, seemed to have him scoring.

Bob Dale is a banker and an idealist, which is probably a combination you could only expect to have coming out of the United States. Over lunch he gave us an introduction to his business philosophy which seems to boil down to honesty as the best policy and, though I certainly didn't say it, I had the feeling that he is going to find this a shade naive as a working principle here in Japan. He is what he calls a total abstainer, something which may not last long out here, either. His wife says this is because he hasn't yet got over seeing and hearing himself being cheered down his college football field. Alicia served sherry and a white wine, Emma Lou sipping both and telling us that these days the Californian wines were better than the French or German, at which our hostess put on an expression which said that, though she had trained herself to accept liberal views, there were still some heresies which remained anathema.

Alicia must have shown her usual candour in what she had told the Dales about me. I was introduced to an Emma Lou putting checks on her curiosity and a Bob more than a shade uneasy in the company of someone who could only be classified, even when you kept a tight hold on charity, as a scarlet woman. He didn't relax until it became plain that I was really interested in his banking career and then suddenly he remembered that all sinners are entitled to forgiveness. I could just feel this thought coming from him while I was prompting an account of his interview in the Kansas City head office of his bank for the Tokyo appointment.

Tonight I have the curious feeling that the Dales are going to become important in my life, this very much like the feeling I had with Marie and Armand, that also from a first meeting, almost as though the accident of contact wasn't only that. I can't believe that there are relationships in our living organized for us from 'outside', and yet at times I find myself believing what I don't believe. This probably comes from not having a defined personality, or at least not one that I can define to myself. I look at people like Aiko, or Alicia, or Kentaro who seem to have absolutely fixed identities, wondering if these are the result of the accident of their circumstances, or something deliberately achieved. Kentaro could well be living by a set of rules drilled into him at an early age, but Aiko has clearly invented her own, these not in any way part of the world into which she was born. The hereditary factor may simply be the gift of a strong character, and strong characters arrive in life demanding a set of rules by which to operate. The rules can either be handily provided for them or laboriously acquired, becoming as vital to the identities using them as Mosaic Law to orthodox Hebrews. It is people like these who make a real impact on their environment and people like me who make none at all. I should be ashamed, but I'm not.

4 Hongwanji Machi,
Tsukiji, Tokyo,
April 19, 1909

Propped up in bed on an imported mattress I am back to doing what I did on the ship coming East, pretending that I am not keeping a journal, telling lies again, this time that I want to make notes on business matters so that Emma Lou won't be tempted to ask what I am writing under their roof.

I am staying with the Dales simply because I am not organized for emergencies like double pneumonia, tending to live with the blithe belief that these things happen to other people. Even in early March I was dragging myself down to the store where my performance must have gone a long way towards confirming old Hiro's thoughts that my usefulness to him is about finished. Emburi San did her best to cover for me while I blundered about the department or sat at my desk unable to think, but what she couldn't cover up was the way I looked, which made me chary of mirrors.

I thought I had a stubborn cold that wouldn't shake off until that morning when my alarm went at quarter to seven and I tried to push back the heavy quilt, finding I couldn't. What I was able to do eventually was crawl to the inner vestibule to meet the postman and it was he who got the word out about my near total collapse in a maidless house. Before noon Dr Ikeda arrived to take charge once again, and I was very glad to see him. He gave me an injection and about two came back to have me buttoned into a ricksha fitted with its winter hood up, the lower waterproof cover over my legs about the only thing that kept me from toppling forward into the road between the shafts.

I was less than semi-conscious through great stretches of Tokyo to St Luke's in Tsukiji, and the only thing I can remember hearing from Dr Ikeda after we arrived was an apology: 'So sorry, hospitaru bery furu. No private prace.' I didn't care whether I had a private place or not, all I wanted was a bed, and I got that, in a ward mostly of post-operative patients not one of whom, in the whole time I was there, disgraced herself by giving the slightest sign of pain endured. Japanese women bring so many admirable qualities to the process of being alive that I can understand Aiko's frustration at not being able to whip them up into concerted action against their much less admirable males. If the meek really inherit the earth then the women should have Japan, but I don't think they are going to.

Later I had the chance of a private room, but I didn't take it for two reasons, first, mobile fellow patients were looking after me in the ward rather better than the nurses, and second, I am no longer being financed by a member of the Japanese aristocracy. My visitors were Aiko back from a crusade in Sendai, Alicia bringing all sorts of thoughtful little presents like lavender water and handkerchiefs, Emburi San to present old Hiro's offering, a box of not very expensive pink and white rice flour dumplings tied up with ceremonial pink and white string, while she herself gave me a Formosan pineapple not easy to eat in bed, but sweet of her. Emma Lou Dale came every day when the crisis was over, treating me more like a favourite sister than someone she had just met once for lunch.

I was really startled when she announced that I was coming to them to convalesce, my immediate reaction a rather brusque no I wouldn't dream of it, which clearly hurt her feelings for she didn't come for two days after that. Alicia did, however, to tell me that

Emma Lou was pregnant and frightened. It would have been worrying enough having a first baby in Pasadena surrounded by loving relations, and the idea of this happening in Tokyo where, beyond Bob and a borrowed house, there was nothing but strangeness, led to a sequence of fears, the one opening out of the other. Alicia told me that I *was* to go to the Dales to recuperate, allowing Emma Lou to fuss over me.

I have enjoyed being fussed over. The Dales have inherited the furloughing missionaries' cook and maid, but Emma Lou insists on carrying trays herself and I hope my being here is of some use to her, for there is certainly no way I can repay her kindness. I am sure that Bob had serious qualms about allowing me to occupy the guest bedroom in a mission house but if there were any protests his wife stamped on them. I have slumped into protective warmth just as I did in that little house not far from here while waiting for Tomo to be born. This is a recess from real living and I don't want even to think about what is going to happen when I get back to Matsuzakara's.

So far Emma Lou has said nothing about her pregnancy, not even a hint, and I can't raise the matter until she does. I wonder how Alicia found out? Through Dr Ikeda at the hospital? She has missed her vocation, she should have been a detective.

4 Hongwanji Machi,
Tsukiji, Tokyo,
April 22, 1909

I was downstairs for a couple of hours today and when I came back up here and settled again into this welcoming bed I said something to Emma Lou about being in their debt forever, and she said we are here to help each other, surely, then began to cry. It all came out, the baby three months on the way, and her terror not just of the unknown in that, but a sense of the alien all around, people talking a language she can't understand, and even in this house sitting on other people's chairs and lying in other people's beds. She had been looking for a place to which they could move and make a home of their own but had seen nothing that she could begin to imagine as that. Had I ever had a house in this country that I felt was my home? I could see that Alicia had told her about the shack in which I am living now so we skipped that and I went back to the house Kentaro had rented for me. As I described it, Emma Lou's eyes grew bigger and I knew she had heard about the kidnapping of my baby, and suddenly I was back to banging Misao's head against the matting and went silent. After some time Emma Lou said: 'You're brave, I'm not. I just wanted to stay home, that's all. I thought Bob was settled in California. That's what usually happens when they come from the Mid-West. They don't want to go anywhere else. He never told me he wanted to come out here to the Orient. You know this, I never even liked going to a Chinatown back home. There's something about those places that scares me.'

I don't know what use I can really be to Emma Lou. Am I supposed to tell her that having a baby in a strange place is nothing to worry about? I am not going to lie to this girl.

Takayama,
Miyagi Prefecture,
July 16th, 1909

Kentaro's dragon has moved again, this time in a manifestation new to me. The beach here forms a crescent between two bluffs, each about a hundred feet high, on which the summer shacks are set amongst old pines, about thirty of these weathered grey wooden boxes that in winter are shuttered against the southeasterly storms that build up terrible force over unthinkable distances of ocean. An after-lunch close-down of all activity is traditional, something I accept happily enough, though I don't go to lie down on my canvas cot, taking the hammock swung between two trees. Today I broke the rules and a little after two walked past houses that might have been suddenly evacuated, not one of the hundred or so holiday-makers in sight, even the children forced to take naps, their scooters abandoned in rank grass, a baseball bat lying on a path. On some of the verandahs privileged foreigners' dogs lifted heads to watch me go by but not one of them broke a heat-enforced peace by so much as a growl.

I have got into the Japanese summer habit of carrying a paper fan wherever I go, flicking this back and forth for the little private breeze you have to perspire to produce, but otherwise I think I look decorous enough, certainly feeling half suffocated by the way I have to dress. I packed two long-sleeved white blouses for this holiday and by continual washings have worn nothing else, conforming to what is accepted as genteel in Takayama because I feel I should for Emma Lou and Bob. Particularly for Bob. I am very necessary to help him with Emma Lou just now, and he is appreciative enough of that, but at the same time since coming to a place where the population is about ninety per cent missionary he has had some bad attacks of unease about sharing a roof with a woman of my background, or rather being seen to share a roof with her, which is why I never settle into that hammock without checking that my skirt is down over my ankles. In this country it is impossible for a foreigner to come to a community of other foreigners without being followed by a case history. Mine didn't mean that the Dale household was ostracized, there was just no fraternization, no neighbour showing up on our verandah with a freshly baked pumpkin pie.

When I reached them the sands were totally empty, the sea with just enough strength to crunch together small pebbles at the water line. A few miles out, not seeming to move, was a sizeable sea-going sampan, its two ribbed sails set for the wind that might be coming. Grey overcast screened the sun but let its heat through, and the sea was so flat it had a burnished pewter look, visibility clear to the horizon. I was sitting on a sand dune staring over the water when that horizon lifted.

What had been a perfectly drawn line where grey sea met a lighter grey sky was now serrated, like the teeth of a very fine saw blade, and topping some of these teeth, flecks of white. The thing coming towards me had its own colour, purple turning to green under the uneven frill of white along that broken crest, but the sea between me and it was still flat, still polished.

I wasn't frozen by terror, I could run, already climbing the path to the bluff when the fishing sampan began to mount the tidal wave, sucked up to a summit where a sudden whipping of foam covered the boat before it was tossed down the slope beyond. Where the path turned towards the sea again, perhaps twenty feet higher up, I saw the *tsunami* inflating itself for the assault on the coast. Blood thumping in my ears had kept out the roaring, but I heard it then, almost animal, a great, continuous bull-bellow.

The wave struck as I neared the first of the pines, hitting the cliffs, impact an earth tremor. I fell. I didn't turn my head to see the ocean mount the land, wanting only to shut out the noise, continuing to crawl upwards, half expecting a tentacle of water to come probing for me. When I did look the beach was covered, and the sword grass dunes beyond it, a plantation of young larches shivering in a lake of swirling brine.

I stood to stare at the suck-back, a huge rake drawing down trees, grass, fishing nets, a wooden hut, scoring the sand and tumbling rocks to well beyond what had been low tide mark, exposing the gouged bed of the sea floor itself. Then I saw another vast wave coming.

There were two more *tsunamis*, smaller than the first, but repeating its pattern, as though sent to complete the destruction, that earthquake from cliff impact first, then the hideous thunder of dissolution against an unresisting beach, the suck-backs scraping flat what had been small hillocks of dunes. The last wave left behind it a sea of uncrested swells that might have been sent to us from a distant great storm, but there was still no wind, and a returning silence was punctuated by the howling of dogs.

I have spent the rest of the day dreading tonight, of what might happen in moonless dark, conscious as never before in Japan of the almost total physical insecurity in which everyone has to live out their lives in this country. Many of the natural disasters are localized, with a kind of personal quality, almost your district devil adapting his works to create a recurring terror. In these islands it isn't the vast earthquake or the huge flood that keeps fear at the back of the mind, but more the threat of an endlessly repeated pattern of lesser devastations, the seventeen typhoons that hit the island of Kyushu annually, and never miss a year, the volcano hanging over the peaceful valley, napping in the sunshine, sending up its innocent, thin white plume of smoke and then, suddenly one night, becoming a red, erupting boil whose lava may not reach your fields, but whose ash and pumice will, suffocating the rice crops.

I will never be able to look at an ocean's horizon again without remembering that these can lift. After those waves at Takayama there was no sign at all on a flattening sea of a two-masted sampan waiting for a wind.

Takayama,
Miyagi Prefecture,
July 17th, 1909

In a disturbed community Emma Lou, not surprisingly, is more disturbed than most. She is obsessed by the idea that her baby will be born prematurely and if this should happen while we are still at Takayama they will both die. It is no use telling her that we chose this resort because it is quite near Sendai where a friend of Dr Ikeda's is the professor of obstetrics at the university and that this professor has been alerted about Emma Lou's case. Not that there really is a 'case' that I can see, for there don't seem to be any complications foreseen beyond a slightly too narrow pelvic bone structure which is apparently unusual out here and worries the doctors a little, I think, though Emma Lou herself doesn't know anything about this.

I can certainly remember periods of acute depression myself when I was carrying Jane, but these weren't chronic, and I wasn't submerged in them. I think pregnancy has in some way greatly increased Emma Lou's feeling of the unreality of everything around her, as if she can't really believe that she is in this strange place, Japan, and that this is happening to her here. It is my guess that she blames Bob, not for fathering the child, that isn't the resentment, it is much more that he is responsible for placing her in this setting where she has to act a role, for which there have been no rehearsals, against scenery that is for her weird and unnerving. After those terrible waves she just lay weeping. Today she is up again, but not really moving, lying in that long chair on the verandah. She ought to have some exercise.

Bob and I have discussed taking her back to Tokyo, but the city heat was driving her crazy. I ought to go myself, I can't really afford this time away from Matsuzakara's when there is considerable uncertainty about my future in the store, yet it is impossible to leave these two on their own. I have a sense of being needed by Emma Lou in a way that I haven't felt from anyone since coming to the East, almost a total dependance on me. Bob has really caught the infection of his wife's fears and here, where he can't escape to his office, is beginning to wear the heavy guilt of the man responsible for it all. What a lot of nonsense is talked about the joy of having a first baby, it can be absolute hell all around.

17

Letter from Mary Mackenzie to Marie de
Chamonpierre in Rome

97 Nishi Kogura Machi,
Otsuka, Tokyo,
Feb. 19th, 1910

Dear Marie,
   I am horrified to realize that it is five months since
your last letter and nothing done about this from my end.
We always have excuses and mine are that since last
autumn I have been in one of those periods of change
which seem to hit me whenever I appear settled in a nice
comfortable rut. Actually, that isn't quite the case this
time, for I could see what was coming from some distance
off and, slack character that I am, refused to do anything
about it. The fact is that I am no longer one of Tokyo's
queens of fashion (if I can claim that I ever was), having
been dismissed from my job at the department store at the
end of September. From a sort of peak when I could do no
wrong everything started to go downhill. I was sent to
Osaka to open a department in the Matsuzakara branch
there, hating every minute of it, living in a dreadful half-
foreign hotel, with continual indigestion from half-
foreign food, and totally friendless. I had some

*introductions to people in Kobe, but it was too far to go,
even at weekends, so for seven months I had my work
which went from bad to worse, plus my own company.*

*I can't really blame them at Matsuzakara's for what
has happened. After I got back to Tokyo I should have put
all my effort into redeeming my reputation with the store,
but instead I seemed to have no 'go' left, and capped this
by coming down with pneumonia, which meant that the
department had plenty of time to learn it could get along
without me. Finally, on top of everything else, I took a
long summer holiday at a beach resort with friends, so it
really isn't surprising that old man Matsuzakara's
patience was exhausted and it became his painful duty to
get rid of me. I was very angry at first but, as with so
many of what look like injustices in this life, seen from
even a short distance away you begin to realize you
weren't completely the wronged victim. However, lest I
seem too noble, let me say that Hiro Matsuzakara will
never be one of my favourite characters in this land of the
rising men and the subjugated women.*

*While I am still talking about myself, which is ninety
per cent of the time in my letters to you, I'll just round off
about where and what I am now. I still live in my little
Japanese house in the far from fashionable suburb of
Otsuka, this a construction become so frail with age that
in the last sizeable quake I thought it was coming down
around my ears. I also have a job, or a series of jobs, these
found for me by friends who have become in my Tokyo life
something like what you and Armand were to me in
Peking. They are Americans, he is a banker, and in
consequence knows many American missionaries. When
Bob suggested that I might teach English in mission schools
I was totally flabbergasted, for reasons I really don't have
to explain to you. The Dales know my history and I would
have thought that the last thing they would want to do
was risk sponsoring me amongst the more solemn-minded*

of their countrymen. I think it was the wife who bullied her husband into doing this. Possibly, too, my obviously blameless life over the last few years—I have been working too hard for it to be anything else!—gives me a reformed sinner rating, and if so I am very glad, for it means I can go on eating.

Don't get the wrong impression, I am not a full-blown teacher shaping the destinies of young Japanese boys and girls; far from it, just a sort of special tutor for the backward ones who are too stupid to be affected in moral matters, or really anything else, by their instructor. I discovered after I had taken it on that I am doing a job for which no one else could be found, and one of the many things that is odd about it are the hours, late afternoon and up to nine p.m. I don't mind about this since evenings at home in this little house weren't really any great joy, and I now get back here for a late snack, fall between quilts, and sleep solidly. I don't have a maid, but the greengrocer's wife has supplied her daughter for casual cleaning, and I have mornings and early afternoons free to do my shopping, which I rather like.

After some years of a running war with charcoal braziers in my kitchen I have bought an oil stove to cook on, an American model, very grand, two burners plus a real oven instead of a tin portable one, and all this has seen me becoming rather gourmet about my food, needing a solid midday meal before I sally forth to face the totally blank faces of my assorted pupils. The stove has the added advantage that it really warms a place that used to be like the inside of an icebox, which is probably why I am becoming a kitchen girl. Before I was modernized, and endured chilblains all winter, I used to think with almost sick longing of that wonderful ugly stove in Peking, or your steam heating.

Sometimes I think about the dream flower land that was conjured up for me by those books on Japan you gave

me to read in Peking. I'm not being nasty, Marie, when I
suggest that your trips here were probably in the cherry
blossom season and your excursions out from the best hotel.
I remember you being ecstatic about Nikko, which I have
yet to visit, but you really couldn't have thought the cities
beautiful? In my possibly prejudiced view, and
remembering Osaka, Japanese cities are the most hideous
I have seen. Tokyo has charm but, aside from the Imperial
Palace with its green moat, not much to look at. In every
direction from a not very attractive red brick commercial
centre there stretches for what feels like hundreds of miles
(when you are in a bouncing tramcar) grey little two-
story houses, with grey tile roofs, the only trimming to this
huge, overloaded poles carrying the electricity and
telephone wires. The lanes are better, narrow and
twisting, and I am quite fond of my lane, but it is not
beautiful.

Since you were here the country is beginning to show
the scars of industrialization. Last autumn I went on an
outing with a Japanese friend to the same beauty spot
beyond Tokyo we visited together only four years ago. Then
we travelled by train, our view a pattern of rice fields,
and thatched roofed villages, and little shrines hidden in
clumps of tall trees, all these with the backdrop of the hills
which were our objective. This time we went by electric
railway, and the only thing I really recognized was that
backdrop of hills. In place of rice fields were factories with
black iron chimneys, and the villages had been replaced by
shack communities to house the factory workers. The
shrines were still tucked into their groves of tall
cryptomeria but didn't give the feeling they would survive
for long.

Tokyo is becoming bloated. They are reclaiming land
out into the bay and putting down factories on ground
still so unsettled the buildings have to be specially braced
against earthquakes. Did you know that if you were to

*come back to Japan for that holiday, and travelled via the
Pacific, the fastest ships for your journey are two Japanese
vessels, both built here, the Tenyo Maru and the Chiyo
Maru? When we were living in Peking there was scarcely
a Japanese passenger ship of any size that hadn't been
built in Britain. Now they will never use a British yard
again, except for ships of war. Apparently they haven't
quite acquired the skill for these yet, though they soon will.*

*I know you will be protesting, and I can hear you
doing it, but these are not a gentle, gracious people living
in their world of yesterday. Most of the women still do, but
practically none of the men. Even amongst my less than
average intelligence male pupils the learning is all
towards one end, practical matters, and practical means
one thing: making in Japan every single object from
pencil sharpeners to monster ocean liners, so that before
long they will need nothing from the outside but raw
material. When I went to Matsuzakara's we were buying
in almost all our cloth from Europe, when I left it was all
coming from local factories, even imitation Scotch
tartans. It is the speed of this change which is almost
frightening.*

*Perhaps part of my unease from all this comes from the
fact that when I was working in the store I did have a
sense of doing something in this country that no one else
could do so well, even though I hadn't been trained for the
work. Now I live on a sort of fringe, tolerated, but of no
importance, not even an object of much curiosity these
days. Allowing for this, I still don't think I am imagining
a markedly changed spirit in this land, the emergence of a
contempt for the West which the Japanese have been able to
copy in such a short time and soon may overtake. I can
now read the language well enough for the newspapers
and in articles and editorials there is a kind of strutting
arrogance which puts you in mind of the goose-stepping
companies of soldiers often to be seen in the streets.*

*I was interested in what you told me about Count
Kurihama as military attaché in London. Either his
social manners have greatly improved since I knew him,
or that natural reserve appeals to the English. We have no
communication of any kind. I made it quite plain before
he left for Britain that I didn't want any in future. I am
no nearer to knowing what is happening to my son than I
was when I last wrote. In my mind, sometimes, I try to
follow his growth as a child, but this is really all phantasy.
The truth is probably that if I met my Tomo in the street,
a little boy with his hand in the hand of a Japanese
woman, I wouldn't know him. I can still feel almost
totally destroyed by thoughts like that coming suddenly,
but the state doesn't last long. I don't speak about him,
even to people who knew me when I had my child, only to
you like this. I'm pretty sure my American friends think it
unnatural that I never talk about either of my children.
Jane will be six, growing up without me. Best that she
should.*

*Somehow I cannot picture you in Rome. Washington,
yes, the Pierce-Arrow motor-car, the house you described
with its lawns open to the pavement, even the city itself, I
could see it, but Rome, no. Rome to me is school textbook
illustrations of ruins, and Father Tiber, and Romulus
and Remus, fused somehow with His Holiness the Pope
living alongside that huge cathedral. I can't see kitchens
and sitting-rooms in Rome, particularly your kitchen
and sitting-room, particularly since you have admitted
that Armand and you have 'taken' part of a palace! How
splendid that sounds! Is there a grand curving staircase
for you to come sweeping down in one of your gorgeous
gowns, with dinner for forty by candlelight in a marble-
floored salon? You see, it is all outside my 'ken', as they say
in Scotland. In my world the arrival of a new American
two-burner oil stove (with oven) is the big event of my
year. But, separated as we are in so many ways, my*

affection for Armand and for you doesn't change. And I
value your letters so much.

Yours,
Mary

PS In Rome you have surely gone back to a carriage
again? Or did Armand have his beloved Pierce-Arrow
shipped across the Atlantic? Someone told me that the
inside of these motorcars, in the passenger compartment,
have gold-plated handles to the doors. Bob Dale, of whom
I have written, wants one day to import an air-cooled
Franklin into Japan. He says these are the best motor-cars
in the world. I tell him that the ricksha is ideal for Tokyo's
muddy streets, but he hates riding in them, saying that
men were never meant to do the work of horses. I am sure
Bob thinks that living in China destroyed my conscience
and he may be right; however these days I am very moral
and don't ride in rickshas. I can't afford to. It is the
tramcar for me.

97 Nishi Kogura Machi,
Otsuka, Tokyo,
April 7th, 1910

I spent the first really glorious spring Saturday with Emma Lou and
Bob, one of those days when Tokyo pretends that it hasn't given us
a snivelling, bitterly cold winter, and because I had to change near
to the entrance gates I went for a walk in Hibiya Park before going
on to the Dales' new house. The early iris were out and I found
myself in the middle of one of those solemn flower-inspecting ceremonies that have an almost religious feel, family parties with subdued children, all keeping strictly to the paths or grouped in tidy
clumps at strategic points. Cherry blossom viewing is an excuse to
get drunk, but the iris apparently appeals to a different type of citi-
zen who believes that the arrival of spring should be greeted with
decorum. The whole park is very decorous, the warmer days not
saluted by a riot of bulb colour, not a daffodil or a crocus to be seen,
just that occasional patch of purple set against evergreen plantings

arranged in a manner that is only a gentle disciplining of the natural. I think of those ovals and squares of packed flowers in Edinburgh's Princes Street gardens, patterns as set as the design for a hearthrug, wondering what the Japanese would make of that ruthlessly imposed formality. I think they would be shocked at an insult to nature.

Emma Lou is pregnant again. She told me this after lunch when Bob was out in what he calls the 'yard', working away at some scheme of his own because he says he can't get the gardener to do what he wants. I had the feeling before Emma Lou gave me her news that something was rather damping down her joy at being the mother of little Bob, whom she calls Junior. Perhaps facing it again has brought back into mind what she went through to have Junior. Since there were no complications about the actual birth, at least that Bob was told about, the new father seems absolutely delighted by the prospect of more Dales to fill up the large rooms and long corridors of this house. I wouldn't be surprised if he felt that Emma Lou, with that first success behind her, ought now to be settling happily to the task of building up one of those really outsize American families of the kind the *Saturday Evening Post* features in its illustrations of Thanksgiving dinners. Emma Lou is perhaps not quite so sure that she wants to be the vehicle for upholding this great tradition.

I don't really care for the house that Bob, foolishly I think, has bought. It was built by an Englishman in 1895, back in those wonderful days when to be a British business man in the Orient saw you hailed as a kind of messiah of the new progress and you could live like a prince. The house is of solid brick, cracked in places by tremors, particularly the ceilings, and I wouldn't care to be under all that heavy plaster in a really big shake. They have spent a lot of money on the place already, certain to spend a lot more, and the kitchen boasts all modern conveniences, hot and cold water to a shining white porcelain sink, and an electric icebox, the first I have ever seen, this a huge great white thing with what looks like a fat wheel on its roof. Every now and then it starts to click in an alarming manner. Emma Lou is very proud of her monster and tells me that it is quite impossible to keep food in a hygienic manner without one, so I don't suppose I will ever be eating hygienic food in my own house. I didn't even ask the price of importing that box from California, I should imagine more than I earn in a year.

The Dales' new servants gave the impression they were rather awed by having to work surrounded by all this domestic splendour, really expected to be technicians, not only knowing how to deal with the icebox, but having to cope as well with an electric carpet sweeper which is noisy enough to be an express train at full speed going through a station. My not very enthusiastic reaction to all these joys of modern living could be because I can't afford any of them. Still, what would I do with an electric carpet sweeper when all I have underfoot is straw matting? As for the icebox, I'd be in terror that it would explode during the night and burn down my house. For me even the Dales' gramophone, which is supposed to bring the world's greatest music into your home, is a kind of horror, unnaturally thinned voices coming out of a background scrape almost like fingernails down a blackboard. Until they can get rid of that scratching I will also do without a gramophone.

All this is making a virtue out of what I can't have. The Scots tend towards this, sanctifying poverty, believing that salted porridge and oatcakes, added to a mental diet of high thinking, have put us a lot nearer the throne of the Almighty than any of those self-indulgent English are ever likely to get. I don't have to look hard for traces of a puritan arrogance in me, and in a way this has been very useful in the life I have to lead now in Tokyo. At the back of my mind is the feeling that there is a kind of virtue somewhere in not just being able to walk into a shop to buy a pair of shoes, but having to save for six months before you can re-shoe your feet, perhaps cutting out a meat meal a week in order to manage it. Somewhere, somehow all this is recorded in your favour in a big ledger, credit marks in black, while the rich of this world, wallowing in their luxuries, are getting those red debits on every page which will see them moving into eternity with a mortgage they will never be able to pay off.

Bob Junior is a very healthy baby, fair like both his parents, so I can play with him without being reminded of Tomo. He is being fed on imported dried milk, Emma Lou much put off the fresh kind by that alleged scandal about cows being infected with tuberculosis bacilli because the diseased animals give more milk. I am not sure I believe the story, and continue to get my bottle delivered daily. If Japan's bugs had been going to kill me they would have done it by this time. Compared with China this is a pasteurized paradise.

97 Nishi Kogura Machi,
Otsuka, Tokyo,
August 19, 1910

An extraordinary day following on that weird letter last week from Bob Dale wanting to see me in his office at noon today on an urgent private matter and asking me, if I met up with Emma Lou before this appointment, not to mention the matter to her. I did the sensible thing when you get a communication of this kind, nothing, no letter and no telephone call, though Bob had underlined the bank's number in red. I really hadn't intended to go and then, as I might have expected of myself, curiosity was too much, and by eleven this morning I was getting on a tram for downtown.

The Kansas and Midwest Warranty Trust Banking has the plaque for its Tokyo offices, in English and Japanese, on the cement wall of one of the just completed office blocks in Nihonbashi, ground floor with its own direct entrance from the pavement, quite spacious inside, marble-faced square pillars and that slightly hushed air the better banks strive for, the feeling you are in the outer sanctuary of a temple to the real gods of our time. There was a great deal of mahogany about, not a wood you see much of in Japan, and this must have been imported, already carved to a taste that certainly wasn't local. Behind an ornamental grille sat a Japanese teller alongside a miniature American flag which, either by design or accident, was rippling in the breeze from an electric fan. The only other human visible was a lady typist, operating her machine by the hunt and peck method I used sometimes at Matsuzakara's for foreign letters. At her rate I'd be surprised if output reached two letters a morning. Though in Western dress, which included a white shirtwaist, she was Japanese, too, her hair done in that bun-on-the-roof style I gave up long ago. Somehow Bob's outer office employees gave the impression that they hadn't yet quite found out why they were here. For a moment I thought the teller was going to shout for help.

Bob must have been clock-watching and expecting me, though I hadn't said I would come. A mahogany door opened and he came out, a professional smile making him look not quite himself, so that if I hadn't seen him in it I might have wondered, as one does with undertakers, what his private life was like. We talked for an hour and at the end of it I was still not, as Bob would put it, in the picture, certainly not a picture that could in any remote sense involve me. What did come across was that Kansas and Midwest Warranty Trust, under its local manager, was making slow progress in its appointed task here in Tokyo which was to put good US dollars to work *inside* the Japanese economy. Midwest Warranty have invested in expensive marble and mahogany as part of its bid to be the first American bank ready to use its money to help expanding local industry. An assessment of the situation had suggested rich veins lying waiting to be exploited by financial mining, but to Bob's pained astonishment, those prospect surveys had overlooked one little point, which was Japanese reaction to a heap of Midwest US dollars helping to run their businesses.

It had been quite a simple reaction: thank you so very much, *no*. Bob just couldn't believe they meant this, feeling that his approaches had been wrong, so he tried a selection of new ones, discreet advertising, person to person contact via introductions, even to knocking on doors without introductions, which I could have told him was totally hopeless in this country. Wherever he went he met politeness and that Japanese convenience phrase: *'Ah, so desuka?'* which can mean anything, but quite often means that way to the exit. The disillusioning message had finally reached Bob that the new industrialists out here preferred to do their own financing, prepared to struggle along with a yen that still hadn't become a really stable world currency.

I was quite worried about the implications of all this on Emma

Lou and Bob's life in Japan, but couldn't see where I came into things, at least in terms of a solemn appointment in his office. Also, since I have taken to having my main meal midday I get hungry about half past twelve, and at quarter past one I was *really* hungry and not expecting Bob to ask me to join him where he usually lunches, the Imperial Hotel grill, because in a place like that we could so easily run into someone who would later run into Emma Lou at the American Club. At a quarter to two I suggested we adjourn to the little place behind the Ginza I used to use from Matsuzakara's.

As I chewed at pieces of age-toughened ox I suddenly had the not very brilliant idea that the Baroness Sannotera just might, through her husband, be able to offer useful contacts. He was shocked. He didn't want the Baroness anywhere near Midwest Warranty, she was a radical who had been jailed for insulting the Emperor. And further it was most unwise for me to have any contact with the lady, particularly now that I worked in mission schools, and I was stiffening against this advice when suddenly he plunged into the real purpose of our meeting.

Bob's idea is to loan *me* money. I sat staring at him while he gave me the picture of Midwest Warranty's new policy for Japan. If the native industrialists didn't want any of his dollars, then he was going to use these to finance foreigners to take yen from the Japanese. Simple, as an idea. His bank's operations would be adapted to the country, taking on what amounted to agency functions, arranging for distribution, showrooms, and so on, in fact wet-nursing new enterprises from abroad that might not otherwise be prepared to gamble on the chance of a market in Japan. In my case the financing would be for an exclusive salon offering Western fashion clothes, this later perhaps to be expanded to much cheaper, simple lines that could be made in large quantities and then marketed through those new selling outlets that are opening up in cities all over the land, the department stores.

As I listened to all this it became quite obvious that I had been 'investigated' as a possible commercial proposition; he knew a great deal more than I had ever told either him or Emma Lou about my time at Matsuzakara's, how I had started out adapting for the local market clothes from Western fashion magazines and then gone on to doing quite a bit of straight designing on my own. What he did not know, and some instinct kept me from telling him, was that I had never put these designs on paper for myself, working out ideas with material direct on to one of our imported frames and then having sketches made by Emburi San. It was my assistant, also, who at a later stage was responsible for the detailed paper patterns sent to the workroom for the sewing girls. It wouldn't be easy to open a salon without Emburi San's help, and also without those girls trained to work on Western style garments. I sat there thinking about the possibility of using Bob's dollars to buy away from old Hiro practically a whole Matsuzakara department, and Bob is dead set against any hint of bribery and corruption. There wasn't a red wool embroidered motto hanging framed on the wall of his office, but there might well have been.

He had stopped chewing piecrust and was watching my face. He asked what my thoughts were. I said they turned towards staffing problems. He reached out across the table to cover my hand, then as quickly took it away again, glancing around the restaurant.

97 Nishi Kogura Machi,
Otsuka, Tokyo,
August 22nd, 1910

I have spent the last three days full of doubts, suspicious of my first reaction to Bob's offer, not just uneasy about whether I can do what he wants and even half succeed, but also wondering whether I *want* to do it. I've got used to living again without real responsibility, the work I do now miserably paid, a complete blind alley and sometimes very tiring, this largely from the feeling that I am getting nowhere with a succession of pupils, but I can and do go to bed without worry except perhaps on one of the muggy nights of 'earthquake weather'. If I do what Bob wants I will have to work and work, with no time for the reading that has become my chief pleasure, maybe almost a vice. And at the end of that work there could be failure again, another Osaka.

There was a violent thunderstorm two nights ago, lightning seemed to split my tightly closed shutters, and I lay remembering that typhoon when I was on the *Mooldera*, and how I prayed not to be allowed to die on the way to China. Again I have an infantile wish to ask the Lord to send me a sign indicating whether or not I ought to open the Mary Mackenzie dress salon in the ancient capital of the Shoguns. I suppose, if I look at it squarely, I am really very lonely. Work could be a cure for that.

97 Nishi Kogura Machi,
Otsuka, Tokyo,
August 23, 1910

Probably because I am disturbed and uncertain as to what I should do, I am suddenly as conscious again of Kentaro as in those days when I sat in a garden by a fishpond waiting for the sound of a gate sliding open on metal runners. Always, just before we met, that intense awareness of him took possession of me, and I know this was something he felt too, if less completely. I would see it in his eyes as he came towards me, as he certainly saw it in mine. It was as though by the very act of coming to me, deciding at a particular time to do this, he shut a door on all the other areas of his living, making himself totally available for a limited period. What he gave me was rationed by those disciplines that drive him, and which even now, after much longer in this country, I don't really understand. But one thing I do know, I was not just his foreign mistress, it was not only the pleasure our bodies gave each other, there was a comfort of mind in it, too, as real to him as to me, even if he did shut off that comfort as he shut the gate on leaving. Oh God, it is the comfort I have never had since, and long for as much as I long for the feel of his body on mine.

It is so hot tonight I have just crawled out under my net to open a shutter, risking burglars. Anyway, the most casual enquiries about me in the lane would make it plain that the foreign woman's house wasn't worth breaking into. This light has brought a thousand mosquitoes to batter against my net. A train whistles and a temple puts its gong message across the city. Lying here, I do not believe that

my sudden intense feeling for Kentaro means that he is coming to
me. It is just that for some reason, somewhere, he has opened a
door and gone into a place long unused, making himself available
again.

97 Nishi Kogura Machi,
Otsuka, Tokyo,
August 24, 1910

My second 'secret' meeting with Bob has seen him rather shocked
to find out just how much I had learned while I sat at the feet of
that great teacher of modern commercial practice, Hiro Matsuzakara. Bob had planned to let me have seven and a half thousand dollars, fifteen thousand yen, for the salon project, this to his mind
generous. I didn't think it was remotely adequate, pointing out that
I would require premises in downtown Tokyo, preferably just off
the Ginza, that I would have to employ a really competent assistant
and pay her a generous salary as well as needing at least six sewing
girls for a start, plus their machines and a reasonably comfortable
place for them to work in. On top of this there was a stock, at a
rough estimate at least three thousand yen's worth which had to be
on shelves and hangers when we opened. I had no intention of
starting to work with anything less than thirty thousand yen of capital behind me.

Bob sat staring at me as though he wouldn't have credited this
hard streak in the woman he had helped to find subsistence work as
a teacher of the mildly retarded. He said that for anything like a fifteen thousand dollar outlay he would have to consult head office in
Kansas City by letter, not just cable. I said that was fine by me and I
would go home to await developments, which called his bluff. With
no more talk of head office we moved on to the terms of the Midwest Warranty's loan to Maison Mackenzie.

The terms were fascinating. Half the money I was to get would
be an outright loan to me personally, repayable over fifteen years at
the modest interest rate of only four per cent, which looked beautiful. What did not look so beautiful was that half of the capital sum
sunk in my business by Midwest Warranty secured for them a sixty

per cent holding, this holding to be operative even when I had paid off my half of the loan. Further, during the years of my slaving to clear indebtedness, forty per cent of the profits from the business were to go straight into the bank's coffers, an arrangement to be continued in perpetuity. That sixty per cent holding made Bob's bank my boss, able to sack me at any time with as short notice as I had got from Hiro Matsuzakara. Also, if the business went bankrupt I remained saddled with that seven thousand five hundred dollars as a personal loan, presumably teaching English again to pay it off.

My reaction to all this was to suggest to Bob that if Midwest Warranty had been operating back in that century they could have offered Shylock some really sound tips. I went on to say that under no circumstances would I be part of any arrangement which gave the bank sixty per cent of my business, but that I would be prepared to let them have forty, along with twenty per cent of the profits.

Bob found my proposition quite unthinkable and we went our separate ways to lunch, me to the little place behind the Ginza with its ox meat and two vegetables special. My appetite wasn't as good as usual and I skipped the pie, having what was advertised as American coffee when I looked up to see a Japanese woman about to leave the restaurant. She was neatly dressed in grey silk, skirt and small bolero jacket over a plain white blouse, the outfit perhaps a little too formal not to be finished off by a hat. It was very hot in the restaurant but she looked cool. The way to the door should have kept her half turned from me, but her head came around and after seconds I got a tentative smile. I felt a stab of excitement. Maybe the Lord in His mercy *had* sent me a sign. It was Emburi San.

18

Emperor Meiji, the God Aiko shouted at, is dead. Last night, with two million other people packed along the route, I watched the first stage of his journey to the Imperial tombs in Kyoto. It was a pageant from five hundred years ago and the people moving through it, silent, were ghosts. Today the unreality remains, the capital completely shut down, not a tramcar running, no clattering clogs, no factory hooters to wake me. From the windows of my new flat the view of roofs is like grey waves rolling in against this hill, and the black bath-house chimneys, with no smoke from them, might be posts caught by a high tide. The continuation of last night's clamped-down stillness is eerie in daylight, and I wait for the reassurance of familiar sounds, something simple like the bean curd seller's horn, but hear nothing.

In a way this reminds me of Queen Victoria's death. I was seventeen when Edinburgh went into mourning for a monarch who had ruled longer than any other in British history. Overnight colour drained away from those stone streets as women went into black. It was as though no one had ever realized that an old lady could not live forever, and to all those who had expected somehow to spend their days safely tucked under the quilt of her reign it was almost frightening to have survived her. Mama was quite certain that the rule of the flighty and probably immoral Prince of Wales, now so strangely a king, would soon see a rapid decline in standards of public and private behaviour. The tears shed in our house, and all over Britain, were for an irreplaceable mother figure. For months prayers in churches for the new monarch held the only slightly veiled plea that in His great mercy the Lord God of Hosts would not abandon us, or the Empire, to a grim time of decay and collapse. It seems likely that similar prayers are now being said in Tokyo temples where the gongs are silent today. Like those suddenly bereft Victorians, the Japanese are in a kind of shock at the thought of their great Emperor, the giver of the new constitution, their guide through years of change and foreign wars, replaced by a son reputed to be half mad.

I watched the procession from the relative luxury of a folding chair in the area in front of Hibiya Park reserved for the American Embassy and important US citizens, these including Bob Dale. I was on Emma Lou's ticket. She is too near the termination of her fourth pregnancy to have any wish to attend a funeral, even an Emperor's. Early September should have been warm, but it wasn't, a chill more than autumnal after rain, and by one in the morning, after we had been in our places for four hours, I could have done with my Peking fur coat which is still in service though Emburi San hates to see me arriving at the shop wearing it.

Bob is being extremely nice to me just now, this not unconnected with the profit figures he has been turning in to Kansas City recently on what he likes to consider is our joint business and he is especially pleased with my current scheme to change Japan's mourning colour, at least for ladies in Western dress, from white to black. This is quite a big project in a way since it goes against a tradition reaching back a few thousand years to roots in China, but I have hopes of pulling it off amongst my clientele and if I do this could create total panic in the foreign dress departments of stores like Mitsukoshi and Matsuzakara who are now fully stocked with autumn and winter outfits in assorted colours. I must admit to having gambled on Meiji's dying, for when there was convincing talk weeks ago that he was, even our commissioned work was put to one side in favour of total concentration on black, court dresses, street clothes, everything. There is already plenty of evidence that our two modest show windows in a Tokyo side street are watched very carefully by the fashion conscious and when the blinds go up on these tomorrow it will be to a display of jet. I have not wept for Emperor Meiji as I did, practically on Mama's instructions, for Queen Victoria, but I shall be wearing mourning for him.

In Japan drama of any kind never hurries and the Son of Heaven's funeral certainly didn't, it was well past midnight before the street lights, disguised as ceremonial lanterns, went out, leaving not a lit window anywhere. Noise thinned and then died, as though on order. The procession brought its own light, this pale, torches burning on pine resin, the men carrying them spaced at about every hundred yards. The procession moved at about half a walking pace, footfalls completely deadened by the two-foot layer of silver sand laid over all the roads on the route. There was no clopping of hooves as the Imperial Cavalry came by, the horses held on tight rein but not snorting. The marchers on foot looked dressed for the *Noh* drama, in medieval robes with the flowing lines which said China, not Japan, all in white except for some of the headdresses. Banners had black characters on white, fastened top and bottom to white painted bamboo poles. Elaborate though all this was it was also almost without pomp, the opposite of a state funeral circus in the West, as though here the object underlying pageantry was silence.

Then, in the distance, silence was broken. I felt a prickling on my skin. The sound was half groan, half creak, and came spaced at something like thirty second intervals, growing louder, aggressive intrusion into an arranged stillness, a lament that held nothing plaintive, just the grim, uncompromising and somehow immediately recognizable voice of death. A cart moaned towards us, two-wheeled, simple design in unpainted wood, the Emperor's body housed under a curved roof, the coffin screened only by gently flapping side curtains. Pulling the cart were seven white oxen, one behind the other, seven heads waggling from side to side as thick legs went down with an almost timid caution into soft sand.

After the cart came priests, completely silent when I would have expected some kind of chanting, and behind them military and naval officers of high rank, four abreast but under a new discipline from that sand beneath their feet, unable to march. They were all in uniform, and presumably be-medalled, but seemed to have been placed in a planned gap in torchlight which diminished them to shadows.

We were kept in the dark for more than half an hour after the last of the torchbearers had rounded a corner, and we waited like that, comfortless, until the groaning faded and was gone. The disguised street lights came on, but in pairs, and in no hurry, not really in any pursuit of death's processional, and for a long time there wasn't much movement amongst the crowds, no attempt to break through the looped rope barriers. When finally we were released there wasn't much talk either. I doubt whether anywhere else in the world such a vast number of people have begun to make their ways home in such stillness.

> Sueyama Apartments,
> Surugadai, Tokyo,
> Sept. 15, 1912

When I got to the shop today it was to find Emburi San weeping, something I have never seen before. She told me that General Nogi, Japan's Duke of Wellington, the great hero of all her mainland wars, has committed suicide. He left a note in which he stated that his life was now over since he could no longer be of service to his beloved Meiji, and in this he also deplored the corruption and moral depravity which in recent years he had seen seeping into Japan partly as a result of Western influences. In so far as I can make out this is a direct appeal to the military caste to return to the old disciplines of the warrior code, and I should think will have enormous impact in the country. I can see Kentaro taking something personal from this, a message from another world demanding an almost ruthless new dedication. Kentaro, like Nogi, belongs to the old aristocracy.

The papers here linger lovingly over that suicide, describing how General Nogi returned to his house on the evening before Meiji's funeral where he and his wife bathed and donned ceremonial kimonos. They sat down before the place for formal ornament in their drawing-room in which the only object was a portrait of the late Emperor. His wife handed him a cup of rice wine which he sipped. He then picked up a dagger, stabbed her to death, and immediately afterwards ripped open his own bowels with a short sword. There is a great deal of high-flown journalistic verbiage about Nogi now continuing in another world to serve the Emperor he had loved, with both of them watching continuously over the future destiny of Japan. An almost hysterical false note in all this really frightens me. I have a son growing up somewhere in this country who is now seven years old.

Sueyama Apartments,
Surugadai, Tokyo,
October 18th, 1913

That last entry in my notebooks provides an ironic comment on this one. We are now in the middle of a wave of riots in Tokyo, these coupled with wild scenes from deputies to the Diet, this all stemming from the very thing General Nogi was warning his countrymen against, huge corruption. It looks as though the Prime Minister, Admiral Yamamoto, will have to resign, no great loss to the country, but what has really shaken everyone is the scale of the bribery that has been going on, first from Siemens wanting to sell wireless equipment to the Navy, and then an unholy alliance between Vickers and the local Mitsui Company over the contract to build the cruiser *Kongo*. The size of these bribes is staggering, a Japanese rear-admiral getting well over four hundred thousand yen, and a vice-admiral more than three hundred and fifty thousand. Two directors of the Mitsui Company, two Englishmen and a German are about to be put on trial here in Tokyo on corruption charges.

Bob is being pretty unbearable about the whole business.

Emma Lou says he suffers from a Mid-West prejudice against anything and everything that comes out of Europe, and especially out
of Britain, that latter feeling something I suppose I may have con-
tributed to! I have given up our weekly lunch meeting at the
Imperial because I got tired of being lectured on the theme, or its
variations, of civilizations on the downward slope. According to
Bob, the British Empire is starting to crumble because our firms
resort to bribes instead of really going out into the market-place
to sell a sound product only on its merits. I have tried suggesting
that the expanding US oil companies haven't exactly a lily-white
record, but he shouts me down, saying that the American eco-
nomic structure is built on the sure foundation that you can be a
good business man and a good Baptist at the same time. Maybe
you can, I don't try to argue that point. What I feel is a bit unfair
is his week-long, hawk-eyed inspection of the Mary Mackenzie
shop books just to make certain that Midwest Warranty is, in fact,
getting its twenty per cent profits and not a false entry disguised
eighteen per cent.

I am worried about Emma Lou. After four sons and a daughter,
well on the way now to that magazine illustration Thanksgiving
family, she really ought to be wearing the expression of the mother
in the picture, practical spirituality. But she isn't. She has grown
thin, almost to the point of scrawniness, and though dressing
expensively from our shop, wears her clothes as if these had ceased
to mean anything to her. I have bouts of feeling, and probably looking, like this but always with me the symptom of a hidden wish just
to let go and not fight. I don't think it is this with Emma Lou, more
as though she deliberately doesn't want to look attractive, almost
purposeful about it. It is terribly difficult for either of us to talk
about anything personal, confidences as alien to Emma Lou as they
are to me, neither of us really able to lay out the contents of our private living to have this pawed over. There was never any probing
from her side to find out what it feels like to have a Japanese lover,
or to live without knowledge of what is happening to a son, and
precious little news about a daughter. A good few of the women I

have known would have taken a chisel and mallet to the stone of my reserve, chipping away until it cracked.

She has asked me to spend August with her in a house she has taken at Karuizawa, and I think I had better go, even if this means enduring Bob's weekend lectures on the coming decline and fall of the British Empire.

Sueyama Apartments,
Surugadai, Tokyo,
January 9th, 1914

I was thirty-one yesterday, have been in the Far East for eleven years, for most of them looking after myself, and I ought at this age and from this experience to be a balanced, sensible woman about ready to hunt for the first grey hairs. Instead, when I got to bed at about half past one this morning I heard the temple gongs announce the hour until seven, not even dozing, lying thinking about a third-generation Minnesota-born Norwegian who was, he said, debauched by Harvard into becoming a Bostonian. Some people seem tailored to fit their names, and that is John Hansen. I haven't asked how tall he is but it must be at least two or three inches over six feet. He is conscious of extreme height and is perpetually just slightly bent to keep in contact with the rest of us down below. He is so fair that going white will make little difference, with a long, bony face and long bony fingers, and I swear his American has a Norwegian accent, but he says that this is because I have never before run up against a cultured New Englander, and the way he speaks is upper-class Boston, something he worked hard for five years to acquire because in the international foreign correspondent business unless you come from Boston you haven't a hope in hell.

We were introduced by Bob Dale seven weeks ago, but have actually known each other for some three hundred years, in various forms, John suggesting, very much in his cups of rye whisky, that one of them must have been as a couple of Japanese 'semi' insects screeching on the same branch. I never sing and neither does he, but we had both been trying to up amongst the pines above the moat in the outer precincts of the Imperial Palace, to which the public are admitted if they conduct themselves with proper decorum and respect. There couldn't have been any police on duty because we weren't thrown out. This isn't love, it is too enjoyable. But I can lie in bed and make a Gregorian chant out of his name.

Neither of us has any sense of future, he has a wife and two children living in a place called Waltham. Her name is Elizabeth and three years ago she told him that if he refused to settle to a decent job, and continued to wander about the world writing pieces for the *Christian Science Monitor*, he could consider their marriage as finished for all practical purposes except that she would expect half of the cheques he received and he needn't think he could cheat on her because she knew somebody well up on the *Monitor* staff and could easily find out exactly what John was earning. Which is why, he says, he will be poor forever, and is looking for some nice, warm-hearted woman ready to keep him in the style to which he would like to become accustomed, and with no questions asked. He doesn't think I am rich enough yet but if I really keep at it and open a factory making corsets I may qualify.

I had been missing joy. We make it together. He doesn't mind about Elizabeth any more, but loves his children, a boy and a girl, which is sad. All these years I have never really talked to anyone about Tomo, but I did to John. What he said was: 'You poor bitch.' Then he bought us another drink.

I am drinking too much, something I have never done before. It just happens, I suppose, because I am keeping pace with him. If I don't, he says he can see a Scotch Presbyterian reformist glint in my eye, and he's had that before, in the New England version. Tokyo has always been Kentaro's city to me, in which I was allowed a place on sufferance, but now John and I own it. At the moment what we own is a winter snarl of snow and sleet and inches of mud in every street, but when the spring comes we will take over the plum blossom and the cherry blossom, and then the beach at Kamakura for the hot weather. He has to go to Shanghai in March, but only for two weeks.

Sueyama Apartments,
Surugadai, Tokyo,
February 2nd, 1914

John would like to move in here with me. He hasn't suggested it, there hasn't been a word said on either side about it, but it is what he wants. I want it, too, and yet there are all kinds of bars. The extreme respectability of these apartments is not one of them. Some of my neighbours are Japanese 'modern girls' being maintained in so-called foreign style by business gentlemen whose main domestic addresses are elsewhere in the city. From that point of view it wouldn't matter at all; from mine it would for some reason.

I have been trying to think why. I suppose part of it is still Mama in Edinburgh in spite of what I have made of my life since then, but another part is how I have been living since I broke from Kentaro's protection. One of the reasons I endured that wretched little Japanese house, and then my teaching English and that whole pattern was a probably ridiculous feeling that I must completely own myself again and that some sort of respectability in the eyes of the world was part of this. I am terrified of losing what I have with John, taking up the attitude that would lead to this, or even just saying the word that would do it. But if I open this door and have him move in I will be living again in defiance of the world around me, and I know what that means, a label that would stay with me for the rest of my life.

I can't fool myself either that there would be any security with John, that is not on offer. Already what we have is threatened by habit. Yesterday when I was waiting for him in the lobby of the Imperial he came in, saw me, raised a hand, then turned aside to talk to a group of three pressmen, keeping them from the bar while he told some story that had them all laughing. It was nothing really, and yet it wouldn't have happened two weeks ago.

Last night I woke up with the thought that in Tokyo it may be known that I can never have another child. Foreigner gossip goes round and round in circles here and I shouldn't let myself feel sick at the idea of what might be said about me in bar talk that John could have heard before we met. I wonder what it would be like to live in a society where you just took what you wanted with no thought or worry about consequences to yourself or to others. Would it be bliss or hell?

Sueyama Apartments,
Surugadai, Tokyo,
July 9th, 1914

I have taken to visiting my neglected friends again. Alicia is suddenly almost frail, and was rather cool, perhaps because we don't meet as often as we used to. It could also be that she has heard about John Hansen and thinks, as she would probably put it, that I have 'broken out again'. These days she is seeing a good deal of the wife of the British Ambassador, and the Embassy appears to have taken her under its wing, which I suppose is natural enough; as we grow older we seek our own kind, losing the inclination to experiment.

I went to see Aiko, too. There is a rumour that she has a Japanese radical leader as her lover, but if this is true then there was certainly no evidence of a man in the little house where she now lives surrounded by what I can only call squalor, her indifference to minimal comfort as marked as her total lack of interest in dress. She has, of course, nothing but contempt for my business, regarding it as a form of pandering to the subjugation of our sex, part of a male conspiracy to keep women content with fripperies, treating as sophistry my argument that since convention, and most climates, demand that we wear clothes it is not a bad idea to make these as attractive as possible, or at the very least neat, tidy, and clean. I have long had a sneaking feeling that Aiko doesn't really share her race's belief that personal cleanliness is equal to godliness.

Emma Lou is now certainly the friend with whom I am most at ease, not a hint left of the hysterical girl of that time at Takayama. Once she expected the world, through Bob, to offer her everything on a platter, but has come to realize that to clutter your life with hopes of this kind is a waste of time and the sensible thing is to settle for what you have in hand, looking around to notice how much worse off some others are. It is almost the old evangelical count your blessings, and is out of character in some way. There are times when I seem to sense something explosive under this new calm. She is much more intelligent than I thought when we first met, and growing more so, whereas Bob seems to me to be sinking deeper and deeper into the sagging chair of his dogmatisms. I think he has really done very well, financing a whole string of foreign companies with a potential for penetrating the Japanese market, none of these really big, but enough of them to give him the feeling he is achieving at least part of what he set out to do in this country.

When I was with Emma Lou on Tuesday for a cup of the tea I taught her how to make, she surprised me by asking suddenly if John Hansen and I were exchanging letters. I said that if three from me and one back from him could be called that then we were doing it. I also told her without any prompting that after his two weeks in Shanghai John had gone on to Hong Kong, then to French Indo-China, then Singapore, and that there was now a project for a series on the Dutch administration of Indonesia which would take him to Java. Emma Lou may have heard things in my voice that I wasn't meaning to have it convey for she said, quietly: 'Don't waste yourself again, Mary.'

It was probably good advice but I didn't know how to acknowledge it, so I had another cup of tea. So did she. Then the children descended on us. Emma Lou is training a new amah to help look after them, a raw country girl clearly terrified of American young, and not without reason.

Sueyama Apartments,
Surugadai, Tokyo,
August 4th, 1914

John is in Yokohama staying at the Grand. He didn't admit having been in Japan for two days before telephoning, but did say he had come on the French line *Porthos* and I know when she docked because we have been waiting for a long overdue shipment of Belgian trimming lace which was in her holds. He has asked me to lunch tomorrow at the Imperial. When you have decided to deal firmly with something that has become a bit of a problem, lunch is a good time to choose, no soft lights, no music, and poor waiter service.

I have no cause for any bitterness, that flare-up between us was mainly the result of a form of starvation from my side, I wanted it so much that it happened. It is humiliating to realize this, and to have to meet him again knowing that truth. But I am also curious to see how a man like John parcels up something like our relationship for discreet disposal. I know what a Japanese man would do: nothing, simply go away without a word; but in American society women have secured the right to be deferred to, their feelings officially respected. There is that beautiful fetish of equality which I have seen even Bob acknowledging in his relations with Emma Lou, probably as a result of having been at a co-educational college. The Englishman, like the Japanese, still hasn't allowed his life to be complicated by such foolishness.

Sueyama Apartments,
Surugadai, Tokyo

Lunch with John was certainly memorable, but not for the reasons I was expecting. I was almost half an hour late, held up by a fitting for one of our more temperamental clients who had managed to antagonize even the usually bland Emburi San. John was already at a table, with two whiskies waiting. He stood up, came around to pull out my chair, then said almost in my ear: 'Mary, last night at eleven Britain declared war on Germany. I've just come from the press agency. The cables came through too late for this morning's papers.'

I sat down really without any reaction at all, this only beginning to come as John, drinking his whisky, talked. The murder of an Archduke in a Balkan town hadn't meant a thing to me, an item eclipsed by a train crash on a branch line from Tokyo in which two people had been killed and fourteen injured. That was real, I had travelled on the line with Aiko.

For more than ten years now European politics have really been totally beyond the areas of my interest, and I found it hard to believe that the assassination of a man about whom I knew nothing at all was going to lead to a war involving most of Europe and probably a good bit of the world beyond it. John says that is what will happen but I wonder if he is taking an American view of another European flare-up that won't really become a lasting fire? After all, the Kaiser has rattled his sabre often enough, but the fact remains that he is a cousin of King George, and the loved grandson of Queen Victoria who insisted on measuring her for her coffin.

John believes the fighting could go on for years and, if it does, this will give Japan her real chance to make herself the dominant power in Asia. No one in the West will have any interest in what is happening out here, particularly on the Chinese mainland, except perhaps the United States, and even with them attention will be the other way, towards Europe. John is pretty cynical about Japan as the gallant ally of Britain and France, saying that if her military brings this country into the conflict it will be to make quite sure that no one makes any protest about Japanese expansion on the Asiatic continent.

I was suddenly very depressed, but John was excited. He sees himself as a man with a role to play all through a time of upheaval and change, and a role he has designed for himself. He sails on Tuesday for the States on the *Mongolia* without telling Boston he is coming, in this way avoiding a cable ordering him to stay on covering events in the Far East. He plans to get to Europe quickly, if not for the *Monitor* then some other paper. We said goodbye in the lobby, and he promised to write, but he won't, and neither will I.

Sueyama Apartments,
Surugadai, Tokyo,
September 17th, 1914

John was right, Japan has come into the war on the side of the British and the French, after three weeks of seeming indecision. Could Kentaro, still in London, have played a part in all this, his despatches convincing Tokyo that the Allies will withstand the Kaiser's hordes? Anyway, Japan has struck her first blow against Germany by taking Tsingtao.

I have come to hate this flat with its little box rooms and its view of roofs to the horizon. I keep thinking about a house in Yokohama, preferably up on the Bluff, from which you can see both Fuji and the sea. It would mean commuting but the new electric trains do the distance between the two cities in under forty minutes.

I begin to feel like a war profiteer, all the signs point towards no austerity here, quite the reverse, a sudden great enthusiasm for everything British, including clothes from Mary Mackenzie. Western dress is the fashionable thing, though as yet I haven't read any suggestions in the press for any form of women's auxiliary service that might require uniforms I could make, this giving me the excuse to expand into a small factory.

At the British Embassy they are having parties to turn sheets into bandages. Alicia has declined, saying she is too old for war work, and I have not been invited. The Ambassadress is said to smoke cigarettes openly at these gatherings. Is Marie doing the same these days?

19

꿈

Sueyama Apartments,
Surugadai, Tokyo,
May 28th, 1915

The sinking of the Lusitania, *with the drowning of so many Americans*
on her, seems to have focused all United States attention on
Europe, and the militarists here certainly haven't been slow to take
advantage of the situation. Japan's twenty-one demands on China
are outrageous. Issued to any other country they would have meant
war, yet it would seem that this clear statement of Japan's plans with
regard to China is going to be allowed to pass almost unnoticed by
the rest of the world.

The demands include total territorial rights forever in the Kiao-
chow peninsula and Tsingtao which Japan took from Germany last
year; the exclusive right to colonize South Manchuria, together with
total freedom to exploit Inner Mongolia for any mineral resources
that may be there. The Port Arthur peninsula, seized from Russia
while I was in Peking, but still completely Chinese territory, is to go
to Japan on a ninety-nine-year lease and there are to be yet more
mining rights granted in central China while at the same time no
harbour or any other territory may, from now on, be leased to any
other foreign power. To cap all this, as a kind of crowning insult, it is
suggested that China would be 'wise' to accept Japanese advisers in
her government and in her army, this latter with the idea of joint
Japanese-Chinese military forces at some time in the near future.

Perhaps my sense of shock from all this is a bit unreasonable since I was born into a country whose king is also Emperor of India, and whose empire was continuing to expand while I was a schoolgirl. I can remember what the captain of that ship along the Chinese coast told me about how we acquired Wei-Hai-Wei to which we are no more entitled than the Japanese to Tsingtao, perhaps less so since we didn't even fight for it. If Kentaro had been out to defend those twenty-one points, which he certainly would never do to me, but may be doing in London, I can imagine what he would say. This would simply echo the views of the ruling caste of which he is a part and it wouldn't totally surprise me if he got a sympathetic hearing amongst the ruling caste in England. Japan was to become the protector of Asia just as Britain was the protector of India as well as a good half of Africa from Cape Town up to Cairo. He might have added that Japan's imperial expansion was certainly taking place a little later than the expansion of the other 'great' powers, but could scarcely be condemned on this account. I can also see him suggesting politely, over the port at some country-house weekend, that the British were in no position to admonish their Oriental ally in the war against Germany for trying to do in a limited way in the Far East what Britain had done in a huge way throughout the whole world.

I couldn't have refuted these arguments, at least not from the point of view of someone defending British policy, and perhaps I am being sentimental about those twenty-one demands which I found so detestable, this because I felt a kind of affection for the Chinese that I don't really feel for the Japanese, or am ever likely to. This is not being rational, I know. When I was in Peking I didn't speak the language, my contacts very limited from this, and half the foreigners there had recently run the risk of having their heads chopped off and stuck up on staves. My personal life wasn't exactly glitteringly happy while I was there, either, and yet I believe that if I was now taken from this part of the world for the rest of my days, it is China that would come into my dreams, a procession of camels tinkling through the Hatamen, an old woman with jade in her ears smiling at a new bride, the Summer Palace floating on its hills, a wicked old woman on the dragon throne. I dare say the Chinese need discipline, either from within or without, but I can't see the Japanese as the right people to administer this. I suspect that as conquerors they go with rock-hard hearts, demanding total submission from those they conquer. Sometimes I feel that the truth about the Japanese is that they have hard hearts for everything that is not contained by these islands and their national 'way'.

Sueyama Apartments,
Surugadai, Tokyo,
June 11, 1915

In a war that looks like tearing the world apart I am making money and hunting for a house. I ought to feel guilty, I have twinges of it, but being at least a partial outcast from it has thinned my sense of duty towards the country in which I was born, indeed, for any country. I still have a British passport, but I feel stateless, and very remote indeed from those ladies rolling bandages at the Embassy.

I have been down in Yokohama on odd occasions over the last month, just wandering around by myself. There is a great deal of new building going up on the Bluff, which was once almost a for-eign concession and still largely occupied by Europeans and Ameri-cans, but with a fair number of newly rich Japanese moving in who don't want to live in native style and are building themselves con-crete mansions to match their neighbours. It was next to one of these places being built, cement mixers busy, that I came on my house, a survivor from another day, modest, withdrawn under its heavy tile roof, and with the wooden fencing about the garden sag-ging, some of it about to collapse.

There was no resistance to my invasion, the gate bar was rotten. I stood looking at something I knew was going to reconcile me once and for all to the country in which I will live out my life, which is asking a lot of a house and garden. I had been passing nothing but rosebeds in front of the concrete palaces. The rose resists this country, you can make it grow, but it blooms saying it hates it here. I stared at weeds, a dried-out carp pool, and stepping-stones, the only colour green, restful to the eyes. There was also a very aged pine suffering from needle fall as a result of having had to endure the last few winters without one of the straw overcoats the Japanese put on these trees in the autumn to help them survive for centuries beyond their normal life span. The house was considerably larger and of much better basic design than that shack in Otsuka I had abandoned with no tears, but even more ruinous, with tiles off the roof and sags that weren't an architect's art, just rotten timbers.

I don't know why all this presents the kind of challenge I can't resist, and I am certainly mad to want the place. It will ruin me to make the house habitable and to restore the garden, adding a new crop of domestic worries to my business ones.

For information about a property nobody seemed to want I went to the nearest police station. He was a fat policeman, fond of himself, wearing a white uniform and sitting in a cane chair that looked too frail to go on supporting him for much longer. His head was shaven, with his cap, wearing its spotless white summer cover, on the desk in front of him. There, too, was his sword of office laid longways behind a writing set. He looked up at me and I knew at once that his considerable experience of dealing with foreigners up here on the Bluff hadn't warmed him towards us at all. Also, I was a woman who had to be shown her place. If Aiko had been with me there would have been a flaming row in seconds, but I was made wise by the hissing serpent of my desire and, after bowing, plus asking to be excused for troubling him, I sat down on a bench to wait his pleasure. An alarm clock ticked. The policeman dipped a pointed brush in black ink and did a little careful calligraphy, this with the flourishes of a scroll painter, then looked at me again to say: 'Nani?'

It was as economical a way to ask me what I wanted as could be found, his tone not even touching the fringe of politeness. At Matsuzakara's, and in my own shop, and from contact with fishmongers and grocers and tram conductors, I have learned quite a lot about women's language, and think I have become quite good at it for a foreigner. It starts with omissions, words one must never dream of using, these exclusively for the male, then allows you other words that most men would rather cut belly than let slip from their lips. Few Western women ever bother with these subtleties, but I offered them as obeisance to a plump officer of the law, explaining that I was a helpless female from Tokyo who could only throw myself on his mercy for help with my problem.

Oh, it worked! It worked so fast that in only moments I was drinking tea produced on shouts to back living quarters, this brought by a wife who didn't always worship her lord according to the best traditions. Never in all the time of his service up in this suburb had the policeman met a foreigner who came as near to understanding the true heart of Nippon as I did. And when he heard what I wanted, which was to preserve and live in one of the few remaining truly Japanese houses in the district, the artist lurking behind a uniform and a bad case of obesity came out from hiding. He, too, on his rounds had looked at the ruin of what had once been great beauty and felt the deep pity of it.

The house had belonged to an elderly couple who had lost both their sons in the Russo-Japanese war and when the old man died his widow, rather than face the world on her own, had slit her wrists and bled to death. Naturally, as a result of this, the place was haunted and unrentable and the dilapidations had started. The heir was a nephew who ran a shirt factory at Omori half way to Tokyo, a modern man who had no use for such an old house which was anyway too far from his work, and for some years the property had been a liability to him. Recently, however, with the sudden boom in building on the Bluff, the land had acquired real value and the policeman believed that the factory owner was now asking a ridiculous price, though in so far as he knew no offer for the place had as yet been accepted.

I left a sub-station leaving behind an ally who promised, if I was successful in getting the Misune property, to do everything within his considerable powers to see that I found honest tradesmen to help me repair it.

Sueyama Apartments,
Surugadai, Tokyo,
June 19th, 1915

I don't know a great deal about the newly popular science of psychology but have heard the theory that a woman living without a man for as long as I have tends, at my age, to go odd in one way or another. My friends, however, haven't offered me the charity of this nonsense, screaming that I am a fool, but since I was expecting this I took my negotiations for a ruined property to an advanced stage before I told the sources from which the money will have to come anything about what I had done.

On the Monday morning after my Sunday meeting with the policeman I went down to Omori to visit the Misune Shirt Factory. Before many years are out Mr Yunkichi Misune is going to be defended by a huge staff and secretaries trained not to give you an appointment, but I caught him while his only defence against the world was still just an office boy with a lisp.

I didn't use my women's language plus meekness on the shirt maker, he wouldn't have appreciated the performance; a young man of about thirty, certainly not much more, who is what Bob calls a go-getter. And he is go-getting so fast that before I had been with him for ten minutes he told me he is already selling his shirts in Burma. The fact that he has achieved world markets from a factory set up inside what looks like an abandoned school was a bit of a surprise until he showed me his equipment, this shining and new, the most modern cloth cutting machines imported from Germany only months before the outbreak of war. One man, working from a chalked top layer pattern can cut twenty-five other layers of cloth at once with precision and total neatness, and I watched quite fascinated with thoughts of possible Mary Mackenzie mass produced simple dresses not entirely remote from my mind. My very real interest soon had Mr Misune accepting me as a kindred spirit and when we got back to his cubbyhole of a chairman's office the inevitable waiting green tea was ignored, a bottle of Osaka Scotch whisky produced instead. It would have been bad tactics to say no to this, so I sipped the repulsive stuff slowly.

Mr Misune had already had an offer for the family homestead on the Bluff, which was bad news. I gathered that it was quite a good offer but he had decided to hold out for a better one, which I didn't care for either. It was clear right away that he regarded the house as a complete write-off and was thinking only of land values, and I was careful not to let slip even the smallest hint that I was hoping to preserve the ruin. I had a feeling, too, that for some reason he didn't much like whoever it was who was trying to buy his property, and that he did quite like this foreign woman who was really interested in his machines. I asked how much he wanted. Looking at me from behind glinting glasses he said six thousand yen, which was clearly at least a thousand more than my rival's bid. I said five thousand and we fought our way to five and a half, settling there.

I didn't let Bob Dale know what I had done until three days ago. I had to tell him then because I want to borrow eight thousand yen from Midwest Warranty, which is what I am going to need on top of my own savings of about three thousand before I can hope to move into my new home. Bob is quite appalled that I want to add this sum to the loan I already have with his bank and has demanded security in the form of a proportion of my holdings in Mary Mackenzie which will give him total control of the company if I can't meet repayments. Ten days ago I would never have believed that I would come to want a house so much as to put myself at risk in this way.

Both Bob and I are steered through the intricacies of Japanese company law by a Eurasian lawyer called Harry Nishimoto who went down to Yokohama to see what I had done and came back with the suggestion that I ought to be certified. I am a bit shaken, but with my head still unbowed, and I more or less ordered Harry to proceed with the deal as agreed verbally with Mr Misune, and also in an exchange of notes which I think would be binding as mutual statements of intent. So I am really into this, with no withdrawal now, and probably am in for a year or so of horrors during which builders will find that the fabric of the house I want to preserve is not rotten in places, but all over. However, I shall meet each blow as it comes, I hope with unshakable fortitude!

Sueyama Apartments,
Surugadai, Tokyo,
June 23, 1915

A very curious development in the matter of the Yokohama house. I was in my office behind the shop working on the books which continue to show us healthy, but perhaps not healthy enough for the expenses ahead of me, when Emburi San came in to say there was a man out front asking for me, someone she had never seen before. We don't often get men in here, a few American husbands, one or two French, never British and certainly never Japanese, except delivery boys.

At first I thought my visitor was a Spaniard, decided olive skin, very dark in a sleek way and with such a high forehead his eyebrows almost seem to be midway between chin and the start of straight black hair that was rather long and combed straight back without a parting. His tailor was not in Tokyo or London, my guess being that the suit came from Paris, moulded to a slim figure. He was carrying a cane which is not something you often see here. Perhaps because I haven't had a great deal of contact with Eurasians, other than Harry, it didn't occur to me that this man had Japanese blood. Then he told me his name, Peter Nasson, and I knew who he was, the head of Nasson and Company, Silk Exporters, one of a handful of Eurasian families who have almost cornered this particular trade and become very rich in the process, the Nassons the richest of them all.

He looked the sort who might come with his wife to help her buy clothes, and I glanced around for the woman who should have been flipping through the readymades. The two of us were alone, Emburi San away on a sudden mission to the sewing room, her feet creaking the stairs. Mr Nasson chose not to sit in my office, but I did, waiting for him to state his business. He came to the point at once. I had bought a property on the Bluff while he had been in the process of negotiating for it in order to make it part of the garden of the house he was building next door. He suggested that there was something far from straightforward about the way I had nipped in while his deal was pending, to undermine this, clinching the matter before he had been given the time, or the opportunity, to perhaps improve on his offer.

Today was certainly hot for June, but I was suddenly a lot warmer than the weather warranted. I told him I had been househunting, found the place I wanted, and had offered for it. His eyebrows went up into that thinker's forehead. He said: 'Househunting? Surely you mean to tear down and rebuild?' I said I meant to preserve with love and care. He smiled. It was the kind of smile a company chairman might use to suppress any slight hints of revolt amongst his directors. There was something like pity in his voice. 'I will give you six thousand yen for that land.' 'No.' 'Six thousand five hundred.' 'No.' He took a deep breath, so deep it stretched the cloth of his suit. 'You'll bankrupt yourself trying to save that place. And when you have I may decide to buy the land off you. Good day, Madame.'

I followed him out into the salon. 'You'd tear down that house and destroy that garden?' He was almost at the door before he turned. 'Naturally. The house is useless and I don't care for Japanese gardens.' I shouted: 'You'll never get your hands on my place!'

There was some satisfaction from the surprise on his face. He went out quietly, closing a glass panel with great care, a gentleman whose breeding was in marked contrast to that of the yelling virago he was leaving. I stood fuming, determined to plant quick-growing poplars between my house and his cement monstrosity. Now I am a little ashamed of my performance, but only a little.

Sueyama Apartments,
Surugadai, Tokyo,
July 6th, 1915

Dinner at the Imperial was pleasant, the place very warm, ceiling fans stirring a tepid air, but we had a refreshing iced soup that was new to me. Mr Nasson had brought the recipe from Switzerland and given it to the chef, and it made an effective start to the studied perfection of the meal. He didn't make a visible fuss over the food but I knew that they were sweating in the kitchens to give him no excuse to, and, of course, everything had been ordered in advance, there was no question of my being offered a choice. He is certainly the kind of man who, in Europe, would send back a wine not completely to his taste but there is no point in doing that here because, so he tells me, all wines are sick by the time they reach here and never recover full health. All I know about wines is that if they are on the acid side I suffer.

There was no attempt made to disguise the fact that the purpose of a most expensive meal served in the Imperial yesterday was to repair an unfortunate contact and to establish the kind of climate between us in which I could be brought gently to see reason. I think his aloof manner is defensive, rooted in perhaps two things, first that he is Eurasian and, second, that he inherited money and a company, which really means that he has only to be clever enough to maintain the business he was given. And selling silk to world markets that are clamouring for it really doesn't put one's administrative skills to much of a test.

The matter of my house and land was not mentioned at dinner, but it will be, perhaps during a projected trip to Miyanoshita in the motor-car Mr Nasson has imported from America. He tells me that the road up is dreadful, not much more than a mountain track, but the views are worth the terrors of the journey.

Letter from Mary Mackenzie to Marie de
Chamonpierre in Rome

Mampei Hotel,
Karuizawa,
August 7th, 1916

Dear Marie,
  It was so good of you to find the time to write to me.
You say that in Rome you are not exactly in the front line,
but I should imagine that practically everything you
think and do is governed in one way or another by the
war. Out here the truth is that it mightn't be happening,
except for the booming prosperity it has brought to Japan,
with her new markets that are in so many cases just
replacements for British goods which can no longer be
supplied. I open my paper with a sense of guilt sometimes
and particularly after this horrible summer with its
dreadful slaughter in France and the failure of Sir
Douglas Haig's offensive against the German armies. I
was interested in what Armand says about tanks and how

if they had been used in the recent battles the Germans
might easily have been smashed. He is probably right when
he says that the Allies are handicapped by old-fashioned
thinking on the matter of making war, but I have always
had the feeling, from what I have read of him, that Mr
Winston Churchill, who advocates the use of these tanks, is
rather a harebrained young man. Certainly it doesn't
look as if our leaders have much idea of what they are
doing.

You ask for news of me and this is really that, in a
small way, I am part of this Japanese boom, more
prosperous financially than I would have believed possible
only a few years ago. Recently my main interest, aside
from business, has been the massive repairs needed to the
house on the Bluff in Yokohama in which I am now
settled, up here for a two-week holiday after the move. You
and Armand must come to me for a long visit. Basically
everything has been kept in Japanese style, some chairs to
my own design made by a local carpenter, plus certain
conveniences as well, like flush wc's (two of them) as well
as a modern kitchen with an electric icebox. I promise you
would be comfortable, and I think charmed as well. So,
when this war is over, I will expect you.

Some time next year I will be opening a branch Mary
Mackenzie shop in the main street of Yokohama, the
Motomachi. This is really because I can see a great influx
of tourists into Japan the moment this war is over,
especially American tourists, and I am planning a pretty
trap to lure their dollars away from them! This will be an
emporium offering the most superb silks and brocades,
featuring Japanese materials in readymades of various
kinds that can be worn by Western women (and perhaps
men?), the idea being to get right away from the now
inevitable kimono. The project is something quite
different, really, from my Tokyo business. And if I am
clever enough I can't see it failing. I might pay retaining

fees to a special squad of the ricksha coolies who wait at pier number one for the big liners to dock, the idea being that new arrivals are whisked away from the bottom of gangplanks and delivered directly to my tender mercies by wild-looking Orientals who 'no speakee English', or French, or anything else! The travellers will be so relieved to find me and my staff who can understand them that they will loiter amongst my alluring wares while their wallets are still plump with travel money.

You see how disgustingly commercially minded I am getting? It is a racial trait that lurks somewhere deep in the core of most Scots, only needing the right circumstances—these usually far from home—to bring it out from hiding. After all, at the union of the two kingdoms hordes of us went south with Royal James, our one object in that descent on London being to loot the place. And ever since, we have dug ourselves into England's empire, in many cases great chunks added to it by Scottish effort. There was a time when you French worked hard to bring a leaven of civilization to the wild tribesmen of the north but, alas, this never really 'took', and we have remained raiders at heart, subject to strange compulsions that the rest of the world can only look at slightly askance. As I grow older I have more and more sympathy for my English husband with whom I still have no contact of any kind. To do myself some justice though, I never blamed him in any way for what happened, for I knew perfectly well that it was all me. Further, as an observer, you knew this, too! It is one of life's little miracles that you and Armand remained my friends.

What you said about my visiting Europe after the war has made me wonder about that. Until very recently the answer would have been that I didn't have the money, but now I do I still think it improbable that I will ever leave Japan, at least to go as far afield as the other side of the

*world. There are a number of reasons for this. I couldn't
be near it without visiting Scotland again but there
would be no welcome for me there. As well as never
having had a word from my mother in answer to all my
letters from Japan, I also have not had so much as a
postcard from any of my other relations; two aunts, an
uncle, cousins, who all seem to have cast me into outer
darkness, perhaps on a command from Mama. Over the
last few years I have written her lawyers three times
simply to ask how she was, just some basic information. I
have had three ruthlessly formal replies stating that she
was well, nothing else.*

*It may puzzle you that such an unforgiving attitude
should be part of living amongst a people with a wild
streak, but it is awareness of this streak in all of us which
makes our middle classes so determined to serve
respectability at all cost. Maybe if I went back to
Edinburgh it would be as a tourist viewing the sights and
returning to a hotel bedroom with sore feet to stare at that
castle on its rock.*

*No, out here is the bed I have made for myself, and the
thing for me to do is lie on it, especially since I am now
able to afford a very comfortable mattress. I will always
be a foreigner in Japan, of course, and at one time this
would have worried me, but it doesn't any more. When I
was living as Kentaro's mistress I tried to bend my
stubborn will into some sort of conformity with the
Japanese way of doing things, even seeing myself as some
kind of adopted subject of the Son of Heaven, mortifying
the natural flesh that is me in a bid to do this. All
absolute nonsense; the Japanophiles, those Western converts
to the Japanese way, are simply objects of amusement to
the natives, who laugh behind politely raised hands. I
laugh, too, these days, but without raising my hand.*

You must come and see me in the little museum of old

Japan of which I am the foreign curator, and this right in
the middle of a suburb containing many examples of the
most horrible new-rich housing you will ever see anywhere.
Until that happy meeting at pier number one in
Yokohama, my very real love to you and to Armand.
    Yours,
    Mary

17 Ura Machi,
The Bluff, Yokohama,
September 11, 1917

Emma Lou's news yesterday was in a way a shock. Since moving down here I haven't seen anything like as much of them as I used to, and though she asked me to come up and stay in Karuizawa with her either in July or August I didn't, largely because we chose the summer period when business is slack to make extensive alterations to the shop, and I had to be available during this. Japanese builders do eccentric things if you are not watching them.

At the beginning of September I was away for a week at the Kamakura Hotel, having told no one where I was going and spending my time in and out of the sea from that wonderful beach. It seems that Emma Lou has been trying to get in touch with me ever since she returned to Tokyo. She is sailing on the *Empress of Russia* for America on the sixteenth with the children, but without Bob. There was something cryptic about this announcement over the telephone which made me uneasy, and I tried to get her to come downtown to have lunch with me, but she was too busy packing and making what she called the final arrangements for Bob. She has asked me to come to the ship at half past ten before a noon sailing. All this is very unlike her, but I can't just ring Bob up to find out what has been happening, and I realize suddenly that it is quite a long time since I have even seen him briefly, this at the end of May.

Upheavals amongst one's friends are what you have to expect out here, relationships being continually undermined by home

leaves or appointments to countries thousands of miles away. Someone coming back to Japan after a five-year absence would be very
lucky to find, amongst the foreigners still living here, even a handful
of the people he had known before. I seem to be as durable as a
marble slab in the cemetery, but then not so many returnees would
go out of their way to look me up, even if they were feeling lonely.
Somehow I had always thought of the Dales as fixed, too, and in
recent years Emma Lou has stopped talking about Pasadena.
Instead of going back to the States for their last long holiday they all
went down to the Philippines for three months on a house exchange
basis with other Americans.

I wish there was some way I could find out what is going on
without seeming nosey. I am certainly not looking forward to that
time before the *Empress of Russia* sails.

17 Ura Machi,

The Bluff, Yokohama,

September 16th, 1917

Two large whiskies have made me more depressed than I was before
them. Probably I should have gone along with Bob to the Grand
Hotel to give him support during the ritual of drinking himself
unconscious, particularly since I don't believe, though he is no
longer a total abstainer, that he has ever before set out to get drunk.
I just couldn't go with him, even though he asked me to, and I
don't believe he really wanted me there as a witness. Perhaps, with
no witness, he won't do it, but if he does they are trained to deal
with these things at the hotel, and will tuck him up in a bed at the
end of it. I didn't suggest that he come back here with me, he
would certainly have refused even in his present state of mind. The
reformed scarlet woman has had a relapse again and I think he
would have been very unhappy if I had said yes to staying with
Emma Lou in Karuizawa. He has always been secretly uneasy about
my friendship with Emma Lou.

Poor Bob getting drunk now, and me near to wanting to. I will
never forget Emma Lou's face as she shut that cabin door, having

sent Bob away on some ploy, and after herding the children into their four-berth and a sofa cabin across the passage. She stood looking at me for a moment before she said: 'Well, go on, ask why I am doing it.' I said I didn't know what she meant, wasn't she just going on holiday to the States? 'No, I am not just going on holiday to the States. I'm going to Pasadena and getting a house there. And the reason I'm doing this is because I don't want any more children. If I stay in Japan I'll have them, whether I want to or not. That's the way things are.'

What I said finally was that if she didn't want any more children there were surely ways this could be arranged without having to take a house in California and leaving her husband in Tokyo? Her answer was in a louder voice than I think I have ever heard her use, even with the children. 'There is no other way! Not with Bob!' After a moment she added: 'I wanted you to know.'

The thing that makes me feel sick now is that I really had nothing to say to her. We heard Bob's voice in the side passage to the cabins, the kids shouting at him. Then he opened the door to stand staring at us, hating two women for what he guessed had passed between them.

The *Empress* liners are known for the speed with which they slide away from the dock after that final siren blast, but today everything seemed in slow motion, a deliberate lowering of the gangway, an even slower cast-off while passengers shouted messages from the promenade deck and, back in the second class, a schoolteacher returning to the States was being serenaded with a Gospel hymn by a platoon of her girl pupils. Bob and I were side by side, but he was a long way from me, staring up at an Emma Lou surrounded by his children, the youngest being held high so that she could throw a paper ribbon down to her father. Emma Lou must have determinedly bought those ribbons and handed them out, for soon Bob had a cluster of them in his hands and then I had one, too, that voice I knew so well shouting from above: 'Catch, Mary!' So I caught my long green strip and held it until the *Empress of Russia* finally did move and all those ribbons snapped to litter the dock and hang like the debris from yesterday's party down the steel plates of the ship's sides. The three-piece war economy orchestra up on the deck started to play, but wasn't anything like loud enough to drown out the screeching schoolgirls.

Bob was crying. I felt a terrible certainty that Emma Lou, in the distance no longer a recognizable face, was standing there dry-eyed.

17 Ura Machi,
The Bluff, Yokohama,
October 7th, 1917

Every morning a ricksha calls for me here at seven forty-five to take me to Sakuragicho Station for my train to Tokyo, always the same puller, a barrel-chested young man wearing his sweat band at a jaunty angle across his forehead who cracks jokes as we travel, quite often suggesting that it is time I got a motor-car. He says that when I do he will give up pretending to be a horse and sit in state behind the steering-wheel. I tell him that if he drove a motor-car with the same abandon he shows in manipulating a ricksha we neither of us would live long. The make he fancies he calls a Rosu Rossi, and it took me some time to translate this to Rolls-Royce.

This morning Komoro and I were held up as we tried to cross the Motomachi, the obstacle being a long column of marching soldiers. Marching isn't really the word for it, they were doing the Japanese variation of the German goosestep, something that I would imagine is still completely grotesque even when performed by smartly uniformed men, and these men certainly weren't that, in dress for active service, baggy trousers under ill-fitting tunics, the packs on their backs looking thrown together.

There was nothing we could do but wait at the intersection until what must have been a whole regiment went strutting past, with the people along the street deferential to them, standing in shop doors almost to attention. Komoro, I know, has been quite skilfully avoiding military service and I didn't think this spectacle would appeal to him much, but I was wrong. He had managed to light the stub of a cigarette with one hand, the other holding the shaft to keep me on

a level keel, and when I asked where he thought the soldiers were
going he turned his head to say out of one corner of his mouth: 'To
the station for China. One day we'll be marching all over the
world.'

I missed my train. I didn't get to the shop until ten.

20

❧

17 Ura Machi,
The Bluff, Yokohama,
June 9th, 1923

Armand has sent me all my letters to Marie, which makes me sad that I have kept none of hers. He has not told me what she died of, but I think I can guess since he says she was ill for more than a year, refusing to leave him alone in Bangkok while she returned to France for treatment. Perhaps she was afraid of surgery. More likely she knew that it would do her no good in the end. Her last letter to me was only four months ago, but there was no mention of illness in it, though perhaps I should have read through the lines of her complaint about Bangkok's endless, humid heat, and how she longed for that holiday in Japan. She was seven years older than me, which would make her forty-seven.

I used to think of Marie as a woman who had everything, particularly when I heard from her during my first years in Tokyo. Her every word came from another life which seemed to be at the core of what was happening in the world, while all that was happening to me was sore feet. If ever there was someone cut out to be a successful Ambassador's wife it was Marie, wit, charm, great power over men, and I know well from what she said to me in Peking, and from her letters through the years since, that this was what she wanted above everything. Armand, at fifty now, is not the French Ambassador in Bangkok, and in all their postings Marie must have had to play second fiddle to some woman with probably half her talents. I am sure this has been a great pain to him. He had money, and social position, but lacked the drive which pushes you to the top in the diplomatic service, or anything. The fatal flaw there, if it is a flaw, was that he wanted a role in life not for his own sake, but for his wife's. At heart he was a botanist.

What will he do now? He will still be thin, with those sinewy arms in which you could almost see the bones under the tendons stretched over them. For me he had gentle kindness. I'm sure that when I knew them he had never looked at another woman as he looked at his wife, that extraordinary concentration of love down a long dinner table. I can't believe that there was ever, for him, a Siamese girl in a little house up a side street, but I could be very wrong here. I remember the Swatow Consul's wife saying that Western widowers in the Far East soon marry again. It will be a curious little shock if I hear of Armand doing that.

When, like Marie, you have no children you pass so quickly into oblivion. I believe that this is the one thing that really terrifies a Japanese, man or woman, the idea that when they die there will be no children to say prayers at the family altar to their departed spirits. That great sceptic, Kentaro's relative and spy, Assistant Professor Akira Suzuki, believes in nothing that cannot be logically demonstrated, but I am certain would still be horrified at the idea of no ceremonial period of mourning, plus the prescribed prayers, after his body had been cremated. I must say that he has taken out pretty good insurance against this happening, three boys and two girls, all being raised in strict patterns of Western philosophical enlightenment, but at the same time undoubtedly being trained to do their traditional duties towards the family dead. This is somehow basic to their national ethos, like cricket to the English, and as totally incomprehensible to anyone not raised within the mystery.

I wonder if Tomo, now almost certainly betrothed, at least, to the daughter of his adoptive parents, would pray for my spirit if he was given the news of my death. He might, I suppose. There is one thing, however, about which I can be quite certain: Jane

Collingsworth has been brought up without any instructions to decorate her evening prayers with a request for God to bless Mummy.

17 Ura Machi,
The Bluff, Yokohama,
June 11th, 1923

It must have been re-reading all those letters I wrote to Marie which has sent me back to my notebooks. I have always been a little superstitious and there is no doubt that her death has made me uneasy, as though it was a reminder, not only of what a long past I now have, but also how easily everything I have worked for could just be written off overnight.

I am not going up to Tokyo today. Emburi San can look after things perfectly well, as she told me quite emphatically over the telephone. Sometimes I think she could run the business better than I do, and in a number of ways is far more contemporary. I find the postwar fashions hideous, one of the worst periods for sheer ugliness in women's dress in history, these up and down lines, too short skirts, and the waist hung on the hips. Now as never before clothes are designed by men who hate women. Emburi San tries hard, but I find it almost impossible to dress Japanese even in careful adaptations of these fashions. For one thing, women here were never meant to show those legs sat upon from an early age, for another they almost all have long backs, which puts the new waists on them not much above where the knees would be on a tallish Western woman. If things go on like this I'll be back to dressing court ladies in floor-sweeping gowns and cartwheel hats decorated with ostrich feathers.

Having a day off in the middle of the week when I am not ill is a strange feeling, I don't quite know what to do with my morning. I thought about telling Komoro to get out the Dodge and drive me down over that rutted track to Kamakura, but I don't really want to sit alone on a beach in this heat eating sandwiches or to lunch with the foreign sahibs in the hotel. If he hadn't been in Shanghai Peter

would have come with me, delighted at this sign that I am beginning to take things more easily. I wonder if I am, or is this only a
brief departure from norm?

I am just in from a garden that has only one thing wrong with it,
a backing of *kiri* trees as a windbreak which makes it too hot in
weather like this. Otherwise it gives me more pleasure than the
house. It is exactly eight years today since I first saw the place and
knew at once that this was where I was going to live. Peter says I
won't marry him because I couldn't bear to have him in here mess-
ing it up, and it is certainly quite true that I would never contemplate moving into the thing he allowed a half-American, half-Russian
architect to erect as a monument to the Nasson money. There is also
the fact that I really have quite enough of Peter as it is, with him as
the man next door.

This garden really isn't mine at all, restored by my money, yes,
but it is still six-eighths the possession of a good many generations
of my predecessors who, being Japanese, still haunt the place for
two weeks every year at the Festival of the Obon, led by poor Mrs
Misune who slit her wrists. Another eighth goes to Sato the gardener, leaving the last eighth to me, my portion shared with Saburo
the cat without a tail I got to deal with the rats and who has stayed
to deal with me. I am a forty-year-old spinster with her cat, if someone with my past and present can hope to be so classified. The
British Embassy certainly hasn't got around to awarding me that
status and now, on account of Peter, won't ever do it, leaving me
barred from those receptions which are quite celebrated in Tokyo,
all of them watched over by a portrait of King George the Fifth, and
attended only by those who cannot find a decent excuse to stay
away.

Before the World War Peter used to go to Embassy ceremonial
occasions, like Empire Day, but now he has even less chance of getting through those portals than I do, forever to be unforgiven for
what he did in 1912. About then, sensing what was coming in
Europe, he renounced his British citizenship along with his father's
name of Williams, taking his mother's name of Nasson and her
Swiss nationality. There was logic as well as an instinct for self-

preservation behind this move, for Peter's father was half British, half Japanese, whereas his mother was all Swiss, which made him just a quarter of a Briton with a good solid claim on neutrality through the years 1914–18. As he puts it, no invitation to the British Embassy for the rest of his life is a small price to pay for never having seen the mud of Flanders. A divorce from his wife, who now lives in Deauville, was part of his loss at this time, too, the lady English and a patriot who only lives in France because the climate is so much better. Somehow I can't see Peter as a married man and I tell him that he only suggests marrying me because he likes to have his brand stamp on everything within his orbit.

I have never before put down on paper what I feel about Peter, and I find myself staring at the words, suspicious of them. Twenty years ago the idea of having as a lover someone who could calmly admit to being a physical coward would have appalled me. The Samurai warrior was a big part of Kentaro's attraction, the mystery of a man who could sit facing the rising sun offering prayers for his dead soldiers. I never got in behind the mystery. The curtain at times seemed to be rising but before anything was revealed it dropped again. Peter is not mysterious. He mocks me by our similarity. With him I have nothing to defend, it would be a waste of time. Married, we would quarrel too much. This way, we each have our houses to withdraw to, the separate identities they offer by a physical environment, the studied perfection of the more than slightly bogus Japanese for me, a concrete horror glittering with the evidence of Nasson money for him. From either of our bedrooms on a fine morning we can see Mount Fuji, the peerless one.

The garden is now very hot. Up here with the *shoji* pushed back for the sea breeze that hasn't yet arrived I can feel heat radiating past me skywards. The geriatric pine, under careful nursing and winter wraps, has recovered its needles and these days its gnarled limbs are crutched by wooden props. I am pretty certain Sato says prayers to that tree when working around it, and there are times when the idea of a venerable vegetable growth having a soul doesn't seem too weird to me, at least not when I am out as a guest in my garden. There is another tree which Sato dislikes almost to the point of bitterness, this probably in the main because he can't identify it. He comes from Kyushu where a sub-tropic climate, or near it, rears many exotics but he has never seen a tree like this one. With positive hatred in his voice he calls it a foreign thing. Actually, it is totally inoffensive, doesn't grow very fast, and has quite pretty pointed leaves which take on a reddish tinge in autumn. When you crush one of these between your fingers it gives off a faintly gingerish smell, and though a bushy habit makes it a little out of place in a formal Japanese garden, especially where it grows up near the focal point of a stone lantern on a miniature hill, I am still not letting Sato touch it. I have warned him that if I come home one day and find that tree gone he will go, too. Its odd-plant-out look somehow accents, for me at any rate, the carefully maintained perfection of everything else around it. Sometimes I see Sato straightening his back and pausing to curse my tree, but it survives.

> 17 Ura Machi,
> The Bluff, Yokohama,
> June 17, 1923

Peter, back from Shanghai, insisted that I go up with him to a performance of the Tokyo Symphony Orchestra, saying that the programme, being totally sentimental, ought to appeal to me. We went in his Morris Cowley, which is what the British call a 'saloon', windowed in like a hearse, and stuffy with engine smells. I much prefer my open Dodge touring car and my ex-ricksha coolie chauffeur.

The concert included the 'Fingal's Cave' overture which ought to have brought tears to my Scottish eyes, but didn't, Liszt, and finally Tschaikovsky's Sixth Symphony. Programme notes in Japanese and near-English told us to look out for the love theme in the work, stating: ' . . . at first quite loud sadness becoming more softly and not often, then only to arrive at last like small echo in booming death cave'. Peter said that after this information we should be ready for anything, including a big laugh, but I found myself waiting for the little theme, moved by it, wanting it to be much stronger at the end than the pathetic little suffocated whisper it became.

I was conscious of Peter watching me and in the car driving

home he was suddenly quite vicious, saying that I was like a world traveller trying to move around with a heavy trunk stuffed with my own past, and it was about time I learned that all any of us need is a very light suitcase. When I didn't say anything to that he came in to the attack again. According to him, I have a large personal area for a misty dream, this dedicated to the sacred figure of my warrior, now a general. Couldn't I see that I had got a big damn nothing out of the dream? I said I had a son from it. He said: 'Where?'

I could have cried out then. I *had* been back in the dream, listening to that music, seeing Kentaro again in the Tsukiji garden looking down at his son for the first time, then, later, squatting on the matting making a little procession of origami toys. Peter was trying to make me cry, but I didn't do it.

He says that I should go through that big trunk to throw away everything that won't fit into the light suitcase. He may be right. Actually, quite a lot has been got rid of already. When Richard was killed in France in early 1918 I didn't beat myself with shame at what I had done to him; all I really felt was relief that I was free of a man who had refused to divorce me, this from what I could only see as a kind of malice, though it may have been principle. Jane, now nineteen, I remember on her birthday. Tomo, soon to be eighteen, comes through a door into a shadowed room much more often, but I can never manage to see his face, and always his father seems to be with him, as though to keep me from doing this.

I might rent a house in Karuizawa for August and take that psychic trunk with me to sort out the contents once and for all, as Peter suggests. I wonder if he suspects I have hung on to this box with my journals? He can't have seen it, it has always been hidden and locked.

Noki Besso,
Karuizawa,
August 18th, 1923

I was down this morning at the tennis courts watching the men's singles semi-finals for the Karuizawa Cup. It was a hard battle between an American called Wendels and a Japanese youth, Kenichi

Massami, who lost in the last set. It was only when they were coming off court that I saw how young the Japanese player was, no match physically or in years for the American. Then, as he straightened from picking up a towel, the Japanese boy looked at me. He was angry at losing. His look could have come straight from Kentaro.

I tell myself that dozens of Japanese youths from the wealthier families are summering here in Karuizawa, and that I must not do now what I have longed to do often before and never permitted myself, set in train some kind of investigation. I did find out that the Massami family are from Kyoto, which I have a feeling is the kind of place in which Kentaro might have wanted Tomo to be brought up. And if that boy was a *yoshi*—? No! I must *not*. Oh God, I came up here to empty that trunk!

Noki Besso,
Karuizawa,
September 2nd, 1923

This is a place of wild rumours after yesterday's earthquake. One is that Fuji has erupted and smothered Tokyo and Yokohama in burning ash. I don't believe this, and neither do I believe that a vast wave has come in from the sea to pour over the capital and its port. The only thing we know for certain is that it isn't a local disturbance as we thought yesterday, something connected with our volcano. My guess is that we were on the fringe of a huge shock centred in or near the Tokyo area. Even here it was bad enough to shatter all communications down from these mountains, no telephone or telegraph, and the talk is that at least seven of the forty railway tunnels between us and the Takasaki plain have collapsed. Certainly there have been no trains.

The American agent for Harley-Davidson motor-cycles came up here on one of his machines last week, finding the track almost impassable then because of mud from recent rains and when he tried to go down again this morning the track had disappeared under a landslide. It looks as though we are imprisoned up on this plateau. All those wild stories heard over the years about what will one day happen to these volcanic islands don't sound so wild now. At the community notice board I heard a man say that if there was some vantage point at the edge of these mountains from which we could look down we might find that the sea came right up to them, half of the country having slid down into that vast hole on the ocean floor known as the Tuscarora Deep. The stories will get even wilder before we hear what has really happened.

I brought only one maid up here with me. Toba San, usually so cheerful, is in a dreadful state, convinced that her family down in the disaster-prone Izu Peninsula have been wiped out and that Cook has been killed in our Yokohama house. I try to calm her down, but there is something horribly infectious about the girl's panic, and the way she continues showing an almost total lack of the usual Japanese emotional control, her eyes streaming tears whenever I look at her. Certainly there is a grim sense of doom hanging over this valley, as though everyone feels that the terror which has struck elsewhere is somehow on schedule for us soon. I keep looking at the volcano Asama which looms over this place, and I see others doing it, too, but the only sign of activity from the crater is the usual thin, almost innocent-seeming plume of white smoke drifting away. Last night there was a red glow reflected by low cloud, but this is quite common. The village food shops are emptying fast, with queues forming to buy tinned goods and the question wherever there is a clump of people is: 'Have you had any news?' The last I heard was of a party being organized to go down to the plains on foot, but this isn't going to be easy if the track has gone, the railway to us used a cog system to get up what are practically precipices.

One thinks almost endlessly about the people down in the cities and I can't get away from a feeling that by being up here I have somehow evaded an experience that should have been part of my life. The earthquake was at midday, when Peter was quite likely to have been at home. Emburi San, in charge of the salon, would probably have been getting rid of the last customer for the morning and thinking about sending out for her usual sandwich and milk.

Aiko is also in Tokyo. I saw her last month when she came to the salon just before I left the city, and with that quite crazy request. I was supposed to go into the cubicle where the wife of the Minister for Home Affairs was being fitted for a gown to ask that lady to use her influence on her husband to get Katsugi, the radical leader, out of Sugamo jail. Since she married that man I really think Aiko is a little bit unbalanced, though perhaps the only real change is that these days, instead of going to jail herself, she spends her time trying to have her new husband's sentences reduced or quashed. If he were my husband I would prefer him in jail. The only time Aiko brought Katsugi to my house in Yokohama he had a good look around, ate everything in sight, and then called me a highly paid lackey of the ruling élite, which I didn't feel was a very good description of what I do for a living. I think Aiko got the message then that I didn't really care for the company of her revolutionary, though I am still much concerned about her, particularly now.

How long are we going to be trapped up here under this damn smoking mountain?

The Imperial Hotel,
Tokyo,
October 16th, 1923

Like everyone else in this city, I have become anaesthetized to horror, destruction on this scale producing its own drug to blunt one's reactions. There are nearly three thousand people packed into this hotel, its lounges, lobbies and many corridors turned into dormitories. The only reason I have got in, arriving back in Tokyo when I did more than a month after the earthquake, was simply because last spring I opened a small shop in the arcade here as a kind of trial run for the much more ambitious project planned for the Motomachi in Yokohama. So now I sleep surrounded by brocades and silks and tourist gewgaws, which must be the only collection of this kind of merchandise within a twenty-mile radius that hasn't been reduced to ashes. I am *not* open for business. Anything that could be of any use has gone from these shelves to the refugee supply stall upstairs and when I look around at the too much stock I have left, so carefully selected by Emburi San and me, it seems, in these circumstances, a load of rubbish. I stay in this little cell most of the time to be available to any of my staff who have survived the holocaust. They all knew about this shop and they ought to learn, in time, that this hotel has survived intact. So far only one has been, the youngest sewing girl. She survived because she was at home with a heavy cold that day. She hasn't much hope for any of the others, including Emburi San because she has heard that in the area behind the Ginza the fire came quickly before thousands who were trapped in the wreckage could be dug out.

I don't want to think about it. There is so much that one mustn't think about. Peter was found under the crumpled heap of his concrete house, one of the known dead. There are probably two hundred thousand who died no one can say where or how. I still haven't heard anything at all about Aiko, though it has been confirmed that the Baron Sannotera was killed in his office. On September first, just before noon, Bob Dale, that former total abstainer, was in the hotel bar above me here, experiencing one of the world's most devastating earthquakes with a whisky glass in his hand. Afterwards, from what I hear, he did impressive work with the rescue squads. Soon after I arrived we met in one of the food queues, and I thought he was suddenly looking a lot older, but then we all are. He has been down here a few times, but we didn't have very much to say to each other. That seems to be a common condition, you see people sitting staring at pieces of the decorative stonework to be found all over this hotel, as though using it for some kind of self-hypnosis.

The Japanese, with their long experience of natural disasters, seem to have evolved an almost unique understanding of how to deal with these. They get up on their feet again quickly, shake themselves, cremate their dead, and turn once more to living. Here in Tokyo most of the streets have already been cleared, some trams are running, and Bob Dale is taking me to Yokohama tomorrow by electric train, these operating again. I funked going down there alone. My cook and her two children have survived unhurt, the police got a message to me from her native place in the country to which she has gone. Toba San, who made the journey with me from Karuizawa, is in Izu, but I haven't heard yet what she has found there.

I can't read. No one seems able to, you don't see people in the hotel with books open. For something to do this afternoon I tidied this place, really to get those garish brocades out of my sight. Under a bottom shelf is what I brought down from Karuizawa, a suitcase of summer clothes and a basket containing household linen, together with that box of letters and my journals, the symbolic trunk that Peter told me to get rid of, and I meant to. Well, I haven't, and I won't now. I lugged that suitcase and basket through a chaos of packed trains and stations where we had to change in order to get here, and the symbolism of the box, if it has to have one, has altered, becoming the only link now left to connect me with those dead years.

Yesterday I went out for a walk. It is only when you are outside this hotel that you really appreciate the miracle of its survival, the new Imperial finished only last year to plans and under the supervision of the American architect, Frank Lloyd Wright. A more improbable building to resist a vast earthquake is difficult to imagine, since it is built entirely of stone cemented together without any steel frame at all, the design said to have been inspired by Mayan temples. There isn't a crack anywhere in the building, its narrow windows and low construction resisted the fires that burned right to its back and side doors.

There is another even more impressive survival, the massive walls beyond the moat which surround the Imperial Palace. Here the stone is unmortared, huge rocks just fitted together and apparently completely undamaged, topped off still by those old pines that show no signs that I could see of scorching. The residence of the god who lives amongst the Japanese is unaffected by the disaster immediately beneath him, though it is rumoured that the god himself, accompanied by what these days amounts to his keepers, was safely away enjoying the hill air of Nikko. When I turned from the palace to look south ruin stretched to Tokyo Bay, though I could identify the

Ginza by a line of burned out shells that had once been its department stores, including Matsuzakara's.

The Imperial Hotel,
Tokyo,
October 17th, 1923

I minded the ruin of Peter's house much more than my own. Mine
was somehow purged devastation, broken tiles, but the rest almost
clean ash from burned wood; his great slabs of that concrete piled in
on itself. I didn't ask how they had found his body, the heap looked
as if no squads of diggers had disturbed it in any way, and those
huge pieces of fractured cement still had their white outer coating in
places, as though the fire had missed this pile. The view from the
Bluff, in autumn sunshine, was better than it ever had been, all
obstructions cleared away. Fuji was serene.

As we were walking back to the train for Tokyo, along what used
to be the Motomachi, Bob asked me if I had kept in touch with
Emma Lou. I said we had for the first two years, then she hadn't
answered a letter and it had become cards at Christmas which had
stopped, too. He told me that they had been divorced, adding: 'I
haven't told anyone here yet. It's just happened. Emma Lou went
to Nevada where you can divorce your husband if you can prove his
dog bit you.'

A cart pulled by an ox had the crown of a road still fissured and
scarred from heat, the load new tiles. I couldn't see any building
ready for tiles, but there had to be one somewhere. Bob and I were
separated by the ox, a curious deferring to the solemn-eyed beast
that would probably end up as inedible meat in a 'foreign' restaurant, or perhaps tourist 'sukiyaki'. When we joined up again I asked
Bob why he had kept on that big house for six years. He said: 'I
guess I kept it on because I went on hoping she'd change her mind
and come back. Good thing she didn't. It would have fallen on her
if she had. It's just a heap of bricks.'

I remembered then that Peter had told me Bob was known to be
going to the Yoshiwara. I really had nothing to say to him, just as I

hadn't been able to say anything to Emma Lou on the boat. In the train we sat staring out at the blackened sites of factories, some of them with metal chimneys still standing, most of these heat twisted. He said suddenly: 'I'm going to manage our office in Shanghai. Let me tell you, Mary, you won't find our new man here so easy to get a loan out of.' He laughed.

The Imperial Hotel,
Tokyo,
November 3rd, 1923

Harry Nishimoto, who became Peter's lawyer, too, has just been to see me here, the day after he got back from hospital in Kobe. He was on pier number one at Yokohama seeing a friend off on the *Empress of Australia* when the dock split under him. He remembers going down into the water with huge blocks of concrete crashing all around, and then nothing until he came to on board the liner at sea en route for Kobe. He was lucky, only a leg fractured in two places.

Harry's news is startling. In this disaster-prone country it has been his firm's policy for years to carry duplicates of all important legal documents in their Kobe branch office, and amongst these was Peter's Will. If he died suddenly Peter meant to have the last laugh on me. I have been left the house he knew I didn't care for, though a heap of rubble rather spoils the joke, and there is no point now in his ghost hanging around to see what I would do with my inheritance. His legacy means that, in addition to my own ground, I have another four acres of adjoining land on the Bluff. It would have been nearer five if a large chunk of Peter's garden hadn't collapsed on to the ruins below.

Harry doesn't think the Bluff is ever going to recover as a residential area but says he might be able to find me a speculator who would buy my land, though I needn't expect much for it. He was shocked when I said I intended to be that speculator and was authorizing him to buy for me all the land, plus ruins, that he could acquire on the Bluff for the forty thousand yen I had available.

Harry would do a great job protecting new widows from sharks; he gave me a little lecture on the sensible handling of available assets and then, when he saw I was still bent on fiscal lunacy, asked what that forty thousand represented in my affairs. I told him that before the earthquake there had been forty-three thousand eight hundred in my account at the Yokohama Specie Bank which would still be to my credit when they got their records sorted out, because I had my bank book to prove my claim. In addition I had the goodwill of a vanished business, some potential in a matter of months from the little shop in which he was sitting, and that I intended opening another shop in Yokohama just as soon as it could be built. I also told him I meant to re-build my house on the Bluff exactly as it had been, down to the last detail, this in the best Shinto religious tradition for reconstructions.

I think his leg was hurting him, or he needed a drink, for his voice seemed to hold pain as he asked where, if I spent all my capital buying land on the Bluff, I expected to get the money to re-start my business and rebuild my house? I said I would borrow from the bank the thirty thousand yen I estimated I would need for the house and the shop on Motomachi, doing this on the security of the land he was to start buying at once.

Harry thinks I am headed for commercial suicide. I believe in that high shelf above Yokohama once again becoming the most desirable residential area in the city. In five or six years those empty lots scattered amongst the newly reconstructed mansions, and belonging to me, should be worth at least a quarter of a million.

21

🙞

A copy of the Last Will and Testament of Mrs Isabel Mackenzie arrived this morning from her lawyers in Edinburgh. Since I am a minor legatee there was really no need to send me that copy, but I am pretty sure that Mama left instructions this was to be done. When I saw the fat parcel from Scotland I couldn't think what it might be, but the bulk was from all my letters home for over twenty years, each still in its envelope, yet all opened and presumably read.

I have been sitting here trying to imagine what the arrival of those letters meant to Mama after she had stopped writing to me. Was she waiting, before she answered one of them, for some indication that I repented my sins? I always signed them with love, but there really wasn't much love in what went before the signature; behind everything I put down there is a kind of resentment at still being classified the outcast. If I had tried even just a little harder I might have broken that barrier between us.

The mention of me in her Will is as cold as ice clinking in a tall glass. 'To my daughter, Mary Mackenzie, formerly Collingsworth, I bequeath the contents of her father's library.' She hadn't cared much for father's library, disliked it, in fact, but had clearly kept those books safe behind glass all this time. My first reaction was to write to the lawyers telling them to sell the books and give the money to a suitable charity, but I have decided to send for them. The father I never really knew may, in a way, be available through those volumes.

The Will is quite simple. There are other small legacies; five pounds for every year in her service to a woman whose name means nothing to me, so Jessie and the Cook either died or left. It would seem that Mama only had one maid of all work for those twelve years that had earned a faithful employee a total of sixty pounds as a remembrance. There was a larger amount, two hundred this time, to the Elizabeth Atkins Grant Home for Fallen Young Women in Glasgow, this followed by a distribution of jewellery, of which there was a good deal, to assorted relatives and friends in Edinburgh. Finally, Jane was the sole legatee of the residue of the estate, this cancelling, after probate, an income of three hundred pounds sterling originally paid annually to Richard Collingsworth on behalf of his wife, but continued to the Collingsworth family from 1906 on the understanding that the income was for Mrs Mackenzie's granddaughter, Jane Collingsworth.

This is the first I have heard of an income paid by Mama to Richard on my behalf. I can remember very clearly indeed my worries in Peking about a dowry, these the result of what Marie said about diplomats having to marry where money is. Three hundred pounds a year doesn't seem a great income in these postwar years of inflation, but in China at the beginning of the century it would have gone a long way towards paying our living expenses.

Richard managed that little matter very neatly, and I'll never know how he did it. What I do know is that Mama must have stinted herself to find that money every year, a huge sum out of an income that could not have been more than seven or eight hundred. There was never one word in her letters that would have given me a clue to this situation and she must have gone on paying that money to Jane as a matter of pride. I can see now how she was bound to have felt a certain bitterness against a daughter whose choice of a husband had created her impoverishment and she would have believed that I knew all about those payments. Poor Mama and that dour, stubborn Scotch pride. I suppose there is a lot of this in me, too.

17 Ura Machi,
The Bluff, Yokohama,
April 13, 1924

Today I ordered the trees for the restoration of my garden now that the bulk of the work on the house is finished. I really only have memory to guide the contracting gardeners, as with the carpenters on the house, for there has been no trace of old Sato since the earthquake. Komoro, my ricksha coolie chauffeur, turned up all right, tracing me to the Imperial Hotel, but only to tell me that the Dodge was a heap of twisted metal and that he was going back to his native place to become a farmer. He went with my blessing and some money, likely to be better at farming than he was at driving.

My determination to have this house and garden as near as possible to what they were isn't just a personal madness, but something shared with countless thousands of Japanese who, in an unstable natural environment, achieve a stability of a kind by this sort of continuity. The shrines at Ise, where the Emperor makes regular reports to his ancestors, are of wood and straw, rebuilt dozens of times over the centuries, but always to precisely the same plan. And in this country it is almost as easy to replace your garden as it is your house, no question at all of putting in young trees and waiting for them to grow, you buy your trees of an age and size you want, these then delivered and planted by experts who will guarantee to turn a piece of waste ground into a mature garden in one year flat. This never ceased to amaze me when I saw it happening before the earthquake on some vacant lot, but now all over Tokyo and Yokohama whole gardens are arriving from the undamaged surrounding countryside, transported on carts pulled by oxen, or tired horses. Everywhere the traffic is patient for these loads, as though acknowledging them as symbols of a re-birth; a vast pine, with its roots in a huge straw-matting bundle, holding up a procession of unhonking automobiles and motor lorries.

The trees I have ordered are of fairly modest size, six twenty-year-old *kiri*, and an only seventy-year-old pine as replacement for a two-hundred-year-old charred stump. This is a compromise with cost; I could have had another two-hundred-year-old, along with crutches to support its aged limbs, for a price—a thousand yen. I might have been able to beat them down to eight hundred, but they wouldn't have gone below that. These days it is a seller's market for trees.

17 Ura Machi,
The Bluff, Yokohama,
April 19th, 1924

A team of workmen are due to start today preparing the ground for my garden, which arrives early next week. I am staying home to supervise the digging. The only things growing here now are weeds, or so I thought. The seeds of these couldn't have survived that scorching, so they must have arrived on the winter winds. I had a look at the almost pure charcoal of my old pine before climbing up the mound to where the stump of the ginger tree stuck up like a creosoted stake. I couldn't believe what I saw fighting weeds for its share of sunlight: a new green shoot come up from a nest of blackened roots, this already bearing nine of the unmistakable, aromatic leaves. I pinched one to make sure and got the ginger scent on my fingers.

I have no belief in omens except when they are good ones. This is a good one. I am back in a house still perfumed by newly planed wood, feeling an absolutely ridiculous joy. I shall stay with the diggers all day to make quite certain that an artificial hill is once again crowned by that stranger tree.

22

17 Ura Machi,
The Bluff, Yokohama,
October 11, 1928

Today saw the end of a series of flaming rows with Harry Nishimoto,
the end because I gave him my final instructions, stating that if he
wouldn't do what I told him my affairs would be out of his hands.
To hear him talk now you would think that the four hundred and
eighty thousand yen from the sale of most of my land on the Bluff
was the direct result of his brilliant planning, but right here in this
notebook, and only a few pages back, is the clear evidence of what a
lunatic he thought me when I insisted on buying up here to the
limit of my then available funds. He wants me to convert the yen
from the sale into something like two hundred thousand US dollars' worth of assorted stocks and shares on the New York market.
According to Harry, all the indicators are not just set fair, everything points to the present boom going right through the roof, and
that by buying on margin I could double my capital in a year. He
has sheaves of brokers' letters full of juicy forecasts about the American economy and says that everyone is buying on margin these
days.

Well, I am not going to. Buying on margin means that if shares
go down you have to cover the drop or end up with nothing. It may
be a Scotch thing, but I like my money in something you can see
and touch if you want to, which is why I have decided to become a

landlady. From the big sell-up I kept back, as well as this place, a four-acre lot further over on the Bluff, and on this I intend to build two three-story blocks of flats for rent to give me an income, a decision that has brought Harry as near to foaming at the mouth as his shrewd business man image of himself will allow.

Fighting him has left me feeling a little tired, and summer in the Motomachi shop was pretty exhausting, too. I think I must go away somewhere for a rest before starting to deal with architects and builders, not to mention all the complex new legislation about foreigners owning property in this country.

A year from now Harry is going to have for me, itemized in detail, the profits I would have made on those New York margin buys if I had taken his advice, and he ought to get some pleasure out of that. I wonder what commission he has from his American brokers? Pretty good, I should imagine. And, of course, he sees no chance at all of a percentage on the flats I am building. I hear that his Italian wife is proving to be very expensive.

> 17 Ura Machi,
> The Bluff, Yokohama,
> October 23, 1928

I have been to Nikko. It took me twenty-four years to get to the tourist mecca which is a top priority must on all the ten days in exciting Japan schedules. The tourist board here have come up with a new slogan to help keep the hotels full—'Nippon, the land of colour, courtesy and charm.' Well, maybe.

Nikko is sensational in a way, an orgy of wood carving covered with red and gilt lacquer, these buildings set against the sombre green of huge cryptomerias, but after one day my feet were as sore as they used to be when I worked in Matsuzakara's, endless stone steps to climb for yet another spectacle of a glittering temple against a dark background.

I may have been a little jaundiced by the fact that my visit coincided with a descent on the place by nine hundred passengers from the round-the-world cruise liner *Carinthia*, all of them with sorer feet than mine, and sagging at the knees from the weight of photographic equipment they carried. Everywhere you looked there were little groups arranging themselves against a cute Japanese setting for a permanent record of travel to be pasted in half a thousand snapshot albums. I thought I would be all right since I had avoided the Western-style hotel, but the Osana, which had been recommended to me, turned out to be one of those charming native inns that have been mentioned in the guide books, and I got back in the evening to find a banquet of bad semi-European cooking disguised as Japanese cuisine being served to two hundred of the round-the-world adventurers. Service for the rest of us was non-existent; after my bath I had an hour's wait before my meal tray arrived, this loaded with what could have been, and probably was, chilled rejects from the big party downstairs. They must have had geisha in, or imitation geisha, for I could hear the twanging of a *samisen* poorly played, a screeching voice offering the visitors what was probably the delicately veiled insult of the latest brothel ditty. A sliding door was pushed back and I looked up, meaning to tell the maid what I thought of my dinner.

Kentaro was standing there. He was wearing the one-layer cotton hotel kimono and was flushed from his bath, or *sake*, or both. A Japanese woman would have pushed herself up to bow. I didn't move. He said: 'How are you?' I said: 'Very well. Thank you for asking after all these years.' He stepped on to the matting, pulled shut the almost all paper door, as if for privacy. I said: 'You're looking very fit.' He said: 'I'm all right,' and went on standing there, looking down at me. I told him I had heard he had been made a general. He said: 'Please don't mention it,' then smiled.

I can never see anything even faintly resembling that smile on a stranger's face without a stab of feeling. I remembered the dragon under Japan. I don't know what he was remembering. He stood there for what seemed minutes, not a word between us, then suddenly turned, slid open the door again, clapped his hands and shouted: '*Oi!*' Almost at once there was an answer from one of the elusive maids. When the girl arrived he said: 'Clear away the meal. Lay out the quilts.'

In China long ago I asked myself if this was love. I still don't know. All I know is that, whatever the condition, for three days I was weak with it, and still am, remembering. The tourists had gone next day, Nikko returned to an autumnal emptiness, and though the painted buildings continued to glare at us even under a grey sky, their garishness was a little subdued, the mausoleums suggesting history rather than show places. We wandered amongst them according to some plan in Kentaro's mind that he didn't reveal to me, which was in keeping with a man who never reveals anything, but walks in the contained silence of a totally private identity even when using words to others.

I walked with him, asking no questions, for I didn't want his answers. If I had asked him how Tomo was Kentaro would have said he was well, and if I had wanted to find out what our son was doing now he would have said he didn't know. I could have reproached him with what he did to me all those years ago, but if I had he would have said nothing.

What I do know now is that he has kept track of me always. There have been long times when I wasn't aware of this, years even, but little that I did was hidden from him. He knew of my relations with Peter and probably had even been informed about the Norwegian Bostonian. I can sense, too, a continuing curiosity, as though he felt an unwavering interest in how a woman like me, with no backing from her own people, would make out amongst his. I wonder if he thinks I have made out quite well, or does he find me hardened by those years of aching feet and a half-frozen heart? Oddly, perhaps, I don't really much care what he thinks of me, I just want to be with him when this is possible.

I did try one experiment. We were having our evening meal at the inn, the food much better now the foreigners had gone, Kentaro shovelling his in from a lifted bowl and with considerable noise. We might have been living in the same rooms for twenty-five years, except that I was not maintaining a respectful silence, talking about Karuizawa, asking if he had been there, to which he grunted an assent. I said that I had been going up every summer since 1923, sometimes only for a week or ten days, but always during the all-Japan tennis tournament on those courts of packed volcanic pumice, where the ball has an elasticity of bounce I haven't seen anywhere else. For three years I had watched a very promising player who seemed to have suddenly disappeared from the tennis scene, and I wondered what had happened to him. The name was Kenichi Massami. Kentaro put down his rice bowl, poured some tea into it, then drank, not to waste a grain. He said: 'Never heard of him.'

On the third day we went to the tomb of Ieyasu, the dictator who for so long ruled Japan with intelligence and an almost contemporary liberalism but then suddenly, towards the end of his life, turned on the foreigners he had admitted and the religion they had brought with them, starting a wave of massacres that was to end in the martyrdom of thirty thousand Japanese Christians and the closing of the country's doors to Westerners for two hundred years. I knew that Ieyasu, ever since, has been worshipped as a god, and to the museum-shrine holding relics of his living—some clothes, armour, sword, court dress—I took with me something like the scepticism of the stout Protestant visiting Rome, refusing to be impressed.

We had the place completely to ourselves except for the attendant priests who were not even interested in a Japanese man accompanied by a foreign woman, as though they needed a good few days to recover from that assault by world travellers, curiosity limp meantime. Kentaro walked on slightly ahead past the glass cases, something he does naturally and only checked for a time when I said that he was always on the alert to disown me quickly if a situation arose in which it would embarrass him to be seen in my company. He didn't like that, and I hadn't meant him to. This is the first time since we became lovers that we have ever been seen together in a public place, and it looks to me as though he had carefully chosen an almost empty Nikko out of season in which to make the first tentative experiment.

One of the priests followed us from the museum, I thought for a tip, but it wasn't that; apparently they are supposed to accompany all visitors to Ieyasu's actual tomb. Kentaro dismissed the man almost angrily, and though in informal Japanese dress, with bare toes thrust into the thongs of low wooden clogs, he looked then very much the general. We were left alone for the climb up what seemed to be a thousand steps, in some places three of these carved out of one piece of rock, all of them worn down by the feet of pilgrims through the centuries, and slippery with green moss. There was nothing but those steps and vast cryptomerias flanking them on both sides. Sound was wind through the tips of the trees and a rushing of invisible water, no bird call or hint of human noise.

It was not because I had slipped on the moss that Kentaro held out his hand and I took it. We went on climbing that way, saying nothing, up and up against the steep face of the mountain into a designed loneliness that after a time began to make me just slightly dizzy and half afraid, but then, beyond this, brought a calm that seemed to seep through veins like a slow-acting drug. I did not look at him or he at me, eyes down to those sloping steps most of the time though at each of the paved landings before another flight we paused to lift our heads and in a complete silence acknowledge a deepening isolation from the rest of the world.

The shrine tomb was in complete contrast to all those glittering temples in the valley, plain wood under plain tiles, the sweep of its roof carried on upwards by trees growing out of a gradient that looked too steep for roothold. Kentaro offered a prayer to the man-god, this almost brief enough to have been a greeting, then turned back to where I was standing by a stone font. With that between us he said: 'I have a friend, a diplomat, who has an American wife. It has been successful.' I said nothing. He stared at me. 'My wife has been dead for two years. You knew?' 'Yes.' He looked at the long-handled dipper on the font. 'We can now marry.'

It seemed to me then that even the wind over the tops of the tall trees had dropped to leave a clear field for thunder coming down the mountain, Ieyasu's anger at this deliberate defiance of his proscription on foreigners. What I said was foolish: 'Have you thought

about this carefully?' 'Yes.' 'If we marry, is Tomo then acknowledged as our son?' 'No.' 'Would I be able to see him?' 'No.' 'Then
we won't marry.'

We didn't travel back to Tokyo together. Kentaro came with me
to the station of the electric railway and at the turnstile for the platform said: 'I will come to you in Yokohama?' That was a question,
not an announcement. I said: 'Yes.'

23

&

17 Ura Machi,
The Bluff, Yokohama,
December 2nd, 1941

This afternoon, for the first time in months, I walked over to the flats which I now hold only by proxy, since foreigners are no longer allowed to own property in this country. I still collect the rents and pay all the bills for maintenance, though how long this will continue is anyone's guess. My excuse today was that I wanted to watch the sailing of the *Tatsuta Maru*, the gardens of the flats offering a clear view of the harbour, which my house does not.

What I saw down there looked like the perfectly normal departure of one of Japan's crack liners for the voyage across the Pacific, except that I couldn't see any of the usual paper streamers fluttering at this sailing. I hadn't dared to bring field glasses; in the present tension the police pounce on the least hint of 'spying', and for a foreigner to show any curiosity about almost anything is asking for a visit from them, with the very real possibility of arrest on some ridiculous charge.

Harry Nishimoto is on board the *Tatsuta* in a last desperate bid to get out of the country in which he could be called up for national service of some kind, though I told him he is far too old for any risk of that. He has really become rather a pathetic figure, at the end of a decline which goes back a long way, I think right to the Wall Street crash and the departure of his wife not long after it. He never seemed to come to terms with the Depression, or adapt to it, as a man with his legal training should have been able to do, especially a man with his knowledge of the intricacies of Japanese law. He ought to have given up dual nationality long ago, renouncing the American citizenship he had from being born in Hawaii, to really settle here.

He wanted me to leave on the *Tatsuta* with him, but what on earth would I do arriving in the States as an immigrant at the age of fifty-eight with no money? Everything I have is tied up here. Also, I don't want to leave Japan. After thirty-five years in one country you don't have a 'homeland' in any other, or even the potential left for making one. I have not become a Japanese subject because that would be play-acting, but experience has made me a kind of Eurasian, as it did with Alicia. She left instructions that she was to be cremated, which is apparently still anathema amongst Anglicans, and I am told that the Bishop of Tokyo was seriously worried about her damaged prospects of being resurrected from an incinerated body.

Aiko has also been trying to get me to leave Japan. She has become something of a trial, aging rapidly ever since Katsugi divorced her in favour of that younger woman, now really an old suffragette talking of yesterday's battles and not much interested in today's. If I did go she wouldn't have too many friends left, but I don't suppose that would worry her, and I have a sneaking feeling that she rather has an eye on this house, very ready to offer to care-taker it for me if I decide to flee from the wrath to come. Well, I have not fled, and that ship now sailing out of the bay was probably my last chance to do it.

The publicity machine here growls continuously, like a rabid dog, at America and Britain, with much talk of A.B.C.D. encir-clement, this standing for America, Britain, China and the Dutch. Since there is nothing I can do in the situation except wait, I am managing what is really a pretty high degree of norm by simply only glancing at the papers and never switching on the radio. A few friends come to see me, but I don't go to see them. There is hostil-ity to the foreigner again in public transport and even on the streets.

I have seen this happen often enough before, waves of anti-Western sentiment, the worst after the American Exclusion Act, which branded the Japanese as yellow Asiatics and not fit to set foot on US soil. At that time I couldn't blame the people around me for the hard looks I got, and I don't now either, for this time they are the victims of the militarist propaganda machine, being groomed to think what the ruling generals, including Kentaro, want them to think.

He has not been to visit me again since he came back from China in 1939 and was scarcely in the house before I asked him what part, if any, he had played in the rape of Nanking. It was something I had to know, but I didn't find out. He turned in a swish of silks from the Japanese dress he always wore when he came to me, and a moment later his clogs clattered over the flagstones to the gate.

I have never seen Kentaro in uniform, not even in China when his formal dress was always European, with nothing to hint at army connections, almost as though he was making a point of pretending not to be a military attaché. I remember a reception at the German Embassy when he turned up in a frock coat that didn't fit too well, as though mocking all the medalled chests around him of soldiers who had never smelled a battle.

17 Ura Machi,
The Bluff, Yokohama,
Dec. 6th, 1941

I have had a letter from Jane. It is hard to believe, even though the pages sit on the table in front of me. She doesn't say how she got my address, she must have traced me through the Embassy.

She is a widow. Her husband, a colonel, was killed in the fighting on Crete earlier this year, one of those episodes in the new European war I read about with no sense of it having any possible bearing on my life. At thirty-seven Jane is left with a son of twelve and a daughter of nine. She writes of her marriage as though they had been very happy. Her words seem to come from an understanding I would never have thought possible. She and her husband bought a house in Shropshire ten years ago, a big rambling place with a garden she can no longer keep up since she is working as a driver for civil defence. I am offered a home with her.

This is the child I had always thought would get on perfectly well without me, and who has, but who still seems to want to make contact with a woman she can't remember having seen. The Collingsworth influence can't have been anything like as strong as I was expecting, or she has shaken it off.

How can I write? I never wrote to the child, or the girl, or the woman. What will I say to fill this great gap of years, or at least indicate I would like to attempt to do this? I have hunted for some hint that she wrote out of duty, driven by the mistaken idea that she has obligations to me, perhaps because of the money Mama left her. Yet all I find is an impulse from warmth. This from the baby with the watchful eyes, who never seemed to need me.

I cannot tell her about Tomo, and why I must stay here. If Japan declares war on Britain, how would she feel about a half-brother belonging to the enemy? And what is there to tell her anyway about the baby I had for an even shorter time than I had her, except that he has followed his father into the Army. This is the one thing that Kentaro, after two whiskies too many, told me about a Kurihama son put out to foster parents.

17 Ura Machi,
The Bluff, Yokohama,
Dec. 9th, 1941

The papers rejoice, but I wonder if the Japanese people really feel that what happened at Pearl Harbor has switched the whole course of history in their favour? I do not believe that the entire American Pacific fleet was destroyed. There have been enough wars in my time for me to be suspicious of all official reports. And in this country we have been lied to by the press and radio ever since the Japanese invaded China in 1937, so the habit is well established. I wonder what will happen to the *Tatsuta Maru* now? After Pearl Harbor it certainly won't be making towards Hawaii or any American port. It has probably turned and is racing back to Japanese waters, with all those miserable last minute bolters aboard. I will probably meet up with her passengers again when, in due course, I am taken to an internment camp.

Meantime I stay in this house and look at a garden which will be here long after I am gone, that is, unless the Americans manage to do what the papers say is impossible, bomb Yokohama and Tokyo. The fire bombs used in Europe would find wonderful fuel in these cities. When this war is over, is there going to have to be another huge transplanting of trees?

Last night I didn't sleep. If Tomo went into the Army at eighteen or nineteen, as I expect he would, then by now he should be an officer of considerable rank, possibly a major. The higher you go the safer you should be. But Jane's husband was a colonel. If Tomo is wounded or killed I won't even know. He is such a stranger my heart wouldn't be able to tell me.

> 17 Ura Machi,
> The Bluff, Yokohama,
> April 11th, 1942

Some days, reading the papers, being forced to accept the truths lying under the exaggerations, I feel like a ghost returned from another age and, as a punishment for distant sins, forced to watch the crumbling away of everything I had once known, and lived in, and believed to be solid forever. Hong Kong has gone, and Malaya, and Singapore. The Philippines have collapsed, two days ago Bataan surrendered, and the only Americans still fighting are crowded into the rock fortress of Corregidor which is under constant bombardment.

One of the Tokyo dailies had a gloating piece yesterday about how all over Asia could be heard the marching feet of white prisoners, both soldiers and civilians, all now the slaves of the god-Emperor. Burma is to be next, and after that the armies of the Mikado will march into India. The Japanese flag will, before long, be hoisted in Canberra and over New Zealand, which has already been given its new Japanese name on Tokyo-printed maps. Singapore, re-christened Shonan-to, is now the nerve centre for a vast advance in three directions from it, south, east, west. To the north of Malaya the whole of the Orient is already Japanese.

These are the facts. I have to make an effort to stretch my belief in the possible to accept them. The Far East I have known for nearly forty years has been wiped out like chalk marks from a blackboard by a wet cloth, but I can't really feel it yet, living here as I do, with Toba San still to look after me, the streets of the Bluff still quiet. Maybe I am waiting for the audible sounds of war to reach us as a convincing argument, but they haven't come. Behind my high board fence this security doesn't seem in the least fragile. It is only sometimes, out in the garden, that I feel uneasy, and I wonder if I should have restored it so carefully, whether a lawn with rosebeds wouldn't have been better after all? I am conscious now, too, of a kind of affectation in my life in almost totally Japanese rooms. The ginger tree, grown sizeable again, remains the stubborn stranger.

24

MS *Gripsholm*
At sea,
August 3, 1942

That woman is at last playing bridge, which ought to mean that I have this cabin to myself for a couple of hours. If she tells me just *one* more time how lucky I am to be on this ship instead of being left behind in Japan there will be an explosion. I hope it doesn't happen in the dining-room. Ever since we sailed she has been complaining about the ghastly mistake the Purser made in assigning her to this cabin down on E Deck with me. She rates *much* higher in the ship than E Deck, because even though she has been working as a typist at the British Embassy, that is not her real status at all, she is the widow of a man who had just been made First Secretary in Kabul when carried off by a heart attack. Since his appointment had not actually been confirmed there are some doubts about her rights to a widow's pension at First Secretary level, which she claims is why she stayed on in Tokyo to work at the Embassy. It is my bet she stayed on in Tokyo because the last thing she wanted was to be returned in a hurry to a London under Nazi air attack.

It is probably the state of shock I am still in which makes me find Mrs Burke's chatter so excruciatingly difficult to endure. I am *not* lucky to be leaving Japan. I wanted to stay on in my house until they came to take me to a camp for enemy aliens. Well, they came for me, though not as escorts to a camp, four policemen in white uniforms.

Toba San had gone grey under a summer tan when she came up to report that we had visitors.

It was all so appallingly polite, as though the four had been given strict instructions to avoid any hint of unpleasantness. The late Countess Kurihama could not have taken exception to the tone of the language used to me, but a thick layer of courtesy sugar did not disguise the bitter message. I had one hour in which to pack two suitcases, after which I would be driven down to pier number one, where the *Gripsholm* was already embarking enemy diplomats and others entitled, under international law, to repatriation. It was no use my pointing out that I had no right to repatriation and did not want it, the spokesman for my visitors bowed and said: 'Ah, so?' He then stated that the orders concerning me had come from a very high place. I asked to be allowed to make some phone calls, but this was not permitted. I was reminded that time was getting on and I had my packing to do.

I went upstairs. What do you take in a couple of cases when you are suddenly to be pitchforked out of a world in which you have lived for the greater part of your life? I filled one with clothes, not very well chosen; I find I am short of shoes, only two pairs and no slippers. I shut the lid on that bag and opened the other. Books? Too heavy, and also replaceable, though some of them stared at me from the shelves, including one volume, out of the original six from KYS to PAY, of the Encyclopedia, this for some reason shoved into the household linen basket and taken to Karuizawa in that summer of 1923. Waugh, Linklater, Auden, Isherwood, Waley, all said that they did not want to be left in Japan. I took the Prokosch novel I was reading, *Seven Who Fled*, then poured letters and journals over it, slamming that lid, too.

Toba San arrived too late to help me, red-eyed. I found my bag and wrote her a cheque for two thousand yen. In so far as I knew my account at the Yokohama Specie Bank was still unfrozen, but I told her to get the cash next day. She was to go on living here for as long as she liked, but mustn't feel that she had to look after my things, which would probably be impossible. She did something then I have read about, but never seen, threw her apron up over her face, making howling noises behind it.

It is something, I suppose, to have the servants you are leaving weep for you. How many other people, when they heard about what had happened to me, would? There is nothing like living in a country as an enemy alien to really thin down the roster of your friends. On the stairs, made less steep than is usual in Japanese houses, I lugged the heavier case, Toba taking the other, and I thought of what Peter once said about needing no trunks for your travels in living. I was being forced to take his advice this time, for whatever was ahead of me wasn't going to be much assisted by a great load of experience from the lost years, if only because so much of it was experience totally meaningless in terms of life in the West.

Philosophy got me past the weeping Toba and out to the car all right, and I didn't look back at the gates in that fencing, or at a curve of tile roof with a hint of pine reaching up to it, but at the end of the road, through the windscreen, was Mount Fuji, snow at the summit still shining in late afternoon sun. Tears reached my eyes then.

There are no tears now. I feel dried out from any kind of grief as we sail south into the tropic sun, our ship glowing with light at night as a proclamation of neutrality, though there are no other lights in these seas that have already seen so much death and will see so much more. The ambassadors on board all stick together, the top aristocrats of our temporary society, a little like deposed monarchs trying to pretend they still have some importance in a crumpled world, surrounded by their courts of wives, secretaries, chancellors, all of them playing yesterday's protocol games. I rate beneath the governesses kept on because it wouldn't have been right to send the poor old things home straight into the bombing. The Swedish crew and stewards are slightly aloof, standing back from the violence to which their particular type of civilization has made them immune. I seem to sense their contempt for all these assorted relics of a wrecked order, though they are very polite, like the four Japanese policemen who called at my house on the Bluff.

Kentaro put me on this ship, the last act in his enduring duty towards a woman he got with child on a Chinese hill thirty-seven years ago. Everything he has done for and to me has had a kind of inevitability in terms of the man himself, though I think he might have managed, after considering the matter very carefully like he did that proposal of marriage, to tell me about Tomo. After all this time it would have been safe enough, our son's life long since set and remote from us both, but the Count Kurihama confines his risk-taking to his soldiering.

MS *Gripsholm*
At Singapore,
August 19, 1942

I could be imagining it, but I feel an almost morbid curiosity permeating this ship ever since we came alongside the dock here this morning. It is as though everyone on board wants to see as much as possible of how the great new colonial power is operating here at its southern base. Not that there is much to be seen from the boat or promenade decks, godown roofs separate us from the rest of the dock area, which in turn is like a no man's land between us and life in the city. We can just see people and traffic in the distance, with the Japanese flag flying on ships and buildings, but not much else, the pier beneath us deserted, though there is a gangway down to it. If there are soldiers or police on guard to prevent anyone approaching the *Gripsholm* they must be stationed beyond the shed, for there is no sign of them. No one really knows why we have stopped here, but it is rumoured that the ship is to take on mail written by prisoners of war and internees. At lunch I heard someone say they had seen what looked like a gang of POW's, naked to the waist under full sun, at work unloading a freighter. Immediately after that a man at the same table told us in a loud voice that he couldn't wait to get to South Africa for a change from Swedish food.

The almost unbearable heat in this cabin keeps that woman out of it during the day, and I am blessedly alone, if perspiring.

MS *Gripsholm*
Singapore,
August 20th, 1942

It wasn't the heat that kept me awake last night, I kept thinking about something that happened in Yokohama just before this ship sailed. There was an enormous horde of pressmen and photographers on board, all out to get pictures and, if possible, stories from the departing enemy diplomats. It wasn't because I thought anyone might want a story from me that I went up to the boat deck, it was cooler up there, and I sat on a bench which did not give me a view of the city or Mount Fuji, just an off-sea breeze. There were other escapees from the crowds down below and when I saw what was obviously a reporter, with a cameraman in tow, coming from a companionway, I thought someone else was the target, but the young man was after the human interest angle, and must have seen a picture of me somewhere, perhaps in police files.

I was addressed by name, no uncertainty about that, the reporter polite enough at the start—how did I feel about having to leave a country in which I had lived for so long? I said sad to be going in these circumstances, and looked at the sea while the cameraman moved around me, clicking away as though I was one of those movie stars on the slide who, before this war, always seemed to come to Japan to help them recover from nervous breakdowns. I suggested that all this was a waste of film in view of the still limited use of pictures in Japanese newspapers, and for some reason this made the reporter turn nasty. Did I have any plans to return here, if permitted to, after the Imperial forces had completely crushed the Allies? I said I had no intention of coming back until Tokyo and Yokohama lay in ruins and the Occupying Forces were in need of a controller of Japanese Customs. I meant to apply for that job since I thought my business experience in this country gave me unique qualifications to do it well.

It was a lunatic thing to say, but I was suddenly wildly angry. So was the reporter. He took a step forward and I thought he was going to hit me, but after glaring for a moment he turned away, shouting for the cameraman to follow. If that piece of arrogance on my part was reported in the Japanese press I could easily be taken off this ship here in Singapore and put in an internment camp, or much worse.

August 20th,
Afternoon

The ship has a loudspeaker system to all decks. I was in the cabin wearing very little when I heard my name called, asking me to report to the Purser's office. I had to dress, and did this, feeling frightened. There was a repeat call before I was out in the corridor.

The Purser didn't look at me as he said he had received an order from the port authorities that I was to go to the main lounge and wait there to be interviewed. I asked him what right the port authorities had to give orders to a Swedish ship sailing under the protection of the Red Cross, even though it was tied up in Japanese-conquered Singapore? He stared at a ledger. 'Madam, they could put a platoon of soldiers on board in five minutes and there is nothing we could do to stop them.' I didn't ask if he thought he would soon be removing my name from the *Gripsholm*'s passenger list.

The lounge is air-conditioned which means that it is pretty crowded most of the time. There were three bridge games going and nearly all the chairs occupied, but one alcove near the now closed bar hatch, usually very popular, was empty, almost as though it had been cordoned off. In it was a long corner settee, a table and chairs. A blond steward indicated that I was to wait there. I walked across the room conscious of eyes watching. Whatever was going to happen to me had a capacity audience. I sat down on the settee and looked at people looking at me until, rather sheepishly, they returned to books, or bridge, or chat. There was noise in the lounge again, though not enough to cover the sucking made by a door with rubber sealing as it was pushed open.

A Japanese officer had come in from the foyer. He stood looking about, his head turning quite slowly from right to left, his hand on the hilt of his sword. The blond steward pointed me out. The talk and games and reading had stopped again. The soldier came towards my table, the links on his scabbard chain clinking, his boots heavy on linoleum. I felt just slightly sick.

My visitor didn't register very clearly in the physical sense, all I really noticed was that he was of about average height for a Japanese, and that under the cap he continued to wear his head was shaven. His ears seemed to stick out more than most Oriental ears and he had heavy dark eyebrows. His uniform was tropic beige colour with an open-necked white shirt. Just beyond the table between us he stopped, brought his heels together, then bowed, still with a hand on the sword hilt. It was the bow of a military man for a civilian woman, the politeness only a little more than minimal. I returned the greeting without rising. This seemed to surprise him. He said nothing for a moment, then came out, in bad English, with words that at least half the lounge must have heard: 'You Madam Ma-ken-shi?' I nodded. He introduced himself: 'I Major Nobushige Ozaki.' He pulled out a chair to the full extent of the chain holding it to the floor and, carefully managing his sword, sat. The chill in my heart hadn't much thawed. I said: 'It might be well, Major, if we spoke in Japanese. For privacy.'

That made him turn his head to the watching eyes, which at once disengaged their interest. Few of these people would have more than a slight acquaintance with the language of the country in which they had been living. In his own tongue the Major did not shout, for which I was grateful.

He asked if I would like tea, as though this was his ship, which I suppose it could have been if he had wished to make it so. I thanked him, but said no, my politeness careful. I kept glancing at the glass doors to the foyer for any hint of more Japanese soldiers stationed out there, but could see no sign of them. They might be waiting at the gangway. The Major said that it was very comfortable in this lounge after the heat outside, then pulled a handkerchief from an inside pocket of the uniform jacket to dab at the beads of perspiration on his forehead. He seemed to find it hard to look at me directly, surprising in a military man of his rank. It could be that he found this mission distasteful. The four policemen who had put me on this ship hadn't enjoyed their assignment either.

Our talk languished. I felt an almost ridiculous need to get it going again. Since the information seemed unlikely to be classified as of use to the enemy I asked if he was a regular soldier. He said he was in the Air Force, then added: 'I come from Lieutenant-General the Count Kurihama.'

I must have been continuing to breathe up until then, but tightly. Now I felt as though I had been freed to really fill my lungs with artificially cooled air. I think I held my eyes shut for a minute, and when I opened them he was staring at me. I said stiffly: 'I hope the General is well?' 'Yes, he is very well. But unable to visit you. You understand?' 'I hadn't been expecting a visit. Are you an aide of his?' 'No. I come only to deliver his message. He wishes you to lead a happy life in future.' I said: 'Thank you,' reminded of those pumice courts in Karuizawa, the elasticized balls bouncing back and forth over the net, like our words.

There was silence again. The Major reached into that inner pocket, this time producing a wallet. I was sitting very straight, as I had been since this man came through the glass doors. Kentaro was about to do, through contacts in Singapore, what he could not have done easily in war-rigid Japan, offer me more money. The wallet was laid on the table, then opened flat. What came out looked like a postcard until turned over; then I saw it was a photograph. The Major pushed this across the table.

The picture had been taken in a Japanese garden that looked as groomed as my own, a woman standing just to one side of a stone lantern, and in front of her, arranged according to age, like steps, were three children, two girls and a boy. The boy was tallest, about ten, perhaps more. He was smiling. I knew the smile.

Words had to be pushed past a constriction in my throat: 'Your wife and children, Major?' He nodded and said: '*Hai.*' I didn't have to ask if he was a *yoshi.*

We both sat very still. Perhaps my eyes should have been hungry for his face, his hands, the stiff figure in the chair, but I looked at the table top. I would not embarrass him. He had come, under orders, not knowing what to expect from a foreign woman. He must not take away anything that might be shaming in the memory. I said:

'When you see Count Kurihama please give him my sincere thanks.'
I could sense his relief. There was to be no scene. I had learned
the proper disciplines, which gave dignity to the ritual of showing
me a photograph of people I would never meet, but who were now
to be regarded as my relatives. I had the wildly funny thought that
when I died I would be duly acknowledged as an ancestor at a
Japanese family altar, but I didn't want to laugh.

We talked like strangers sharing a table in a crowded restaurant,
about the humidity of southern regions, the tastelessness of most
tropic fruit. Our quietness had faded almost all the interest in us,
apparently no real drama on schedule from the reserved corner of
the lounge. A man loudly rebuked his partner for her bidding and
she snapped back at him. Those voices seemed to disturb the Major
and, as though feeling he had to cover them, he said: 'When you
return to Japan after the war I hope you will visit Nagoya.' He had
told me where he lived without being asked. I said: 'Perhaps. And
we may meet then.' He smiled. It was not Kentaro's smile. 'If I am
not in my native place in body when you come, I will be there in
spirit.' That clamp on my heart again was this time from a different
fear. 'Why do you say that?' His answer was simple: 'This will be a
long war. I am a flier.'

He did not believe that Japan could win or that he would live to
see the peace. I wanted to cry out in protest, but he had come to
feel safe with me. We both sat very still, now looking at each other,
until he reached across the table for the photograph. This went back
in the wallet which was then stowed away carefully in that inner
pocket. His left hand went to the sword hilt, which meant that he
was getting up, but before he did he leaned forward and said in a
low voice, almost as though afraid of being overhead: 'Life has been
good for me. I must now return to duty.' He added the conventional phrase: 'Please take the greatest care of your health.'

This time I stood for my bow and his was not for a woman of little importance. He turned and thumped towards the glass doors. A
moment later I followed him out of the lounge, eyes on me again. I
went up to the boat deck and when I reached a rail between davits
Major Nobushige Ozaki was already down the gangway and walk-

ing towards a car parked in front of the dock sheds. He did not look
back at the ship. A soldier got out of the driving seat and opened
the car's rear door. Even after this had been slammed I could see the
back of Tomo's head through the rear window. The car began to
move, going quite slowly over a rough surface, then disappearing
around the end of the sheds. I tried to find some vantage point from
which I could see it passing through the dock gates, but wasn't able
to reach one in time. From a wing of the ship's bridge the blond
Swedish officer of the watch stared down at me.

About the Author

Oswald Wynd (1913–1998) was born in Tokyo to Scottish missionaries and spent his formative years in Japan. He attended the University of Edinburgh and joined the Scots Guards in 1939. During World War II, Wynd spent three years as a Japanese prisoner of war; it was at this time that he began to write seriously. He is the author of many novels, including *The Blazing Air* and *Death the Red Flower*. Under the pseudonym Gavin Black, Wynd wrote many well-received thrillers. He died in Scotland.